MORE PRAISE FOR
FREEBIRD

"Jon Raymond's wonderful new book *Freebird* poetically wrestles with the big and the small: how globalization and international conflicts reconcile with the personal; how the amorality of war affects individual psyches; how impulsive post adolescence mirrors impulsive old age. And the undercurrent of this increasingly suspenseful story is a fascinating discussion of environmental mutilation, at once a tangle of benign bureaucracy and calculated avarice, which Raymond tackles with equal parts sensitivity and expertise."

—JESSE EISENBERG, AUTHOR OF *BREAM GIVES ME HICCUPS*

"*Freebird* is such a timely book, considering the current deep divisions between right and left. A new classic for the collapsing political landscape of America."

—KIM GORDON, AUTHOR OF *GIRL IN A BAND*

"*Freebird* is an intelligent and absorbing multi-generational story of an American family, written with great sensitivity, insight, and verve."

—PATRICK DeWITT, AUTHOR OF *THE SISTERS BROTHERS*

"[*Freebird* is] the rare work of fiction that feels more timely with each passing moment."

—*SEATTLE WEEKLY*

"Thanks to Raymond's loose, masterful style, *Freebird* is an arm wrestling match between hilarity ⸳

—*INTERVIEW*

FREE BIRD

JON RAYMOND

 TIN HOUSE BOOKS / Portland, Oregon & Brooklyn, New York

Published by Tin House Books, Portland, Oregon, and Brooklyn, New York

Distributed by W. W. Norton & Company

Library of Congress Cataloging-in-Publication Data

Names: Raymond, Jonathan, author.
Title: Freebird / by Jon Raymond.
Description: First paperback U.S. edition. | Portland, OR : Tin House Books, 2018.
Identifiers: LCCN 2017035138 | ISBN 9781941040836 (softcover)
Subjects: LCSH: Families—Fiction. | Domestic fiction.
Classification: LCC PS3618.A985 F74 2018 | DDC 813/.6—dc23
LC record available at https://lccn.loc.gov/2017035138
ISBN 978-1-941040-83-6

First US Paperback Edition 2018
Printed in the USA
Interior design by Jakob Vala

www.tinhouse.com

For my grandparents

Death is the Wealth / Of the Poorest Bird

—EMILY DICKINSON

1

Two survivors walk into a room . . .

It could almost be a joke, Anne thought. They walk into a room, though, and then what? They see a duck? There was definitely a joke in there, she knew it, but where did it *go*? Where was that weird non sequitur that took it somewhere else? Somewhere hilarious?

It was possible the whole premise just wasn't that funny—two survivors, ha-ha. No, it wasn't, Anne thought. To witness her father, one of the two survivors in question—this troll-like barrel of a man, his Stalin mustache drooping, eyes bagged, balancing his tray of trout, Jell-O, and iceberg lettuce on the cannonball of his paunch—straining to hear whatever this shriveled old woman with the nimbus of white hair, survivor two, was saying, got her much more weepy than jolly. Maybe in Florida this kind of meeting happened all the time, maybe in certain neighborhoods in New York. In Israel, obviously. But what were the chances of two ancient Polish Jews, scarred refugees of the twentieth century, bumping into each other in a convalescent-home dining hall near a soft-serve dispenser in the outer reaches of the San Fernando Valley?

She watched the old woman pointing at her dad's chest, talking, talking. Her arthritic knuckles trembled with gaudy rings.

The old lady might be talking about the day's meat loaf, and she might be talking about the Eichmann trial—it was impossible to tell. As hard as Anne tried to pick out her voice amid the clamor of silverware, she could never quite catch its timbre.

Just don't freak him out, she thought straight into the woman's brain, and tonged a few more tomato wedges onto her plate. I love you, I feel for you, but don't go and fuck up all the work I've done by freaking him out with your blood-soaked memories. The old lady clearly had no idea how many favors Anne had pulled just to make this day possible. The sheer volume of groveling she'd done among city commissioners and nonprofit executives was practically insane. In the end she'd gone all the way to the lieutenant governor's wife to land a place on Fountainview's waiting list. The last thing she needed was the ghost of history dropping in and spooking her dad halfway through the tour.

It'd been hard enough just getting him to agree to the tour. For a guy who almost never left his house, he had a curiously high opinion of his own domestic abilities. After four falls, three ER visits, and what may well have been a minor stroke, he still held on tightly to the ideal of himself as the hale, middle-aged, Pacific Gas and Electric career man circa 1975, capable of scaling electrical towers with his linemen and riding his motorcycle home along winding foothill highways at night. The notion that he wasn't fit to live alone hadn't yet truly penetrated his skull. For this reason, the day's mission—triggering in him some recognition that the time had come to accept, nay, to welcome, organized help—was not to be derailed, no matter what.

Anne watched him navigate the obstacle course of wheelchairs and mobility scooters, pausing at the logjam near the muffin baskets, narrowly avoiding the projectile of a speeding busboy. By the time he'd toppled into his chair, he was openly exhausted, his breath almost violent, his trembling fingers gripping the table's edge for support. His skin was the pallid color of old cheese and he couldn't seem to lift his head from his chest and somehow he'd spilled most of his ice water into his salad along the way. And yet, still, she knew, he'd argue that getting up on a ladder to prune the neighbor's cypress hedge was a great idea. Unbelievable.

"I think she likes you," Anne said once the wheezing had abated.

"What?"

"That woman," Anne said. "The one you were talking to. I think she likes you."

Her dad grunted, either uninterested or uncomprehending, she wasn't sure.

"You guys must've talked for, like, five minutes," Anne said. "What did she say?"

"She loves to talk," he said, leaning over his plate to start extracting the small bones from his fish. "She thinks her daughter's the only one who ever studied the law."

"So. You didn't talk about anything . . . else?"

"Why would we?"

Anne smoothed the linen onto her lap and exhaled with some relief. If the old survivor lady was already exiting her dad's mind, all the better. They could just leave that box of hobgoblins closed for now, thank God. Maybe someday they'd go back and ponder the meeting, maybe Anne would even coax her dad out with some leading questions, but there was no need for that today, and maybe never. In the end, what was the point, anyway? The childhood horrors her dad and the old woman shared were either so obvious as to be not worth mentioning or so incomprehensible as to defy explanation, so why scrape off the old scabs? Especially when there were so many other, more pressing matters to worry about, like low-sodium meal plans and the men's book club selections, for instance.

If they got lucky, Anne thought, shaking oil and vinegar onto her lettuce, watching her dad pull apart the shingles of his fish as if he were defusing a land mine, the old woman would stay out of sight for the rest of the visit and for any subsequent visits they made, and the vast, frigid silence that had enclosed her dad's life story for the entirety of her consciousness would remain as it always had, undisturbed. After they'd signed all the papers and paid their first month's deposit, then fine, she didn't care. Let the floodgates open. Her dad could walk around Fountainview with a golden Star of David stitched to his sweat suit, if that was what he wanted. Just so long as she knew he was safe.

After lunch, Anne and her dad met Cassie, the manager, and revisited the room in question one more time—the studio apartment, as the management called it. The space was clean and well proportioned, sporting fresh, not wholly ugly wall-to-wall carpeting and windows that looked out onto the gardens where Anne approvingly identified mimosa and angel's trumpet edging the trimmed lawns. The square footage was a lot smaller than he was accustomed to, but that didn't matter much. Years ago, his needs had shrunk down to precisely the dimensions of a soft chair and a medium-sized flat-screen TV.

She watched him looking out the window without expression and wondered if he might finally be coming around to the idea himself. Maybe after four decades in his ranch house in Sun

Valley, California, he was finally ready for a change. Of course, she could grasp how the prospect of facing his final years (God willing, years) in this place would seem off-putting. Who'd ever choose this geriatric cruise ship if they didn't have to? But she could also see how the new place could be all right. Squint your eyes and it was cozy, simple, decently lit. Plus all those opportunities it afforded. Her dad never had many close friends in day-to-day life—plenty of acquaintances, sure, but close friends, not really—and maybe this was the place those friendships would finally bloom. Maybe, perish the thought, even some romance.

Soon enough the tour was bringing them back to the starting point, Cassie's office, a small, glass tank off the main lobby. Cassie guided them to a sofa and offered to answer any more questions they might have, but by now Anne possessed all the information she needed, from the emergency response team specs to the timetables for weekly qigong lessons. The only question she could think of was, How many people had already died in room 282? How many corpses have you guys pulled out of there, anyway? Instead, she nudged her dad and asked if he had any questions, because if so, now was the time to speak up.

"How about it, Dad? Anything you want to know?"

Her dad, nestled deep in the recesses of the soft couch, was barely awake. His mustache held some minuscule particles from lunch, and his eyes were almost milky with fatigue. They'd pushed him well past his nap time, and all the walking had taken its toll, so it was surprising when he seemed to rouse and mutter that he did in fact have a question. First he had to clear his throat, however, a process that took almost a minute, with much hacking and hawking of phlegm, but afterward he wrestled himself to the edge of the couch and addressed himself directly to Cassie:

"How much?" he said. "I'd like to know how much all this costs, if I may."

Cassie accepted the question, like everything, with great, buoyant optimism. "Well, Mr. Singer, that all depends," she said. "Ninety percent of the entrance fee is refunded, you know, and, pricing average housing values, you can equate the equity in your home to the cost of entering Fountainview. Monthly service fees include utilities, weekly housekeeping, linen service, a dining plan, transportation, maintenance—"

"I know, I know, miss," he interrupted. "But how much?" He was more stern this time. "What number do I write on the check every month? That's what I want to know." Even now, a faint Polish lisp clung to his voice.

Cassie held her smile in place and tilted her face in Anne's direction, seeking cues on how to proceed.

"Dad," Anne said, "I think what Cassie is saying is, it depends on a lot of factors."

"I'd like a ballpark."

Anne looked at Cassie, assenting to a round number.

"Seven thousand a month," Cassie said. "That's not an official quote. But maybe in that area."

Anne's dad pursed his lips and drew his chin toward his chest, exhaling loudly. Whether the figure struck him as offensively high or surprisingly low was hard to tell—he had strange ideas on the relative costs of things—but in any case he wasn't going to reveal anything more in this room. The tour was now officially ended.

It wasn't until they were bouncing over the speed bumps in the parking lot, blond Cassie receding in the rearview mirror, that Anne finally allowed herself to ask her dad outright what he thought. She couldn't avoid it forever. His answer, unsurprisingly, was monosyllabic. "Nice."

"That's it?" she said. "Nice?"

"That's what I said," he said. "It's nice."

"Nice." Steering out of the parking lot to the side street and angling toward the roaring traffic of the main artery, she pondered the word. The word itself was meaningless, more a way of avoiding a conversation than an actual attempt to transmit significance. She could tell by the way his head retracted even deeper, his hunch becoming almost turtle-like, that he was withholding something, and whatever deeper opinions he harbored were going to have to be extracted by cunning or force.

"It's kind of amazing, isn't it?" she said brightly. "Better than I thought it'd be. Cassie seems sweet."

"It's very nice," he said, this time with a mild nod for emphasis.

She gripped and regripped the wheel. The words couldn't be construed as enthusiastic, exactly, "very nice," but he'd said them vigorously enough that they caused a mild flutter of hope in her chest. He was reiterating himself, and that must mean something. "Very nice" was a notch above simply "nice." What had he ever called very nice before?

The traffic roared by in waves, and at the first opening she gunned out into the flow, batting away the positive thoughts she normally so scrupulously prohibited herself from thinking. If her dad decided to move into Fountainview, so many of her troubles would be resolved. No more nights lying awake, wondering if he'd fallen down in the kitchen or keeled over in the shower. No more nagging fear about his secret sugar binges, his inadvisable driving, his stubborn stair climbing. It would cost them, but she didn't care. Who deserved this level of care more than her dad, who had endured so much? She'd find a way to cover Aaron's college, and as for her own dotage, well, that was a long way off. So many apocalypses were possible before that time came. He could think of Fountainview as a gift to her sanity if that made him feel better.

Jockeying her way into the left lane, she reminded herself that this was not the time to push her dad too hard. But, at the same time, she didn't want to lose any momentum. They had to make this decision quickly. If they could just agree in this moment that the visit had been a success, if they could bookmark his good impression, the following conversations would go all that much easier. If they could establish that Fountainview was in fact "very nice," that was a start.

They arrived at an intersection and slowed into the field of glinting glass and chrome, and in the relative quiet she could hear her dad mumbling, his words too low frequency to decipher.

"What?" she said.

He muttered again but still too quietly. She craned to hear. "What?"

"I said, it's very luxurious, that place," he said, suddenly loud.

And immediately, whatever blossoming hope she'd been nurturing wilted and burned.

"Luxurious." She could tell he'd been sitting on this word all morning, waiting to unleash it at the most opportune time. The word had probably entered his head back at the library, in the gym, at the cedar-lined sauna, and he'd been building his case against Fountainview ever since. "Luxurious" was a word with no positive connotation in her father's vocabulary, a synonym only for waste and self-indulgence. "Luxurious" was a mode of experience only for other people, never himself. And so, two minutes onto the road, the golden door to Fountainview was already closing and locking behind them, the darkness of the future regathering in thick folds.

When they got to his house, Anne dragged her dad out of the passenger seat, cradling his elbow as they staggered up the walkway. She helped him through the door, disabled the alarm, and installed him in his recliner, his soft, fitted shell facing the gray face of the TV. She placed his remote in his palm, and within moments he was watching *Ellen* at top volume.

She straightened the newspapers, organized the recycling, and made sure the refrigerator was stocked with the weekly cache of damp turkey sandwiches and cartons of egg whites. She inspected his pill collection, counting out the lozenges and pink dots and pale asterisks in each tray, then again as the minor chords of a crime show boomed through the house. "You doing all right, Dad?" she called, but there was no answer. He was fast asleep.

Outside, rush hour was congealing across the city, and she figured she'd wait it out. She discovered a warm Amstel Light in the kitchen cabinet and sat on the back patio to respond to her day's calls, cursing the ineptitude of everyone in her professional and personal network, if not the whole ingrate army of society itself. *Three connections between L.A. and Denver? Sounds crazy. Anything better? Pretty sure the plastic cups are in the top cabinet. The VERY top.* Often she had to wonder if the people she worked with were genuinely stupid or just so bored and frustrated, they fucked up on purpose simply to have someone to talk to. She wasn't sure she'd ever know.

In the end she was left to stare at the empty sky. Without Fountainview she had no great options. What was she going to do with her dad? Sipping her skunked beer, she found herself bewildered as to how life would proceed. How had this duty fallen to her? she wondered. She feared that the punishment for her own goodness was only beginning.

She stared at the clouds and tracked the movement of a quiet thought arcing like a shooting star through her brain. Maybe, she thought idly, just maybe, her dad should just die. That would sure solve everyone's problems, wouldn't it? The house would transform into college tuition. Her savings would become a nest egg. All her daily guilt would be lifted. How easy it would all be if he just gracefully bowed out and stopped breathing. And before the thought was even finished, before the glowing tail had faded from view, she was already scolding herself: Bad wish, Anne. Very bad. Don't ever think that. Never again.

2

Ever since he was a child, Ben Singer had despised baseball. It was a game of zero hustle, no meaty physical contact, no flame-engulfing accidents, no perilous flips, spins, or even dismounts, a sport of millionaire morons dressed up in children's costumes, spitting on their own shoes. Not to mention, the food they served at the ballparks was disgusting. For upward of forty years he'd been making the case against baseball one bar stool at a time, and it was only very recently that he'd begun to wonder if maybe in this he'd been wrong, too.

Today, seated in the bleachers of his former high school, watching a brightly colored squadron of young men arranged against a singular opposing batter in a white jersey, Ben was forced to wonder if maybe all his tirades against baseball had been wrongly conceived. Maybe all those baseball-loving fuck-heads had a point. On a sunny summer afternoon—the smell of cut grass and citrus mixing with the smell of hot dogs and stale popcorn, the sounds of the kids yelling, the crack of the bat—baseball was proving not all that bad, maybe even kind of great, a form of deep communion with the American grass and earth itself.

In a way, Ben could see, he'd never really had a chance to like baseball. He'd been reared in a deeply anti-baseball household, after all, the son of an anti-baseball father, himself the son of a man who'd certainly never heard of baseball, and thus in a way he'd been brainwashed from the start. His dad—an immigrant from Kraków—had never truly had any feel for the pageantry and passion of the great American sports institutions, nor for the pleasures of American spectatorship in general. Football he could vaguely understand: that was just the violent acquisition of real estate. Basketball: at least that took a certain African dexterity. Those men, his dad allowed, were like physical gods. But baseball: what was that? "They don't even run," he'd scoff, pausing to rap the TV's thick glass with his knuckles. "They just stand there scratching their nuts. This is a sport? This is golf." Golf being the most ridiculous pastime invented by man.

By adolescence Ben had taken for granted that baseball was a mistake, a hoax perpetrated by stupid fathers on their stupid sons, and over the years his prejudice had hardened, excluding him from many a loud, dudish conversation. Among the guys in his platoons, he'd often been construed as eccentric and deranged, although admittedly he probably would have been viewed as eccentric and deranged by most of the redneck goyim he'd served with anyway, baseball being only the smallest of his differences. But today, at last, leaning back against the dry, chipped wood of the bleacher, the heat of the American sun warming his face, he was understanding many things about America and baseball he'd never known.

The game, as usual, seemed stalled out between events, but for once he felt the low-burning suspense. The catcher, a fluid, blond kid, was madly signaling the pitcher, a mere noodle, who silently confirmed something before averting his gaze. The kids in the dugout were almost drooling, they were so hypnotized by the stasis. In the bleachers, the parents and siblings and girl-friends were also happily entranced. Baseball, he realized, was a mode of group contemplation, a meditative discipline unique to the psyches of America's soft, defenseless potato people. This was the place the happy people pooled their attention to renew the happy life they knew as their due.

The crack of the bat. A tepid roar. By the time Ben located the ball, rolling in center field, the batter was almost at second, and then, in a snap, the ball was back idling in the pitcher's mitt, getting fondled and massaged, and the signals between pitcher and catcher were starting up again. The mothers and fathers were pushing more fingerloads of yellow popcorn into their faces. A plane crawled through the upper reaches of the atmosphere. Strike one, the ump called, over the corner of the plate. And at this Ben had been there as long as he could stand.

He made his way through the scalding parking lot, the setting of much long-ago mischief and romance, thoughts of baseball still turning in his head. This was only his third trip back to Sun Valley in twenty years, and, walking the gravel shoulder of the road into town, he was barraged by long-dormant memories. Over in that yard, a euphoric water balloon fight. In those bushes, a bleary kegger ending with police sirens. Over there, an evil, brown dog. After all this time, he was pleased to find the local sunlight still recognized him, clapping him on the shoulder with a familiar heat, and the whoosh of passing cars still carried a familiar scent of minerals and gasoline. Soon the first buildings of downtown were passing on either side, bringing more vaporous impressions, and he felt confirmed in his intuitions that the visit was a good idea and that the old haunts might hold the secret not only of his past but possibly of his future as well.

A year ago he never would have been here. A year back, and two, and three, he would have been off at war, fighting on the front lines of America's campaign for freedom, guided still by the great truism that had dictated his actions since he was fifteen years old, the single axiom he'd ever deemed worthy of a tattoo. Even now the words stretched across the taut curves of his deltoids, shoulder to shoulder, in a plain, unadorned, antique typewriter font: "We sleep safe in our beds because rough men stand ready in the night to visit violence on those that would do us harm." A year ago he'd had no reason to question that truth, but, like so many of his truths these days, it was under violent siege.

The sentence was George Orwell. Some people assumed Winston Churchill, but those people were wrong. Others said Richard Grenier and they might have a point. In any case, Ben still remembered the first time he'd read the sentence in the pages of the *New Republic* magazine at the Village Drug Store, not two blocks from where he currently walked—how electrified he'd been, how deeply and intuitively he'd known the sentiment was correct. Yes, he'd thought, this placid American life is not what it seems. It is in fact as fragile as a soap bubble, an aberration of history, and all these people, these soft-skinned children, mothers, salesmen, and professional athletes, exist in their comfort only because their world is ringed with far-off sentries. Most people, he realized, had no idea this was the case. They enjoyed their American happiness in blissful ignorance. But the horror of his father's childhood had opened him to a different reality. Without armies: ovens. That was a fact. From that day onward, he'd taken the quotation as a fundamental postulate of his life.

One of his goals for the trip to Sun Valley had been to locate that Village Drug Store and possibly even re-create that youthful, epiphanic moment, but, as it turned out, not surprisingly, the building was gone. In its place was a bland plaza studded with concrete benches and a flagpole, which seemed appropriate. The flag, like so many flags these days, was wadded at half staff, although Ben had no idea what the day's tragedy might be. When had all the flags in the country gone permanently half-staff? he wondered. And what was the smell that flowed out of Subway's doors? Was it supposed to smell like bread?

He sat down and watched three teen skateboarders testing their mettle against some concrete steps. They weren't very good, but they were okay to watch. One of them had those stupid white dreadlocks, and another one wore an oversized T-shirt with a peace symbol on the chest.

The peace symbol reminded Ben of another Orwell quote, also excellent but not deserving of a tattoo: "Pacifism is objectively pro-fascist." How could he explain that sentiment to this ignorant skateboarder? What it meant to him—as he'd lectured many times on many continents, mostly to men about to parachute out of planes or storm jungle encampments of insurgent guerrillas—was that the struggle against evil was always already enjoined. Evil was real. Evil was out there, seeking to enslave you, and you had the choice either to fight evil or become an appeaser of evil. There were no spectators in the fight. Those cement stairs where kids wasted their days doing ollies: menaced by evil darkness. The infrastructure that allowed that Subway to dispense its food product: thanks only to the pain and sacrifice of tireless soldiers somewhere off in the shit.

For twenty-four years Ben had been one of the rough men visiting violence in the night in the name of freedom. He couldn't even remember all the violence he'd visited. He'd visited violence in Honduras, hanging with the last of the contras before Ortega crept into the dustbin of history for the first time. He'd visited violence in Bosnia, eliminating the murderous henchmen of Milošević. He'd attempted to visit violence in North Korea one time, but sadly that mission hadn't gone off. He'd spent three days in a ghillie suit, sitting in a trench in the DMZ, shitting into a sluice, waiting for the appearance of Kim Jong Il from his bomb-resistant underground concrete bunker, but the dictator had never materialized. Intelligence had been wrong, much to his chagrin. Oh, how he would have enjoyed pulling the trigger on that one. To have killed a totalitarian monster. It would have made for a very good day.

For the past few years, he'd mostly been visiting his violence in Afghanistan. He'd been knocking around in Kabul and the northern provinces, putting the hurt on Taliban chieftains and various recalcitrant goat herders slow to accept the civilizing hand of the American liberation. He'd prided himself on the surgical nature of his violence-visiting and had genuinely enjoyed his place in the hierarchy of his nation's armed forces, his status as a deadly weapon in the hands of the men who guided his people down the treacherous path of their destiny. He'd lived happily in the darkness, knowing his actions guaranteed the light-filled life back home in the States.

And then, about a year ago, there had been a change. The poles had reversed. Every intuition had turned inside out, and ever since then the light and the dark were no longer so easy to tell apart. The men in charge didn't seem so unimpeachable, and all those he'd opposed had ideas that weren't so easy to dismiss.

The change, as far as he could tell, had started in Kunduz during the mission to kill the savage warlord Abdul Rashid Mazari. For two weeks, Ben had been stationed on a rooftop as satellites drifted in and out of position, beaming images to the suburbs of Virginia, accumulating data. He'd been happy enough to wait—that was his job, after all—and he'd packed in enough meals for a month, as well as a smartphone loaded with history tomes. It all would have been easy enough if not for the rancid smell that had plagued him from the start.

The smell had been truly terrible. A dying-animal smell, a rotten-meat-in-the-hot-sun smell. A little reconnaissance had revealed the source to be consistent with the nightly screams emanating from a nearby apartment window. As it turned out, the screaming and the stench originated from the exact same spot, the body of a young boy, maybe nine years old, with an infected wound on his leg, probably the result of an errant IED. Ben's explicit orders had been to avoid all engagement with the locals, but in this case he'd gone ahead and broken them. The smell was too awful, and one night he'd stormed into the house, tied up the parents, and treated the boy's leg with some good old-fashioned American antibiotics. He'd done this five more times, encountering successively less struggle and fear on the part of the boy and his family, possibly even some looks of damp gratitude, and by the time the order to debrain the warlord came in, the leg was showing some definite signs of repair. He'd completed his mission with all the attendant pyrotechnics and never saw that kid again.

He should have taken a break about then, but, as it happened, the boy and his infected leg bumped up against another significant event in Ben's tour of duty, the trip to Bagram and the mission to rescue two SEALs in the mountains of Barai Ghar. That mission had been a clusterfuck from minute one. A Chinook had been downed on the top of an unnamed peak, and Ben's team had been assigned to snatch the survivors before the savages arrived to lop off their heads. Their helicopter had followed the first helicopter's path over the mountaintops, into the navel of the world, as the local dirt farmers called it, and at the designated coordinates had crept downward to the frozen, godforsaken landing zone. Why the LZ was rutted with narrow tracks, and why there was an unmanned, vintage eighties, Russian-made anti-aircraft machine gun sitting there, no one knew, but according to the gunship all was clear. Optical heat sensors picked up no human-sized signatures. It was at the sight of the decapitated donkeys and goats hanging in spindly trees that the major sirens went up. Obviously, the LZ was already inhabited by hostiles.

"I'm looking at donkeys and goats here," Ben's pilot radioed to base.

"No enemy combatants on the ground," said the gunship.

"I see goats in trees." That was when the rocket-propelled grenade punched a hole in the electrical pod, passing through the left mini gun ammo can, and exploded in the interior of the aircraft. A second later, another RPG hit the right-side radar pod. Another exploded in the snow by the right front and peppered the Chinook with shrapnel. Another hit the right-side turbine on the tail.

So much for trusting a screen more than your own eyeballs. The cathode ray tubes spooled down and faded to black. Out went the multifunction displays, the navigation systems with GPS, the automatic flight-control systems, the radios, and every other operating component. Out went the generators and down came the bundles of transmission and hydraulic lines, splashing burning-hot liquid everywhere in the cabin. Only when the electricity goes out does anyone get real, Ben flashed. Only when the power disappears does anyone start seeing again, thinking again. This was a new lesson for him.

Ben had survived the ensuing firefight, just barely. He'd been flown to Kabul, then Germany, then DC, where he'd recuperated adequately enough, though not so adequately that the SEALs were any longer an option. At age forty-one, he was well past the sell-by date, anyway, and by all standards ready for the downshift into a life of consulting. It was in this period that his moral inversion had become complete. "Consulting," it had turned out, was another word for "bodyguarding," and his first client had been an executive for a major multinational construction company. Ben's job had been to accompany this vice president on his tours throughout Central Africa, visiting various oil fields, consulates, government buildings, river deltas, and so forth. In this capacity, Ben had enjoyed a front row seat to the daily routines of a corporate master of the universe, a very nice man named Michael Holmes, who never said an unkind word to anyone because he had Ben standing next to him with an AK-47. You get up into the upper echelons of power, Ben had been told, and there are basically two kinds of arrangements: a nice guy surrounded by assholes, or an asshole surrounded by nice guys. In this situation, it was the former, and he was the asshole. Back and forth between mind-crushing poverty and mind-crushing opulence he'd traveled with this nice man. To Europe to visit a son at the Sorbonne, to

Dubai to make deals with the sheiks, back to Africa to walk the perimeter of the oil field on the edge of the slums of Nairobi.

All of these experiences, taken together, back to back, had demolished some of Ben's basic foundations. When the time had come to re-up his contract, he'd bowed out, and ever since then he'd been wandering alone, his mind a fiery collage of images. Festering leg wounds, burning helicopters, starving babies, prep school graduation parties, greasy blood spurting from a savage warlord's head. Not to mention the ghosts. They'd become regular visitors of late, these void-eyed apparitions unable to communicate whatever searing message they'd been assigned to deliver. So far they only stood there, mute and terrifying, hovering in half shadow, casting shrieking headaches and stabbing ear pain, but who knew when they might reach out and touch him? No matter where he went, the images and ghosts plagued him. And none could answer his one, simple question: why was one kid left to die and another sent to play baseball?

Such was his inner turbulence as he stood across the street from his father's home, a stucco ranch on a Peanuts-style cul-de-sac. He'd been thinking he'd call on his dad today, surprise him with his sudden arrival, but he could see that wasn't going to be the case. He didn't want his dad to see him in this state, so fried, so freaked. It was so strange: here he was, a guy who'd built entire telecom stations in hurricanes, swum miles in the Indian Ocean surrounded by tiger sharks, and parachuted from low-flying planes into minefields surrounding terrorist encampments, but he couldn't make himself walk up and knock on his dad's door.

The sun was sinking, and the pictures continued to flash in Ben's skull: bleeding wounds; dismembered goats; suburban parking lots. Every image encapsulated an entire world of experience, and all of them were at war with one another. If only they'd stop for a second, maybe he could string together a thought, but they strobed on and on, ever more harshly, to the point where his head was ringing with pain. He fashioned a mental baseball bat and began swinging at random, smashing the images as they appeared, splintering them into tiny shards. It was almost calming, in a way. Thwack, thwack, thwack. His mind became the sound of wood thwacking hard earth. He stood on the sidewalk feeling the woody report in the bones of his face. He doubted this was happening in anyone else's brain, this mental smashing. None of his dad's neighbors were prone to suffering in this way. They were all too happy sucking on their barrels of carbonated sugar water, running mazes on their handheld phones, enjoying the bounty of this good, American life. It was a life he needed to discover some way to join, now that his nights as a rough man were done—he knew that.

His eyes roamed his childhood street, seeking respite in all the old places. He didn't dare look at the neighbors' windows because there might be ghosts, and he didn't want to look at his dad's house because it was almost vibrating with mysterious, pent-up energies. In his heart he still believed that Orwell was right, but he had to admit, the burning sensation growing in his chest argued otherwise. It was possible the postulate of peace through violence might even have some fatal flaw. Staring at his dad's roof, imagining flames shooting skyward, napalm spreading over the earth, all manner of burning death, feeling his head slowly separating from his body, he began to wonder the once unthinkable: What if America was not imperiled by enemies on another continent at all? What if all the potato people enjoyed their supersized happiness not thanks to the rough men but simply because? After almost three decades of extreme clarity on the matter, he was no longer at all sure. And without that clarity, there were other big questions to answer, too. Namely: if the enemy wasn't out there, then what the fuck had all that violence even been for?

3

How could electricity feel so good? Aaron wondered.

How could a charge born in some far-distant river or wind farm, sparked by copper-coated turbines spinning against giant magnets, flowing into high-tension lines strung across deserts, forests, mountains, and farms, pouring out of the speakers in a bath of vibrating sound waves, bring his body to this state of such killer feeling? The guys on the stage, if you could even call it a stage—it was more like a small clearing in the corner of the warehouse—were sorcerers, he thought. These three schlumpy dudes in thinning T-shirts and ratty cargo shorts had come down from the mountains, mud on their faces, God-delivered guitars in hand, to unleash their druidic powers on the world.

The chord shifted, and a new plateau of energy rose. He was still stoned enough to think he could see the music itself, a pale, multicolored fog billowing from the amps. And just when he thought it could not possibly get better, more gorgeous, the voices came back. He'd forgotten about them! He'd become so lost in the drone that he'd forgotten all about the human voices that had been there at the start of the song—the start, how many ages ago?—and he'd forgotten the terrible, awesome, hypnotized authority of the harmony. It was like a choir of demons boiling in lava, he thought, some kind of rapture in Hades.

The band was called Warship, and it was a thousand times better than the other bands on the bill. Penis Butter and Jism, they were just local punks; Fedders, from New York, were toothless emo pop; Gobbet, the metal outfit, were great, but not great in a way that was exactly pleasurable to listen to, more like a Viking Wehrmacht division razing the land with incendiary riffs. These guys, though, were artists. Warship. Aaron had never thought about the name before. Warship. Worship. The double meaning was kind of pretentious, he had to admit, but deep in their gnarled drone he'd forgive them that affectation. They were owning it, at least. There was no question these dudes were lifers.

The final feedback jam was not perfunctory, and Aaron's ears were still ringing as he shuffled down the broken stairs, and ringing still when he got to the sidewalk and smoked a cigarette, the magic spell conjured by the din already evaporating from his nerves. He wasn't that high anymore, just burned out and shaky, and as passing headlights flashed on broken glass and fellow showgoers trudged by at dazed, postcoital speed, the everyday current of acid criticism again began rising in his blood.

He surveyed the other showgoers on the sidewalk, the part-time punks and belated Goths, the eternal hippies and bewildered jocks, and silently judged them. He could ID a published poet and a photographer with pictures in a museum, so they said, and a whole, elaborate hierarchy of shoes. He saw the filmmaker, Dan, talking to the bassist of Powerstrip, making some plan of future collaboration. And then there was Dana Star, only seventeen and already known for the video she'd screened a month back. It wasn't a very interesting video—home-birth footage cut with hard-core porn—but the idea had been so obvious, it had almost seemed necessary, and people had been talking as though she was some kind of comer ever since.

Over near the streetlight, he spotted his buddy Karl deep in conversation with the brain-fried panhandler people called Mr. Africa. Karl loved Mr. Africa and sought him out after every show at the Ooze, soliciting his cracked notions about lost languages and God's quantum will, confirming his theory that crazy black guys were inherently more cosmic than crazy white guys. "Crazy black dudes have it *down*," he liked to say. "Better fashion, better theories, better hats. Crazy white guys are just a bunch of mumbling pants shitters. What white guy would ever be Sun Ra, dude? He could never be white." Aaron was still trying to figure out whether Karl's ideas were blatantly racist or not, but at the very least they were better than the covertly racist ideas of the people who treated Mr. Africa like some kind of mascot or pet. And it was possible they were even more advanced than his own ideas, too, which generally just led him to keep his distance.

Aaron had another cigarette, arranging his shoulders in a zombie hunch, arms adangle, glad to give Karl his space. If nothing else, the rap with Mr. Africa meant they weren't talking about the sunporch in Echo Park anymore, thank God. All night long, between bands, out at the burrito cart, Karl had been laying into him about the sunporch. According to Karl, his uncle's friend Duane had a sunporch attached to his living room, and he was willing to rent it to them for a mere three hundred bucks a month. Split two ways, Karl said, that was basically nothing, and thus for basically nothing, if they could just get their shit together, they could take possession of a space. And with a space—a space!—they'd have everything they needed to start their lives of insurrection and poetry. Not that Karl ever said anything about insurrection and poetry—that would be too corny—but that was the tacit understanding between them. From this sunporch in Echo Park, they would commence their journey into the great lore of the scene, moving beyond any known category or school, unearthing all manner of secrets hidden to the vast population of squares.

Aaron liked the sunporch idea, and he was flattered that Karl, a person of such strange promise and adventure, would want him as a roommate. But unfortunately he was already committed to a handful of other plans next fall. His mom, for instance, assumed he was going to college, as did his dad. His grandpa wanted him to visit Israel, preferably soon. And then there was Joel Sterner, another friend, with whom he'd promised to drive around Mexico, a plan advanced to the degree that they were already shopping for cheap vans. At some point, he could see, some people were going to end up being disappointed, and, as much as he liked Karl's sunporch scheme, he didn't see the point of adding yet more disappointment to the list.

Normally they would have driven to Chow's, but because Karl had almost no gas, they had to walk. The trip was fifteen blocks and took them through a veritable obstacle course of ghetto traps, starting with a shitty bodega where prison-built dudes loitered, followed by a park where a knot of kids was torturing a rat, and then a vacant lot where a guy was twirling nunchakus, at every station of which Aaron's white skin glowed with invigorating vulnerability and self-doubt. At last the beacon of pink neon appeared and they crossed the final boulevard, shaky but unhurried.

Inside, Chow's was hot and loud, jammed as usual with time travelers from every epoch and dimension. Rockabilly dudes, Confederate colonels, drunken gurus, gold prospectors, wasted fairy queens, gypsy witches. The ubiquitous guy with hair cut into harsh bald patches, as if he'd been in a fight with a hyena, was there, as was the torpedo-headed guy in a motorcycle jacket with the extravagant muttonchops. Most of the crowd's costumes were not that amazing, but a few were impressively fully fleshed, not that it really mattered one way or another. In this room, no one really cared who you were. The only real crime was not pretending to be someone else.

They found a free booth patched with duct tape and ordered a mound of cheese fries from the tattooed ghoul who paused at their table. The sound of a brawl in the kitchen flared and ended with an explosion of glass as the sizzle of frying grease roared on like a monsoon. Karl had gotten onto the subject of taking a shit on acid—the terrible stench, like a ghost rising from the toilet with clanking chains, the terrifying wiping experience, like sucking one's own hand up one's ass—but as soon as the steaming pile of fries appeared, he took it as a signal to switch gears and return to the unfinished business of the sunporch, and their future.

"Duane is into it, dude," Karl said, extracting a cluster of moist potato strips from the heap. "We can move in whenever. We just say the word, dude. We're in."

"I never met Duane, did I?" Aaron said, although he knew something about Duane. He was a self-proclaimed collage artist and long-ago drummer, now a carpenter specializing in custom cabinetry for tech moguls. Aaron only brought up the subject hoping to lead them into a digression, possibly a whole new conversational galaxy.

"Duane is cool," Karl said. "Very philosophical dude. Very gentle. Deep soul. Killer pad. I told you there's an empty pool in the back, right?"

"I think so."

"And I told you Jeff Johnson's moving in, too, right? Fucking amazing dude. Total shredder. And funny as fuck. He's taking the pantry. The sunporch is by far the best spot, though. Good air. Good light. Hang a sheet and we've both got our own private pied-à-terres." He drew out the last s into a long zzz sound, curing the word of its pretensions.

Aaron nodded, folding another pinch of fries into his mouth. He chewed slowly, savoring the grease, but not slowly enough to outflank Karl.

"So, what do you say?" Karl said. "Come on. Let's do it."

"I want to," Aaron said. "I do."

"So let's."

"I'm just not sure if I can, is all."

"Why?"

This time the question came with a certain hardness and left a glassiness in the aftersilence. It seemed even Karl was getting worn out by the unresolved tack of the conversation and couldn't understand why his friend was being so adamantly evasive. He wanted some kind of agreement to occur so they could move on—they both did—and thus Aaron, against his earlier vows about keeping his other plans to himself, knowing it was going to open a whole new, seething pit of issues, went ahead and dealt the card he'd been hoping to keep facedown.

"The thing is," he said, "I might have a plan with Joel in the fall. We've been talking about driving around Mexico. I'm not sure what's happening. We might get a van and do it."

"Joel Sterner?"

"Yeah."

"Oh," Karl said, with a rare kick of surprise in his voice. He was usually seven steps ahead, or at least five steps off to the side, but this was information he hadn't anticipated. He wasn't ashamed to show he was knocked off balance.

"I see. Okay. I get it. I see what you're saying." His face darkened, and Aaron immediately felt a grave confusion enter his mind. He didn't want to throw away the sunporch just yet, and he definitely didn't want to offend Karl, not that he'd ever thought that was even possible. He'd never imagined Karl as vulnerable to something as conventional as rejection before. But he didn't want to ditch Joel, either. His two friends led toward such diametrically different lives; he didn't want to miss out on either one.

"It's not for sure or anything, though," Aaron was quick to add. "Who knows if we'll get our shit together. But if we do, I don't want to leave you hanging, you know? I want to get the sunporch. It sounds awesome, it does. I just, you know, I don't know what's happening, and I'm still trying to, you know, figure it all out . . ."

Aaron's mealy words petered out in a shrug, and when Karl spoke again it was soberly, and with a wise broadness of vision.

"I get it," he said. "I love Joel. He's awesome. I see how it is. I guess you just have to make a decision. That's all."

They continued eating. Aaron chewed without pleasure, disgusted by his own weak duplicity. He'd been thinking he might be able to avoid a decision in this matter, that fate might intervene and decide his future for him without any conflict or choice or rejections on his part at all. Surely, he'd thought, something would fall through, and he'd be left with whatever remained. It was a feeble way of blazing a trail, he realized, but he'd managed to convince himself there was even a certain Zen sagacity underneath, a principled passivity in the face of illusion. If he just waited and did nothing, destiny would have to step in, wouldn't it?

Aaron kept picking at the fries as a guy with a ridiculous mohawk held court in a packed booth across the room. The kid was pale as chalk and cadaverously thin, his body an ideal rack for his studded biker jacket and pale-blue mesh shirt. It was an impressive display, fashion-wise, very London 1978, and Aaron continued watching as the kid mimed a full Sid Vicious routine, snarling and snaring the salt shaker and shaking it on his friend's head. He instinctively hated this tenth-generation clone, this model with his mall-bought personality. He was not a lifer, he judged. Anyone could see that pose would never carry him far.

Karl blew his nose and inspected the discharge before plunking his napkin on the cold fry plate. His eyes were also fixed on the liberty-spiked punker, and to Aaron's surprise he seemed almost amused by the costume, maybe even impressed. A smile was coming over his face. Usually he wasn't moved by such derivative efforts.

"That guy wants his ass kicked," Karl said with admiration.

"I don't know," Aaron said. "Pretty stock, I'd say."

"In this neighborhood? That takes some balls."

"His mom's Navigator is parked outside."

"No," Karl said, brooking no argument. "He's cool." He lifted his snot napkin and took another huge pinch of fries. "I was just reading this book about Nazis," he said, chewing wetly. "That dude is like a badass storm trooper or something."

Aaron kept his eyes on the punker, puzzled by the turn of subject. Nazis? He couldn't tell whether Karl was being stupid or advancing some hurtful, ulterior agenda. Karl knew Aaron's family's story, of course, but his sense of political history could also be embarrassingly limited and off base. If he had some kind of twisted Nazi-chic fascination going on, Aaron didn't want to hear it. Not to mention, this kid didn't look like a Nazi.

"Okay," Aaron said. "I don't know what that means, but whatever . . ."

"The book was about goose-stepping," Karl said, obviously proud of his extracurricular readings. This kind of academic knowledge was normally Aaron's purview, and he was gladly poaching. "I've always wondered why they did that, you know? I mean, what was up with that? Goose-stepping? Kick, kick, kick." He bashed the underside of the table with his feet, unconcerned by the bothered looks from the neighbors. "The Nazis made themselves look so fucking stupid. Walking down the street like a bunch of fucking Rockettes. What was the point?"

"It was the style," Aaron said. "The Prussians started it. Armies actually still do it all over the world."

"Yeah, but this book was saying it was all just a way of fucking with people's heads. The Nazis knew they looked like total faggots doing it, but they were basically telling the people: Come on, laugh at us, you bitches. We are so fucking badass, we can walk down the street looking like total fucking faggot morons, and no one is going to call us on this shit. That's what that guy's doing. He's goose-stepping around, saying, Fuck you, motherfuckers! Suck on this! I dare the world to call my shit. He fucking rules."

"I wouldn't call him a Nazi for that."

"I would. He's a fucking awesome faggot Nazi."

Aaron sipped his drink, staring at the congealed remains on their plate. If this was Karl getting back at him for his indecision about the sunporch, picking some kind of meaningless fight, he was doing a good job of getting under his skin. He hated the frivolous Nazi talk, and even more he hated being thrown outside Karl's circle of logic, if "logic" was the word. He wondered, cringingly, if Karl's theory could somehow be construed as anti-Semitic or offensive in any way. He knew his grandfather would certainly not approve of the theory, but then again any mention of Nazis was strictly forbidden in his grandpa's presence. The Holocaust was an event so sacrosanct, it was never discussed, and thus, in a sense, any theory would be offensive. But dragging the storm troopers through Chow's, tossing them around like they were nothing? That didn't seem right, either.

The kid with the mohawk was now stripping off his jacket and flexing his pitiful muscle, inviting his fake Nancy Spungen to touch his small lump, and the whole room was pretending not to ogle him. The goose-stepping theory was aggravatingly glib, Aaron thought, but it was hard to think around, too, he couldn't deny that. There was something to it. So the verdict was still out. Was Karl a racist? An anti-Semite? A genius? An idiot? Who could say? He might be all of them at once. Part of the fun of renting a sunporch with him would be figuring that out.

4

How long ago had she stopped being happy here? It was so hard to tell from inside her fog of unhappiness. If Anne's unhappiness had taught her one thing, it was that it was the nature of unhappiness to make everything, past and present, appear as the same long, continuous unhappiness, an eternal force binding every unhappy era, even those that might have seemed otherwise at the time, into one unbreakable, unhappy life. Aaron's birth: unhappy. Falling in love: not that happy. But wasn't there some ebb and flow to it all? She'd been happy before, she remembered. Wouldn't she be happy again? But seriously, what could ever happen in this room that could possibly make her happy?

She knew the Bureau of Sustainability was a fine place to work, as fine as any, most likely. The organization's mission was unimpeachably correct—ecological stewardship of the municipal infrastructure, with an eye to global leadership in the arena of sustainable technological innovation. The pay was adequate, as were the benefits. And the office itself was a perfectly comfortable environment in which to while away one's working years, a realm of thoughtful, ergonomic furniture, modular bookshelves made of reclaimed wood, and whimsical cubical decorations proclaiming the cheerful individualism of all those who toiled here. If exotic air plants, foreign-movie posters, Japanese toy figurines, and friendly dogs roaming the maze of workstations signaled happiness, this was surely heaven on earth.

So why, then, did it all make Anne feel like sawing off her own head? Alice, her neighbor, wasn't helping matters. Her endless phone conversation about green this, nano that, eco-eco-eco, was like a vise tightening on Anne's skull. For at least twenty minutes, her voice had been flowing over the cubicle wall, piling sustainability jargon into a giant, stinking, nonsensical heap. "The retrofitting technologies are going to be game changers in the sustainability category." "The real game changer is the emergence of the social-performance corporation." Fuck that. The next time anybody stuck the prefix "eco" onto an innocent noun or verb, she was personally going to stab that person in the face.

She sipped her coffee and tried blocking Alice's voice from her head, but she didn't know where to turn. Her desk was a dreary tundra of work shit. The window in front of her was a tableau of brutalist state office buildings and unused lawns. The air was a cocktail of orange blossom room freshener, off-gassing carpets, and recycled farts. She'd been sitting in her chair for forty-five minutes, and thus far she'd managed only to open her email page, and that only in case anyone walked by and doubted her productivity. Not that anyone noticed or cared. Among the many bothersome aspects of her workplace environment, the one truly excellent thing, the thing that kept her clocking in day after day, week after week, was the incredible lack of oversight.

Her boss, Susan, was almost never there anymore, too busy off nursing her own minor celebrity as an eco-guru at environmental symposia around the globe. And, since Anne's job title, assistant to the director of the Bureau of Sustainability, made her neither answerable to anyone else, nor directly responsible for managing anyone else, she lived her days in a gilded cage of benign neglect, free to pursue whatever personal agendas she chose as long as the basic work duties for Susan got done. Today, the personal agenda was the locating of a live-in caregiver for her dad. Following the trip to Fountainview and the subsequent thirty-second conversation they'd had about the experience ("I'm not going there," "You're sure?" "Yes."), it had become apparent that he wouldn't be moving into managed care just yet, and that meant he was going to have to accept a live-in nurse to make sure his house was reasonably clean and his meals were hot. A paid roommate would be easily as expensive as the tuition at Fountainview, she'd already calculated, but without the sauna and fine china in his face, her father might not suspect it. She had power of attorney, which meant he would never have to know the true numbers.

She looked over her crimped notes, the crossed-out names and phone numbers, a few with scratched words beside them. "No English." "Weird vibe." "Phone disconnected/bad sign." She'd assumed it would be easy to find an angelic helpmate, considering the amount of money she planned to spend, but the search was proving harder than expected. Didn't anyone want to take her money to wipe her father's ass? But, as it turned out, the market had once again beaten her to the punch, mopping up all the best caregivers in a seventy-mile radius. They were already wiping the asses of Mr. Cody and Mrs. Hutchinson, Mr. Johnson and Mrs. Margolis, all the ancient lawyers and surgeons of yesteryear. What was worse, the best caregivers tended to stay on their assignments for years at a time, what with modern medical science expanding the twilight years into perpetuity. She was left in the awkward position of hoping one of her friends' parents had a sudden aneurysm just so she could scoop up the help.

She went through the list one more time, ranking the options. The best ones were brown people, of course. Not only were they a little cheaper; they also hailed from tribal village cultures that ostensibly valued the elderly and paid them due respect. Fijians had an especially good reputation. Mexicans were also highly rated. Russians were to be avoided, though Bosnians were all right. All the new arrivals were in the game, it seemed, elder care being the new immigrant grocery store, America's entry-level rung on the ladder to fortune.

She had her eye on Temo. He was Fijian, with a long line of illustrious clientele, the most recent being Mark Felt, a.k.a. Deep Throat, the Watergate informant—yes, that one. If Temo was good enough for Deep Throat, she figured, he was surely good enough for her dad, a much less renowned and demanding character. From what she'd discovered, Temo's current charge, a Mr. Dimond, was on the verge of entering hospice care and likely didn't have long to go, though who could really say? It was also possible that Mr. Dimond would hang in for a long while yet. These end-of-life ordeals were so hard to predict. He might die and come back to life or take refuge in an iron lung like some immortal hot dog under a heat lamp. The life-extension technologies these days were truly appalling. She was starting to think her own generation might never die at all. They might nurse themselves along forever, cloning their organs and filtering their blood, surviving on the cusp of death until the sun exploded and they all evaporated in a wave of solar heat. Which meant the search for a live-in nurse would only get worse.

She stared out the window at the building across the quad. It had once been such a vivid, pleasing view, the palms abutting the silver rectangle of the building's face, the bellies of the distant clouds lopped by the building's roofline, but today it all looked dim and unmagical. Ugly architecture hosting scenes of endlessly boring, futile effort. An affront to the human spirit. Or even worse than an affront. Less than an affront. Nothing at all.

She called Aaron, her son, but he didn't pick up, and upon putting down her phone, she decided, for no more reason than she'd had two seconds before, that Temo was the one. The others all had some kind of problem, and she was willing to wait a little longer. In the meantime, she just had to figure out some temporary measure. So far, the only idea she'd come up with was Aaron.

Aaron was such a complaining little shit, she hated to ask him to take out the trash, let alone tend to her deteriorating dad, but she really needed somebody present in case of emergency. He had the time, what with his half-day senior schedule, and in a few weeks, once summer started, he'd have all the time in the world. Plus, there were other motives, too. Aaron would be leaving home soon, and this could well be his last chance to store away the old family memories, and it could be the last chance for her dad to bask in his grandson's presence. It would be a mitzvah for both of them, she thought, and possibly even for humanity at large. The stories had to be passed down, as terrible as those stories might be. And so it was decided. She would ask Aaron to lend a hand, if not for her father, if not for her son, if not for herself, then for the legacy of the Holocaust itself. The only question now was how much to pay him.

That done, she got down to real work, zipping off a memo to Susan, currently in Atlanta, providing a bullet list of updates on the seven projects she was interminably shepherding through the bureaucracy, positive it would go unread but wanting the memo placed somewhere in the data stream as proof of something or other, her existence, maybe.

Midmorning, she sat through a meeting that epitomized everything she despised about her current station in life. It took place at a nearby state building, in a windowless conference room, at a much-too-large table, with four representatives of overlapping regulatory agencies tasked with formulating strategies on how best to increase public awareness about the solarization pilot project in the Richmond neighborhood. The agenda should have been incredibly simple to address. The solution, obviously, was door flyers. And yet, unbelievably, the people at the meeting refused even to directly address this strategy, instead veering sideways and filling the whole late-morning time slot with a vapid, aggravating, willfully stupid exchange of abstractions upon abstractions about abstractions. The "communication" with the neighborhood would have to incorporate a diversity of languages because the assumption that English was the common language was Anglocentric and offensive to the realities of the current public sphere. The "communication" would also have to be carefully phrased so as not to offend renters, who likely did not have the power to decide upon their property's fate but who could be construed as allies in the larger campaign. The "communication" would also have to avoid any reference to public funding, as suspicion of the government was rampant at every level of society, for different sociopolitical reasons, some of them quite legitimate in the larger historical frame. Anne was amazed by the energy expended simply to ensure the complete inoffensiveness of the designated "communication," as if all the lavender-scented padding against any possible scrape or bruise or hurt feeling weren't fundamentally offensive in itself. In the end, the meeting was adjourned, like so many, without consensus, the nature of the "communication" to be decided at a later date, after all the bureaucrats had returned to their respective cubicle farms and polled their colleagues about what form of media best served their common constituencies, by which time Anne would have the fucking flyer ready to go.

She went back to the office and extracted her sack lunch from the refrigerator and decamped in Victoria Boberg's empty office for some privacy. Victoria Boberg was on maternity leave, and her glassed-in office space had become a favorite tank for personal phone calls among the staff. Every day, it hosted a revolving cast of secretaries, architects, HR people, and interns scheduling their children's pickups and confirming their blind dates, the pictures of Victoria's kids and husband privy to all manner of secret dealings.

Anne's agenda wasn't secret, per se—she just wanted to clear her head—but as long as she was taking space in Victoria's office, she felt compelled to look busy. Thus, she took out her phone, and once her phone was out, she decided to go ahead and make a few calls, lunch being a good time to dispense with some of her most desultory obligations. Since most people were out of their offices during lunch, she could usually leave some quick return-messages without becoming entangled in unnecessary conversation. She found a nearly masochistic pleasure in the nonproductive, zero sum game, especially since she'd recently learned the real definition of "masochism." It wasn't pleasure in pain, as she'd always been led to understand, and which had never exactly squared logically in her mind, but rather the hastening, the controlling, of inevitable pain. Pain would come, that much was a given. The masochist simply preferred to get the pain over with on his or her own schedule. Now, that was a deviancy she could understand.

The first name on her list was Mark Harris, whom she'd been ignoring in her email queue for going on two months and who, in the past week, had escalated his attack to phone calls, a bold move, and one she had to admire. She could sort of recall meeting Harris at a conference in Denver. She had a picture of a tall, energetic, golden-haired man with a confident, thrusting jaw. Like a Greek discus thrower or a javelin hurler, someone in a short toga. A quick googling informed her he was a "green developer" hailing from Portland, Oregon, known best for erecting an entire neighborhood of LEED platinum high-rises on some brownfields along the riverfront. In Denver, they'd talked about—now she remembered—bioswales.

She was midway through her first granola bar when his self-assured voice suddenly leapt into her ear: "Anne! Fantastic!" he said. "Thanks so much for getting back! I was just thinking about you. Seriously. How are you doing? It's been a long time. Too long."

Mark Harris's sporty bark ignited a whole branch of suppressed memories in the recesses of Anne's head. Now she remembered him, all too well—how he'd dominated her for a solid half hour in the Denver Marriott, selling her on the carbon-neutral grocery store chain he was trying to develop. The banks were afraid to touch him with a ten-foot pole, he'd complained, stuck too deep in their old, industrial-era paradigms, thus unable to manifest a truly radical future vision. Now she remembered why she hadn't been answering the calls. His eco-salesmanship had been so unabashed, so craven, she'd never wanted to talk to him again. She coughed, forcing down the last granola bite, wincing as the rough corner scraped along the back of her gullet.

"Mark," she choked. "Hi." She pounded her sternum, holding the phone away from her face. "I'm fine, fine." *Cough.* "Sorry if I've been kind of hard to reach lately. Busy times around here."

"No worries, Anne!" Mark spoke like a carnival barker, intolerant of any doubt. "You're an important person, I know. I'm low on the list. I get it. No problems. I'm just glad we're on the phone now. I have to tell you, I've been blown away by your work for a long time. That coalition you organized to stop the marina development in Santa Monica, I don't think anybody saw the numbers there, but wow. I almost shat my pants when they pulled the plug on that one. That was some David and Goliath shit, seriously."

"Oh, well, you know . . ."

"It seems like every solid piece of city legislation I read has your fingerprints all over it. So thank you again so much for taking this time. I'm truly grateful."

"Okay, Mark, whatever," she said. "I'm glad we caught up with each other today, too. So what's on your mind, anyway? What's happening?"

"Well, it's complicated," Mark said, slowing down the pace. If she'd been hoping for some brisk volley and a rapid sign-off, she was already disappointed. He was launching into a long preamble about how delicate the coming subject matter was going to be, how he'd really like to talk to her face to face if possible, and before she knew it she could feel the time burning away. She could tell she was going to have to manage the pacing herself if she wanted to keep this conversation moving, even at the risk of sounding like a rude bitch.

"What are we talking about here, Mark?" she broke in. "My lunch calendar is packed for six months out. Tell me what's on your mind."

"Well," he said, with undiminished good cheer, "I can tell you it involves your city's wastewater supply, I can tell you that much right now."

"Uh-huh. And?"

"And I can tell you I'm looking for some help landing a permit to put that wastewater to good use. That's the short version. But seriously, Anne, I'd much rather give you the details in person. This is a big project. It isn't something I can really describe in one go."

"It sounds like you need someone in the Sanitation Department," she said decisively. "They're the wastewater people. How about I give you the number of Damon Hardy, all right? He's been over there ten years. Very good guy. Let's see, let's see . . ." Wastewater, she was thinking, scrolling through her contacts. No, thank you, Mark. The subject of wastewater had dominated her life for a solid ten months back in 2003. She'd had enough talk of brown water, black water, filtration, and repurposing to last the rest of her life. This was Sanitation's problem, and she couldn't wait to throw it in their lap.

"I'm telling you . . . ," she said, struggling to cue the right contact on her screen, "I just . . . I just . . ." Her mind, divided between the phone and the monitor, was having trouble concentrating in either realm.

"I've been doing research, Anne," Mark said, breaking in gently. "I've been watching you for a long time, and talking to a lot of very smart people, and everyone agrees you score really high marks on getting things done at city hall. I'm pretty sure you're the one I want to talk to. Come on. Have lunch with me. We'll enter into a discussion and see where it goes."

"No, it's Sanitation you want, believe me . . ."

"I talked to them. I know Hardy. Seriously, I've been calling you for a reason."

"Well, then, you probably want to talk to Susan, my boss," she offered, going for one of the most common weapons in her arsenal. A conversation with Susan was almost impossible to schedule, and few people had the patience to wait. If she couldn't pass the buck to Sanitation, she'd pass the buck up the ladder to Susan, and up there the buck was as good as lost.

"No," he said, still genially, but with unshakable conviction. "I know all about Susan. We've met a few times. I know Susan's a big name and everything. She's moving up in the world. But let's just be honest here for a second, all right? We all know how the big names work. The big name isn't really a doer at a certain point. The name is just the brand. The people doing the actual work and making the actual decisions all live under the big name. I happen to think you're the one who does most of the work and makes the decisions for the brand named Susan Jacoby these days. In fact, I'm pretty sure about that. She might be the name, 'the mayor whisperer' and all, but you're the Susan whisperer. That's who I want to talk to."

"The mayor whisperer whisperer," Anne said, unable to resist. Apparently Mark had read the *Los Angeles* magazine profile of a year ago that had caused so much loathing among the staff.

"Right. That's where the leverage is."

Anne was flattered by Mark Harris's interpretation of her power. And what he was saying was not even entirely untrue. In fact, his opinion confirmed a long-held fantasy she had of herself as a political consigliere in the classic mold. The power behind the throne. The adviser providing the theoretical frameworks, creating the literal verbiage so the queen could appear informed. The interviews she'd ghostwritten for Susan had been quoted publicly by cabinet members! But part of her job was also concealing that fact, and she had the presence of mind to demur.

"I think you've got the wrong person, Mark," she said. "I'm a member of a team, that's all. And we don't have any power over the water."

"Just have lunch with me, Anne," he said. "Worst case, you eat a nice lunch. Best case, there's something in this idea for both of us."

Everything in her body told her to say no to Mark just one more time. One more no and the natural, rhetorical structure of their conversation would have run its course and they could respectfully hang up and move on. They might pretend some later conversation was in store, but they'd both understand that the fundamental rejection had been established. On a basic, subverbal level, she could already feel herself turning away, forgetting that Mark Harris had ever existed. And yet, sitting there in the private cell of Victoria's office, watching Megan Pong biding her time to take her place and Alex Mead jockeying for the next position, seeing the green architects at their standing desks, these sullen, defeated eunuchs of sustainability, knowing her own shit desk was waiting for her ass to return, Anne had another thought, too: maybe, just maybe, it was time to quit listening to her own goddamn intuitions so much. What good had her intuitions been doing her lately? Maybe it was time to finally start acting against her intuitions, to zag instead of zig, and go have lunch with a clown like Mark Harris. Why not? And it was under this counterintuitive logic that she went ahead and agreed to put something on the books.

She returned to her desk and succumbed once again to generalized hate. Her coffee was cold, the smell of someone's bean dish was overpowering, the succulents on Alice's ledge were tired and dusty, as always, and as they always would be. Her phone buzzed angrily near her hand, a series of dumb spasms against the wood. According to her monitor Aaron had taken approximately three hours to return the call. Or maybe Temo's client had died—how wonderful that news would be.

But the call wasn't her son, or Temo. It was Ben, her brother. How very odd, she thought, to see his name on her tiny screen.

5

The Pentagon wished it could design something as perfect as a hawk. With the slightest tip of its wing, the raptor navigated the open sky, cutting cruel pathways across the turbulence of the rising thermals. It swooped and turned. It floated. It sank. And for long moments at a time—sometimes ten breaths, Ben counted—the hawk would pause, hovering like a geosynchronous satellite over the arid earth, scanning with its black, stony eyes for any moving food on the ground below.

Ben sipped from the canteen and watched the mild rocking in the hawk's body as it held its airspace. He admired the bird's single-minded resolve, the stark hunger that drove every movement, every turn. Whatever beauty the bird shed was a mere side effect of its overriding killing motive. Ben watched as the feathers tippled again and the sleek body arced out over the cracked lake bed on another sweep for prey. On any other day he would have waited for it to return, taking in the fast, graceful chase of shadow over earth until the taloned bird screamed overhead like a B-25 Mitchell, but on this day he had to go. He still had seven miles of desert to walk, and a hundred fifty miles to drive, just to get to dinner.

He didn't want to go to dinner, but he didn't see how to avoid it. The dinner was at his sister's house, with his dad and nephew, too, none of whom he'd seen for going on five years, and thus not showing up would be an insult of the most grievous sort. Three days ago it had sounded like a great idea. After a month in the desert, basking in the deep silence and solitude, he'd assumed he was ready. He'd become serene and untroubled by all the ghosts and violent death visions that had plagued him so badly in the city. He'd even become happy, in a way, visited by regular upwellings of love for his family. At times he'd almost been overpowered by the gushing feeling, as if his soul were physically attached to theirs at the ends of invisible, thrumming strings. Space and time seemed to disappear, and they all found each other in a warm alternate dimension, laughing and hugging in the dappled sun. It had been during one of those tender surges that he'd called his sister and agreed to have dinner at her house. But within about a minute of hanging up, he'd begun doubting it was for the best.

He hiked past a giant pile of broken limestone, an alien stretch of eggshell brittleness, and the border of a pristine salt flat, barely noticing the wonders of color and light that surrounded him. All he could think about was dinner. Why had he ever said he'd go? It was a terrible idea. What he really needed to do was stay put. He needed to remain exactly where he was, keeping exactly the same quiet schedule. He needed to wake up with the pale moon and spend the afternoon observing the sprawling ants and make conversation with the occasional tarantula and horned lizard, if he felt so moved. What he didn't need was to go into the city for dinner. Not when he'd been loving his family so perfectly from afar.

At a boulder with a mashed face, he descended into a canyon's balm of shadow, emerging onto a patch of powdered earth where his RV waited. He'd chosen the spot for practical reasons—easily defensible, a safe five hundred meters from the main road, well beyond the accuracy range of an M16 or M4 carbine—but he'd come to appreciate it for the ancient walls and clean, sandstone smell. With a blast of sun-heated water from the plastic bladder on the roof, he rinsed the dust and sunscreen off his body, and then he stood still, allowing the air to swarm him gently from all sides. He saw no way out. His family would never forgive him if he failed to show. It was so ironic, then, he thought, that the very desert silence that had nursed him back to health was already pushing him back into the cruel static of the grid. The silence had been too strong, too healing. And so it was with a forlorn sense of duty that he stepped into his trailer and slid on his slacks and cross-trainers, suiting up for dinner with all the grim discipline and conservation of motion of going into battle.

Half an hour on the road, and the billboards were back, blaring their news of fast food, Indian casinos, and top-forty radio stations, their endless, unabashed promises leading always to exactly the same horseshit. Mile by mile, the grid took him in. After a life of blindness, he saw the grid in all its accreting history now. The grid of power. The grid of entertainment. The grid of mindless consumption. "The grid" was no longer even the right phrase, was it? It had evolved into something not so gridlike at all. An organic creature, curvaceous and multidimensional. A bulging, Day-Glo, genetically engineered octopus with wet tentacles snaking everywhere, sucking the world of its nutrients. Although maybe that wasn't right, either, he thought. "Octopus" made the grid sound too sentient, too conscious. The grid was a zombie, a frictionless fractal of sound and color, as dead as a kaleidoscope.

He curled down the San Bernardino Freeway, cresting the San Gabriels into the grid's very belly, the diamond fields of Los Angeles herself, her lights just shivering to life beneath the scurf of orange-brown sunset. Speeding along 101, he scanned the eight million lights for Anne's light. One of the lights was hers and one of them was his dad's and one of them was his old friend Bill Wren's. It was strange to think how every point of light out there marked the home of a sister or a daughter, a grandfather or a girlfriend, that singly each dot of light housed the promise of love. And yet, collected together, draining energy from faraway dams, hollowing out the very guts of the world, the lights became something decidedly other than love. The lights became a pox on the land. How? How did the singular points of decency add up to this collective evil? Where did the toxin enter the system? One person, one light—that was fine. Two people were fine. Maybe three was the number of avarice and destruction. That was occult, kabbalistic thinking, he knew, but he couldn't get the thought out of his head. Three was the tipping point. Three was the warp in the math. One plus one plus one added up to society, and society was a disease, without mind or morality.

As he entered Echo Park, the traffic gathered on every side, and suddenly the racing electrons of L.A. jumped in amplitude. He'd tried to prepare himself, but the onslaught still took him by surprise. Drifting along with the traffic, he wished only that he could turn back and take refuge in the silent desert again, already pierced by the knowledge that the desert had allowed him to forget—namely, that he'd left L.A. to avoid committing some terrible act.

He made his way to Anne's street and beached his car at the curb. Mercifully, her neighborhood was quiet and still. Anne's house was a modest Spanish bungalow, a little white cake of stucco fronted by a lima-bean lawn, bowered by eucalyptus and figs. The neighbor's rock wall made a tidy border. Here was a modest American life with some dignity and grace.

Ben sat in his car, trying to catch his breath. His sister would see through him in this racked state, he knew. She would see everything, just as she always had. His dad would also see through him, see what he'd become. Maybe it wasn't too late to call in sick, he thought. He could tell her he had food poisoning or strep throat. Maybe he could drive away and ram the car into a wall, call from the hospital. That seemed a bit extreme. Why couldn't he just open the door and walk up the path?

He was still trying to send signals of strength into his arm, telling it to go ahead and pry open the door's latch, when Anne materialized on the front steps. Her slim shadow was unmistakable in the golden light, that cocked hip and bowed leg. At the sight of his sister's telltale posture, he was reinvigorated. His days-long torment magically lifted. What had he been thinking? It was her! His sister. His dear sister, his precious older sister, his person, his puzzle. The one who'd shared the woolen blanket on Saturday mornings at the heater vent near the wooden stairs. The one who'd fought for the tapioca in the fluted cups in the yellow refrigerator. The person he loved more than life itself.

He pushed himself out of the car and strode up the walk, and before he knew it he was taking Anne in his arms, feeling the delicate bones in her back, so light they almost seemed hollow, breathing in her smell of cornmeal and a hint of cilantro. He could have stood there hugging her for a year and a half, crushing her gently into his chest, but eventually he had to step back and face her, beaming. He stared into her hazel eyes, feeling her hands on his forearms, relishing the last moments before the pure, natural, unblemished love between them would have to be tested.

"About fucking time," she said.

"Missed you, too, sis."

"Drive okay?"

"Pretty much. I got here anyway."

"Feel those muscles. You are such a specimen."

More hugging and laughter ensued. Hugging of his nephew, utterly transformed in five years, and hugging of his dad, undeniably old, and then a tumble inside the house, into Anne's bastion of superliberalism. In a blur, Ben caught sight of rice-paper lamp shades, hanging Paraguayan rugs, the framed woodblock print of the organizer Joe Hill. Even the beer was leftist, a thick brown bottle decorated with hand-tooled vines, emitting a perfume of molasses and gardenias, so unlike the piss water favored by the studs of the military.

"So how long are you around, anyway?" she asked. "I guess you're on leave or something? Between assignments?"

"More like retired," he said, pulling on the welcome beer. "I've been out for a few months already. Just taking it easy for a while. Figuring things out."

"Oh," she said. "That's big news. Where've you been?"

"Around."

"You could have called."

"Well . . . you know . . ."

"You'd have to kill me if you told me what you were doing? Top secret? Is that it?"

"Something like that."

"Well. But I hope we get to see a little more of you. That'd be really nice."

The task of establishing the night's chemistry fell to the siblings, which only made sense. Aaron was practically a stranger to Ben, whereas Ben's dad was like a mute rock, giving nothing except the simple fact of himself, which—if you were willing to understand it as the deepest, most unconditional stolidity and love, merely expressed on a frequency far below any human sensory perception—was generally enough. There would never be any surprises or tests from his dad. They would always pick up in the same wordless place they'd left off. He didn't even need to go home to know that.

So for the benefit of the generations on either side, Ben and Anne performed their rapport. Anne started by asking him about work and former classmates, and he asked her about work and real estate. They talked about the weather. And soon enough, unsurprisingly, questions of politics were finding their way into the conversation. It was a topic they'd been debating for many years, across many administrations and many wars, with rare moments of accord, and, although he didn't want to get into it now, to quit at this point would almost be strange.

"How go the wars?" Anne asked him, jauntily. "How are all those hearts and minds in Afghanistan doing, little brother?"

"They seem all right," he said, mumbling into his beer. "Like you read in the papers. You know."

"Papers lie," she said. "Come on, Ben. Give us the real shit."

"I don't know," he said. "I'm out of it."

"Oh, come on, give us something. You were there a long time. We want to be educated."

He shrugged and drank. She was trying to be light, he knew, expressing interest in what she thought of as his area of expertise, but the undercurrent of judgment was impossible to miss. She just couldn't help herself. She had to jockey for the ultimate angle, almost without knowing she was jockeying. She was a bottomless geology of love and judgment, layer upon layer, the bedrock, after all these years, still yet to be touched.

"Don't disappoint Aaron," she pushed. She was on the couch with her feet tucked under her legs, the very picture of domestic comfort and leisure. "I told him you were a master of the game. I told him there's probably nobody better at it in the whole world."

"I don't know what you mean," he said.

"Yes, you do! You practically invented the game!"

"I don't know what game you mean."

"You know. The Most Dangerous Game."

At these words Ben inwardly moaned with dismay. Now he understood what she was talking about. She was casting back thirty years, to that fateful night in the family van, on the way home from her volleyball practice, the heat of a Round Table pizza box seeping into his knees, the night he'd made the joke about someday wanting to hunt human beings. It was a joke that had never been forgotten. It had just been a stupid, passing, teenage thing to say, with no significance other than mild shock value. They'd read the story in English class that week, and everyone was making the same crack. And yet Anne had filed it away as ironclad evidence of his essential blood thirst. Ever since, she'd held him to that stupid, insignificant moment. "How's the people hunting?" "Bag any humans in

Baghdad this year?" He wondered how much of his life had been a response to her withering, unfair judgment. How many sacrifices had he made just to prove her wrong?

"Your mom thinks she's really hilarious," he told Aaron.

"No kidding," Aaron said.

"Does she get up your ass all the time, too?"

"Oh yeah."

"Oh please," Anne said. "Don't be such pussies. I thought my guys were supposed to be tough."

Mercifully, the buzzer on the oven went off, and the theater of conversation shifted to the kitchen, where Anne and Aaron began chopping onions and peppers and kindly shouldered the conversational yoke for a while. In the lair of hanging copper skillets and dangling garlic ropes, they rambled over topics of easy familiarity like Aaron's teachers and his friends' drug use and sexual proclivities, keeping everything nice and breezy, if extremely local in reference, and Ben gladly took the chance to drift into his own private lagoon of reflection.

Aaron was handy with a chopping knife, he noted, as an only child of a single mom should be. He also noted that Aaron's child's body had molted since the last visit, evolving into the body of a tall, thin young man. His face didn't look much like Anne's, Ben thought, the Polish and Hungarian Jew features a fleeting shadow from certain angles, at best, but his dad's face, as he recalled it, was deeply imprinted. The face of the blond, bum surfer, the uprooted Okie fried by the western sun. It looked as if Aaron would end up with his father's perfect Aryan proportions when he filled out, too, probably also his dad's haplessness and sloth. What a burn, he thought, that that loser had somehow asserted genetic dominance in the pool.

And his own dad: he was so old. Off in the corner he sat in pathetic isolation. He'd never been a big talker, but he'd at least been a vigorous, healthy presence in a room. In the past years his skin had turned papery and sallow. His eyes were puffy and muddled. His body, once a solid boulder of muscle, was more like a sandbag, with much extra heft sagging around the midsection. Even his clothes—stained Old Navy sweats and a wash-worn T-shirt—were a downgrade from the old days of perma-pressed pants and flammable leisure shirts. Ben wanted to pull Anne aside and ask her about his health, his memory, his general state of mind, but he didn't see how.

Gazing at his dad's down-turned face, feeling the realness of his physical presence, Ben sensed the ghosts returning again, more of them than he'd ever seen in one place. It was a whole crowd of shadow-gutted faces this time. Eyeless, voiceless faces, wavering in the air, shooting razors of pain straight into his skull. The pain was probing and fantastic. Webs of pain winding through his brain's nerves. Ben knew he was the only one in touch with the ghosts, but it was difficult to keep acting normal. The ghosts clustered around his dad's body, offering up their premonitions or memories or warnings or curses—Ben had no clue. He tried to listen to the words flowing between his sister and his nephew, but nothing could really penetrate the sizzling in his head. Who were they? Ben wondered. He could barely see them through his watering eyes. The pain tolled in his head like a bell. They wouldn't stop coming around. And now they had some kind of designs on his family.

It was the tacos that finally brought him back into the moment. Gusts of beef brisket were wafting through, and after a month of protein shakes, jerky, and convenience-store bananas, the smell held an even stronger power than ghosts. Shakily, Ben managed to dig a chip into Anne's homemade salsa, tasting chipotle and jalapeño, and forced the ghosts back into the walls. To keep things going in the right direction, he tried joining the conversation, thinking this might be a good time to establish some avuncular connection with his nephew.

"So hey, Aaron," he said, wiping his eyes, "you have a girlfriend these days or something?"

"Uh, no," Aaron said.

"No? How come?" He wasn't asking in a pointed way, but only out of curiosity. He realized the interrogation was probably no fun for Aaron, but he had no other great moves. What was an uncle supposed to do?

"I don't know," Aaron said.

"I mean, you're a good-looking kid."

"Eh."

"Shit, I wouldn't worry about it," Ben said. He dipped two chips at once and scarfed them down. "I never had a lot of girlfriends at your age, either. Girls scared the shit out of me back then, to be honest. I mean, they didn't scare me"— he checked himself, wanting to be precise for his nephew's ravening teenage mind—"they just bored me. I guess that was it. It wasn't their fault. They just didn't share my interests."

"Ha! I'll say," Anne cut in. "Judo and staff fighting? Not a lot of teenage girls in those dojos of yours. What about you, though, Ben? Any romance in your life these days? What's going on in that department for you?"

"Nothing," he said.

"No?"

"Uh-uh. It never really seemed like a good idea, what with the career and all."

"Oh, come on . . ."

"No, it's true. I see all the guys in the forces getting married, and it's always so much crap. They don't give a shit about their women. They like the idea of a little lady back home, but the truth is, actually sitting there on a lawn with their kids and their neighbors is like death to them. Worse than war. They don't have the guts to deal with the boredom of family life, you know? No inner resources. Anyway, I never wanted to treat a woman like that. Better just to get whores."

"Uh . . ."

Anne and Aaron were staring at each other, and Ben understood he'd gone too far. "Anyway," he said. "You playing any sports, Aaron?"

"No."

"Any plans after graduation?"

"Not really."

Ben loaded another chip and gave up. Better to let his nephew return to mincing peppers into atom-sized bits. He could tell from Anne's scrupulously blasé chopping that he'd hit on a household nerve with the postgraduation question, and he was tempted to keep exploring the sore spot but figured for Aaron's sake he should probably back off. Instead he fetched his fourth beer, brewed, he found, near the Russian River in Mendocino County by grateful, anticonglomerate artisans who enjoyed hang gliding and rock climbing on days off. Beer was proving a good antidote to ghosts.

Anne's tacos turned out to be much more elaborate than their mom's had been. They'd eaten her tacos as a twice-weekly staple, but there was no crumbled Safeway hamburger or canned refried beans here. Instead it was organic beef, heirloom beans, handmade tortillas, and guacamole with many minuscule flecks of seasoning. And yet, still, the sight of the old family meal made Ben's nerves tingle hotly in his nose and eyes, bringing on a shot of consciousness around the tragic endurance of his motherless family, how inconsolably they all still missed her. "The tacos look amazing," he said, and Anne patted him on the shoulders, understanding, or not, the rich depths of the compliment.

When the tortillas were ready, the arrangement of the bowls on the table achieving a perfect picture of bounty, Ben gently helped his dad into his seat, and without any preliminaries or prayers, the family commenced building their tacos. Warm tortillas circled the table and flopped onto plates; spoons flashed in bowls. Beans as mortar, next meat, next cheese, next the batting of cabbage and onion sprinkles. They all had their own methods of construction.

The quiet was welcome and hearty at first, nothing about whores or organized slaughter to distract them from the eating pleasure, but soon it became prolonged and awkward. Anne and Aaron filled the space by talking about the provenance of the beans, and Ben's dad groused about the spice level, but nothing caught. How sad, Ben thought, if they were already at the end of their news. How badly he yearned to break through and acknowledge the moving reality they were sharing, this rare miracle of togetherness. If only the clean, loving silence of the desert could descend on them and allow them to feel the brevity of their time on earth. He was still searching for the right way of expressing himself when Aaron, pinched perhaps by the same feelings, opened the way.

"So, Uncle Ben," he said, catching the corner of Ben's eye, "you went straight into the army after high school, is that right?"

The question sounded casual enough, but the topic had obviously been on Aaron's mind. Ben could sense an unfinished argument between Aaron and his mom somewhere in the background, and it occurred to him he was possibly being used as a proxy of some kind, but he didn't care. He was just glad to have a topic. And maybe his nephew, on the cusp of leaving home, actually had an interest in the nature of human will and destiny. Ben had some definite ideas to share on that topic, if anyone cared.

"The navy," Ben said. "SEALs are navy. But yeah, right in."

"And you always knew you wanted to go."

"I wanted to join the SEALs, yeah. I'd come to that conclusion through my reading and thinking at about your age."

"Why?"

Ben built himself another taco, weighing his words, sensing an opportunity before him—a rare chance to speak to his family with some profundity, possibly even on multiple registers at once. He could speak to Anne, for instance, with a measure of confession in his voice, a nuance of apology, insinuating that he'd possibly been wrong in certain presumptions over the years and that he was almost ready to acknowledge that fact. Not quite, but he was getting there. He could speak to his father, meanwhile, in a voice of gratitude. Everything he'd done was to honor him, and if he'd made mistakes it was only in an effort to understand and protect his legacy. And he could speak to his nephew in a tone of wisdom and inspiration. This is my story; learn from it what you can. You are stepping into a world full of danger, so beware. Three elegantly separate, customized meanings, one for each listener. But mostly, he had to admit, the words would be for Anne.

"I wanted a test," he said. "I wanted to go out and do the hardest thing possible. I wanted to see how heavy a load I could take. That's just me, though. I had the idea it'd be good for the soul."

"Good for the soul?" Anne said, mildly incredulous.

"I wanted to sacrifice something," he said sincerely. "Does that sound so weird?"

"Kind of weird," Anne said. "Yeah."

"It might sound weird in this day and age," he said, turning to Aaron, "to sacrifice anything. Most people don't give a fuck. It's all just me, me, me, all the time, fuck the rest of the world. Who gives a shit where my shoes come from, you know? Who cares about that kid in the factory in Pakistan? Just give me my shoes. Shit, that kid would take the shoes, too, if he could. Just dumb luck, really. But that's not how I ever wanted to be. I didn't want the shoes. I wanted to give something up. I wanted to give up as much as I could to secure the safety of my family, and my country, and all the people I loved. I don't know if that's what I ended up doing, but that was the goal. I wanted to serve." He took a swig of beer, letting the words hit their respective targets. "That's how they get you, by the way," he added. "Your good intentions."

"'Good intentions,'" Anne echoed.

"That's what I said," Ben said.

"And you feel like it worked out?" Aaron said, meeting his uncle's sincerity with his own. "Your service?"

"Hell if I know," he said, draining the beer. "I can say I've seen the best and worst that a man can do out there. I can say that much. And I can say I've been tested to the absolute limit, physically and mentally. What I found out wasn't exactly what I wanted to know, but what the fuck? You can't go back in time and be any smarter."

"I never understood the whole valor thing," Anne said. Her fingers were covered in hot sauce, and she licked a rivulet off her pinky. "What kind of idea is that? Valor only makes sense as some virtue in the military. Valor."

"I'm not talking about valor," Ben said.

"And would you do it again?" Aaron said, maintaining sincerity. "Join up again?"

Ben looked each of his family members in the eyes, ignoring Anne's arrows of cynicism. "I don't think I was wrong to go, if that's what you mean," he said. "If I made any mistakes, they were honest mistakes. I think I went for good reasons. And if I hadn't gone, then, well, shit, I wouldn't know what I know now, and I wouldn't want that. I'd never want to not know. But now that I know, and I've seen what I've seen, I have to be true to that, too. So things are different for me now, yeah. I . . . I don't know what I'd do. I don't really know." His gaze had fallen to the table; he was losing his thread.

"I bet you've seen some crazy shit," Aaron said.

"That, I'm afraid, is very true."

Ben stared at the stray beans on his plate. He could sense Aaron was rapt, and that was gratifying, at least. It made him wonder if possibly Anne hadn't been poisoning her son's mind against him all these years after all. Was that conceivable? The hope was enough to keep him at the table, anyway, when his main desire was only to walk to the car and drive back into the silence. But he saw his young nephew so rarely. In a sense, they barely knew each other. And here they were, blood kin, eating tacos and drinking beer in his sister's dining room. Ben thought he might even sense an understanding growing between them, maybe even a chance to make a real impression on the kid. Had he seen crazy shit? Oh yeah, he'd seen crazy shit. As it happened, he had dozens of excellent, top-secret, shit-crazy, action-adventure stories in his pocket, ready to roll.

"I probably shouldn't even tell you about this . . . ," he said, and proceeded to recount a vintage yarn about the time he'd blown up a Tomahawk missile in the desert of Kuwait. The story commenced on an aircraft carrier on the Indian Ocean. It involved a jump out of a helicopter into the raging waves, a secret contact in the dunes. The demolition of the stray, misfired missile in the sand, followed by a moonlit race back to the water. It was a good story, a test of endurance, with no victims involved, only heroes, and Aaron made plenty of hums and squawks of disbelief all the way through. It would all have been perfect if not for Anne smirking and shaking her head the whole time from her perch off to the side.

"What's so funny?" he said as the story drew to a close. "That really happened, you know. That's the kind of thing we do all the time."

"It's just funny, that's all," she said. "What you do."

"I wasn't trying to be funny," he said. "People have no idea what we do. Sitting in their fucking SUVs, drinking Starbucks in their heated seats. Taking their orders from Google and motherfucking Facebook. How would they ever know?"

"No, no, I know," she said.

"They think everything's real under control, but they have no fucking clue."

"I'm not arguing. Calm down. All I'm saying is, you did it. You're an action hero. You became your guy. Arnold. It's amazing."

Ben tore a bite off his taco, his heart sinking. "I don't know what you're talking about," he said, though he had a guess. He chewed on the no-longer-so-delicious taco, waiting for the next inevitable lash of criticism to come.

"You know . . ." She lowered her voice and fogged her eyes and let her mouth fall open: "Ahhh-nold. Your idol."

"I never wanted to be Arnold," he said.

"You worshipped Arnold. Don't lie."

Ben shook his head. This was another of his sister's fixed ideas, another imaginary skeleton key to a secret box that didn't exist. She was wrong, but try telling her that. Aaron, for his part, wasn't following at all.

"Schwarzenegger," Anne explained. "Ben loved him. His whole room was filled with Arnold posters."

"I had one poster."

"You did not!" she said, thrilling to the memory. "You had, like, eight. I remember. And, come on. How many times did you see Terminator?"

"I don't know."

"You know exactly how many."

"Maybe twelve."

"In the theater. What about on video?"

"I never wanted to be Arnold," he said to Aaron. "I don't even know what your mom is talking about. She has some hypothesis she's working on, but she's way off base." How deeply he resented the idea that his life had been spent chasing a Hollywood fantasy, when in fact there had always been real principles, real convictions, involved. Real blood.

He reached for a new pile of tortillas when out of nowhere, the dagger came: "Whatever. You loved that Nazi. Admit it."

Ben was shocked. The word "Nazi" was never uttered aloud within hearing distance of their dad. Even the word "German" was almost forbidden. If the topic of Germany or the Holocaust or even Volkswagen or Mercedes came up, a force field surrounded them, and they picked their way clear as quickly as possible. They'd always been led to understand that he didn't want to talk about those days. The memories gave him nightmares and made it impossible for him to sleep. Could something have changed that drastically in the past five years? Could some kind of glasnost have descended around his father's memory of the camps? Ben couldn't believe that was the case, and when he flashed over to see the expression on his dad's face, he found he was correct. The only reason Anne had said the heinous word out loud, the only reason she'd brought down the lash so mightily, was because their dad was fast asleep.

He drove back to the desert the same way he'd come in, winding through the city to Highway 10, heading east, putting the racing electrons behind him, and then, at last, he entered the calm, stark emptiness of the desert land. He never should have gone into the city. All the calming work he'd accomplished had been undone. His mind was again ablaze with terrible thoughts.

Yes, he'd loved Arnold as a child, it was true. He couldn't deny that fact. But he hadn't loved him for the reasons Anne thought. It had never been about the silly glamour, the cheap machismo. He'd never cared about any of that Hollywood crap. What he'd loved about Arnold was only one thing, and that was the incredible willpower the man represented. He'd seen

Arnold as the heroic protagonist of the ultimate immigrant story, the ultimate maker of his own American destiny.

There was no argument. Everything Arnold accomplished had grown from his own body, his own complete mastery over his physical instrument. He'd been born a regular kid in Thal, Austria, the second, unfavored son of a small-town police chief, and he'd been smitten by the promise of American freedom and American strength. Inspired by the American bodybuilders Steve Reeves and Johnny Weissmuller, he'd built himself into a seven-time Mr. Olympia, a living icon of his ambition, the Austrian Oak. He'd invented muscles that no one had ever seen before. That selfcreated body had led him to the barbarian roles. Those dumb parts in turn had led him to the action roles, which had led him to the comedy roles, all of which had led him to politics.

Governor Schwarzenegger. Who could deny that pinnacle of accomplishment? And still, even so many years into his story, everything flowed from the muscle, the superdefinition he'd willed from his meat. Who could argue with that kind of drive? With that kind of man? There had been times Ben had almost wished they would change the U.S. Constitution so that Arnold could become president, if only to complete the incredible story of his rise.

But now, again, he had to wonder if he'd misread the secret of the world. If he'd seen all the evidence but been mistaken about the big picture. The telling shadow, the puff of smoke— they were in different places than he'd thought. It was possible he had been wrong about everything, Arnold included. It was possible he was nothing but a fool.

He was tempted to call Anne but figured he was already arguing with her enough in his head. No need to hand over even more talismans for her crowded necklace of judgment. Besides, he knew on the deepest level that she was wrong. Arnold was a Nazi, sure, but not in the way she said. He was a Nazi only in the way that everyone was a Nazi. Her mistake, like Ben's own, had been assuming that the Nazis were someone else. That they were the bad guys out there in all their villainous forms—the drug dealers, the Communists, the leftist totalitarian thought police, the terrorists. His whole life had been spent searching for Nazis in faraway lands, and, as it turned out, all this time they'd been right there at home, shopping for Cheerios, pumping gas, watching the new Batman installment in their home entertainment modules. They were his fellow citizens of the eternal corporate state. All this time he'd wondered: who were the ones who'd send his family to the ovens? Look around, they were there.

So he'd been wrong. And Anne had been wrong. Everyone had been wrong. But to give up and seek forgiveness now would be the most cowardly, ridiculous act. What soldier in the world didn't dream of living out his days under the sweet, tragic cloud of disillusionment and loss? "Durch Nacht und Blut zur Licht," said the black, red, and white of the German flag. "Through night and blood to light."

No, he would not live that lie. He'd understood the risks when he'd walked into the recruitment office. He still believed in evil. He still believed some people needed to die. He would not enter the light at this late date. Driving into the desert darkness, the Nazi moon casting cold light on the mesas, he vowed he would stay in the darkness and the blood. He would stay there fighting all the way to the end.

6

The whole grandpa-sitting arrangement Aaron had agreed to try out was still a little vague in his mind. The duties were not entirely clear, and the hours were a bit blurrily defined, but he figured he'd come to understand the requirements once he got started. He was definitely supposed to make lunch for his grandpa, that much he understood, and monitor his pill intake, and if possible do some housecleaning, including the bathroom if necessary. And in exchange for all this attention, he was to receive fifty dollars a day, more if he stayed longer than the minimum five hours. It was better than some jobs he could think of, and, seeing as the opportunity had fallen entirely into his lap, always the best way of acquiring something, he'd agreed. He definitely needed the money, one way or another.

Whether the commuting time counted toward his hours, he didn't know, and he didn't want to ask. He was going to assume it did, which was why he didn't hurry through his morning routine on his first day on the job. He climbed out of bed, still numb from the thirteen straight hours of immobility, a near record, and stumbled into the empty, sun-drenched kitchen where the dishes were still piled in the sink, no note necessary to tell him he was supposed to move the mess into the dishwasher. He found himself a clean bowl in the cupboard and poured some flax cereal, thinking about the night of dinner with Uncle Ben. What had that been about, anyway?

Aaron poured another bowl of cereal, ending in an avalanche of flax dust, and when he was finished he put the bowl among the other dirty dishes and found a clean mason jar and drained the orange juice. He fit the mason jar into the dirty dish puzzle and brushed his teeth and hurried off to the car. He didn't have time for dishes anymore. Already it felt as if he was running late.

Traffic was sluggish, but that was all right, assuming he was on the clock. He had no great eagerness for the day waiting for him on the other end. He might even have gone looking for a better job if it weren't for the family-obligation factor. His mom hadn't had to tell him that spending time with his aged grandfather was a good idea, whether remunerated or not, though of course she had, more than once. "Get his story," she'd said. "He's not going to be around that much longer, and it's an amazing, important story. You should know it." "I know, I know," he'd said. "I'm not kidding," she'd said. "The things he's seen . . ." "I know!"

He regretted the snapping. He hadn't meant to do that. He wanted to get his grandpa's story, too, of course, just like everyone else, no matter what his mom and grandpa assumed about his complete American callowness. They thought everyone under twenty years old was as stupid and narcissistic as Miley Cyrus and Justin Bieber, which said more about their own ignorance than his generation's. But he also knew the story was basically ungettable anyway, trapped inside his grandpa's impenetrable skull. He was happy to look for an opportunity to pry it out. But in all his seventeen years, he'd never seen one yet.

His grandfather's house was a modest California suburban ranch going to pot. The ceramic roof tiles were starting to slip, the bristly bushes along the front wall had grown to block most of the windows, and the expanse of white pebbles covering the front yard needed a good vacuuming. Walking the path, noting the cobwebs in the cacti, Aaron girded himself for the mausoleal atmosphere waiting inside. Maybe other grandchildren looked forward to spending time with their grandfathers, hanging out with old guys who dispensed folksy wisdom and went fly-fishing or whatever, but not him. The salary he'd be receiving was exactly to compensate for the experience of his grandfather's gravitational field of boredom.

Inside, Aaron found his grandfather, as usual, bonded to the leather of the recliner, fast asleep. His mouth was open, and his breathing came in ragged, uneven gasps, between which the whole body seemed to shut down, only to jump-start with the next violent intake of breath. He sucked air, he died, he sucked air, he died. Again and again, the system crashed and rebooted, as flecks of spittle deposited in the edges of his lips, catching in the giant, hairy leech of his mustache.

Aaron listened to the rolling catastrophe as he strolled through the house, taking stock of the decorations. He peered at the framed photos of his mother and his grandmother on a bench in San Leandro; the hotel painting of the clipper ship in heaving waves; the patently racist ceramic busts of the Irishman, the Mexican, and the Chinaman, the mick, the spic, and the chink. His grandparents had picked them up on a trip to Cancún back in 1955 or so, and they'd remained on the wall through seismic cultural changes, pushing the whole household scene beyond mere boredom, into something like low-grade horror.

He went outside onto the deck and called his friend Joel, who was deep in a session of *Skyrim*. Between bone-crushing sword strikes and a blast of dragon breath, he managed to get out that he had a lead on a possible van on Craigslist.

"It'll go fast," Joel said, grunting as the thwip, thwip, thwip of arrows parted the air. "We should check it out today. You got time?"

"I'm at my grandpa's," Aaron said.

"Nineteen sixty-nine VW," Joel said. "That's a superior year, my dad says. They run forever if you treat them right." He paused for the death groan of an armored sentry. "And this one looks like people were kind. Only four grand."

Aaron didn't have anything near two thousand dollars, and even if he did he still wasn't sure he wanted to spend it on a Mexico-bound VW bus, but he told Joel to go ahead and send him a picture anyway. He hung up feeling curdled by his own duplicity and indecision. He still hadn't mentioned anything to Joel about Karl and the sunporch because he still wasn't sure what he wanted to do, and also he didn't think Joel would even understand the debate. He'd say, What the fuck are you even talking about? Joel didn't give a shit about bohemian sunporches. He barely even gave a shit about music. Compared with the political mission of driving around Mexico and witnessing firsthand the lives of the campesinos in Michoacán and Chiapas, everything was insignificant.

At some point, Aaron knew, he needed to tell Joel he might not be going on the fact-finding mission to Mexico. But then he heard the toilet flush, and he quit worrying about it. He was on duty.

He intercepted his grandfather staggering out of the bathroom, attempting to tie on his sweatpants. There were piss stains on his crotch and some crumbs on his belly from the crackers he'd been eating, and, since his fingers seemed unable to loop the drawstring, Aaron stepped forward and jerked the knot into place.

"How's it going, Grandpa?" he said.

"I was sleeping," his grandpa said thickly, and yawned, his hot, sour breath enshrouding Aaron's face. His head was right at Aaron's chin level, and Aaron had an intimate view of the leathery pate, coated in a few remaining gray hairs, with bits of fluff and dandruff scattered on the surface.

"Yeah, I got here awhile ago," Aaron said.

"Are you hungry, sweetheart?" his grandpa said.

"I just ate. Thanks."

"You're sure?"

"Yeah, I'm good."

"You're sure?"

His sweatpants safely cinched, Grandpa Sam headed for the kitchen. Trained by generations of Yiddish women to equate food with love, he wanted only to put something in his grandson's mouth. He opened the fridge and bent over, sticking his head almost all the way inside. "Loaves and Fishes came yesterday," he said. "I have sandwiches."

In fact, Aaron was a little hungry, but he knew he wanted nothing to do with his grandpa's depressing food supply. He'd seen all the old, corroded pickle jars and squashed, plastic-wrapped sandwiches in the refrigerator, and they were the opposite of appetizing. The much better option today, by his reasoning, would be to fabricate some errand and eat out at a restaurant.

"So, what do you want to do today, Grandpa?" he said. "You have anything you need? I can drive you wherever. Maybe we should get out of the house. It's nice out."

"I don't need anything," his grandpa said. He was probably already plotting household chores Aaron could do, little cleanup jobs, yard duties, a thousand insignificant improvements to the domestic sphere. Another reason to go somewhere was to avoid all that business.

"Come on," Aaron said. "I can drive. You should use me."

His grandpa closed the refrigerator and went back to his recliner and pulled the lever to sweep his legs into the air. He lay there, eyes closed, as the clocks throughout the house ticked out of sequence.

"Grandpa?"

Grandpa Sam's eyes seemed to be closed, but they might have been open, too. Aaron could see a tiny slit of wetness inside the dark lids, a little crevice of gleaming life. It was possible his grandpa's eyes simply didn't shut all the way anymore, another small malfunction in the aging machine. Or it was possible he was not asleep, just resting, just staring up at the white ceiling, noting, or not, the strands of cobweb drifting in the sluggish air. The clocks kept ticking. At last he stirred, and his eyes opened all the way, finding Aaron nearby.

"I guess we could go get my pills," he said. He didn't seem to care one way or the other, but if his grandson wanted to go somewhere, he was willing to indulge.

It took about forty-five minutes to get to the car. Putting on shoes, taking a shit, brushing his teeth, combing his hair, feeding the cat, flattening some boxes in the garage, all took their time.

At last, Aaron commandeered the driver's seat and made a show of adjusting the mirrors and repositioning the wheel, knowing his grandpa was a tyrannical backseat driver and not wanting to give him any excuses to get started. He would have turned on the stereo, but he knew that would only cause a snit. His grandpa didn't like distractions on the road, and that included music, most of which he found jarring and incomprehensible even under the best of circumstances, and, since Aaron already felt a little guilty about forcing him to evacuate his house, he kept his hands off the tuner as he crept out of the dank garage.

Without music, the main option for entertainment was conversation, and Aaron figured this was probably as good a time as any to begin the inquiry into his grandpa's horrific life story. The best way to get the ball rolling, he assumed, would be to pose some innocuous questions about current things in hopes they'd naturally lead backward in time. Maybe he'd even end up skipping over the worst part, jumping to the ancient shtetl life in Poland, and then work his way forward again. He'd see. Starting simple seemed like the proper strategy, he thought, because God knew he couldn't imagine how to broach the topic directly.

So as the garage door sank and they headed down the street, he asked his grandpa how long he'd been living in this house—a banal but sincere point of clarification. Ever since Aaron could remember, he'd known this to be his grandpa's home, and he honestly didn't know what place had come before.

"What?" his grandpa said. The question struck him as so obtuse as to be nonsensical. To anyone but his grandson, he wouldn't have bothered responding at all.

"I mean, how long have you been in this house? A long time?"

"Eh." His grandfather gave the air a limp, dismissive flick of his hand. His eyes were glued to the road, his mind solely on judging Aaron's driving skill. Issues of brake control and signal timing far outweighed any questions of bygone real estate.

They arrived at an intersection, and Aaron navigated his way to the other side without incident. They slid past the brick fire station and the newly painted elementary school, also without disaster. A few more easy, uneventful blocks elapsed before his grandpa seemed to relax a bit and recollect a question had been asked.

"Long time, I suppose," he said.

"Uh-huh," Aaron said. "But how long, exactly?"

"How old is your mother?"

"Forty-five?"

"Forty-three years ago, then. So not very long."

To Aaron, it sounded infinitely long. In what universe was forty-three years not long? Forty-three years ago Americans were driving Gremlins and Dodge Darts. Forty-three years ago they were listening to the Temptations and Henry Mancini on top-forty radio. The world had not even witnessed *Star Wars* yet. Not to mention all the technological stuff.

"And where'd you live before this, Grandpa?" he asked.

His grandpa shrugged almost without shrugging. He expressed his shrug without any movement at all. His sweatpants jiggled with the vibration of the car. "Oakland," he said. "Petaluma. A few places. North." The memory extraction seemed almost physically painful to accomplish.

"And what were you doing up there?"

"Oh, I don't know."

The car glided along Vineland, and his grandpa took refuge in the changing sights. He seemed sad, although maybe not sad, too. Maybe he just couldn't remember anything. The sign for Jack in the Box came and went. They passed a row of frowsy palms. Aaron was giving up on getting any more information when his grandpa dispensed another random batch:

"In Petaluma, I worked on a chicken farm," he said.

Aaron received the information quietly. He didn't want to rattle his grandpa with too much enthusiasm, but he was pleased by the fresh nugget. He'd never heard of a chicken farm before. He knew about Oakland—the place where his grandpa had met his grandma and where his mom had been born—but that was the extent of his American family history. Auschwitz–Oakland. That was the jump cut. The notion of his grandfather raising chickens in between was a new and bizarre sidebar. The idea of his grandfather standing on dirt was bizarre, for that matter. In Aaron's mind, his grandfather was a creature solely of the suburban sidewalk, the strip-mall parking lot, not raw, organic earth.

"The owner of the farm, he hired Jews from the city," his grandpa went on, not entirely displeased with the memory himself. "Cheap labor. But he was a good man. We became very good friends while I was there."

"You fed the chickens? And killed chickens? And everything? Really?"

"I drove a truck."

Aaron pondered his young grandfather, fresh from war-torn Europe, hot wind blowing in the window of his International Harvester, chicken feathers floating onto the road shoulder. Up in Petaluma, wine country, with that same mustache, darker hair, younger muscles, more oomph. It was a hard picture to muster as they joined a line of cars waiting to turn onto Strathern, and far from the ugly stuff he was really seeking, but he was glad to have it nonetheless. After seventeen years, they'd finally started down the road.

They had to go to the Walgreens for the pills. In the water aisle, they got trapped comparing prices on bottles and pallets and then ran into a woman his grandpa knew, a rouged scarecrow who laughed timidly at all his moth-eaten jokes about nuns falling down stairs and priests in airplanes. After filling the prescription, his grandpa wanted to drive past his friend Rick's house for some reason, and they drove by his front lawn three times in hopes that someone would be standing outside, but no one was. And then his grandpa had some banking to do, though it didn't seem like any money actually changed places. He only wanted to sit across the desk from the bank manager and talk about average interest rates.

For lunch, they returned to the Walgreens strip mall and ate at the Black Bear Diner, a pancake-and-hamburger chain decorated with many sculpted bears. It wouldn't have been Aaron's first choice, but it was the only place deemed properly inexpensive, and thus there was no argument in the matter. Aaron could have tried to convince his grandpa that the food one ate, the substance that nourished one's body and soul, might possibly be worth spending an extra dollar or two on sometimes, but it wasn't a debate he wanted to take up.

Chewing on his dry Swiss mushroom burger, he worked to fabricate some further inquiries into the past. More details about chicken farming? The Oakland years? His beginning in the electrical engineering career? For no particular reason, he decided to go with Oakland. There had to be more images to pluck from that era.

"So," he said, shaking a fresh puddle of ketchup onto his plate, "tell me about Oakland, Grandpa."

"Mmmphh," his grandpa said, his mouth loaded with French-dip sandwich.

"You were in Oakland after the chicken farm, right?"

"Yes." He wiped his napkin across his oily chin. "Before and after."

"Where were you in Oakland, exactly?"

"McKinley Avenue."

"What years were you there?"

"Oh. I can't remember that."

"But what years? Approximately?"

His grandfather took another bite, beef broth drizzling over his lips, and chewed patiently. His face registered no contemplation. At last, wiping his chin again, he said, almost gruffly, "It was in the years just after the war."

The sentence sent a mild charge into the far shoals of Aaron's fingers and toes. He wasn't prepared for the word "war"—not so quickly, anyway. After the war, Grandpa Sam had said. Here they were, only two hours into their day, already knocking on the iron door. Aaron chewed on his burger, playing it cool. The word "war," even in this silly, bear-infested chain restaurant, summoned evil meanings, mud smells, frozen limbs, and Aaron was aware that he was talking no longer to his grandpa but to the spirit of history itself, that whatever words came out of his grandpa's mouth next should be remembered for the sake of posterity. He informed his brain to open the deepest vault to receive.

"Why Oakland?" he asked. "How did you end up there?"

"Oakland was the first place they sent me," his grandpa said.

"But why?"

"Who knows?" He didn't seem pleased to be remembering any longer, but Aaron felt secure in his responsibility to keep pressing. He didn't have to lead him much farther right now, just enough to lay the groundwork. They were only plotting the eventual path, pacing out the perimeter of the fence topped with concertina wire. They didn't have to open the gate today, but they would return to this place when the time was right.

"Come on, Grandpa," he urged.

"The temple in Oakland sponsored me," his grandpa said. "To come to America then, you had to have a sponsor. The temple had all the paperwork done. They said I had a job with one of their members. That's why Oakland. It could have been anywhere."

"And was there a job?"

"No. But I found one. I worked in a bread factory for a number of years. But this is all ancient history now, sweetheart. I don't know why you want to know these things."

"You're my grandpa. I want to know."

If he'd expected a warm smile of appreciation for his dutiful, grandsonly curiosity, he was disappointed. His grandfather didn't smile but simply stopped talking and returned to his sandwich. Watching him put the food in his mouth, the stray bits falling out and scattering near his plate, it occurred to

Aaron that he'd possibly never seen his grandfather truly smile before. Had he ever seen him laugh out loud? Surely not. He could see now from his grandfather's bleary, tired eyes it was time to let the questions rest.

On the way out, Aaron dropped three extra dollars onto the table to supplement his grandpa's meager tip. Grandpa Sam might have been to hell and back in his lifetime, but that didn't mean he knew you left twenty percent.

Back home, Aaron helped his grandfather up the path and eased him into the warm embrace of his La-Z-Boy. He placed the remote in his palm and put the glass of water nearby, using the newspaper as a coaster. He laid out a snack of turkey slices.

He still had some time to fill, so he did some dusting and sweeping, the kinds of chores that let him keep up his own stream of thoughts. He wandered around the house tearing ropy cobwebs from the high corners of the rooms, composing speeches to Karl and Joel in his head. He had such high regard for both of them, he wished he could split himself in two and take both journeys. He also answered all the questions he didn't want to discuss with his family. Yes, he'd told his mom, I'm skipping college, at least for now. Why? Because I want to drive around and drink mezcal in workingman's cantinas. I want to wake up in tiled gardens with parrots and iguanas. Was he going to say any of that out loud? No.

His dad would be okay with the plan, but in a way that only made matters worse. His mom had long ago chalked up Barry as the most lazy, self-absorbed, insecure (or maybe overly secure, it was hard to say—insecure or overconfident, they kind of panned out the same in the end, by her reasoning)

bum she'd ever met, with no earning power or sense of duty
to his family and his community whatsoever. The youthful
chemistry they'd once felt—the love that had created Aaron,
no less—she openly admitted had been almost entirely carnal,
the case of a hot stud walking into her estrogen cloud at exactly
the right time. But for all her shit-talking, Aaron respected his
dad and understood he'd come a long way in his life. As the son
of a midwestern rancher deep into belt whipping and Jesus,
Barry was almost heroic in his unflappable passivity. He may
have been an eighthgeneration hippie, among the last dudes
to discover the fashions of Haight-Ashbury and the sonics of
Frank Zappa, but he was the first generation in his bloodline to
get there, and that counted for something.

As for his grandfather, none of these questions would even
make any sense. To be born a Jew, with the weight of that history,
and to drive around Mexico? A person should never go out
seeking experience. People should consider themselves lucky if
they never had an experience at all. That was the lesson of his
grandfather's life. How could Aaron possibly explain that he
might skip college in pursuit of this nebulous experience, that
he wanted to throw away all the hard work of his ancestors and
become something unheard of, something even he didn't yet
understand? What would his grandpa say to the prospect of his
wasting every privilege he'd ever been given? How would he feel
knowing his grandson only wanted to burn his time in the most
useless, unredeemable way possible? And yet that was what
Aaron could feel rising in him, that wasteful, destructive urge.

As for the true ambitions that flooded him on a daily basis,
those were so extravagant, they could barely be thought, let
alone spoken aloud. Sunporches and Mexican road trips were

only the beginning of the fantasy. His dreams ran to radiant glory and blinding, obscene fame, a life ruined by fame. He wanted, when he really got down to the true desire running in his veins, a life that could be called revolutionary. There, he'd said it, at least to himself. A revolutionary life. Was that too much to ask? To be a song by the Clash. To be a song by Neil Young. He wanted to be the song "Powderfinger," a living being of infinite soul and beauty in his mind. And how disappointing it would be if he failed to wreak this havoc on the world, if he failed to change the course of human thought.

By the time he came back to his grandpa's lounging area, his mind had cooled, though he was no closer to figuring out what he planned to do.

"Okay, Grandpa," he said, tossing the last of his paper towels in the garbage can. "I'm heading out now. I'll see you tomorrow, all right?"

"Oh, you don't need to come tomorrow, sweetheart," his grandpa said from his sarcophagal chair. The TV cops were sneaking through a basement with raking flashlights, but the suspense level was low. There would be no bodies discovered in this room, anyone could tell.

"No, no," Aaron said. "I'll be here."

"I won't be here, though," his grandpa said.

"Oh?" Aaron said. "Why not?"

"I'm going out of town."

Aaron frowned. His mom hadn't mentioned anything about travel plans.

"I didn't know you had any plans this week," he said gently.

"I'm going to Oakland."

"But . . . how?"

"In the car," his grandpa said, as if that were obvious. He was fingering the remote, preparing for his coming hours of glorious TV. So many cops were behind the screen, preparing to entertain him.

"How long will you be gone?" Aaron said. He was no longer sure if this was real or fantasy.

"Not very long," his grandpa said. "I only have to get something. All that talking we did, it made me remember."

"What do you have to get?"

"Something at the bank."

"You can call the bank. I can help you if you want."

"No, no, for this I have to go there. This isn't something for doing over the phone."

"What is it you have to get?"

"My gold," his grandpa said. "I think it's time to bring it down here. Before I can't anymore. Before I forget."

"Are you serious?" Aaron couldn't believe he was serious. Or could he? He wasn't sure. Gold?

"Oh yes."

Aaron watched his grandpa lying in his recliner, the top of his head with its spots and greasy patches under the thatching. Aaron was skeptical of the mission but also curious. Could this be true? Did it matter?

"What time do you want to go?" he said. "I'll drive you."

7

There were so many red flags flying on Mark Harris, it was hard to know which one was the reddest. The mere choice of the Beverly Hills sushi restaurant he'd insisted upon for lunch was a red flag, with its lacquered bar, its gigantic, pretentious displays of birds of paradise and calla lilies, its intimidating, canted mirrors, and the coup de grâce, the glass bathroom stalls with the doors that frosted when they locked, an electrical charge somehow turning the clear panes opaque. Pure flypaper for the crass, rich, and insecure, Anne thought, stepping from the chamomile-scented chamber.

When Mark himself had appeared, the flags had raised and snapped stiffly in the wind, practically flying off his every article of clothing: his trendily plaid oxford shirt, still creased from the package, flagrantly open around the neck; his absurd, crosshatched designer jeans (Why does anyone ever wear anything but Levi's? she wondered; men should know this by now); his grotesque sport shoes, multicolored piles of scientific webbing and buttresses upon buttresses, with those silly aerated soles. Every single sartorial choice was dubious, if not some kind of crime against decency.

And under the clothes, still more flags—his fatless body, superfit from what he'd let slip was his near-professional

Argentinian martial arts regimen; his sharply defined jaw, framing fine, symmetrical features that had never once known struggle or despair; his porcelain hands, if porcelain were soft. The entirety of his clean, pink skin that smelled delicately, spicily, of aftershave.

All in all, Mark Harris was the very embodiment of the guys Anne had been fighting against her entire life. She'd fought them in high school, strutting around in their Top-Siders and madras shorts, taking bong hits and extolling the virtues of Ronald Reagan; she'd fought them in college, stumbling on the fraternity steps in their grass skirts and sombreros; she fought them daily in the office, killing time in their fantasy basketball pools, succeeding wildly beyond their efforts or intelligence simply because they understood each other so well, having consumed all the same albums and movies and TV shows at all the same junctures in their pampered lives. She'd spent her whole life hating these guys, these unapologetic winners in life, almost none of whom had any idea the fight was even on, having never been forced to recognize their own grotesque privilege and dumb luck, let alone account for it.

She'd googled him, of course. He'd started out rich, no surprise. His fortune had been handed down from his banker father, and, to Mark's credit, he'd amassed another fortune on top of that one. Real estate was his game, and in particular green real estate, whatever that meant; it seemed like an oxymoron to her. He'd developed a prime tract of riverside brownfields in Portland, erecting a pod of mirrored silos for aging baby boomers within yards of the major medical-research hospital. After that bonanza, he'd developed a sustainable convention center, the first passively heated structure of its gargantuan size in the nation. From there he'd graduated to "green stadiums," less an oxymoron than an outright hypocrisy in her book, mostly on the grounds of state universities, inciting controversies over the ecological footprints and rumored sweetheart deals with resource-gobbling sports programs. He was now, at age forty-seven, as rich as humanly possible, splitting time between a few cherry-picked projects at his design agency, his martial arts, and his winery.

Yes, Mark Harris was the enemy, the epitome of the entitled capitalist overlord. So why, then, did she find herself liking him so much? Sitting across the table from him, staring at the Oakley sport glasses pushed back on his blond head, the manicured, professorial beard on his toned, ruddy cheeks, knowing full well the history of sickening injustice that had spawned him, she found herself strangely amused. Why? He was not amazingly intelligent; he wasn't a good listener; he had horrible taste. But he was funny. And, even more than that, he was funny in a particular way that she was helpless against: he was a pervert.

"Wontons," he said, peering at the menu. "I think I'll have the wrinkled wontons today. Extra wrinkled. Yeah. Mmmm. Wrinkled wontons. Nice."

"Okay, Mark," she said. "You do that."

"Or maybe some tight, cold, wrinkled wontons would be better," he mused. "Long, hot wontons or cold, tight wontons? I just don't know. What do you think, Anne? You like wontons? Are you a fan of wontons?"

"Please stop saying 'wontons,'" she said, understanding too late how methodically he'd been leading them to this place. All his little questions about exotic menu items, all his teasing little intimations of scat and sex, had been ways of gauging her limits, seeing how far he could go, and, having coaxed a small chortle from her, he felt he had all the encouragement he needed. He stayed on the word "wonton" for another two minutes, whispering it, mouthing it, adding prefixes—loose wontons, slippery wontons, baggy wontons—letting the joke bloat from the merely puerile to the mildly funny to the momentarily hilarious and leading her to chortle again, louder this time. She resented being cast as the straight man already, but she couldn't help it. Her brother and all his friends had trained her in appreciation of the boyish game.

"Pupu," he said, changing gears. "I'd like a pupu platter. With some poon-poon on the side."

"Oh God. Please."

"You don't favor the pupu? Well, your loss."

"Seriously, Mark . . ."

"Sorry. I'm just talking about eating some pupu here. I don't know what you're thinking . . ." He giggled at his own juvenile riffs, too rich to give a shit what anyone thought.

Anne raised her menu, not wanting to reveal the smile he'd induced. Mark Harris was such a ridiculous, pathetically childish person, but his childishness was almost an act of mercy in a way, preemptive forgiveness for whatever passing image flared to life in one's head, an invitation to honesty and maybe even intimacy of sorts. At the very least, it was the thing that allowed her to look past all the red flags for the course of a lunch date, a lunch that he was paying for, after all, and that was going to be obscenely expensive when the bill came.

"Wow," he said, his attention suddenly captured, doglike, by movement on the other side of the patio.

"The salmon *tataki* sounds good," she said.

"Wow," he said again. "I mean, wow."

"Okay, what, Mark?" she said, eyes still focused on the menu. "Are you going to tell me?"

"You should just look at that lady over there," he said. He was openly staring now, daring her to follow his gaze.

"I'm not looking," she said.

"Just look," he said.

"No," she said. "And stop staring, seriously. It's rude."

"I'll stop if you just look."

Anne refused to look, keeping her eyes glued to the word *"donburi."* She wondered if this was an average meeting for Mark Harris. Thus far, not a word about business had been spoken; instead, there had been only this constant initiatory hazing. She guessed his locker-room antics served him well in most situations. She'd just never seen such an energetic specimen of his type.

A slight displacement of air and a readjustment of Mark's gaze told her the object of his attention was passing nearby, and just to make him stop bothering her, she took a quick peek. The object turned out to be a woman so obese, she could barely walk. She was like a hippo, lumbering on her giant trunks, wearing sheer yoga clothes, with golden princess slippers and a glittering tiara and hot-pink, manicured nails. She was like a monstrous five-year-old child, probably the overfed wife of some despotic Hollywood producer, deformed by wealth and patriarchy and celebrity worship and likely a large dollop of mental illness to boot.

"Okay, okay. I saw her," Anne said, turning back to the menu, disgusted on every level—with the woman, with Mark Harris, with herself.

"She sure is fat," he said.

She didn't respond.

"I'm just kind of amazed, is all," he said, still tracking the woman's halting progress across the patio. "How do you get up in that, anyway? You'd drown."

Anne dropped her menu, aghast, and stared at Mark. Was it possible he'd really said something that insanely awful? Was she supposed to just let that pass? For a second they stared at each other, probing each other's eyes for clues of character, judgment, wisdom, intention. His eyes were hazel with brown bursts around the pupils, flanged by long, sensitive lashes, and they didn't look apologetic in the least. But nor did she sense anything really malicious in his eyes, either. If anything, Mark Harris looked as shocked as she was by the words that had just jumped out of his mouth. He was a radio, as blameless as a transistor receiving its signals. Once the initial horror of his words wore off, they both started laughing, helplessly, for almost a minute.

During the laughing fit, Mark Harris looked as if he was suffocating, astonished by his good luck in a dining partner. He'd said something truly terrible, and here she was, still with him. Anne, for her part, tried not to encourage him any more than she already had, but she couldn't help succumbing over and over again to the indefensible comedy of the situation. Her cheeks trembled; her ribs hurt. When they'd finally recovered, sighing, wiping their eyes, Mark made another few halfhearted plays to milk the joke, but the laughter was all dried out, and in the end he settled on raising the day's real agenda, water.

He daubed his eyes, his voice cracking around the edges. "So, Anne. Anyway. Phew. Sorry about all that. I'm really embarrassed. No excuse for that. It's not really how I think . . .

or, not how I want to . . . or . . . you know. I think we were here to talk about something important, right?"

"So I was led to believe."

"Well, this is what I want to talk about," he said, and held up his glass of water. He took a gulp. "Water."

"Okay," she said. The endorphins must have flooded her bloodstream, filling her veins with some natural tranquilizer, because she found herself willing to entertain whatever presentation came her way.

"You guys are on the verge of a major water crisis down here, you know," he said. "L.A. has maybe a few years of water left, and that's it."

"That's what I always hear," Anne said.

"Do you know approximately how much water your city uses every day?"

"Not offhand, nope."

"Over a billion and a half gallons a day in the greater Los Angeles area."

"That sounds like a lot."

"Yep. It is. And you know how much comes out on the other end as waste?"

"Nope." If there had been any doubt the joking was over and he really wanted to talk about wastewater, his next monologue erased it. She was almost impressed by how fluidly he'd transitioned from crassness into salesmanship. Not many people could compartmentalize themselves that cleanly.

"Three hundred million gallons of wastewater a day are generated by the system," he said. "Most of that ends up in cleaning pools down in Terminal Island. The effluvium gets pulled out, turned into biogas and fertilizer. And then the leftover water gets pumped into Santa Monica Bay. You've got a pipe that leads five miles out, spilling all that stripped water back into the ocean. Right now you guys are only reusing a tiny fraction of the wastewater you produce, and most of that's just going to golf courses. So that's what I want to talk to you about. I'm interested in purchasing the rights to Los Angeles County's wastewater. I want to see that wastewater put to use."

Anne was returning to her senses now, coming back into her professional wits. The instinctive critical faculties were coming back online, one by one. "Still sounds like you probably want to talk to someone in Sanitation," she said. "I can give you some names if that would be helpful—"

"No, no," he cut her off. "I don't see too many supportive voices over there. I'd much rather buy the city's brown, hairy cornwater from you."

"I don't think the rights to our wastewater are mine to sell, Mark."

"See, that's the thing, though," he said. He dunked a piece of grilled octopus in his soy sauce and held it in the tongs of his chopsticks. "They're not anybody's to sell, per se. The city's wastewater isn't really viewed as a commodity right now. It doesn't really have any agreed-upon value yet. Technically, it's more like garbage. It would be like buying the rights to all your banana peels or your old diapers. But I'm willing to take it off your hands because I'm a nice guy."

"Well, that's very generous of you, I'm sure. But still, Sanitation . . ."

"I'm willing to pay the city quite generously for it. Can't a guy just buy the rights to some brown, hairy cornwater in this country or what?"

"Stop saying that, please."

"Brown, hairy cornwater?" he said, scanning the patio before bringing his eyes to rest on her own. "You don't like when I say brown, hairy cornwater? All right. I'll stop saying brown, hairy cornwater as soon as you sell me all the brown, hairy cornwater. Then I'll stop."

"Why do you want it?"

"I just know that something's got to give here, man. The world can't afford to use water only one time anymore. Especially people living in deserts, like you. There's a global emergency in front of us. People might not like the idea of drinking their own sewage, but, believe me, they'll get used to it pretty quick. A few years from now, no one's even gonna think about it anymore. You'll just recycle your sewage, and you'll assume you always did. That's what I want to see, ultimately."

"And what's in it for you, exactly?"

"For me? What do you mean?"

"I mean, what's in it for you? I doubt this is just a charity mission."

"I honestly believe in the need to reuse this resource, Anne. The future of our species depends on it. But if that isn't enough reason, I'll admit this, too: wastewater is currently a radically undervalued commodity in the world economy. Right now it's just a problem to deal with. In a few years, wastewater is going to be the next oil and gold and diamonds rolled into one."

"You want to become the world's first used-water salesman."

"I want to figure out a way of monetizing this truly priceless element. I want to create a new marketplace to tap its potential for everyone's growing needs. That turns me on, I'll admit. If I end up making some money off the deal in the long run, hey, that's great, too. I'm okay with that."

Anne was again aghast. She could read between the lines here. It might look as though they were just sitting calmly, eating their wildly overpriced octopus, but in reality they were talking about monetizing the very future itself. Mark wanted to own what currently belonged to the people, the very substance of life, and sell it back to them at a grotesque profit. Was evil being born right here in front of her? A man like Mark Harris waking up and deciding he wanted to hang dollar signs on the air, run his credit card through a glassy brook? The ambition was so wrong on so many levels. It's possible this is what the face of evil looks like today, she thought. A guy from Seattle with an iPad and a mesh bag from REI.

But the flush of revulsion passed quickly. This wasn't truly evil, she reassured herself. How could evil be born on such a sunny, fragrant, pan-Asian patio, with dulcet water trickling over pebbled concrete fountains? Bad taste could be born here, but evil? Evil was bayoneting babies in front of their mothers. Mark's silly Enron fantasy was nothing compared with true evil. It was almost a disservice to evil to get too worked up about Mark Harris's stupid plan.

And furthermore, if she was really honest with herself, she found the audacity of Mark's plan kind of refreshing, in a way. Maybe he almost deserved credit for h is absurd, exploitative scheme. It was hypocrisy that she hated most, after all, and he was definitely not a hypocrite—she would give him that much. No, he was more like a dog, utterly simple in his doggish desires, plagued by none of the crabbed self-doubt and fear that thwarted her and her friends' every will to satisfaction. Once upon a time there had been burly, strapping union men who wanted to own the future in the name of the people. Once upon a time, badass liberals with a fuck-you attitude had walked the earth. That had been the righteous fantasy that had led her into this world of public service in the first place. But those days were long gone now. The representatives of the people had become a bunch of dried-out bureaucrats, wimps modulating the level of damage from their cubicle farms, rounding off the last edges of life. She could at least be honest with a capitalist pig like Mark Harris. He wanted to put his stink on the future. A future that was probably diametrically opposite the one she wanted, but still . . .

"I can't sell you the rights to the city's wastewater," she told him, with some small pang of regret. "Sorry to disappoint you, Mark. I'm not an elected official. I don't have that power. I'm not even a lawyer, and it would take a lot of lawyers to do what you're talking about."

"I've got lawyers," he said. "A shit ton of lawyers. And I know you can't sell it to me yourself, Anne. But who can? That's what I need to figure out. Who's got the authority to make this kind of deal?" A sudden, carnivorous interest had entered his voice. So here was the practical question that bedeviled him. Where was the lever he was looking for? Where was the button? Where was the key?

"I'm not sure," she said, with some care. "It'd take some figuring out. There are probably a few ways it could go."

"Susan?" he asked.

"No," Anne said. "It's more complicated than that. You'd need to build a whole coalition."

"The mayor? Most likely the mayor. The mayor would have to sign off."

"We're talking purely theoretically . . ."

"Of course."

"The mayor, yes. You'll want the mayor's signature on the document, whatever it is. That would be important. But also the city council. There are fifteen members, and you'd need at least one or two to spearhead it through the vote. If you really wanted the deal to hold up in a court of law, the council would need a say."

"Which council members would be the best?"

"Randy Lowell oversees Sanitation. No way around Randy."

"Randy. Yeah." He seemed to be fitting her words into the larger puzzle in his mind, confirming the shape that had been established before her arrival on the scene. "Randy Lowell. master of the brown, hairy cornwater." He brooded a moment, then brightened and stood, depositing his napkin in a pile on the table. "Speaking of which. Excuse me a moment. I shall return."

She watched Mark Harris's muscled legs striding across the patio with that telltale jock swagger, the product of a thousand football locker rooms, basketball courts, suburban keggers. He was the enemy, indeed, but she couldn't even really see him as a full-grown man. She saw him as a little boy, another of her brother's unruly childhood pals. As a girl, she'd loved those guys, their destructive urges, their immense lack of self-control. She'd loved the way they threw themselves into each other, hurting themselves so happily, and later on how badly, how pathetically, they'd wanted to fuck her. Boys were so simple. They wanted the simplest things. The problems started when they became men. They shed the simple stupidity and became dishonest and conniving. They started lying and hoarding for themselves. Mark Harris might be a horrible, insensitive, wrongheaded person, but he wasn't ugly in that way, not yet, and she couldn't help it—she liked him.

She sighed, thinking about her men. Her father, who'd never been a boy at all, whose boyhood had been stabbed in a ditch. Her son, who was still a boy but on the verge of manhood, and who refused to give her the slightest inkling as to what he was planning to become. He'd turned away from her for now, needing room to incubate the next self. Her brother, who was neither boy nor man but something else. God knew. A wraith. What boyhood song had sent him off to his wars? What had she missed that had led him into that jungle? And what was his deal at dinner that night? She hadn't seen that little huff coming at all.

Mark Harris was a funny little boy, and as he came gliding back to her across the patio, sunglasses down, face stony and serious, she was having trouble remembering exactly why she was supposed to hate him so much. Just because he'd been lucky enough to stay a boy all his life? Just because he'd gotten what everyone deserved?

"This has been a fruitful conversation, Anne Singer," Mark said, retaking his seat. "I am incredibly thankful that you made the time to meet with me. It's not every day I get to meet one of my heroes of civic planning."

"Ha."

"I'm serious, Anne. I wish everyone could understand what you do. We haven't even talked about the Pomona Green Corridor yet. That was an absolutely incredible win. And it was you who did it. You. I know that for a fact."

"Well . . . I wouldn't exactly . . ."

"Okay, okay, whatever. You've got your modest little worker-bee thing, I get it. You have to. But you and I both know there's a way bigger picture here. In a different world, well . . . who knows what you might get to do. I'd like to see that myself. I'd like to live in the world where Anne Singer is recognized for what she does. Or, even better, where she's pushed to do something she didn't even think she could do. But maybe that's just my fantasy. I don't know. In any case, I think we have some interesting agenda items to work on now, don't you? That's my take-away from this meeting, anyway. I hope you feel the same way."

"Sure, yeah," she said. "Very interesting." Withholding herself seemed the only defense against his implacable charm. Unless it was a collaboration with his charm; she wasn't yet sure.

"You think I'm joking," he said, "but I'm quite serious about this idea. And to show you I'm serious, I'd like to make an offer to you. Right now. On the spot. I'm utterly, completely convinced of your intelligence and talent. Are you listening? This is the offer."

"Uh-huh."

"I want to make you a stakeholder in BHC Industries."

"BHC?"

"Brown, Hairy . . . I think "Cornwater" is one word, right? Cornwater. We'll assume so. Three initials is better. Anyway. First, I'd like to bring you in as a consultant with BHC Industries. Paid, of course. I'm thinking five thousand a month to start with? We can reassess the numbers in a few months. After you've had a chance to put together this coalition you're talking about. And then, assuming we get some traction on the permit, I want to give you points in the final operation."

"The back end, so to speak."

"Ha! The back end of BHC. I love it. Yes."

"I'm honored, Mark," she said. "But unfortunately, that would be a blatant conflict of interest for me. So I'll have to pass."

Mark seemed unfazed by her refusal. "How so, conflict of interest?"

"I work for the city," she said. "You're the private sector. That's like . . ." She bumped her fists together, bouncing them apart like two magnets.

"Is it illegal, though? You seriously can't moonlight if you work for the city? You give up all your rights of citizenship?"

"I can't serve both the public and private interests, no."

Mark rubbed his strong chin, affecting thought. "See, that's something I don't understand. I don't understand why the public and private interests are necessarily opposed. Who said that had to be the case?"

"That's a whole other conversation, Mark. But believe me, the interests are opposed. If we didn't oppose you guys, we'd all be living in a parking lot now. We'd be eating infected meat packed with sawdust. We'd be radioactive."

"Okay. I don't have any idea what you're talking about. But let me ask you this: is it actually illegal for you to consult for BHC Industries? Susan consults all over the goddamn world. She's raking in speaking fees on every continent. Basically, what I'm proposing is a consulting arrangement. I'm a green entrepreneur. You are an expert in the field of sustainability. I see no problem here whatsoever."

"Well—"

"Just think about it, Anne, that's all," he cut her off. "I think you're just surprised how fast this is all moving. Which is understandable. I know everything in the public sector moves

ver-r-r-y slowly. But let me tell you something, Anne." He
flagged the passing waitress, a gesture that came as easily as
breathing. "Out here in the real world, when things happen,
they happen fast. Now is the time to get on this train. You
could end up in a very comfortable place at the end of this
ride. It could be a pretty sweet back end we're talking about.
Oh yeah, back end, BHC . . ." And so it devolved from there.

Anne said she'd think about his proposition, knowing she
wouldn't really think about it, and knowing that their lunch
would soon recede into a dim chamber of her memory, joining
so many half-forgotten lunches and barely remembered
conversations in the murky pit. Maybe they would bump into
each other at a conference somewhere or ping each other
with the occasional email. But Mark Harris was destined for
a kindly haze of acquaintanceship, one name among many
names occasionally beaming into her in-box.

Sitting at her desk, eating her bag lunch, she did the math on
the proposed salary, though. Had he really said five thousand
a month? That penciled out to sixty grand a year before taxes.
With that, plus her normal salary, she could practically send
Aaron to Harvard. At the very least she could allow him to exit
his higher education unfettered by debt, as her own father had
done for her. And if he did really say five thousand a month,
that probably meant she would have to do some real work for
him, get her hands dirty. But maybe not, too. Maybe to him
five thousand a month was nothing. He lived in such an ocean
of capital that money had become a complete abstraction.
Feelings of revulsion, curiosity, greed, wonder, and indignation
braided inside her, never coming to rest.

She put it all out of her mind. She didn't have time to think about Mark Harris or BHC Industries because she had other things on her docket, such as her meetings on the erosion abatement program in La Jolla, which was entering its second year of bureaucratic deliberation, with at least two or three years to go before anything resembling real-life action might happen. The meetings went fine. She liked the head of the committee. He had a kid Aaron's age, and they traded teenage war stories. He was a kindly, patient, self-effacing guy, with a mature comprehension of the ins and outs of public-policy making. He understood that the whole point was the creation of social priorities, the pursuit of long-term endeavors that merited society's collective time and resources.

He was the opposite, in other words, of Mark Harris, who wouldn't stop bothering her with his emails. Two or three times a day, his name appeared in the queue, probably sent from the cockpit of his private experimental plane or the massage table at his martial arts training compound.

"Hurry up," he said.

"Figure it out."

"Let's get this on!"

She didn't respond to most of the messages, and she was mildly surprised, even a little irritated, when they kept popping up. He just kept at it, not in a nagging or belligerent way, but always in a light, funny way, as if he genuinely liked her personality and wanted to share some of his delightful good fortune. He started attaching pictures of fat women to most of his emails. Fat women in bikinis. Fat women covered in grease paint. Fat hippies. Fat Muslims. Rubens paintings, Fertility goddesses. It could have been considered sexual harassment if a person wanted to look at it that way, but Anne didn't. She knew Mark Harris was just a perverted little boy eager for attention, whether good or bad, and that she'd given him the license by not scolding him the first time. He was just staying visible, teasing her. In that, he had exactly the right intuition.

Indeed, he had good intuition. He seemed to understand something about her that most people missed. From the outside, she might have appeared to be the holder of strict principles, a public servant dedicated to the ideals of deep ecology and social justice, a strident warrior of fairness, but Mark had sensed otherwise. He seemed to comprehend that she'd taken the path of public service not out of grand principles but rather because it had been the path of least resistance. It hadn't been hard to find this kind of work out of college. She'd never been actively greedy or materialistic. But to call her an upright pillar of society wasn't precisely correct, either. She was an opportunist, like everyone else, and she was often amazed by her coworkers and friends who honestly believed in their own unshakable moral fortitude. She listened to them make their grand pronouncements, decry other people's weakness and avarice, knowing full well that their principles had never been put to the test.

Here was Mark Harris, testing her. How did he know she might be susceptible?

It was hard to say when exactly the switch clicked in her head. Sometime during the week Susan was off in Costa Rica, presenting her paper on the Pomona Green Corridor, claiming authorship for the seven-year battle Anne had orchestrated, eating swordfish on the taxpayer's dime. Sometime during the week Mr. Dimond didn't die and Aaron didn't come home until three AM two nights in a row. The switch started clicking one of those nights as she was lying awake, waiting for her son to creep in the door. Most likely Mark Harris's scheme, if you could even call it that, wouldn't work, anyway, she thought. There were so many guys like Mark sloshing around these days, guys with elaborate spreadsheets and expensive business cards and killer apps promising to revolutionize the world's energy-consumption patterns, none of whose plans ever seemed to pencil out in the end. They weren't malicious, most of them, just wishful, deluded fools like Mark.

Probably Mark Harris was no different from them. But even if he was different and he succeeded in buying the city's wastewater and selling it back to his fellow citizens at an exorbitant profit someday, what did that really mean? Whom did it hurt? What was public and what was private anymore? Every decade, it was getting harder to tell.

Lying in bed at two, three in the morning, hoping Aaron was not out shooting heroin somewhere, not impaled on a barrier on the side of some highway, hoping her dad was not lying broken on the kitchen floor, cool air tumbling over his body from the open refrigerator door, she felt the switch clicking. Maybe Mark Harris's scheme—which would never work anyway, and which would not really mean anything even if it did—maybe this scheme was the thing that could drag her from the quicksand of her life. She'd been making her way long enough in the world to know this was exactly the kind of thing that might actually lead somewhere. This was the kind of utterly absurd, utterly unexpected side door that took you places. She knew by now that nothing ever happened just by your walking up and knocking on the front door.

When she woke up, Aaron was home, snoring in his twisted sheets, his room reeking of hot beer farts and teenage BO. The next email from Mark that popped onto her phone got a response. She'd do a little nosing around, she wrote, talk to some people on behalf of BHC Industries. Why not? she thought. Truly, why the fuck not?

8

Ben moved through the airport without speaking to a soul, stepping from the deboarding tunnel into the concourse and gliding smoothly through the banks of illuminated monitors, reading the signs. Signs were everywhere—embedded in walls, imprinted on temporary placards, hung on movable pillars—but his eyes tracked only the signs relevant to his mission—those pointing to gate 56.

He entered a tunnel and walked alongside the rolling people mover, keeping pace with the docile herd, then climbed the stairs by twos beside the escalator, overtaking the docile herd. He waited on the platform for the terminal train, and the docile herd caught up, only to soften and seep into the walls of the capsules, filling the whispering cars with its docile flesh.

He followed the ramps siphoning him to the last arcade of food vendors, and he took a moment to peruse the eating options, finding the bread at every food dispenser to be the same bread. They'd perfected some kind of simulated artisanal bread product with the appearance of a brown, hand-baked crust, but underneath the crust was obviously the same empty sponge of the old massproduced loaf. The magazines nearby were all the same, the same as the ones for sale in Los Angeles, in Atlanta, in Terre Haute, filled with the same pictures of the same arbitrarily renowned men and women and their poor, accursed children. He leafed through an issue of *Fast Company,* the monthly hagiography of capital, with a nearly wondrous emotion of disgust.

He took a seat in the far corner of the gate and soothed himself by observing the slow traffic of the taxiing 737s and watching the silent lights and the weightless motion of the luggage trucks drifting on the pavement. His mind became calm, filled with the old, peaceful feeling of the mission. It had always been this way. With the acceptance of the mission came a luminous clarity to the world, a brightening of the colors and a sharpening of the sounds. As his eyes roamed the passing civilians, all the scene's information seemed discrete and knowable at a glance. It had been a long period of muddled incoherency, an era of nagging uncertainty about what, if anything, was worth his attention, but once again he knew which story drove most deeply into the days ahead. Among all the people in the world, only he knew that in a matter of days, weeks at the most, Michael Holmes, CEO of Blackhawk Consulting Solutions, global leader in procurement, construction, and multinational project management, would likely be dead.

Again, the audacity of his idea pierced him with its simplicity. He had spent many months with Michael Holmes, traveling the globe as his bodyguard, and in that time he'd come to understand something of his employer and his worldly domain. Primarily, he'd come to see how phenomenally small the domain was. Not in terms of distances and hectares. Those sums were enormous. But in terms of the groups in which Holmes plied his power, the rooms in which Holmes meted out his influence. Within that small world, no one conducted the theater of corporate power as unassumingly as he. In Persian Gulf hotel suites, Corn Belt football stadium skyboxes, and Benelux leadership conferences, he quietly sowed some of the most destructive ecological and humanitarian mischief on the face of the earth.

If Ben accepted the Mission, the termination of Michael Holmes, the event would surely send a chilling message to the oligarchs who controlled the world's fate. When they read the note he would write, they would understand the significance of what they were facing. If you are a global leader trafficking in rapacious, exploitative behavior: you are a tier one target. If you are a purveyor of gross inequality toward your fellow man: you are a tier one target. For all your treachery, all your greed, you will pay a dear price. You might be Americans, or quasi-Americans, as the case may be, and you are entitled to your pursuits. But know that a vengeful, armed soldier is watching you.

The idea was incendiary, he realized, and very possibly insane. But in the clarity of the desert, the idea had come to him with force. Some change must occur. Some sanity must be asserted. The decent people of the globe must impose their will on Michael Holmes's junta. And there was but one inarguable instrument of change in the world, and that was violence.

Watching the flux of travelers in the concourse, the gradual infill of his fellow pilgrims to the nearby seats, Ben scrutinized the Mission for flaws. He had to comprehend whether his tenets were sound, because, unlike other missions, which came down from the head shed, this one sprang from the moral chambers of his own mind, and he had to be sure there was no mere vendetta here, no adrenalized, soldierly ego being stroked. Did the Mission make sense? He wasn't entirely sure. Did he even believe in the will of the people? He wasn't sure about that, either. But it was at this point that the plan deepened into a richer, more tragic conundrum. What if the people were not even aware of their own will? What if it was the duty of an able soldier to show the people their collective destiny? From this angle, he could feel a distinctly giving, merciful, paternal love driving him.

The Mission could still be worthless, he realized. It was very possible he was on the verge of a terrible, life-ruining mistake. But he had to believe the Mission merited further investigation, at the very least.

Muddled voices came through the speakers, interrupting his thoughts, and soon the docile herd massed again to begin boarding. Ben joined them and shuffled his way into the plane, still not having shared a single word or glancing eye contact with another human being. He took his seat beside the window and girded himself for the coming sojourn. He would go and see and by seeing arrive at a decision. He would harvest and mull. And as the pull of the plane's g-force drew him back in his seat and the plane's body began its long drive into the flesh of the night, he closed his eyes and reminded himself again that no one in the entire world had any idea what he was plotting.

He emerged on the other side of the night over Philadelphia, waking to peer down on its sprawl of brownstones and refineries, just brightening along the red rim of the horizon. The plane circled the airport two times, and as the wings banked he could see the white glints of day refracted on a thousand sheets of glass below, the ground a sprawling, beveled armor, a bronze frieze.

Michael Holmes lived and worked in New York these days, but Philadelphia would serve as Ben's base of operations. It seemed the safer, less scrutinized bet. If to buy a plane ticket was to date-stamp his life, he might as well date-stamp a false address.

As much as possible, Ben had been careful thus far to leave no tracks. Over the past weeks, using a handful of library computer terminals across the San Fernando Valley, he'd done his initial intelligence gathering, careful always to limit each search to four or five queries. He knew the masters of the Internet could draw any signal out of the noise once they knew what they were looking for, and the churning attentions of the government's Web surveillance program were never at rest. Once the Mission was completed, a hundred "Michael Holmes" searches conducted at the Pasadena Library would most certainly ring a bell in one of those mirrored office buildings in suburban Virginia, piquing the interest of some Mountain Dew–swilling twenty-five-year-old with a top secret security clearance. The last thing Ben wanted was to attract the attention of those mole people, and thus he'd labored to bury his pattern as deeply as possible.

As such, his information was partial at best. He had some rough idea of Holmes's current habits, but nothing precise. He knew that Holmes currently commuted every morning from his mansion somewhere on Long Island to his new offices in midtown Manhattan, and that must mean he drove along the Long Island Expressway at least twice a day. Considering his aversion to eating in restaurants or attending parties or even going to the movies, one could surmise he lived almost wholly inside this narrow pipeline. Thus, Ben's first objective was to map Holmes's pipeline.

Exiting the airport, he immediately used his debit card for a cab—Ding! Here I am, it said—and he used it again to pay for a hotel room downtown. Ding! He made a few more purchases with his card—Ding, ding, ding—laying out a plausible binge of provisioning for a day of vanilla tourism. Water. Newspaper. Walking map. The hotel room he got was adequately clean, which was all that mattered, but he didn't stay long enough to settle in. Hitching a small backpack over his shoulder, he walked directly to the bus station in Chinatown and bought a ticket on the Dragon bus—the transport line connecting Chinatown to Chinatown along the Eastern Seaboard—paying cash for a ticket to Manhattan.

Nothing dinged. No one in the world—not his own sister or father, not a single caffeine-addled government mole person—knew this transaction had occurred. He wondered, folding his ticket in his breast pocket, just how long the powers that be would allow cash money to exist. Surely not much longer. It was too clean, too anonymous. It allowed for far too much unsupervised spending. Waiting for the bus to board, he struggled to remember a world without the incessant, compulsory, electronic watermarking, but already he found it was almost impossible to recall. What a world that must have been. A world of such fantastical freedom and opportunity for invention. People hadn't even realized how free they were. The freedom had only become visible as it vanished in the rearview mirror.

The Dragon bus ride was typically Third World, marred by a broken toilet that leaked powerful shit fumes into the cabin, forcing Ben to use his sweatshirt as a gas mask. Breathing through the fabric, staring out the window at the tumbling roadside landscape, a collage of ruined warehouses, choked streams, and battered fences, he tried, as he often did, to imagine what this place had once been. Before Jamestown, before Plymouth Rock, when the Iroquois and Onondagas wandered the land, what had it been? Out West, at least, a person could still squint out the vague silhouette of what God had made. But here, along Interstate 95, even the silhouette was gone, to the point where Ben couldn't feel the spirit of the earth at all.

The industrial ruins got only more putrid as the bus approached New York City, but then, after a switchback down to the river slough, the Holland Tunnel sucked them in, and they zoomed through the incredible tube, emerging on the other side into a living, breathing, heart-pounding city.

Chinatown was suddenly all around him, the streets thick with people, people walking their kids, people selling bedazzled T-shirts and bootleg Fendi bags, people streaming around honking cars, a city alive with everything that a city should be alive with. The Dragon bus bellowed down Canal, and here was the eternal ghetto of America. Tenements with iron fire escapes. Graffitied trucks double-parked. Dirty ice cubes melting into the gutter. And everywhere throngs of dreaming human beings, a docile, corn-fed crowd no longer. Ben could almost feel the ghosts of his ancestors entering his body. He could hear the yelps of the Yiddish boys and girls under the twisting laundry lines, smell the boiling chickens in their iron pots, and hear ever so faintly the clatter of mule hooves on the cobblestones. God, he loved this ghetto, the ghetto not only of his people but of all the incoming tribes. For every generation, the same Hudson light had revealed America. Breathe this air and you are American. Feel this sun and you are American.

Debarking under the Manhattan Bridge, Ben found himself on a Sesame Street block of dented garbage cans and laughing Puerto Ricans, amazed to think how excruciatingly pure that Hudson light had once been. He paused and leaned against a smutty brick wall, letting the light coat him. This was one of the great benefits of being on mission that he'd almost forgotten, this occasional, dumbstruck awe at the world's reality. He remembered that bowl of mole in San Salvador, still possibly the most delicious taste that had touched his tongue, eaten an hour before offing the dwarven cartel boss. What a gift.

He bought a pork bun and descended into the fecal-smelling subway tunnel, sliding his dollars into the machine for his Metro card. He ate the bun with his back to the tile, gnawing the bits of dough off the wax paper, watching his fellow passengers arranged across the platform, admiring their silent acceptance of each other's strangeness. He observed a whole spectrum of small gestures and secret codes passing among them, an encyclopedia of odd clothing choices. He himself would never wear jeans embroidered with giant dragons on the pockets, for instance, but he was so glad that the young Laotian man found them to his liking. Soon the lights were kindling on the tracks, and then came the rushing, shattering noise of the train, and he shuffled through the doors with his fellow citizens and found a seat on the ass-polished plastic bench.

At the Penn Station exit, he rose onto Seventh Avenue to discover the light was not as wondrous in this part of town. The big, inhuman glass-and-steel buildings didn't have the same supple bounce as the tenement brick. The canyons were too wide, and the street racket was too impersonal and aggressively corporate. His day's goal was Madison Square

Garden, and it took him a few minutes to isolate the correct monolith. The building was hemmed in among the many similar boxes, but eventually he managed to locate the proper high-rise and count up to the proper floor. He eyeballed the strip of windows where Holmes spent his days. Where Holmes was possibly sitting or pissing or shitting right now. Not that it mattered. Already he knew he wasn't going to find a decent sight line into the office itself.

He stood on the sidewalk as the foot traffic from Penn Station parted around him. Even here, bits of old New York were visible. There were midcentury coffee shops and postcard stores. There were shoe shiners and shopkeepers in suspenders. So even here, a spark of love for his fellow man glowed in him. What could rouse these citizens to the same love he felt? What could shake them out of their all-American slumber?

Only the slaughter of their common enemy, that was what.

Again it struck him that the Mission was a terrible idea. A monstrous, insane notion. But insane compared with what? he thought. Compared with the continent-sized gyre of plastic debris in the Pacific Ocean? Compared with a world of endless war?

It would hurt nothing to walk the perimeter of the building looking for access points. He pushed through the front glass doors into the main lobby, keeping his brim low, and counted the turnstiles leading to the elevators. He noted the security guards at each gate, the laminated ID cards rising from pockets and purses, and the guards snapping digital photographs of every entering visitor. Handing out their temporary passes, the guards were probably generating more archived information per hour than the last ten thousand years of human existence combined.

Ben exited the building and wandered to the mouth of the parking garage and peered into the darkness. He could make out rows of steel bars fortifying the walls and layers of antiterror barricades stacked along the traffic lanes. He strolled back to Seventh Avenue and scoped the surrounding buildings again, but the only option he could see was going to be underground, in the brief trot from limo to elevator, and he didn't want to do some Jack Ruby number. He wanted to survive the Mission, not only because he enjoyed being alive but also because the Mission would succeed only if he remained at large, a looming threat to any multinational executive who transgressed his orders.

He turned and walked down Sixth Avenue, already recalculating his strategy, seeking new signs. He passed an Internet café with a poster in the window of the great pyramids, an enduring object of civilization and slave labor and a site he had in fact visited with Michael Holmes. He remembered vividly how the camel driver had tried forcing his way into the car, seeking tourist dollars, and how Michael Holmes had claimed he was Canadian, as he sometimes did in the developing world. The man had cried, "Canada Dry!" just as Ben had tossed him onto the sidewalk in front of Pizza Hut. All day they'd imitated the camel driver. "Canada Dry!"

It might be a sign, he thought. And, seeing as he was currently off the grid, with no one on the planet aware of his whereabouts, he decided the time for his next round of information gathering was at hand. He entered the bleak, mustard-colored storefront, paid the man at the counter, and selected a workstation, and for the next three hours plunged into the digital ether, casting through pages for any new, useful dirt on Michael Holmes.

Ding, ding, ding. The bells were ringing, but no one knew to listen just yet. Holmes was fifty-eight years old. Caucasian. Six foot five. He'd grown up on a farm in northern Wisconsin, and he'd worked his way through college tending bar at the country-club dining hall. His tenure at Citibank was notable for its unprecedented profit margins in foreign currency exchange. His philanthropy included the ballet, the natural history museum, and children's cancer research.

But where did he live? Where did his car get serviced? What was his travel itinerary? The most important information was buried under a shale of useless Holmes-related trivia. Ben continued searching screens and discovered again the fact that Holmes lived on Long Island, but in which town? On which street? He peeled through screen after screen and was on the verge of giving up and going home, all the way home, when a gossamer thread pertaining to Holmes's real estate dealings materialized. The thread dated to 2003 and consisted of a handful of postings by Long Island residents about their new, mega-connected neighbor. They wondered if he was going to chop down any trees. Or if he was going to decorate for Christmas. Then, via an attached link, Ben jumped to an even juicier page: an aerial image from the real estate company that had ostensibly sold Holmes his property.

He examined the photo. It was a great mansion on the water, a Tudor thing, with a sprawling, many-chimneyed rooftop and many decks. A giant rear patio led down to a lawn big enough for full football scrimmages. The entire property was encircled by a thick wall clasped by a wrought-iron gate, and the nearest neighbor was a hundred yards away, front door to front door. The home appeared to be accessible only by way of a snaking road connecting to the township of Glen Cove.

The satellite had passed over the property on a sunny winter day, so the trees were bare, the shadows long and sharp. The address was printed on the page, along with the real estate specs.

Ben printed out the image. He cross-referenced the real estate photo with other bookmarked images, pulling up pictures of Holmes with his wife on a patio, Holmes grilling hot dogs. The images seemed to correspond. He was grilling hot dogs on a brick patio with gray, choppy water in the background. The article about Holmes's sailing habit also made perfect sense in the context of this bloated seaside architecture.

Assume this was Holmes's domicile. Ben could see now that he had suspected all along that this was his true objective, but for some reason the knowledge hadn't fully coalesced. Some part of him had refused to understand the simplicity of the Mission. He'd assumed New York City was the appropriate theater, but the Mission had clarified itself once again, one clarification after another. He could tell by the wooded area across from the front gate, the spacious patches of grass, the copious air space, the pyramid poster, that this was what destiny had decreed.

He printed out street maps and deleted his search history and wiped down the keyboard with a baby wipe from his neighbor's unattended bag. Happily, there were no cameras in the store, and when he stepped back onto the street, he knew his image in the mind of the man at the desk was already fading.

The Dragon bus delivered him back to Philadelphia by early evening, and he used his debit card again for dinner at Sofitel, a hotel restaurant where he treated himself to a bloody tenderloin steak. The coming days were taking a new shape. In the morning he'd use his debit card to lay more stations on his false trail, and then he'd buy himself a cheap car, cash. In this car, he would drive to Holmes's Long Island neighborhood and begin his next phase of observation and deliberation. If the signs held, he would keep going. He would watch and wait, as he'd been trained, and return to Philadelphia as many times as necessary before making a final move. He would remain open to the ever-shifting winds of intuition.

Walking back to his hotel, the protein of his meat infusing his blood with strength, he passed Independence Square and crossed the park housing the Liberty Bell. He paused at the glass temple where the bell lived and pressed his forehead to the pane, searching for the darkened shape inside. His breath silvered the glass, and he found himself staring at the dim outline of the cracked icon. A placard said that the Liberty Bell had been cast using the metal of a previous bell in England and that the name had come from a group of abolitionists. News to him.

Ben looked at the icon for a while as a rat skittered in the bushes and a grumbling homeless man wandered through, searching for cans. In the morning, Ben would come back and look at the bell again. Maybe he'd even go inside and join the tourists. It wasn't that he had any great desire to see the Liberty Bell. It was only a hunk of cracked metal someone had put in a box. But if the Mission was truly happening, if the Mission was real, it was exactly the kind of false step that would throw the drones off his trail.

9

"So tell me about Oakland," Aaron said again, but Grandpa Sam didn't respond. He didn't even bother shrugging this time, such was his disinterest in answering any more questions about Oakland and his life decades before Aaron's birth. Much more interesting to him on this sunny, mild California morning were the oncoming freeway stripes and the gradual growth of a turquoise Corolla in the right lane as they gained on it and finally, roaringly, passed. Another half mile of I-5 rolled underneath before he sighed and continued his silent sitting.

Aaron didn't try asking any more questions. For days he'd been making queries about the Oakland years and thus far had learned almost nothing. He'd established the basic window of his grandpa's residency there, 1949 to 1959, or thereabouts, and he'd unearthed the name of one friend, Joe, but almost nothing else. No address, no photographs. He didn't mind sticking to the subject—it wasn't as if they had a lot of other topics to discuss—but the distinct lack of desire on his grandfather's part to continue the interview was profound. Not that his grandfather knew an interview was occurring.

But eventually he got bored. "So. What part of town did you live in again?" he said.

The sound of the engine spinning softly under the hood mixed with the muffled moaning of the wind flowing over the windows and the low drone of the AC. This time it was Aaron who eventually sighed. Fuck it. He was really done with the interview now. For the next five hours he'd just let his grandfather sit there like a loaf of bread and stare unmolested at the flat expanses of soy or cabbage or whatever it was spreading infinitely to either side.

Bakersfield, sixty-one miles.

At least they were making decent time after the morning's crawling start, he thought, what with all its last-minute packing and snacking and methodical locking of doors. The city streets had been brutally clogged, construction intersecting construction, but once they'd crossed the Santa Susannas, the highway had mercifully opened to twelve lanes, and for the past hour they'd been fairly flying across the open-air factory of the Central Valley, the feudal domain of Monsanto, Sysco, and all the titans of agribusiness. Stealing glances at the featureless land, home to generations of Mexican laborers manning the tractors and delivery trucks, and generations of Anglo overlords managing the Mexicans, Aaron spotted not a single living figure in sight.

Bakersfield, fifty-five miles.

What the miles were steadily filing down to, Aaron didn't know. Soon enough they'd arrive in the East Bay, scene of his grandpa's early American apprenticeship, where his grandfather was quite sure his old safe deposit box remained packed with gold, but the truth of that belief was still very much debatable.

The existence of the box itself was a fact; at least that much Aaron had ascertained. Over the past weeks, he'd made a few calls on his grandpa's behalf, and he'd learned a little bit about the Bank of Oakland, if nothing else. The Bank of Oakland, which had at one time housed his grandfather's savings account, no longer existed. It had made it only until 1986, at which point it had been eaten by Wells Fargo. Wells Fargo had in turn been eaten by Washington Mutual in 1999. And WaMu had been eaten not long ago by Chase, one of the few behemoths to survive the great meltdown that his elders had bequeathed to his generation. All of this Aaron had learned from a single phone call with a consumer watchdog agency in Walnut Creek. A quick street-image mapping had located the physical structure of the original Bank of Oakland, still standing on the corner of Broadway and Tenth, the signs over the door having just changed with each new owner.

Aaron had called the branch, thinking maybe, possibly, doubtfully, the antique safe deposit box was still somewhere on the premises. He'd been handed off to four different tellers, explaining his question over and over again, and eventually had discovered that the bank shipped old, delinquent safe deposit boxes to a central warehouse in Vallejo. He'd called that warehouse, they hadn't found it, and a cursory search of his grandpa's mail had uncovered the fact that he'd been paying the monthly fee all along. A call back to the downtown Oakland Chase branch had revealed that the branch did in fact house some old safe deposit boxes in the vault, maybe, possibly, doubtfully, left over from his grandfather's day, and at this point the manager had gotten on the line and things had accelerated. The manager had confirmed that indeed one of those boxes did share a number with the key in his grandpa's possession, 306, and it was maybe, possibly, doubtfully, the case that the key would open the old box. The very prospect of this had filled her, the manager, with almost orgasmic pleasure. It had been a bad decade for banks, PR-wise, and this tale of a loyal, Greatest Generation customer reuniting with his long-lost treasure had all the earmarks of a positive, community-oriented news item. She was ready to help however she could.

So the plan was to open the box on Friday. Today was Thursday, and if everything held steady, Aaron and his grandfather would arrive in Oakland by the late afternoon. They'd sleep in the Marriott Hotel kitty-corner from the bank, and in the morning they'd walk across the intersection and meet the manager, Jackie, who would kindly guide them into the vault. The key would be inserted. The lid would open. And . . . then what?

Aaron was not getting his hopes up. Sure, there was a box, and there might even be something inside the box, as his grandpa believed, but it was highly unlikely it was gold. More likely it'd be some old stamps or old passports or old shoelaces—who could say? His grandpa had been gruffly positive he had orange juice in the freezer this morning, and it'd turned out there was only a bag of frost-encrusted fish sticks.

But the adventure was still worth having, Aaron told himself again. He'd even brought along his video camera, loaded with fresh batteries, in hopes of taping his grandpa for the archives of the Shoah Foundation should the chance come up. Maybe they'd end up in the hotel room tonight, watching *The Big Bang Theory,* quaffing a few beers, and the conversation would turn in the right direction. Though more likely, considering his grandpa's current torpor, the camera would remain in his backpack.

Bakersfield, forty-nine miles.

Aaron blew by a sixteen-wheeler and, gliding back into the right lane, he noticed a rank smell infiltrating the car. Grandpa Sam? No. That was a different kind of bad smell. This was a tangy, harsh, burned-earth odor, and it continued getting worse for miles, until the source became clear. It was the smell of manure. Many metric tons of manure, baking in the Central Valley heat.

Soon they were passing an industrial cattle farm spreading as far as the eye could see, and for the next ten full minutes, they were exposed to the sickening expanse of reddish-brown dirt, barbed wire, looming watchtowers, and thousands upon thousands of huddled cows awaiting slaughter. Field after field of interred animals. Families of cows crouched on the bald earth. No food. No nothing. Just dead brown earth and fence line. And, somewhere among the ugly, low-standing buildings, the charnel house itself. If Grandpa Sam noted the resemblance of the architecture to a concentration camp, he didn't mention it, and neither did Aaron, but the smell of the cows' shit followed them for another thirty miles north before fading.

They ate lunch at a place called the Bagel Café in the town of Dublin, half an hour east of Oakland, because his grandfather thought it would be simpler to stop outside the city and avoid the congestion. Aaron's main intention was to eat something vegetarian after the horror show of the factory farm, but in the end he settled on Asian chicken salad, hunger outstripping conscience. His grandfather ordered a grilled-cheese sandwich and tomato soup and immediately got started on his occasional restaurant routine, which was harassing the waitress with his unanswerable questions and plying her with his *Reader's Digest*–level jokes. Here they came: the one about the whorehouse on a mountaintop, the one about the dog and the cat in the graveyard. Aaron had heard all of them approximately eight hundred times.

This waitress was tolerant. The lunch rush was over, and this old man at table five at least offered a moment of rest. Grandpa Sam took the toleration as encouragement and kept slinging the chestnuts. "Do you want a tip, young lady?" A long, awkward pause. "Here's a tip. Don't bet on the horses." "What's black and white and black and white and black and white?" A long, puzzled pause. "A nun falling down the stairs." Aaron tried to ignore the edge of confusion and mild contempt in the waitress's eyes as his grandpa extolled her beauty and advised her to smile more because America was the freest country on earth. By the time he finally released her, under the displeased gaze of the Bagel Café's manager, he'd even promised to show her his gold treasure on the way home from the bank.

"You'll be here tomorrow, Kari?" he said. He was on a first-name basis with her now. "We'll be here with the bag. We'll show you."

"Okay," Kari said, backing away, and left Aaron's grandpa to bask in the afterglow of his flirtation. Tunelessly, he began humming one of his old crooner songs and fondling the key to his safe deposit box, at which point Aaron decided he might as well capitalize on the rare light in his grandpa's eyes by asking more questions.

"So you met Grandma in Oakland, is that right?" he said. He figured maybe if he piggybacked on the family lore, he could get some traction. The mention of his grandma was a sure way to extract at least a few pieties about her cooking and accounting skills.

"I did," his grandpa said, still a-tingle. "That is true."

"And you guys met at a dance, is that right?" Aaron said. "That's what Mom said once."

"At a dance, yes."

"So yeah, tell me something about the dance."

"What's to tell?"

Aaron slid down in his seat, holding back the first thought that came to mind: How about anything, Grandpa? I'm asking you about your goddamn precious life here. The life you're getting real close to the end of. So give me some details before it's too late, how about that?

Instead, he said, "What music did they play?"

"Oh, I don't remember the music," his grandpa said.

"Come on, what kind of music? I don't need to know the exact song. I just want to know what it was like."

His grandpa stared at Kari, filling a napkin holder, his face too old and slack to express the leer that was probably somewhere in his head. Even at this age, the vain dream of getting laid wasn't wholly extinguished. He barely seemed aware of Aaron's presence, but he managed to mumble out an answer. "Jewish music."

"So it was a Jewish dance?"

"The temple put on dances. Yes."

"So, like what?" Aaron said, genuinely mildly interested now. "Klezmer? Is that what we're talking about?"

"No, no, no." His grandfather shook his head with some vigor, pleased his grandson knew the word "klezmer." This, plus the residual high of the Kari banter, seemed to dislodge a granule of memory from somewhere deep in his skull, sending it through the long bottleneck of his nerves, all the way to his tongue.

"Big-band music," he offered. "There were trumpets, trombones. They always had a bandstand."

"Ah," Aaron said. At last, they were getting somewhere. Trumpets and trombones. That painted something in his head. Suddenly he could dimly see something moving in the past: his youthful grandfather and grandmother standing on the edge of a dance floor in Oakland, horns gleaming, strings of lights shining, shadowy palms buried in the East Bay mist. He could see them standing there, talking but not dancing. That was still too much to conjure. The image was sketchy but enticing and brought more questions to mind. What were the first words they'd said to each other? What were they wearing? Sadly, all the rich, fine-grained, sense-memory details, the flashes of hot life itself, were lost to the ages.

"I didn't know big-band music was Jewish," Aaron said.

"Of course it is. Benny Goodman. He's Jewish."

Aaron laughed. It was true. He'd thought about this before: all music was Jewish music, wasn't it? Gene Simmons was Jewish. David Lee Roth was Jewish. Lou Reed was Jewish. The Beastie Boys were Jewish. His grandpa's big-band sympathies confirmed the thesis again.

He wanted to extract more information in this vein, but the food was coming out, transported in the hands of his grandpa's angel, Kari. They'd made some progress, though, established a new line of inquiry, and it wasn't as though his grandpa was going to start painting an oil picture of those bygone nights in Eisenhower's Oakland. He wasn't, at this late date, going to transform into some raconteur.

They were back on the road within the hour, and almost immediately they hit the outskirts of Oakland, the tangle of highways all ending, confusingly, in the suffix "-80." This final leg took only a few minutes, but his grandfather was fast asleep by the time the off-ramp to downtown swung into view. Aaron parked on the side street near the Marriott and let his grandpa snooze awhile, zoning out on the low clouds seething over the rooftops, testing the air's ocean brine. Downtown Oakland wasn't much to look at, he discovered. It was basically a bus mall, home to a few dozen methadone addicts bargaining their last dollars back and forth.

"I need some money, man, or I won't get my medicine."

"You can't have it, man. I got to pay my rent."

"Come on, baby, tomorrow my check comes."

Aaron pulled out his earbuds and tracked down Benny Goodman on his phone. He landed immediately on a YouTube clip of the song "Sing, Sing, Sing" and opened the window to find a performance that looked pulled from an old detective movie. Benny and his band were in a tropical nightclub, laying the mood for the first make-out session with the buxom moll, or something like that. Aaron gave it a try, listening tentatively at first, worried it was only cheese, but soon with curiosity and even delight, riding the swinging, thumping party number into the era of his grandpa's youth. The music was just cartoonishly fun, the horns bending and swaying, rising and punching their golden, brassy blasts, the clarinet solo slinky and sophisticated. The drumming was truly wild. The guy looked like a sex criminal, with his wolfish, hunchback style, his arms and his spine all out of sync. "Swing" was the right word, all right. To gaze out at modern-day Oakland with that soundtrack in his ears was truly bizarre, the shabby city suddenly shot with sex and optimism. The horns ricocheted over the empty walls, the rolling drums clattered down the littered street. What abundance! The buildings and buses and trees were suddenly strutting all over town. Aaron wasn't sure he'd ever realized quite how ballsy the old music was.

He listened to the song twice and then checked the vintage: 1937. Another quick search confirmed his dark hunch: 1937, the very year Buchenwald opened its gates. In Europe, the nightmare was boiling, and this was the sound of America's Jew jazzman. How those worlds could share the same planet was beyond him.

When his grandpa woke up, they checked into the hotel. Since it was too early for dinner, they took a walk around Lake Merritt. The park was a riot of joggers, skateboarders, bicyclists, tai chi'ers, the whole Eden of Oakland on display, and the smell of weed wafting from behind boulders and bushes almost made Aaron salivate as he imagined the moment later on when he could safely break out his stash.

His grandfather, well rested, sprung from his La-Z-Boy, the spirit of the waitress still with him, shuffled along the path with a whistle on his lips. He stopped and patted a giant pit bull and regaled the owner with the mountaintop whorehouse joke, for which he received a polite guffaw, and then they sat on a bench near the boathouse and let the day's heat soak into their bones. All around them lesbians were necking, hobos were napping, glowing amaretto-skinned men were stretching out in their clinging running shorts. Some happy ducks staggered nearby, and Aaron listened with amusement to his grandpa's little clicking sounds and finger snapping; he was apparently under the belief he could coax them over and pat them on their heads.

"Oakland's changed a lot, I bet, huh?" Aaron said as a warlock with a cybernetic helmet of some kind shambled by. The sheer quantity of weed blowing through was somewhat incredible. He could see Karl digging this rainbow-hued town. Maybe there was a sunporch in these parts for them to crash on.

"Eh?" his grandpa said.

"I bet it's changed here a lot," Aaron said again. "A lot more skateboarders now."

His grandpa sat immobile in the sun. The ducks were frustrating him, but he still seemed to think he had a chance to touch one if he was patient. He held his hand down at beak level, his fingers limply rubbing in welcome. "Still a lot of poor people," he said. "A lot of people doing anything to make a buck."

Aaron folded his arms and observed the ducks, not sure what his grandpa was talking about. The hobos sleeping on the grass were stamped with facial tattoos, having burned their bridges to straight society. Make a buck? Not these people. But such was his grandpa's strange perception.

"I never enjoyed Oakland much," his grandpa said without prompting.

"Oh," Aaron said, scratching his eye.

"It wasn't a very happy time in my life," he said. And with this, Aaron's attention was pricked. Was it possible his grandpa was getting into the spirit of disclosure? It seemed unlikely, and yet . . .

"It was a good thing I met your grandmother," Grandpa Sam said. "That was the best thing that could have happened to me. Before I met her, I was very unhappy here. All I wanted to do was go back home, to Germany."

Aaron sat up straighter. His grandpa had just said "Germany." Aaron couldn't remember ever hearing the name of the dread nation coming out of his grandpa's mouth, let alone hearing it referred to as his home. He wished he had his video camera handy as they stepped onto the hot, uncharted ground.

"I thought you were born in Poland," he said. "What do you mean, back home to Germany?"

"Oh, I couldn't go back to Poland after the war. No. I could never go back there . . ."

Aaron watched the ducks, trying to be patient. He didn't want to disrupt his grandpa's thought process as he slowly wound toward something.

"But . . . I guess I thought . . . So you lived in Germany?"

"I traveled all over Europe after the war. But I ended up in Germany, yes."

"Oh."

"I rode the trains. I didn't have money, but this was my ticket." He lifted his arm and showed his ashen numbers. "The conductors, they would come through the train, and I would roll up my sleeve and show them this, and they would go away. I did the same thing in bakeries and restaurants. For months after the war, no paying for anything. No one would take my money. They knew what this meant. I went everywhere, looking for my family. But I didn't find anyone. And in the end I went back to Germany."

"Why?"

"In Germany they had the DP camps. Displaced persons. They served three meals a day. They gave us beds with sheets.

They even had classes. The DP camp was where I first learned about electrical wiring. I signed up for every class they offered. I knew education was the best way out. The only way out." He patted Aaron's knee to punctuate this lesson.

"And so you were in the DP camp how long?"

"Two years."

"And then here?"

"Yes."

His grandfather breathed heavily, eyes on the ducks, seeming to debate with himself about whether or not to keep going. Maybe it was the smell of the eucalyptus, maybe it was the last glimmer of his flirtation with Kari, but he plowed onward into the past.

"The camps were very crowded," he said. "And some of us were moved into houses and apartments. We were the lucky ones. I was put in a home with a young woman, a widow, and she was a very, very nice woman." He paused as the ducks waddled almost close enough to reach out and throttle, but he only watched them, resigned. "Yes. We got along very nicely. Her husband, he'd died in the war. She had two small children to take care of, and she needed the help. That's why she took me in. We had a very good relationship. We helped each other very much those years."

The lake water was dappled with silver light. A nerd couple, Asian and white, walked down the path, the man's cape flapping around his feet. Aaron didn't want to risk breaking the spell, but he also wanted his grandfather to know he was with him.

"What was she like?"

"She was a very kind woman. Very warm. She enjoyed cooking very much."

"Uh-huh?"

"She made stuffed cabbages every Sunday. She was an expert at stuffed cabbages. She boiled the leaves and filled the leaves with spiced meat and tied them with string. You had a little pile of strings at the end. I remember those strings."

"What else, Grandpa?"

"Oh, I don't know . . ." Grandpa Sam stared at the water, falling into a memory and rising back out. "Her favorite color was yellow. She loved yellow. Yellow curtains, yellow chairs. She was a wonderful woman. And her children, they were wonderful, too."

"And you lived with her before you came to America."

"If you had the chance to come to America back then, you came," he said. "I had the chance. But it wasn't easy once I got here. I wasn't happy at all. Oakland was a very hard place to be. I didn't understand how to make my way. I talked all the time about going back. Going back, going back, that's all I wanted to do. I had to. So I saved my money, and I went back as soon as I could."

"Wait a minute, what?" Aaron wasn't sure he'd correctly understood what his grandpa was saying. "Are you serious? You came to America, and then you left America and went back to Germany?"

His grandfather nodded, and the ducks stumbled back into the water, plunking in one by one. The water parted behind them, black ripples on the silver, their wakes meshing into a shimmering geometry. Aaron's grandpa didn't seem struck by the insanity of his story, but Aaron was agog. To survive the camps and go back? What could possibly make that seem reasonable?

"So, then what?"

His grandpa stared at the stilling water. The ducks had scattered into the weeds. "It wasn't the same when I got back," he said, without feeling. "Someone had moved into my room. And it was true I could make more money in America. So I came back and, thank God, I met your grandmother."

Four hours later, Aaron sat on a bench on Broadway, getting high. He took hit after hit, watching the bud cherry and fade away and the smoke escape from his mouth into the cooling air. Up in the hotel room, his grandfather was watching TV, if not already asleep. The sound of the traffic was abstracted and watery. The last golden light on the top of the eucalyptus was transportingly sad.

Aaron had never heard of his grandfather's German war widow before, the German woman he'd loved enough to leave the land of opportunity. The German woman who'd cooked him dinner in her yellow house. The German woman whose children he might have raised. How utterly strange, Aaron thought, the way history could suck a person in, the little whirlpools inside the torrential flow. A whole life could spin off to the side that way. He wondered if his mother knew the story of the war widow. She must.

He fished out a notebook and attempted to write down the gist of what he'd heard that day, but he was too stoned to concentrate. He couldn't make it to the end of a sentence without forgetting the start. He'd have to jot his entry in the morning. The important thing to know was that he was making progress, working his way ever deeper, back to Oakland, back to Europe, getting ever nearer to the edge of the sucking black hole at the heart.

10

Loading the dishwasher, Anne pondered the many methods of skinning Mark Harris's cat. There were many skinning strategies one might employ, she realized, but surely one skinning method was the best. Skin it from the head? Skin it from the butt? Peel the whole pelt inside out? If nothing else, the cat skinning was an interesting thought experiment to ponder. If she was going to sell off the rights to the used toilet water of Los Angeles, how would she do it?

The water of Los Angeles was touched by many agencies and authorities. Fish and Wildlife, Parks and Recreation, the Port. But controlling hegemony over the city's most precious resource, once it passed down the drain, lay ultimately with the Bureau of Sanitation, as she'd told Mark Harris from the start. Sanitation was also in command of trash, which meant the fleet of 750 trucks hauling more than six thousand tons of refuse a day, and the landfills, and the 6,500 miles of sewer line, mostly leading to Hyperion Treatment Plant and Terminal Island, where the bioslurry was turned into heat-dried fertilizer for nonfood crops in the Valley. All together, the system added up to a sprawling municipal fiefdom, manned by a staff of some 2,800 people, based at a crescent of industry on the waterfront near the airport, and presided over by one Charlie Arnold.

Anne knew Charlie. Charlie had been in the commissioner's chair of Sanitation for around five years, and before that he'd been at city hall, and before that, long ago, he'd been at CALPIRG, the environmental canvassing organization. His job at Sanitation had come as an act of flagrant nepotism by the mayor after Charlie's turns as mayoral campaign manager and mayoral chief of staff, and, although Charlie had always been a competent, dutiful civil servant, he'd surprised everyone by becoming what many now termed a "visionary" of all things eco, a walking PowerPoint presentation on the glories of the green city. He talked about membrane bioreactors, ZeeWeed ultrafiltration membranes, all manner of membranes— internal, external, sidestream, you name it. His greatest triumph was a pilot project whereby tons of bioslurry had been injected into deep fissures in the earth, creating pockets of biogas to later siphon back out as alternative fuel. The program had been regarded as a major success, with write-ups in the industry papers and a *New York Times Magazine* profile. Shit into energy, a perfect circle, the dream.

At some point BHC Industries' permit quest was going to lead to Charlie Arnold's door. How to convince Charlie that ownership of his precious public wastewater should migrate into the hands of a greenwashing speculative capitalist without any particular conservationist agenda was not immediately clear. Charlie was a staunch protector of the public interest, harboring a nearly violent hatred of polluters of all kinds. He was also an arrogant prick. If anyone comprehended the value of the city's wastewater and would fight to protect it, it was Charlie.

Bracket Charlie.

The other unavoidable personage through whom the permitting process would go, as she'd also told Mark, was Randy Lowell, the city-council member who putatively oversaw Charlie Arnold's Sanitation Department. Randy Lowell was in effect Charlie Arnold's boss, or at least his direct manager, and he was not in any way, by any definition, an eco-visionary. He was the child of old L.A. Anglo stock, scion of Okies, a former cop elected term after term by his district in La Jolla, grounded in a hard-core constituency of corporate donors, city commerce club members, anticrime soccer moms, right-leaning megachurches, and certain nonpublic trade unions. He was a devout pragmatist, in other words, with no interest in high-minded principles of equality, justice, environmentalism, or industrial regulation of any kind. He was a "friend of business," as they said, a defender of cops and the people who loved cops, with a reputation for doing his homework and yelling. A lot. A lot of yelling.

Anne had a fine relationship with Randy. Randy liked Anne because she was also someone who did her homework, and they'd shared more than one cutting joke at the expense of some hapless city manager flailing with his Excel spreadsheets. But as to whether Randy was a natural ally? She doubted it. He was not a fan of public giveaways unless he was the one doing the giving, and even if he was a natural ally, it didn't much matter. Ultimately, it was a personality thing. Both Charlie Arnold and Randy Lowell were going to have to sign off on this permit. And unfortunately, Charlie and Randy despised each other. The natural ally of one was the natural enemy of the other. Such was the needle she had to thread.

People thought the government was a hierarchy, but in fact that was not the case. The government was a centerless hive of back channels and side alleys, pitted with private dungeons where personal agendas went to be tortured and starved.

Yes, she thought, folding laundry, downing a second glass of her favorite pink *cava,* the best avenue was going to be the hardest one. She couldn't go top-down on this one; she had to go bottom-up. And that meant cracking the hardest nut first, to mix metaphors. She had to recruit Charlie Arnold, the green visionary, and only then could she take the proposal to Randy Lowell, the pragmatist. From there, the project would move to the city attorney (she already knew which one she'd use—Ed Monk, a blathering know-it-all but ultimately pliable and friendly). And finally, she'd let the mayor in on the impending deal. They could possibly circumvent the full council vote, definitely any public hearings. The mayor was a great connoisseur of secret bargains, and if she could get this all the way to his desk without interference, he'd be impressed, and they would likely be fine.

Mark Harris was going to have to give them all something, of course; it wouldn't be free, but that wasn't her concern right now. Paying the tolls on this road was his problem, not hers. She was only holding the map.

She and Charlie had a traditional place they liked to meet, and when Anne called his office, she reflexively suggested the old spot—a bench in the park near the entrance of the La Brea tar pits. They'd established their meeting ground back during the 1996 Campaign for Clean Air in Schools, during which they'd both served on the regional advisory committee and had put in some ungodly hours dealing with leadership infighting that had threatened to spill into the newspapers. They'd bonded then, recognizing each other as serious people, and they'd continued to encounter each other with genuine affection at every new plateau of their careers. She'd proposed the old bench partly to remind him of their youthful allegiance and also because she knew he probably wanted to avoid crowds at this particular juncture, owing to his current sex scandal.

This was another factor shaping her scheme, too, if lightly. Normally Charlie would have enjoyed mixing with his constituents and fielding what he seemed to think was their adulation, but this was a strange time for Charlie Arnold. A month ago, he'd been caught in a compromising position—i.e., having sex with an intern—and ever since, he'd been keeping a low profile. The girl was a semi-attractive student from UCLA, the daughter of a politically involved TV agent, and their pathetic mash letters had come out on LA Weekly's blog, these sad, lewd sex notes between a middle-aged bureaucrat and a teenage striver, since which time numerous parties had been calling for his resignation. Everyone agreed he'd get through it—the girl was of age, the parents seemed almost proud of the tryst, the blog posting had gone relatively unread—but it was probably embarrassing to Charlie nonetheless, and Anne knew enough to avoid that third rail by whatever means necessary. So she was surprised when Charlie sat down and immediately brought up the news himself. They'd barely traded hellos, and all the gnarly details of his sex life were gushing out of his mouth, and there they were, miles from her own day's agenda.

"It's all true," he said, wheezing from the effort of mounting the small knoll of grass to their appointed spot. He was looking a little thicker around the middle, she noticed, if not downright soft, and his face was getting puffy, a mealy blankness

threatening to swallow his thin lips and small eyes. He needed
a haircut, too. And his shoes looked fifteen years old. And yet,
against all this evidence of decline, his swagger also suggested
he still imagined himself as an irresistibly handsome specimen.
This was both the annoying and tragically endearing thing
about Charlie's character, the desperate self-love that made him
at once human and such an asshole.

"In case you were wondering or anything. God, I was stupid,
Anne. So fucking stupid! I still just can't believe I went there,
you know? She's not even that hot or anything. Just young, is
all. I'm so old, I can't even tell if a person is hot anymore. I just
see the youngness, and I'm, like, Gaahhhcck. I knew it was stupid, but I was just an idiot. What else can I say?"

"Yeah, well, what are you going to do, right?" Anne said,
working to strike the right note between disinterest and
sympathy. Who Charlie fucked was his own business. For
once, she didn't want to hear all the salacious details.

"Never thought it'd happen to me," he said, intent on
wallowing. "I thought I was a different kind of fish. But there
you go. It happens, all right. And, I mean, of course it does, you
know? Look how busy we all are. We're all giving everything
we've got. You pull your head out of your desk and look around,
there's no time for dating. You take what's standing there."

Anne nodded. Already, she could see, his apology was curdling into rank anger and blame. The slide from self-flagellation
to self-justification had taken all of forty-five seconds. She worried it was a mere prelude to long-winded score settling, and
she was right. He began with a broadside against reporters, a
rant about his newfound sympathy for celebrities, and then went
on and on, about sex with interns, sex with married people, sex

with ex-lovers, sex on first dates. Maybe, Charlie theorized, people his and Anne's age were consigned to sleep with only the people they'd already slept with in their twenties. There was only returning to old beds now, never finding new beds. Then a diatribe about his recent computer-dating adventures, the depressing activity of updating his profile, the silly antics of avoiding women after the failure of their outings. He'd literally jumped into a bush in Silver Lake in order to dodge a conversation with a woman he'd reluctantly screwed the week before.

Mostly she just watched the people entering the tar pits, letting his confessions wash over her. There was only a smattering of families and a few tourists out today, shuffling to the ticket booth under the weight of their backpacks and diaper bags. She watched them punching their debit codes, siphoning into the quiet gates. God, how Aaron had loved this place as a kid. They'd gone almost every month to ogle the ancient, blackened bones. What was it about the mastodons that kids found so fascinating? She had to think it was the aura of death they emanated. These tremendous creatures had once ruled the earth, and now they were nothing but dead bones. The kids came to this museum to get their first, happy glimpse at their own unimaginable demise.

A flock of schoolchildren approached the gate, chaperoned by three harried grown-ups, and Anne watched them all congregate at the fence while the teachers counted them off, and then the yelping crowd of princess pink and Spider-Man red descended en masse into the devouring maw, down to mastodon Valhalla. The world just kept making more of these kids. Why had she assumed the world would stop after she'd had hers?

Anne could feel the clock ticking on the meeting's end. Charlie was still being his funny, oversharing self, but surely he had meetings stacked up through the afternoon, and this one had to be low on the priority list. If she wanted to get to the main subject without rushing him, she had to make a move, but she wasn't sure how.

Thankfully, Charlie had his own inner clock ticking. He was a professional, after all. And, as the more powerful member of their duo, he was secretly the one in charge here. It was possible the sexual confessions were even a simple assertion of that power, an imposition of his private life into their mutual head space. It was LBJ taking a shit with his aides in tow. But once he'd deigned the time was right, the lesson imposed, he snapped back into business mode with surprising alacrity.

"But what are we here for anyway, Anne?" he said, clapping his hands, and she could tell all the emotional capital she'd been storing up had suddenly been locked away. All her moist sympathizing had been for naught.

"Lay it on me," he said. "What's up your sleeve, Anne? I know you called me for some reason. I've got a ton to do. It's great seeing you, by the way."

"Great seeing you, too, Charlie," she said, mindlessly brushing her skirt. "I'm glad you're getting through everything all right. That was the main thing I wanted to know. But as long as we're here, I do have a little thing to run by you, if you've still got some time."

"Sure. What's the thing?" He snuck a look at his watch; he was such an asshole, he physically couldn't seem to help himself.

"It has to do with the city's wastewater," she said. "You have some jurisdiction in that area, right?"

"Yeah."

"So, I have a guy who wants to take a crack at recycling it. He wants to filter all the city's wastewater and send it back into the drinking supply or something. He says he's got some hot technology to get it pure enough for consumption, and he's got the capital lined up to build the facility."

Here, she was embellishing on Mark's plan a bit. Quite a bit, actually. But she didn't see any other way. Something she always liked to remember about Charlie: in addition to being a great lover of the air and the water and the earth, he was also a major technophile, a pie-eyed optimist in the grand Silicon Valley model, lacking any of the twentieth-century nausea that Anne had always taken for granted as part of any mature worldview. If BHC could come at him with some kind of shiny gadget, she suspected, some kind of Next Big Thing for the treatment of wastewater, the pitch would be all that much easier. If she could only work in the word "membrane," she'd have him.

"He'd like to meet with you if you have the time," she said, without obvious eagerness.

"Who is this guy?"

"His name is Mark Harris."

"Ahh. Harris." Of course he knew him.

"You know him?"

"Never met him, no," Charlie said, and Anne could tell by the minuscule stiffening of his spine that he was disguising his real, spinning thoughts. "He's on a buying spree lately. He just bought Hoffman-Jenkins, the contractor that hauls most of our sludge. And he just bought a bunch of land south of Terminal Island. He's circling us for some reason. Now you. What does he want, anyway? I'm getting curious."

"I don't know what he wants, exactly," she said, annoyed to lack crucial information going into her meeting. "I'm not a scientist. But he seems pretty serious. He's funny, too. I think you'd like him. Or hate him; I don't know. But he's a big fan of yours, I can tell you that much." She was embellishing even further now, but what did Mark expect if he didn't give her the whole story? If only he knew the level of services he was purchasing.

"Why doesn't he just call me?" Charlie asked.

"He will. I think he wants to go through the proper channels."

"It kills me," Charlie said, grimacing at the sun. "People have no idea how much water we're already recycling. You should tell him to check out the filtration system over in Lakewood. They're keeping four golf courses alive on runoff from the city's washing machines alone. Great pilot program. And no one knows shit about it."

"I think Mark is talking about something on a different scale," Anne said, with due meekness. The last thing she wanted was to belittle Charlie's current efforts. "I think he wants to reuse, like, all of it. He's thinking pretty long-term."

"And you're, like, his agent or something?"

"No. I just fielded the call. He's . . . I guess he's a constituent."

"You think he's that interesting?"

She stared past the trunk of the eucalyptus tree, the insane tangle of roots diving under the sidewalk, and watched the first kids she'd seen go into the museum already streaming out, carrying their new coloring books and polyurethane woolly mammoth shapes. "Interesting" was a code word, coming from Charlie, she knew, a personal query into the character of Mark Harris. He was admitting his high regard for Anne after all these years but also that he had grave suspicions about her client. If Anne was willing to vouch for Mark Harris, maybe he would change his mind. And so, in this moment, Anne held Mark's future in her hands. With a word, she could open this door, and all her hard-earned integrity could be thrown out to sea.

"Yeah," she said. "He seems smart to me. He seems interesting."

The sky didn't open. Thunder didn't call her name. Her voice quietly entered the matrix of Charlie's mind and diffused through the labyrinth of other thoughts, other considerations. He'd absorbed her betrayal of principle and saw her no differently than he had moments before.

They ended the meeting with promises of further talks, future collaborations, better daily contact in general. Anne wished Charlie good luck on his sexual misadventures; he wished her good luck on her spinsterhood. Driving home, she felt generally satisfied with how the conversation had gone. The meeting might not have delivered the killer blow she had hoped for most—he could have fallen on the ground and humped her leg over the mere possibility of giving away the city's wastewater to some speculator—but it hadn't gone badly, either. She hadn't made any huge, humiliating mistakes.

She got home at dusk, with the little red-breasted birds tittering in the bougainvillea, the sound of the street cleaner growling around the block. She unlocked the front door and went for the tea basket, selecting a Tension Tamer and putting on the water. Waiting for the pot to boil, she called Aaron, but he didn't pick up. No news was good news, she figured, unless it was the worst news imaginable. She wondered what her brother was doing out in the desert, under the pale, dimming sky. She sat and stared at the patch of light on the wall, the rays marbled by the old, warped glass, reminding herself that this operation wasn't going to resolve itself in one conversation. This was going to take some stages, some effort, probably even some duplication of effort. She'd planted the seed today, that was all. Now she'd see what hideous plant grew.

11

Ben bought a gray Pontiac Vibe, the ultimate invisible hatchback, for three grand, cash, and visited Holmes's neighborhood on a muggy Wednesday afternoon. He approached the greater New York City area from the south, crossed the Verrazano, and twirled his way eastward into the hinterlands of Long Island, passing the austere saltboxes, the rustic vegetable stands, the all-American main street of Westbury. From there he tooled along the roads running beside the truly lavish properties on the coastline, where the houses were more like castles, cartoons of extreme privilege, and the grounds were planted with money trees and diamond grass. He passed Tudor, Georgian, and medieval manses, gargoyled, topiaried monuments of a gilded time when capital had had no compunction about spreading its leathery wings for all to see. His main thought, motoring along the fence lines, was of utilities. The heating bills here were probably more than the education budget of most central African nations combined.

The invisible Vibe cut through the twilight and passed the entrance of the private road leading to Holmes's estate. Ben continued on for another two hundred yards, until he came, as mapped, to a cul-de-sac near the beach and stood there inspecting the drab, pebbly spit of coastline for beer cans and fishing twine, deeming the litter sufficient to excuse the prolonged presence of a parked car. Then he ambled back the way he'd come, slipping past the private gate, and crept along the private road shoulder, alive with a child's feeling of insurrection, imminent danger, and freedom. This was just pure fun now. He'd done nothing wrong yet, he had nothing to hide. If anyone asked, he was taking a walk on what could easily be construed by an innocent westerner as loose, public land.

His footsteps seemed to explode on the thick leaf litter. From the satellite images, Ben had estimated about fifteen acres of elm and spruce and chestnut contained in the chic belt of private roadway Holmes shared with his neighbors. Already it was plain the woods went largely unvisited. The trees were but a museum, their preservation a brute expression of the homeowner association's untouchable influence.

He almost hoped for some confrontation that would eject him from the Mission, but no confrontation came. The surrounding houses were lodged deep behind reinforced walls, electrified gates, and elaborate motion-detecting laser machines. There were no animals, not even birds, to be seen. He encountered not a single, legible sign to divert his course. He breathed the fragrant air with gusto. The joy of the unilateral mission was something Anne would never understand.

He crossed a shallow ravine and mounted an ellipsis of boulders, already comprehending the topography quantumly better than any satellite map could have allowed. No surprise, the computer had been deceptive. This was an argument with the head shed every day. You want to know where the muzzle flashes are coming from? Stand here next to me. You want to know where the insurgent sniper is taking potshots? Sit here. Don't tell us what we can see with our own eyes.

He met back with the road across from Holmes's front gate. The wall, as expected, was fifteen feet tall, yellow brick, with eight cameras grafted to the lamps and immediately visible. He could see a lightning rod on the roofline. The only big surprise was how deeply the forest floor sank down. He was effectively standing in a shallow bowl, looking up. But even if that hadn't been the case, he still needed a higher position if he wanted to scope the front steps.

Never stand when you can kneel, they say, and never kneel when you can lie down. But in this case he needed a tower. Just off the road shoulder he selected the thickest, most gnarled, most branch-studded option, a horse chestnut with burly arms, wide forks, and broad bloom. It turned out that all the attributes that made for a good climbing tree as a kid made for a good climbing tree now, as a killer, and he heaved himself upward, branch after branch, until the tile roof of Holmes's estate spread into view, and higher still, until he could see most of the front acreage and a sliver of water beyond. As per the satellite images, the driveway ran directly across a broad, groomed lawn, fifty yards from gate to door, where it looped around a concrete fountain and spoked off to a four-car garage. The front door, the prize door, was a paneled oaken frieze planted at the top of seven, graceful, rounded steps.

The sun was now setting, and the sky over the sound was erupting into a lurid orange brushfire. A few sails were visible on the water, and beyond, the trees of Connecticut. Down below, in the clouds of toxic hypoxia, lurked cherrystone clams, mud snails, red crabs, and sand tiger sharks gliding over the weed-covered electricity cables and fiber-optic transmission lines. There were plovers, turnstones, and yellowlegs in the air, turtles and bullfrogs on the banks, black gum and hickory in the surrounding hardwood forests. Depending on how you looked at it, Long Island Sound was many things: a machine, an ecosystem, a highway. But here in Michael Holmes's neighborhood, amid his elite class, Ben knew it was mere decoration, a pretty backdrop for cocktail parties, morning tennis matches, and afternoon rounds of power conference calls.

He closed his eyes and probed the neighborhood's silence with his ears, listening for signs, but heard almost nothing. The silence of this neighborhood was wicked and unreal. In the silent air, he knew, invisible signals were streaming back and forth, spectral voices and pictures and numbers and data swirling. There were thousands of unseen eyes in the sky looking down, a million invisible guards in the tower. Ben knew he was probably being paranoid about the volume of space cameras above, but erring on that side was fine by him. Paranoia was a form of intelligence here. Fear was a form of imagination. He could feel the whole networked system vibrating just beyond the limits of his senses.

Again, he understood a basic truth: the man with the clearest vision is the one on the bottom. He is the one who sees everything. The man on top sees dick. The trick was to stay on the bottom, to hold the low ground. It was the opposite of what they'd always said, of course. You had to stay low and fend off the illusions brought on by any upward progress through the world. The goal was stay low and to be an earth man. Ben was an earth man, all the way. He took his orders from the earth, and he always would.

At 2043, the silence was broken by the sound of tires on the dry asphalt entering Ben's immaculate mind. Through the shiver of leaves, Holmes's limousine slid into view, long and black and gracefully slow, like one of those sharks prowling the ocean floor. The iron gate opened with a low, whirring growl, and the car eased inside the perimeter, swimming the channel to the front of the house. Ben watched, counting the beats of his heart. Gradually, the revolution of the tires slowed, and the car came to a halt. For twenty long heartbeats, nothing happened. The black box of the car idled, still. And then the door opened, exposing Holmes to the open air, sending his fragile skull bobbing six feet, five inches, above the ground.

For two minutes Holmes stood beside the car, talking on his phone. His old pal, exposed. His jaw opened and closed, and the words entered the little box and zoomed into the cosmos, beaming to a satellite in space and bouncing back down to earth like a rain of meteors. The man speaking was just a vague shape, bleary with shadow, a scarecrow with ragged silver hair. If Ben had been holding a gun, he could have completed the Mission right then and there. Was this a sign, he wondered? He shouldn't need signs anymore, only his own bedrock moral sense, but a clear sign would be nice. He hoped this was not the best shot he ever saw. He remembered all too well the five days lying at the border of the DMZ, in wait for Kim Jong Il, the only glimpse of his target coming in the first ten minutes, and after that, a blank concrete bunker wall.

When Holmes's call ended he tucked the phone in his coat and carried his skull up the steps, pausing while his hands unlocked the door and the gold light spilled over his silhouette. Holmes crossed the threshold. The door closed. The car, done waiting, swam out of view to its cave.

Ben acquired a gun from the Camp Fire Club by way of theft. The Camp Fire Club sounded like a children's troop, but in fact it was a hallowed, rich-guy hunting institution founded by Teddy Roosevelt and maintained by diamond-studded Wall Streeters and hedge fund assholes wanting the occasional power weekend in a woodland environment. Ben had done some hunting on Long Island before, and he'd seen the old-money lodges dotting the backcountry. He remembered one of them in particular, secluded and stately, likely unobserved in midweek and easy to break into. Without much problem he managed to find it again, and sure enough it was a bonanza, racked with cut-glass decanters, fine silver, a walk-in humidor, and oiled deer rifles behind glass. They liked their pricey equipment, all right. Ben had his choice of short-action Rugers and Brownings, long-range .280 Remingtons, and French-walnut-stocked .243 Winchesters, but in the end he selected the Echols Legend Sporter, glass mounted with a Leupold LR/T scope, already zeroed and ready to go.

He was still waiting for a clear sign, but back at the hotel he drew the curtains and broke down the weapon, cleaning every component to his satisfaction. He stripped the action and examined the bore, finding it fouled ever so slightly. He used a plastic-coated cleaning rod and cotton swabs soaked in brake cleaner to remove the carbon residue, Hoppe's No. 9 for copper, wiping his rod clean after each trip down the bore. Then he oiled the bore.

As he worked, inhaling the fumes, photons of doubt speckled across his mind. Something in the familiar motions got him seeing himself in his proper proportion to the world's future. Up until now the journey had been a purely theoretical exercise, like hunting big game with a camera. But the next phase, bearing a firearm, would be something else. He could feel his body entering into some cellular revolt against the Mission, his muscle tissue and circulatory system refusing to endanger themselves without good reason.

He turned on the TV for distraction, and like a sign, the face of Shane Larson, the talk-show host, appeared. Larson was a truly reprehensible being, a meat-faced pundit of the angry-right variety. He was the host of the nationally syndicated *Shane Larson Show*, on both TV and radio, the author of bestselling books against Islam and the rights of women, and a reliable supporter of any and all violent death in the Southern Hemisphere. He had a bottomless sympathy for bankers and corporate executives, regardless of crime, and his main goal in life seemed to be goading his audience into armed warfare against the poor and less fortunate. Never had there been an underdog he didn't kick.

Ben recoiled to think he'd once counted himself a fan, had even listened with rapture back in the days leading to the war, seeking ways to justify the killing he'd so badly wanted to do. He'd sucked in all the talk of WMDs and taking the fight to the enemy's home, ignoring the many untruths about Larson's reality. Now he despised Larson and recognized his bullying as a pathetic tool of oppression. Larson was a buffoon and a murderer. He was every racist asshole dad at every childhood barbecue of his life. To see him on the cheap hotel screen now, crawling with digital fungus, was nearly too much.

The sound was low, and Ben couldn't tell what Larson was talking about, only that he was fulminating at typically high pitch. His pink face was shaking, and spittle was collecting at the edges of his lips. Ben wished seethingly he could reach out and pull Larson through the screen. He wanted to beat him savagely while shouting some of his prized Anatole France quotes into his face: "'The law, in its majestic equality, forbids the rich and the poor alike from sleeping under bridges, begging for money, and stealing bread'!" Or: "'You think you are dying for your country; you are dying for the industrialists'!" But maddeningly, Larson was unreachable. He was too far away, too oblivious to Ben's very existence, to be shamed. Soon the segment was over, and the next show was coming on, and Ben, still unsure where he was going, built a suppressor.

12

They arrived at the bank half an hour before opening time and waited for the early teller to unlock the glass door. They could see her inside, a limping blond woman in a too-big pantsuit, turning on the lights, unlocking the teller stalls, then staring at a monitor and occasionally tapping a keyboard as if she was shopping for winter coats on Amazon. At last, with no particular regard for their schedule, she lumbered to the front and ushered them into the marble lobby.

The manager kept them waiting a few more minutes in the soft chairs near the coffee machine, but when she emerged from her private glass encasement, she seemed genuinely excited to shake their hands. Her name was Jackie, and she was a sweet, squeaky-voiced black woman with giant pools of purple makeup around her eyes, almost to the level of a backup singer for Parliament. She examined Aaron's grandfather's key with great optimism. "This looks very promising, Mr. Singer! I think we might have something." And with a quick, bustling wave to her staff, she ushered Aaron and his grandfather, the treasure hunters, down the stairs to the vault.

Aaron had never seen a bank vault before, but, as with so many things, it was much like it was the movies. The door was a giant, round agglomeration of silver and gold discs and spokes, about the size of a car, and after Jackie entered a many-digit code, and a whisper of shifting pistons and cogs emanated through the steel sheath, it opened with the slightest touch. The room revealed was shadowless and clean, and without ceremony Jackie took them into the vault's secret air.

Lining the walls were many small, metal doors, more than Aaron could count, and he wondered what lay inside all of them. Deeds, diamonds, engagement rings, bracelets, tiaras, who knew? A thousand mysteries, a thousand life stories, with a thousand twists of fate, none of which were his concern this morning. His concern was only Grandpa Sam's story, the gold that was the symbol of Grandpa Sam's fate, not that Grandpa Sam himself seemed all that precious about it. He could be watering his lawn, he was so excited to be in the vault. At least Jackie, businesswoman that she was, had some energy. She stalked over to a far corner, crouched down, tucked her skirt into the crease of her bent legs, tilted her head, brushed her fingers over a row of faceplates, yanked on a handle, and withdrew the proper box, the proper mystery, and hauled it to the table in the center of the room for opening.

There, Aaron's grandpa fiddled with the key, unable to fit the teeth into the slit. His effort went on for a full two minutes before Jackie stepped in and inserted the key herself. The key turned, the lid popped open, and sitting inside were three rolls of coins.

At first Aaron thought it was a bust. He'd been expecting something more spectacular—a pile of shining nuggets or a stack of glittering bars, something radiating actual cartoon bolts of brightness. But, judging from Jackie's delighted squeal, these plain, brown rolls were more than acceptable. He watched as his grandpa lifted one of the rolls and stared, turning it end to end. The roll was the size of a candle, and at each butt the coins' heads and tails were visible, and in these spots some of Aaron's fantasy came true. The coins were indeed gold in the most ridiculous way—gold like butterscotch, gold like the gold nuggets in a fairy tale, gold like the gleaming gold coins in a leprechaun's pot. Jackie was so pleased by the sight of the goldness that she clucked like a hen. Aaron's grandpa allowed himself a resigned smile of victory.

Jackie had a scale brought in, and they weighed the rolls and found the coins added up to twenty ounces, placing the worth somewhere in the region of twenty-five to thirty thousand dollars, depending on the day and the buyer. Twenty-five to thirty thousand dollars, compressed into these three slim cylinders of krugerrands. The gold had no use, exactly. It couldn't cure cancer or improve your boner strength. So why did men and women love gold? This was a question for the ages.

"This is quite a day!" Jackie said.

"I suppose it is," Grandpa Sam said.

"Your grandpa is a real card," Jackie said, pinching Grandpa Sam's shoulder.

"Yeah," Aaron said. "I guess so."

Next came picture time. One of the tellers, grinning and clutching her smartphone to her chest, was already lurking near the vault door, and she asked Aaron and Grandpa Sam and Jackie to stand for a few portraits. They arranged themselves in a line, Aaron's grandfather sandwiched in the middle with the gold, and smiled effortfully for the bank's e-newsletter. Then Aaron's grandpa signed the releases allowing him to take his property and also allowing his picture to be used for press purposes in the bank's e-newsletter, after which they shook hands with Jackie a few more times and climbed the stairs back up to the marble lobby.

"You're sure you want to close your account?" Jackie said as they reached the brass door to Broadway, during the warm goodbyes. "We've done a good job for you so far, Mr. Singer. Safe and sound."

"That's true," Grandpa Sam said. "But I need to bring this home now. Thank you very much."

"What about some insurance? I could draw up the papers right now."

"I just want to get home now, thank you."

"Your grandfather is a good guy, Aaron," Jackie said, opening the door. "You should listen to this guy."

"Oh, I do," Aaron said. "Sometimes."

The rolls went into a pouch his grandfather had brought expressly for the purpose of transportation. It was a purple velveteen pouch with gold, tasseled drawstrings and the words "Crown Royal" embroidered on the side. The pouch had been in his grandfather's possession for somewhere around a decade, awaiting some use. With the pouch safely tucked inside Grandpa Sam's fanny pack, they exited into the Oakland morning and belted themselves into the car to start home.

They retraced their way through the maze of cloverleaves, barreling between the noise-dampening freeway walls and zooming past the mysterious townships of San Leandro and Hayward, the pristine, white visage of the Mormon temple in Oakland Hills, bearing witness to their triumph.

To anyone else, Aaron's grandfather might have looked kind of depressed, hunched in the passenger seat, but Aaron was beginning to understand something about his emotional postures. His grandpa's shoulders may have been rounded, his head bowed toward his chest, but his hands were full of action, fiddling constantly with the soft bag in his lap. His fingers twisted the cords, retracted, lay still for a moment in their normal resting position, only to creep back and start massaging the bag again. For Aaron's grandpa, this passed for an expression of near euphoria.

The mood got even wilder as they continued east, and Grandpa Sam leaned forward in his seat to read the whizzing signs. Aaron had never seen his grandpa so fully engaged. He grumbled, not unhappily, as the clusters of fast-food restaurants wheeled by in his vision, to the degree that he almost seemed to be searching for something out there, but of course he didn't say what. That would have been too much, even for this extraordinary mood.

"You need anything, Grandpa?" Aaron asked. "A bathroom? We can stop."

"No. No. I don't need anything. I'm fine, Aaron, thank you."

The exit to Hayward approached, and Grandpa Sam's squinting and muttering started up again, fading as the overpasses and distant traffic signals receded. They were already leaving the dense Bay Area suburbia and entering arid pastureland, the hills sprouting copses of oak trees and occasional power stations and isolated homesteads, the sky dramatically enlarging.

"You're sure?" Aaron said. "Pretty soon there won't be anything for a long time."

"No," his grandpa said, fingering the tassels, but when the freeway merged with the traffic from San Jose and expanded to six lanes, he changed his mind.

"I think we should stop soon, for lunch," he said.

"Lunch?" Aaron said. "Now? Really?" The dashboard said 11:00, which meant they'd been driving for a grand total of fifteen minutes. They'd only just gotten up to speed. Aaron was of a mind to keep pushing. A bathroom pit stop, sure, but lunch?

"Yes," his grandpa confirmed. "I'd like to stop now."

"How about a Clif bar?" Aaron asked.

"No. I want to go to the place from yesterday. I told Kari we'd show her what we found."

With this revelation, Aaron's reluctance edged into outright mutiny. Breaking stride just to visit that girl, Kari, who'd surely already forgotten they existed, was stupid, and he definitely didn't want to eat another meal at her restaurant. A much better plan, by his estimation, would be to keep going and pull over in Bakersfield or somewhere like that and find an amazing Mexican place. But, glancing over at his grandpa's slumping girth, he let go of his reservations. So his grandfather wanted to stop and show off his gold to a pretty girl. Why not? How often did this silly, frivolous side of Grandpa Sam get exercised? And who deserved a victory lap more than his genocide-surviving grandpa? Truly, what was the point of reclaiming the batch of gold you've stashed away for decades if not to impress a girl at the Bagel Café?

Aaron barely had time to peel off the freeway into the citadel of Dublin. Entering from this side, it was all the more obvious what an exurban outpost it was, the last, mirrored extrusion of Bay Area yuppie-dom, at least for the moment. They cruised past the Oracle building and the other anonymous office-park complexes, heading toward the tracts of McMansions marching over the golden hills ahead. At the light, they turned into the nowfamiliar strip mall and coasted into a spot near the diner.

Kari was not at the counter this morning, but Grandpa Sam wasn't dissuaded. He pressed his belly to the glass case and asked for her by name, and he was rewarded with an obligatory search in the back room. A minute later Kari emerged from the kitchen, looking slightly put out.

"Oh," she said. "You guys."

"How are you this morning, my dear?" said Grandpa Sam, with an almost Old World decorum. He enunciated his words and held his posture as erectly as his depleted bones could manage. Within his limits, he almost seemed to perform a courtly bow.

"Did you guys forget something, or something?" she said with the look of a sad, tired Scottie dog. She was a beefy woman, with a flat perm that fell around her cheeks like drooping ears and eyes that were pinched with an expression of enduring, half-comprehended pain. "'Cause I didn't find anything, if you did."

"We only stopped to show you something, that's all," said Grandpa Sam. "I told you the reason we were driving to Oakland yesterday. Do you remember?"

"Yeah."

"Well, come here, Kari. I want to show you something."

His grandfather shuffled over to an empty table and pulled out the purple bag, holding his hand half inside the soft mouth until Kari joined him. As she peered down, her sullen expression shifted into a look of mild interest, mixed with some irritation.

"We went to the bank this morning," Grandpa Sam said. "I think I told you, I hadn't been to this bank in over forty years. And we had a very successful visit. Yes, we did. We went into the vault, and the key I had fit into the box. I don't think Aaron could believe it. Could you believe it, Aaron?"

"Nope."

"And this is what we found, Kari." Without any flourish—he was not a man of flourishes—he pulled the three cylinders from his bag and pressed them to the table, rolling them out like a fan. Kari leaned forward with another uptick of interest.

"That's gold?" she said. "For real?"

"Gold," he said. "Yes."

For a few seconds, Kari scrutinized the precious metal with something like reverence. She picked up one of the rolls of coins and hefted it in her palm, inspecting the edge of the brown paper sheath where it revealed the glowing metal. For a moment the rest of the world, the restaurant, all its smells and noise, seemed to exit from her mind, and she stared like a girl at the golden princess doll of her dreams.

"Heavy."

"It's gold," Aaron's grandpa said. "Gold is heavy."

"How much is it worth?"

"How much would you guess, Kari?" He was very pleased by the impression his show-and-tell was making. He was ready to keep playing the game with her as long as she'd stick with it.

"You're gonna make me guess?" she said.

"Go ahead. Please. Guess."

She started by guessing five hundred dollars. Aaron found the guess slightly moronic, but then again, thinking it over, he realized that only two hours ago he might well have made the same guess himself. It didn't look like that much gold, after all, three little rolls, and if a person had never seen real gold and had no idea how much gold was worth, how was that person supposed to know? His grandpa chuckled, shaking his head, pleased by the low-ball stab.

"More than that," he said.

Next she guessed five thousand dollars, a reasonable tenfold jump, and from there she crawled upward in thousand-dollar increments. By the time she landed on twenty-five thousand dollars, Aaron's grandpa was partly delighted, partly disgusted she'd taken so long. But he hadn't enjoyed so much attention from a young woman since the days he'd first stuffed the gold into the box.

"I told you I'd show you what we found," he said, carefully packing the gold back into his pouch. "I've had this gold a very long time, Kari. A very long time. A person should always have a little gold in their possession. You never know what might happen. You should remember that. Will you?"

"Uh-huh," she said, and disinterest again veiled her eyes. Anything smacking of grandfatherly advice, of useful advice in any category, was not going to find purchase with her, Aaron could tell. She was a person who'd made a life of rejecting whatever good advice might come her way.

"So, you guys eating lunch here?" she said, a beleaguered waitress again. "Or you're probably going out for steaks, huh?"

Zipping up his pack, Grandpa Sam looked over the dining room, examining the many empty seats. Among them was the very booth they'd sat in the day before, and Aaron could see the prospect was tempting. To fall into a routine so far from home? How enticing. Two mediocre lunches in a row? Absolutely, yes. How else might he know exactly what was coming in the hour ahead?

"Yes," his grandpa said imperiously. "We'll eat here, yes."

Kari waited for Aaron to confirm the decision, but he just shrugged. This was Grandpa Sam's day. And, holding his bag against his waist, his grandfather started for their booth, Kari falling in behind, grabbing menus, and Aaron silently falling in, too. It was only 11:10, but once again, if this was what his grandpa wanted, so be it. And maybe they could still make it home by dinner this way.

The lunch crowd was starting to come in, and Aaron felt as though he recognized a few of them from the day before. He also noticed that the waitresses and busboys seemed to be paying them more attention this time. They slowed down a little as they glided past their table, smiling, watching them out of the corners of their eyes. The news of their payload had obviously traveled and conferred on them the mantle of honored guests. Extra bread and butter appeared. Kari came around, filling their water glasses whenever they hit the halfway point. So this is what money brings you, he thought. Service.

His grandpa didn't seem to notice the stepped-up attention. Having completed his mission and fulfilled his promise, he was happy to sink back into his regular languor. Out the window, the sun-baked parking lot beguiled him, and occasionally he touched the drawstrings of his bag to remind himself it was indeed still there. When the food arrived, he placed the bag beside his plate like a sleeping hamster and proceeded to slurp his tomato soup, picking up specks of tomato in his mustache and looking more and more exhausted by the spoonful. The pleasure of his reunion with the gold had burned him out, and the slack turtle face was returning.

Aaron, for his part, entertained himself by ogling the waitress in the next section. She was a fairly generic, sorority-type blond, probably a lover of Pink and the Black Eyed Peas, but something about her willowy body and small, pert breasts was almost cruelly arousing. Her fine, broad shoulders and sweet, full, athletic ass, displayed almost pornographically in the binding black polyester pants bunching up in her panty line, oppressed him. From the way the outline of her nipples kept appearing and disappearing against the thin weight of her blouse, she probably wasn't wearing a bra, either.

At moments she almost seemed to sense Aaron's eyes on her, but if so, it made her only more flagrant in her bendings and reachings. Aaron watched as she leaned over to pour water, craning her neck, on the lookout for more glasses, bathed softly in the light of the Bagel Café's bay windows. Her skin was flushed; her lips were glossed. Before the plates had been cleared, as his grandfather drizzled the last spoonfuls of soup into his mouth, she passed near enough that Aaron could smell her, a breeze of clean, floral Calvin Klein scent, at which point he had to excuse himself and head for the bathroom to masturbate.

Happily, the diner bathroom was private. He sat down on the toilet seat and unzipped his pants, the image of the waitress's ass still seared on his lids. For a few minutes he tried to fabricate some kind of storyline to bring his fantasy to fuller effect, imagining the girl as his girlfriend, waiting for him after work in the parking lot, or in a car, or in the shadowy booths, but in the end he set the fantasy in the very bathroom where he was sitting. He visualized himself opening the door and finding her waiting, the embarrassed shuffle between them, the accidental, grazing touch, the sudden, inexplicable overflow of lust. He imagined the fuzz of her pubic hair against his fingers, the wetness of her slit, the pliant give of those delicate buttocks, and jerked harder.

About fifteen minutes later, he exited the bathroom with his hands freshly washed and his shirt tucked deeply into his waistline. He would have been out much sooner, but due to an unfortunate accident on the hem of his T-shirt, he'd ended up taking more time than expected, pawing at himself with damp paper towels and drying off under the hand blower, all to limited effect. The tuck-in was not a cool look, but he didn't much care. He wasn't going to see anyone he knew driving with his grandfather down I-5 today.

Back at the table, he found his grandpa asleep. His head was tilted awkwardly on his shoulder, and the snoring, while not at its most awful, brain-rattling level, was loud enough to bother the nearby eaters. A spill of cracker crumbs made a sad snowdrift on his chest. Aaron brushed off the dust and checked his phone, figuring he'd wait until the bill arrived to wake up his grandpa. He could see his fantasy waitress off taking an order from a trucker at the counter, but, interestingly, he no longer found her quite so fetching. That silly blond ponytail wasn't his thing, after all.

He was just scrolling through his emails, finding nothing of note, waiting for Kari to reappear so he could flag her down, when he noticed the bag was gone.

"Wait a minute. Wait a minute here. Hold on. No, this isn't right," Aaron said, his voice rising, and he lurched to his feet and stumbled around the booth, searching the floor, the seat, the tabletop, as the whole dining room gradually went quiet and watched. He looked along the baseboard of the booth, where the rug ended and the grit and crumbs of old meals collected. He tipped the chairs and felt the indentations where the legs had been. He enlarged his circle and searched under the neighbor's table and went back to the booth at a new angle. Sometime during his flailing, Grandpa Sam woke up, too, snorting, and feverishly joined the search, peering under his legs, behind his back, also to no avail.

The restaurant manager came over, and one kind old woman approached, wanting to make sure no one was having a stroke, and then, somewhere in the mix, the police arrived. The two cops listened with mild concern as Aaron tried to explain what had happened—the gold, the bag, the drive—and they pulled aside a few people for private interrogations. Aaron and Grandpa Sam waited in the booth as they talked to Kari, the busboys, the cashier, and some neighboring customers, but the questions must have been minimal, because it was amazing how quickly the suspects were released and the room fell back into its old order, minus the gold.

Fifteen minutes passed, and the manager was already back at the counter, thumbing his phone, and Kari and the busboys were again making the rounds, filling coffee cups and clearing tables. A family of 49ers fans was back to eating their roast beef sandwiches and discussing the new uniforms, the return to classic style, the surprising inclusion of the 49ers ligature below the neck. The only sign that a crime had occurred anywhere in the vicinity was the presence of the two cops at the register, straining to understand the tiny, mole-encrusted Mexican cashier, denying that anything had happened.

Even Aaron's grandpa was back to normal, about as expressive as a cinder block. He sat there staring into space, as if the event had already been digested and ten years had passed. Remember that day when the gold was stolen? What a terrible day; thank God that day is gone forever in the mists of time. Since waking up he hadn't said more than four words, the only clue pointing to the incredible disappointment and sorrow he felt being his eyes studying the air, the edges red and wet with a viscous fluid somewhere between tears and chicken fat. Seeing those damp eyes made Aaron want to stand up and murder somebody, to smash someone's skull into wet, bloody bits. Who was it going to be?

It seemed incomprehensible that no one had any clue. He could not believe it. They didn't know anything. They didn't know what shit food they were eating. Or where Iraq was on a map. But, worst of all, they had no idea who his grandpa was, what visions he came bearing. They thought he was just another lazy American like them, stunted by generations of luxury, rendered stupid by the years of unearned wealth, when in fact he was the angel of history itself. He was the angel of fucking history, and he'd been mugged right in front of them, and they had no fucking clue.

He scanned the room again, grading the suspicion level of the remaining patrons. The gaunt trucker with the beef-jerky skin. The Chinese teenager with the silver iPad. Everyone in the restaurant seemed like a plausible suspect. Everyone had known of the bag's contents, that much had been figured out. And thus, everyone had a clear motive, the same motive, twenty-five thousand of them, to be precise. Aaron racked his mind for any forgotten clues, but in his memory, the suspects all looked like that waitress's ass. Every face in the restaurant, white, black, Mexican, Eskimo, they all looked like that waitress's fantastic ass.

He was still seeking clues of possible guilt when the bigger, goateed cop returned from the last round of "interrogations."

He was a solid fireplug of a man, the skin at his collar pink and freshly shaven. He should have been pumping weights at the nearest LA Fitness, not packing a gun. Not surprisingly, he came bearing no real news.

"We'll be filing a report, for sure," he said. "But we don't have much to go on yet. No one has any real information here. But something definitely happened. We know that much. You had a bag of gold, and now the bag is gone. So, as far as we know, anyone on the premises could be the perpetrator."

"Yeah," Aaron said, seething. He was almost more pissed at the police than at whoever had ripped off his grandpa. At least the criminal wasn't incompetent. "So what happens now, sir?"

"The investigation keeps going," the cop said. "We still have customers to track down. Credit card records to check. Video cameras to look at. It could take awhile."

"No video," the other cop said, sidling up. He was the Laurel to the Hardy. Or the Hardy to the Laurel. Whichever one was the thin one to the big. He was notable for his five o'clock shadow, a purplish smudge covering his dimpled jawline.

"Right," the first cop said. "No video in this part of the restaurant. But a lot of data to sift through. A lot of data. You two might as well go home and get some rest. We have your number. Nothing's going to happen today, I can tell you that much."

"So when will something happen?" Aaron said.

"I wouldn't put a specific time frame on it. Could be a few days, could be a few weeks. Could be a few months, even. Depends on the data."

And before Aaron could even register his dismay, the cops exited, returning the restaurant to complete normalcy. All around them, people who had no idea what had transpired less than an hour before were eating, and out in the world many former customers were already forgetting everything they'd seen. Maybe they'd mention the day's event to their wives or children, a little anecdote around the dinner table, in the bar. Through the window, Aaron could see the men and women of Dublin coming and going in the mall's lot, pushing shopping carts, talking on phones, chasing toddlers, dozens if not hundreds of potential thieves flowing in and out of the grocery store, departing the scene for parts unknown. Demoralized, his grandpa sighed.

"Unbelievable," Aaron said.

"No," his grandpa said. "Not so unbelievable at all, I don't think."

"No, I guess not." They sat in silence, buffeted by the noise of the knives and forks on ceramic, the low babble of midafternoon conversation. "So what should we do now?"

"We wait."

"We could be sitting here for a long time, Grandpa."

"It won't be long."

"What do you mean?" If his grandpa had some idea that the thief always returned to the scene of the crime, he'd been watching too many cop shows on TV. Not that the cop shows even believed that inanity anymore.

"I know who it was. It won't be long."

"Who?" Aaron stared at the ceiling, too exhausted to rise to the bait.

"I don't want to say."

"Just tell me."

"There are some things you can't understand," Grandpa Sam said. "You can never understand. But I know. This is something I know. We wait."

13

Mark Harris's ass, encased in form-fitting Lycra, pumped away on the narrow, bone-hard bicycle seat. It was called the gluteus maximus, Anne remembered from high school biology class, and Mark's was a thing of toned firmness, she noted, beckoning her onward with every shifting, clenching flexation. At times it almost seemed like it was winking at her.

She didn't want to think about Mark's ass anymore, so she turned her attention to his shorts instead. The material of Mark's riding shorts was some kind of scientific wicking textile, which meant the padded fabric was somehow drawing the sweat away from his ass skin as they rode, sucking it into the very cloth itself and yet somehow also remaining feather light in the process. He'd explained the whole moisture-wicking technology at great length, something about braided strands of fiber, themselves braided together, or something, but Anne still didn't really understand the science. The sweat had to go somewhere, didn't it? Did it form little pockets or bubbles in the fabric? Was it a sponge? Did Mark have to wring out his shorts at the end of the ride? Or pop little sweat packets like blisters? Who cared?

Such was the chatter in her mind as she passed the one-mile mark on her first bike ride in approximately three decades. Not since she was a little girl rolling down the wide, white sidewalks of Sun Valley with her handlebar streamers crackling in the breeze could she remember the sensation of flying over the ground like this, her feet grinding on the pedals, her hands squeezing the rubbery grips. How, exactly, she had come to be here, stuck behind Mark Harris's sweating ass, piloting a rented carbon-frame twelvespeed, packed into her own ridiculous riding togs, the kind she had always assumed would never touch her body, was hard to say. She'd always laughed at these black tights, this absurd, multicolored shirt, this honeycombed, ergonomic helmet thing. A person might as well hang a sign on their back saying, "I am a total fucking prick." Now that person was her.

Barring the sight of Mark's back end, though, she had to admit the experience was not altogether unpleasant. Blurring trees, speeding grass, hanging sun, were all arrayed around her like proffered gifts. The scents of moist, mushroomy earth and sappy forest blew into her lungs, almost obscenely clean. Even the mildew and decay smells were invigorating. Flying along, she was all of eight years old again.

It was so nice that she wondered if she'd slipped into some alternate dimension, some zone where the normal laws that governed her life were temporarily suspended. Already, she could tell, the past twenty hours were entering the realm of personal myth. In fact, she could almost pinpoint the exact moment the switch-over had occurred: it was yesterday afternoon, 3:30 PM, midway through her phone conversation with Mark on the topic of her first meeting with Charlie Arnold. She had just delivered the basic summary of the meeting's minutes (Charlie's mild openness to the idea of extending a proprietary permit for the city's wastewater) and was heading into the interpretation (the need for some invented technological gadget as a dangling carrot) when Mark had suddenly stopped her and demanded a face-to-face meet-up.

"This is too important," he'd said. "We shouldn't do this on the phone. We need to be together and hash it out. Let's have a strategy meeting this weekend, all right?"

"Uh . . . Okay."

"You can come up here? That's cool?"

"Whoa. Wait a minute."

By Mark's account, his schedule was too packed to allow a trip down to L.A.; thus, it would be much better if she just jetted up to Portland for a night or two. She should see his place anyway, he'd argued, now that they were in business together. The food alone was worth the trip. She'd tried to beg off, offered to Skype as long as he needed, but he'd demanded a visit. He wanted to show her his world, he'd said. And, as she didn't actually have anything keeping her in town—no dates, dinners, or work obligations to speak of—in the end she'd relented.

Within ten minutes, a flight confirmation number had popped into her in-box, and two hours later an ominous American town car stocked with bottled water, single-wrapped Life Savers, and a chauffeur from Ghana was idling at her door. She'd easily made the 7:20 PM flight from LAX, and by 9:30 PM she was on the ground in Portland, where another chauffeur, this one Russian, had met her at the airport and whisked her away, past the dowdy, depressing outlying hotels and warehouses, alongside dark embankments covered in blackberry vines, past foreboding off-ramps to nowhere. The city itself, when it finally melted into view, was much smaller than she'd imagined, a dinky little Lego town, somewhere between a jewel box and Dubuque.

In the morning Mark had appeared in her hotel lobby outfitted for a full-on biking safari. Under the hotel's elk-antler chandelier, he'd flashed open his trench coat to reveal his superheroic costume, with all its ugly Day-Glo stripes and its silly pockets and its padded codpiece. She'd been unable to stop herself from physically blanching.

"I didn't know you were a biker," she said.

"Biking is the new golfing," he said. "This is how we do business this decade. Come on. You're going to love it."

"What? No, no, no. You have fun, Mark. I'll just catch up with you after."

"No, we're biking today. Come on. Get up."

"I don't even have the right shoes."

"We're going to fix that. Now let's go. This is happening."

The preparations had been exhaustive. It was like some awful version of *Pretty Woman*. An even more awful version, rather—getting outfitted in all this douche-wear, assembling all these extraneous, absurd gadgets. Mark had insisted on buying everything for her, playing the consummate alpha host, and then he'd rented her a bike that was admittedly as beautiful as a sculpture, as light as a pinecone. He'd strapped it to the rack beside his own, and in his silver BMW they'd zoomed to the top of the West Hills, heading north along Skyline to the drop point for one of his favorite excursions. And thus, now here she was, zooming downhill through a mossy tube of maple trees, layers of luminous greenery smearing in her vision, and things were getting really fun.

They snacked at a cute little barn on a bucolic river island north of the city, in the middle of rolling blueberry, raspberry, and strawberry fields, near a cute little produce stand surrounded by cute little food carts and beer vendors. All around them, cute, healthy-looking, brown-haired families wandered among the bales of hay, fondling broccoli and kale, admiring the caged farm animals, and for about two seconds the scene sparked some understanding in Anne about why people moved here from Southern California: ahhh, the fantasy of white people stewarding the glorious land. Here we can shop for produce out of rough-hewn wooden bins and drive home to cook it in our Craftsman bungalows, unmolested by any people who might not share our worldview. They were children of Leni Riefenstahl up here, cheerfully doing their morning calisthenics in the wheat fields, happily grinding Jew bones into the dirt. But whatever. Good for them. They were irrelevant to the world at large, thank God. With the first leg of the ride officially ended, the ritual purification performed, Mark, his multicolored shirt jauntily unzipped, his ruddy face drenched in spring sunlight, was ready to get down to the true pleasure of the day: business.

"So, you met with Charlie Arnold yesterday," he said. They were sitting at a picnic table with honey-colored beers before them, their helmets like two bright stones on the wood. Even though no one was within hearing distance, Mark had lowered his voice to a conspiratorial growl.

"I did," she said.

"And he seems interested. That's good news."

"I'd say he's open to being interested," she said. "He might eventually become interested. That would be more accurate."

"He didn't close any doors, is what you're saying."

"No, the door is most definitely open."

"See, that's fantastic," he said, clapping his hands, grinning at the blue sky. "That's the best we can hope for right now, Anne. Fantastic. You're doing great work."

Anne was mildly disturbed by his excess of optimism, but then again, she thought, of course he would be that way. Only a morbidly wishful thinker like him would ever have the nerve to corner the market on one of the very elements of nature in the first place. Gross optimism was a prerequisite for the job.

"I don't think I'd be celebrating anything yet, Mark," she cautioned. "It was only one conversation."

"Ah, but it was more than a conversation," he said. "It was a conversation with you." He tapped her knuckle. "And you mean something to him. You command his respect. It's not just a normal door you opened. It's a special door."

"Charlie makes his own decisions, believe me," she said.

"Don't sell yourself short. You command his respect. I know that for a fact."

"He doesn't even know what I'm asking for yet."

Mark waved off her doubts. "People think decisions get made based on ideas," he said, "but that's not actually the case. Decisions really get made based on relationships. And that's a good thing, Anne. I trust people more than ideas any day. Don't you? So just trust me—you're doing an amazing job. You're putting yourself on the line out there for BHC, and that's a big deal to me. I thank you for that."

Anne wasn't sure what to make of his gratitude, but she accepted it, clinking his thick glass. He probably gave this kind of canned pep talk to his underlings a few times a week, doling out the praise like gold stars. It was a form of social control, maybe even the sentimental flip side of his perverse humor. And yet, despite all her cynicism, sipping her beer in the sun, she found she appreciated the gesture. Even if Mark's praise was utterly fake, or merely self-serving, or a blunt tool of manipulation, the fact that he made the effort demonstrated some level of comprehension about what she'd done, about how much time and energy she'd spent outside his line of vision, and that was more than most managers could usually understand, in her experience. Most just assumed that all the work they didn't witness happened by itself, like plants growing, or the weather.

"So now we just have to figure out how this coalition comes together," he said. "What do you think, wise consultant? What does Charlie need to hear next? And how can I help you in this process?"

"I think he's kind of expecting to hear something from you," she said. "In fact, I kind of told him that was happening. I told him you had some designs to show him."

"And what kind of designs do you mean?"

"I was vague. I didn't know what to say. That's your department."

"What did you mean, exactly, by 'designs'?"

Anne had been hoping for some sort of tacit understanding at this juncture of the conversation. Some gentle mind reading. A significant look or two. She'd done her part and opened the doorway—wasn't that enough? Now he was supposed to carry her across the threshold. But the blank, bovine look on his face told her she was going to have to spell out the next step after all, which also meant spelling it out to herself.

"I don't know," she said. "Designs for whatever it is you want to do with the wastewater. The filtration plant or the bottling factory or the delivery system or whatever. I hope it's something pretty cool-looking, is all. Charlie likes cool. He's susceptible to cool."

Mark scowled, less than enthusiastic about what she was saying. She wasn't sure what she'd expected from him, but it wasn't this. She'd assumed he understood there would have to be some subterfuge in the process, a little smoke and mirrors. The City of Los Angeles wasn't just going to hand over the wastewater without some hard promises on his part.

"I don't have any designs, though," he said.

"I thought you owned the contracting company that carries the waste," she said. "And the land around the treatment plant. Sounds like plans to me."

Mark shook his head. "The plan here is to create the market for second-use water. That's all. The market decides how it happens. I'm only interested in creating the conditions for innovation to occur. That's my role."

"Yeah, well, I don't think that's what Charlie wants to hear. That doesn't exactly motivate him."

"Maybe he just doesn't understand the nature of markets."

To that she had no idea what to say. Was Mark Harris really such a true believer in the magic of free markets? Were they really that far from reality?

"Markets are the key to all creative invention," Mark went on, in a practiced tone. This was apparently one of the postulates of his whole life, much repeated. "And markets operate on the law of desire. Somebody wants something, and pretty soon somebody else decides they want it, too. People compete over the best price, the best cut. That's how demand grows. That's how wealth gets made. But someone has to start wanting something first. Someone has to stick his neck out and say, yeah, I want this. Over here. I want this used water. I want this Cabbage Patch doll. That's got value. This is just basic economics here, Anne. I'm the first wanter in the picture. That's my role. That's it."

"Funny," she said. "I always thought wealth was made by exploiting labor. Silly me."

"Ha-ha. So maybe there are two ways of creating wealth, then. There's fucking over the workers, and there's redefining the nature of reality. I'd rather go the latter route whenever possible."

"Yeah, well, someone still has to build the new reality, you know, Mark. And clean the new reality. And fix the pipes in the new reality. If you want Charlie's wastewater, you're going to have to give him a specific blueprint. I'm sure about that."

"If Charlie is open to the monetization of his resource, I bet we can find the right price."

"No," she said, starting to get annoyed. "See, Charlie doesn't care about monetization. Monetization isn't going to help Charlie. He doesn't control the money flow. The money is for Randy and the city council. They're in charge of the purse. Charlie, he needs something else. He needs romance. Don't you get that?"

Mark shifted on his bench, looking even more uncomfortable. The simplicity of his plan, such as it was, was becoming ruffled and bent around the edges. He wanted to salvage it before it got torn. "So, what are we talking about here? You're kind of losing me."

"He wants some kind of game changer," she said. "Some kind of next-gen technology. A secret machine. He wants to know he's part of the future. Not everything is money, you know."

"Monetizing his resource is what's going to make all those things happen."

Anne shook her head, appalled. Market, market, market. How many times was Mark going to give the same answer to every question? He was autistic for the market. He was a big market queen.

"He needs a good story, Mark," she repeated. "Does that make any sense to you? You need to tell him a good story."

"Okay," Mark said. "So, like what? He wants some kind of miracle machine? Some kind of giant robot squid off the coast that'll turn his shit water into honey? Is that it? He needs to see plans for that?"

"Now you're getting it."

"Great. One giant, shit-eating robot squid coming up."

"Good. Perfect."

They both drank, retreating to their corners, trying to catch up on where the plot had just gone. Anne could feel the beer settling in her gut, fuzzing her brain. Already she was dreading the uphill part of the ride. Meanwhile, Mark had begun gnawing on his lips and casting his eyes at the splinters of the table as if some answer might appear at his fingertips. To avoid watching his pathetic display, she turned her gaze back to the attractive, chestnut-haired families milling among the produce bins and let her irritation flow in their direction. How she would have loved to slap all the organic turnips and melons from their hands and out them as the true racists they really were. I know all about your secret lynchings in the woods, she wanted to yell, even if you don't know about them yourselves. I know all about your secret, *volkisch* dreams.

She turned back to Mark, staring unhappily at his beer, and a half smile of contempt crossed her face. How funny, she thought. All this time she'd been assuming Mark was the devil, tempting her. But ah, look who was the devil now.

They finished the ride, which, barring ten minutes of screaming leg burn, never got that difficult, and parted ways until dinner. The restaurant Mark chose was on the east side of town, and with only a woodstove and a Bunsen burner, the chef turned out some of the most subtle dishes Anne had ever eaten in her life. The roasted trout with charred leeks was so good, she wondered if she had ever truly eaten food before in her life.

And yet, this place made her angry, too. She couldn't help it. The decor was so uniformly perfect, it was almost offensive. The perfect wooden tables, with no adornment to detract from the lovely grain of the pine, the bar with the perfect bouquet of incredible wildflowers in the perfect antique vase, like a perfect, dry explosion of pink and orange and fuchsia. The perfectly good taste displayed everywhere was just another form of narrow-mindedness, she thought. How about some ugly doily or heavy velvet drapes to mar the perfection? The scrupulous curation of the room, of the whole town, felt like a form of ethnic cleansing.

It didn't help that Mark was still trying so hard to get his head around the next step. For a pirate of speculative capitalism, he was incredibly fastidious about taking a risk.

"I'm not sure I'm comfortable with where this is going," he said, picking at his gorgeous beet salad. "It almost seems like you're asking me . . . to lie."

Anne kept herself from groaning. After all he'd done, this was where he drew the line? He was a billionaire real estate developer, a master of greenwashing, a creator of bloated stadiums and mirrored condos, and yet he held so tightly to his graduate school abstractions. A part of her wanted to protect his quaint self-perception, though a larger part wanted to crush him into the dirt.

"I'm telling you to be specific, that's all, Mark," she said, with as much patience as she could muster. "You have to show him something. You have to give him a plan. And I'm just telling you to be optimistic in your assessment of the plan. Optimism isn't lying, as far as I know, right? That's just my advice. As a consultant. The final decision is up to you. Obviously."

He pushed his beets around, and she wondered, flickeringly, if her own conscience should be alarmed. Was she really proposing some kind of fraudulence? But no, she thought, her advice was all within the bounds of fair play. She was only urging a little showmanship on Mark's part, the throwing of some hard elbows. And interestingly, even as the flicker of introspection brightened to a slight twinge, she found she didn't really care. Moral peril was not an entirely unpleasant sensation, it turned out. A good scheme demanded the destruction of some received idea, and they were entering a grand scheme now. The first victim was Mark Harris's own illusion of goodness.

"Look, Mark," she said, breaking into his shell of contemplation. "Look at it this way: we're all on the same team here, right? You, me, Charlie, the city commissioners, all of us. We all want the same thing, which is pure water delivered to as many people as cheaply as possible. Is that not true?"

"Yeah."

"And you truly believe the privatization of the wastewater will be the quickest and most efficient way to bring that reality into being?"

"Yeah."

"So you just need to help Charlie feel comfortable with that reality."

"That's a good way of putting it. Help him feel comfortable."

"And if you don't know the exact details, then some provisional details are okay. It's all moving in the same direction."

"See, now that makes some sense to me."

They ended the night with drinks in a rustic hotel bar, surrounded by the Pendleton clones of the creative class, the shoe whores, the ninth-generation post-punk poseurs, by which time Mark was coming around to the notion that Milton Friedman alone wasn't getting him to the end zone on this one.

"I see what you're saying," he said, stewing over his fourth Macallan single malt since dinner. "I do. I just don't know what the solution is yet."

"There must be some new ideas that could excite a guy like Charlie," Anne said. Her endurance for the topic was turning out to be much greater than she'd thought. After sixteen hours, two meals, and many, many drinks, she was still keeping pace, if not pulling the vast weight of their strategic planning. She could remember these kinds of sessions in the early days with Susan, but it had been a long time since her scheming faculties had been so fully engaged.

"Sure. There are people working on sonophoto-chemical oxidation, photo-Fenton processes, catalytic advanced oxidation. Lots of things."

"So you know something about this stuff."

"I have investments in a few companies that do R and D. Part of the whole eco-portfolio. I read the shareholder reports."

"So there you go. I'm sure any of these things could be great."

A few more drinks and they still hadn't arrived at a concrete solution, but Mark's resolve was strengthening. He wouldn't speculate on the exact nature of the next move, but he was at least willing to exercise himself on the moral necessity of continuing with the plan by whatever means necessary.

"There shouldn't even be a city in that desert," he slurred as the bar sounds crashed around them. "Your city is fucking the whole western ecosystem. Yours and Las Vegas. You all are going to be coming for our water one day no matter what. I'm just trying to even the score here. Let Southern California pay the north for once. Time the north took its due. Consider it a consumption tax. We've got to teach you people to drink your own shit before you come for our watershed."

She laughed at his tirade. He was being absurd, but she didn't mind. She liked Mark better in this engorged state. At last, he was giving her the kind of fearful, paranoid, vengeful thinking she could get behind.

She didn't sleep well that night—the pillows were too fat—and in the morning the town car was waiting again, ready to ferry her back home, following the invisible bread crumbs. Car to airport to car to home, every step greased with capital. How frictionless the world became with immense reservoirs of money on your side. She could get used to this life, she thought, to Mark's life, that was. Belatedly, it occurred to her that she might have been trying out for more than being his consultant on this trip. If so, she wasn't going to think about it now.

Sitting in business class—for only a two-hour flight, such a waste—she accepted a glass of white wine, hair of the dog, and a pile of unopened magazines, spreading herself out to the maximum degree. The plane took off, and the fuzz of mist clinging to the trees and valleys was like a fine mold growing on the fruit of the earth. The city banked in her window and shrank from view, and soon the ancient topography of the western rain forest was scrolling below.

The woods were but a shadow of their former self, a patchwork of clear-cuts in varying states of paltry regrowth, more a giant, groomed lawn than the primordial jungle of yore. It had taken billions of years for God to build this forest and only about a hundred years for men to mow it down. In two lifetimes the entire earth had been pruned and angled and sheared into this last, vestigial geometry.

She sighed and shut the plastic window shade, not wanting to see. She didn't want to watch TV, either—that would only be more depressing—so she reached for a magazine but couldn't find anything worth reading. She sighed and put the magazines back in the seat pocket and leaned back in the wide, comfortable seat. She closed her eyes, hoping sleep might take her, while speeding along at hundreds of miles per hour through empty space.

14

Everything leading up to the killing was the easy part. He just had to drive out to Long Island and climb a tree. It would be only after the bullet left the barrel that the trouble would really begin. Only after the bullet entered Holmes's body, shredding his organs, and all the alarms had gone up, and the dragnet had been called out, that things would truly change. And from that moment onward, the danger would be constant, accompanying Ben for the rest of his life, clinging to his shoulders and jabbering in his ear for all eternity. Once the bullet left the muzzle and stole Holmes's life, Ben would step permanently through the dark curtain of the law, to the other side.

Was it worth it? He still wasn't able to tell. Sitting at the fork of the branch, his deer rifle in his lap, he tried to peer beyond the curtain of the law, but the curtain was too thick, too voluptuous. The curtain was like black wool with heavy brocade, a sculpted drapery allowing past no light, traced with golden writing that couldn't be read.

Ben had felt his share of anguish about his violence over the years. There had been many killings, some of them unsavory. But in the past the killings had always been solidly on the side of the law. All his murdering had been in the name of his country and the Constitution, and he'd always walked away afterward with a clear conscience. But in his new life he would take full and complete personal responsibility for his acts.

Sweat collected under his arms, and a nerve ticked in his neck. In taking complete personal responsibility, he would be stepping beyond man's law into the realm of a deeper law, acting as his own interpreter of God's law at last. Was that good? He sat there with his gun, comprehending that he was on the verge of a sacrifice in the ancient form. Soon he would enter directly into conversation with the burning bush inside his head, casting off the robe of man's lies to become Death itself. And he would have to accept the curdling fear as part of the due.

His body was shaking as it never had on a mission before. Death could be afraid, he now knew. Death could be indecisive. Death was rarely gentle. Death was occasionally sudden. Would he be Death tonight? And if so, which Death would he be?

The moon edged along on its path. His gun sat in his lap, muzzle greasy gray in the darkness, and electric pulses charged through his nervous system, sizzles of energy snapping through his relays. He thought about Holmes and the judgment upon him. Holmes didn't deserve death, exactly, although the case could be made that he did. The case could be made for many things. The case could even be made that killing Holmes was evil. Could evil action bring good result? Now, that was a question for the rabbis. Somewhere a dog hoarsely barked.

He doubted if any commander had ever worried over his orders in the way he worried tonight. No general he knew had ever truly suffered over the massive death he sowed without reason. They should do some killing of their own sometimes, he thought. See how cautious they got after washing themselves in blood. How amazing it was to think that the men making death never killed with their own hands.

Ghosts were flashing in the corners of his eyes, but he refused to turn his head. If he didn't look they would disappear, he hoped. He didn't want them to lead him down a path to insanity.

He looked at the empty road. The killing tonight might be insane. He might be on the verge of perpetrating an insane act. Doing evil to fight evil, casting black magic to coax evil into sight—it sounded insane. But it was a necessary insanity in hunting the particular species of evil he sought. It wasn't the evil of maniacs and slashers he was after tonight, the horrible, incomprehensible evil of rapists and baby molesters. The newspapers and cops took care of that kind of evil. There were prisons for those people. There were also bolts of lightning, venomous snakes, flash floods, hurricanes. Those were not his evil. Those were ugly mistakes in God's design.

No, the evil he was hunting was the systematic kind. The evil he now knew to be always out there, ubiquitous and discreet. The evil not of Hitler but of Germany, everywhere and nowhere at once. It was evil without actors, without authors, the evil that never stuck to a single name. That was the evil he wanted to destroy. The evil of toxic pollution, preemptive war, redlining, and default mortgage swaps. The evil of racist innuendo and unnamed rumors. The evil of nighttime roundups. The evil of anti-Semitism. The evil of history itself.

He knew Anne would not approve of his war on evil. She would most certainly have some simple, obvious arguments against such a mission. But he didn't want her voice tonight. In his mind's eye, he watched himself slowly rising from the waters, face painted, hunting knife clenched in his fist, and mauled her intruding doubts into unbeing, after which he dragged the rent pieces back down into the bracken and continued his wait.

The whisper of the tires came to his ears, and a moment later the car's lights appeared, carving their white trench in the darkness. Ben's senses were so highly elevated, he could feel the vibration of the car's movement in the air molecules. There had been other cars before this one, but he knew this was the car he'd been waiting for: Holmes's limo, cruising down the private lane, slowing at the iron gate, waiting as the gate retracted on its wheels with a distant clank and hum, and floating inside the property line, darkness pouring back into the ditch of light.

At the first sensation of the car, all thinking stopped. The change had come over his system, and there was only his breath now, in and out. Ben lifted his gun in preparation, should his shot come. He nestled the stock into the padding of his shoulder and placed his cheek to the stock. He let his finger rest on the trigger guard, his other hand on the forestock. He looked through the scope to test the flattened optical frame. He watched the limo going through the same motions as the other night, drawing to a stop at the path leading to the front steps. The moon burned a hole in the sky, white hot among cold stars.

The limo's door opened, and Holmes emerged. Ben tracked his skull in the scope, a big, ripe cantaloupe hovering in space. A moon filled with brains. Ben breathed slowly, evenly, letting the stock fuse with his shoulder. The barrel was an extension of his arm and hand. The scope was a lens of his eye. Holmes walked down the path, carrying a paper bag filled with small boxes or something, something not very heavy, not that it mattered what. This was the moment. Holmes was there. Ben knew this man's midwestern voice, his mild halitosis smell. He had shared *injera, mujadara,* and fried chicken with him. But he also knew Holmes had been granted too much power in the world, too much influence on the course of planetary life, and that was a crime. Ben's finger tightened on the trigger, and with a light gasp the bullet was released. He barely noticed the recoil.

A hundred and fifty yards away, blood sprayed onto geraniums, followed by a cloddish tumble of weight. Ben didn't pause to confirm the kill. He knew the shot had been straight and true. He'd felt the taut line from his muzzle to Holmes's brain. He'd felt the perfection.

Down on the ground, time continued to rush onward, pouring over the scene of death, leaving no riffle, no wake. The world had turned slow and ultra-detailed, rich in information about rasping leaves, dispersing gunshot residue, idling engine sounds, satellite flight patterns, but Ben knew there wasn't a moment to spare. Nimbly, he sprinted over the leafy ground, aiming himself toward Holmes's estate. He took the street in two quick bounds and angled for the far corner of the wall, a murky area obscured by hanging fig branches, and using the fig tree as a ladder he scaled the wall, dropping deftly to the soft dirt on the other side. From there, he clung to the shadows of Holmes's property line, spilling himself in quick, decisive bursts toward the water.

He ran lightly, his rifle strapped to his back, emitting almost no sound. The cat's cradle of his heart stretched and shrank inside his chest. Already, there was commotion near the door, but the Holmes estate remained sunk in darkness. He crossed the chemically fortified lawn en route to the lapping water and without a pause plunged himself into the sound. He was in his element again. The water is your mother and solace, as the SEALs always said. He'd learned in BUD/S training that, whenever in doubt, go to the water; the water will save you. He pounded his arms until he'd made it fifty meters out to sea, at which point he jettisoned the rifle, turned north, and swam another three hundred meters. He was slogging away in his heavy clothes, arms and legs burning, when the Holmes estate ignited behind him, every window shining, every corner exposed. But the light didn't reach him in the black water.

The white birch he'd selected as a landmark appeared, and he headed back to land, emerging onto the pebbled shore of Holmes's neighbor's estate. Soaking and winded, he sprinted another fifteen meters to the hole he'd dug over the course of two midnight visits a week before. The dirt, he'd dumped into the ocean; his tools, he'd discarded in a garbage can behind a Chevys restaurant. There was no remaining evidence of his digging work, and there were no witnesses, not that digging a hole was a crime.

The hole was hidden under a plywood board obscured by earth and leaves and twigs and one large, shaggy pine branch. Gently, he pulled the board aside to reveal the hole's black mouth, three feet deep, six feet long, and containing a single plastic garbage bag. He stripped his clothes and changed into the dry clothes he'd stored and put his wet clothes in the bag. The sound was dappled with moonlight, covering any trace of his passage. He climbed into the hole and slid the board—the wig, as he called it to himself—back into place, wedging the edge into the lip of dirt to make a clean seal.

The hole was dark and comfortable. He could hear his ragged breath in his throat, and he could feel the damp earth against his spine. He lay there, momentarily safe. His scent had been expunged from the scene, and the canoe he'd stashed a mile in the other direction would lead his pursuers on a false path. The likelihood that anyone would find him quickly was extremely small. Most likely they'd scour the area and then widen the search, presuming he was fleeing to the interstate highway system. They probably wouldn't even find his Vibe, parked five miles away in the bus parking lot, but if they did, the car, wiped clean, wouldn't give them anything.

He could hear sirens muffled by the fat of the earth, and in the darkness, waiting, listening, senses on high, he farted grandly. The fart was a celebration of the Mission's success, and the smell was sulfurous and terrible, a joy. He squeezed out another two, adding to the noxious fumes, and relished the bouquet of coffee, rotten fruit, and mud. The smell was all his, but, he had to admit, the sound was much like his dad's. The same washboard buzz, the same juicy finish. How many mornings of his childhood had included that noise? His father, bumbling through the kitchen, fixing a brown-bag lunch, farting without shame. It occurred to him, as it had before, that his asshole was probably shaped exactly like his dad's asshole. It only figured. He had his dad's ears and hands. Of course he'd have his dad's sphincter, too.

In the darkness, smelling his own gas, he pondered his dad's body, the body he now owned. Lying there, invisible to himself, he could feel his father's dimensions. His own ribs, his fingers, his pelvis, all were copies of his dad's. He could almost feel the cells of his father replicating throughout his body, filling him in, shaping him. Someday his dad was going to climb out of his chest fully reborn. It was so strange, he thought. His dad, a man so unknowable, unreachable, and unreadable in life, was also so close at hand, nesting inside his very skin. Maybe Ben's soul itself was a hand-me-down.

Thinking about his father led Ben to think about his father's father, and he tried to feel that man's presence in him as well. If his father's body harbored his own father's body, and so on, back into the depths of time, Ben's forefathers must still be lurking in him, too. How far back did it go? He could almost feel the original spark deep in the recesses of the past. He wondered who'd captured the first spark and what ancient knowledge the spark held. Who was the first man? Was it a Jew? In the darkness, his eyelids teeming with strange colors and amoebic shapes, Ben could feel his father and his father's father behind him, running all the way back to the stars.

Hours passed, and Ben dozed, thinking about his father's blood, and his mother's, too. His mother's blood was the good blood, he thought. She'd died when he was only seven, and his memories of her had become talismanic and unreal, but he felt her nevertheless. Her blood was not like his father's sluggish blood. It was smart and full of steel. If only he could bend his blood to her blood, he would, for, as much as he loved his dad, he hated to live inside those same limitations, to be plagued by the same weakness and shame. To be dumb like his dad, oblivious and narrow like his dad. To see his own family murdered and fail to save them. To be ruled by that law. Lying in silence, he could feel the two bloods streaming in his veins, at endless war.

Out in the world, distant movements were becoming audible again. Through the earth he heard footsteps and voices. In the air he heard propellers. His senses groped to comprehend the significance, but he could only guess. He had no smell, no sight, to guide his thoughts. Only his ears, and they were tricky. He heard dogs barking. He heard rumbling sounds. Distant, irregular vibrations. He'd already decided that if the police found him, he wouldn't fight. He wouldn't kill anyone just for doing the job of law enforcement. So he lay there in his hole, resigned to whatever fate God doled out. He lay there, giving up over and over again, until a kind of peace came over him. If they found him, so be it. He would give himself to God's will. Have mercy, he prayed. But do what you will. I submit.

The peace lasted only briefly, and his ears kept straining to understand the movements of the outside world. He'd hoped he would find peace on this side of the law, but he could see now that wasn't the case. This side of man's law was much like the side he'd been on before, dark and inscrutable. Peace wasn't here. He'd been hoping the Mission would part the curtain and send fresh light streaming into his mind, but the curtain was too thick.

The sounds of the outside receded again, and he heard his own breathing. He smelled the moist, clean earth, infused with the brackish water scent of the sound even this far from shore. He heard the minuscule scratching of bugs or worms. How long had he been underground? Already time's movement was becoming turgid and unclear. He farted again, and the hole filled with his luscious smell.

His senses slipped away one by one. He couldn't see, he couldn't hear, he couldn't feel. Without ears, without eyes, he drifted in black space for what might have been hours or, possibly, days. In stops and starts, he screened a mental movie of every memory of his dad he could summon. His favorite: his father, hale and happy, building a rock wall in the garden, healthy legs powdered in dust, powerful hands fitting sun-warmed stones face to face. He saw Anne in his blackness, laughing under an oak tree, and Aaron, wandering a path through a meadow, and for an instant he glimpsed a fountain of light that seemed to flow out of the wellspring of eternity itself.

He rose two days later into a crepuscular world. The forest was murky with evening shadow. He moved the board back onto the hole, breathing fresh air. Someday someone would lift the wig and find the hole, he thought, but by then it wouldn't matter. This earth was already forgetting him.

15

Thus far, Aaron had found only one album on which he and his grandpa could agree, and that was Steppenwolf's *Greatest Hits*. Why this was the album that passed his grandfather's muster, he had no idea. Maybe he'd heard it a long time ago in some bar or warehouse where he'd worked. Maybe someone at his gym or his coffee shop had once told him it was all right. It didn't matter. The point was, they'd now listened to it four times in a row while sitting in the parking lot in front of the Bagel Café, and that organ sound was becoming like a serrated knife peeling back Aaron's skin.

They'd been there for almost four hours now, sinking into the life of the strip mall, becoming one with the poky circulations of the cars, the broken clatter of the grocery carts, the babble of cell phone conversations cut off by the slamming of doors. The day's only action had come when a refrigerated food truck had pulled up and unloaded dozens of boxes of hamburger patties, and the jiggling glare on the glass had threatened to shatter on one deliveryman's trip inside. In all that time, Grandpa Sam had never once elaborated on his theory as to Kari's guilt, though his conviction remained strong. He knew she did it, to the degree that he barely seemed to be hearing the music at all.

"How do you know she did it, anyway?" Aaron asked. "I don't doubt you. I just want to know."

Predictably, his grandpa shrugged. He just knew. There was no way to explain.

So they waited, listening to "Magic Carpet Ride" for a fifth time, that awful drone rising to that cloying, invincible chord progression. By whatever powers of concentration, by whatever flailing sense of intuition, Grandpa Sam didn't seem to mind. He was too deep inside his truth, and he would not leave this post until justice was served.

Maybe he did know something, Aaron thought. It was hard to say. It was not inconceivable that his grandpa's life had granted him some kind of special radar for the doings of evil. Maybe his horrific youth had imbued him with an extrasensory moral compass. Or maybe it was exactly this extrasensory compass that had allowed him to survive in the first place.

It was three minutes after seven when Kari finally departed the Bagel Café, dragging her long shadow along the blighted sidewalk and through the glinting chrome and glass of the parking lot. She crossed the empty spaces and climbed into an old Accord, where she sat for fifteen minutes, talking on her phone. She was still talking when she turned the key and backed out of her space, creeping her way through the aisles to the main strip.

Aaron and his grandfather followed a few car lengths behind, sticking to the protocols of the TV detective. They didn't talk during the pursuit but remained stone-faced, like good partners. When the light changed, she turned right, and they turned right, keeping her always in view.

They weren't hiding from her, exactly. If she'd spotted them, they wouldn't have denied anything. But if possible, they were hoping to observe her without her knowledge, at least for a little while. They had no official authority in this pursuit. The police had told them none too ambiguously that the best thing they could do was head home and get some rest. But the cops hadn't explicitly told them they were not allowed to follow her, either. Not that his grandpa cared what the police said, anyway.

In the best-case scenario, Aaron guessed, the bag would fall out of her pocket while she was pumping gas or something. She would spot them in her rearview mirror and pull over and tearfully repent. They simply didn't have enough information to go on. All he knew about Kari was that she paid her bills by carrying plates of food to geriatric customers at the Bagel Café. If he knew what music she listened to, maybe he could make some predictions. Insane Clown Posse? That was one thing. Rascal Flatts? That was another.

One thing he found out about Kari very quickly: she was a fucking terrible driver. Two car lengths back, watching her drifting randomly between the stripes, stopping joltingly within inches of the brake lights ahead, failing repeatedly to signal her turns, he was appalled by her lack of skills. She was astonished by every obstacle, unprepared for every intersection. Texting while driving should be a capital offense, he thought, at least for her.

He was glad when she turned onto the freeway, heading east, but then she peeled off almost immediately at the town of Livermore, a collection of unremarkable streets that he wouldn't have noticed at all if he were just speeding by. The town was actually larger than he would have thought, built into a depression of land falling away from the highway, obscured by scrubby trees and low brush. He followed her across some train tracks, past some large water tanks, and around a quarry of yellow rock. She turned into a residential area, and he kept with her, going deeper into the dowdy blocks of Livermore, far from groovy Oakland, far even from nouveau riche Dublin.

These were poor homes, identifiably so, ironically, because they were encumbered with such obscene amounts of stuff. Children's play cars, trampolines, three-wheelers, motorboats, ATVs, Jet Skis. Every house was like a magnet of plastic. Poverty wasn't what it used to be, Aaron thought. The shtetl wasn't goats and water buckets anymore.

Kari came to stop at a house much like all the other houses, a shoe box obscured by an unpruned magnolia tree. There was a broken car in the driveway, and the small pad of yard was covered with leaves. A leopard-face blanket covered one window, and a distant, single-prop airplane droned in the airspace beyond the roofline. Aaron pulled over at the curb a few houses down.

"So . . . ," Aaron said, gauging his grandpa's desire to continue the investigation.

"So we wait," Grandpa Sam said with calm authority. One could almost imagine he had some kind of plan, and again Aaron wondered if maybe he knew something after all. Maybe his grandpa had organized secret uprisings in the Kraków ghetto or trafficked in secret communiqués with Polish peasants outside the barbed wire of Birkenau. Maybe he was tapping into some old, spooky skill set he'd honed in the fires of World War II. Doubtful.

Kari was on the phone again, and it took another five minutes before she dragged herself out of the car. She leaned back inside to grab her purse and rose again, glancing around. Her gaze traveled over the street, noting the mattress in the neighbor's yard, the passing shirtless biker with the cigarette, and landed almost immediately on Aaron, at whom she stared directly for the majority of her phone call. She locked her car doors with a chirp, never taking the phone from her ear, and strode inside the house.

Aaron and Grandpa Sam sat there, already caught. The sun was going down, and the street was fading from view. Some birds pecked at a disintegrating paper cup in the gutter near an abandoned fax machine. A school building chopped off a segment of purple sky. The quiet led only to more quiet. Grandpa Sam stared dully at the house. Aaron turned off the car.

In Kari's house, shadows passed by the yellowish curtains. From his oblique angle, Aaron watched the dark blotches shifting on the dingy fabric like brown ghosts. The shadows edged back and forth, folded, shrank, converged.

An outdoor light came on and the front door opened and a young man emerged. He was hard to see through the overgrown branches, but he looked a little older than Aaron, though not that much older. He was very skinny, and his posture was elaborately hunched, almost gnarled, a combination of affected gangster slouch and inborn low self-esteem. He wore a plaid hoodie with Gothic lettering on the chest, and loose denim shorts that made his wiry legs look extra pallid and unhealthy. On his head was a crisp Giants lid. He was blond, blade-faced.

He lit a cigarette, scanning the street, and took long drags. Streams of smoke disintegrated over his head. His gaze came around to the car more than once, pausing and moving on.

"Maybe we should go now," Aaron suggested.

"No," Grandpa Sam said. "We stay."

Aaron sighed, embarrassed by his own cowardice. He'd often wondered what he would do were he ever truly tested.

What if his neighbors rounded him up and sent him to a slave camp? God willing, he'd never know, but he was afraid he might not even put up a fight. He might be the type to just go quietly into the mass grave, take off his clothes, and bow his head. This was part of the reason he'd been testing himself these past years, climbing small rungs on the ladder of self-knowledge. His petty vandalism, his drugs, his sex. He'd been probing the outcomes of various behaviors, wondering when, if ever, there would be true consequences. Thus far, the lesson of his teenage years was that there were almost none.

Here came a new test. The twitchy blond dude was loping in their direction, baroquely limping and establishing his hostile position at the driver's side window. Aaron pretended not to notice, and only when the dude rapped on the glass did he lower the window a few inches.

"Yo, son," the guy said. His smoky, nasty breath poured into Aaron's face. "You got to leave now, son, you get me?"

"How come?"

"Because," the guy said. "Or we're calling the police. That's it." His eyes, up close, were screwed into a look of pleading meanness. Don't make this go badly, they seemed to say. I'm deeply unsure of my own powers, but I'll go the distance if you push me.

"But we're just sitting here," Aaron said.

"You can't be here, bud, period," the guy said. "You gotta go. I'm not saying it again." He flicked his fingers in the air like he was scattering invisible bugs. It was hard to imagine that his displays of authority usually had much effect.

"I'm pretty sure this is a public street," Aaron heard himself say. "I'm pretty sure we can be here if we want to be."

"This ain't a public street, man!" the guy said. "So come on, let's move it. Right now."

Grandpa Sam, over in the passenger seat, was silent but all-hearing. If only for his benefit, Aaron felt the need to hold his ground.

"This is a public street, actually," he said. "See that fire hydrant? That means this is a public street."

The guy didn't bother looking at the fire hydrant. He kept his eyes directly on Aaron and waited a tense few seconds, breathing heavily, before spitting out his response:

"You little fucking bitch."

Then the guy banged hard on the roof of the car. He drew in another lungful of smoke and exhaled almost nothing and bent and glared at Aaron again. He seemed to have something more he wanted to say, but he couldn't find the right words, and instead of waiting for them to come, he just banged on the car again and loped back toward the house. He flicked the butt into the yard as he climbed the steps, sending a skid of orange sparks over the dirt.

Aaron's heart throbbed, and his nerves sang with fear. He'd been positive the guy was going to hit him, but with the front door safely closed, he could breathe again. For a moment the air had turned viscous and highly conductive, but it was returning to normal now. For some reason he'd gotten lucky this time. He'd dodged the beating, and now it was time to go home and celebrate. A bong hit and hotel cable sounded about right.

The Steppenwolf album, barely audible, ended, and Aaron turned off the stereo. He was done with this shitty album, as he was done with this sad, desperate, misguided stakeout. What his grandfather knew about Kari and this guy she lived with was less than nothing.

But, as it turned out, his grandpa wasn't yet ready to go. There he was, unbuckling and pushing open the door, then climbing out of the car in pursuit of the skinny, blond dude, all as Aaron sat there holding the keys.

"Hey. Hey," Aaron said. "What are you doing?"

"Getting out," said Grandpa Sam. He grunted, trying to roll himself free.

"But . . . why?"

"To talk to Kari."

"I'm pretty sure she doesn't want to talk to you, Grandpa."

Grandpa Sam didn't answer. He rocked his body, trying to stand, and again fell back into the car. Aaron didn't feel he had any choice but to get out and help him.

"I don't think she's going to be happy if you knock on the door," Aaron said, heaving his grandpa to his feet.

"I don't care. I'm talking to her. You don't have to come."

"Oh, I'm coming."

Aaron continued trying to reason with his grandpa as they shuffled along the sidewalk to the house. He promised him they could come back in the morning, or file another report with the police, or even keep sitting in the car all night, if that made him feel better, but his grandfather had his own agenda. He seemed to believe this was the moment to seize back his property from the villainous Kari, and any delay would only diminish his natural rights. Aaron shadowed him into the dirt yard, cradling his elbow up the steps, and let him step forward to ring the bell. If only he could understand that the krugerrands were probably already sitting in some pawnshop in the Mission, or on the bed stand of some rat-faced little teenager who didn't even know what the fuck he had. But try telling that to Grandpa Sam. His brain was capable of exactly one thought at a time.

The bell chimed, an ugly, broken clang. No one answered, and Grandpa Sam rang again. He rang five more times before the door finally flung open and Kari, enraged, was before them.

"What the fuck do you two want?" she said. "Huh? Who said you could come over here and sit in front of my house? Huh? This is not acceptable. This is harassment. I'm calling the cops right now, you fuckers."

"We're not harassing anyone," Aaron said.

"Oh, you're not? The hell you're not! You're harassing me just being here, you little fuck. I know what harassing is."

"We're just here, that's all."

"You think I have your fucking bag. You want to frisk me for it? Come on. Frisk me. Is that what you want? Scott's gonna kick your ass if you do, both of you, but come on, frisk me. Go ahead. Right now."

She planted her arms on the doorjamb and stared Aaron down as her boyfriend—Scott, apparently—emerged in the doorway behind her. Aaron wondered if they'd arranged this particular display, if they'd conferred on the roles. Scott was the muscle. She was the mouth. It seemed like a natural division of labor. But he doubted it. He doubted they had put any forethought into their plan whatsoever.

She called them faggots a few times and slammed the door, to which Grandpa Sam responded by sadly shaking his head, confirmed in all his groundless hunches. These people were obviously criminals. What more did a person need to see? To Aaron, the behavior was crazy but not necessarily indicative of guilt. Poor impulse management. But not gold-stealing guilt.

"They won't call the police," Grandpa Sam said.

"Even if they do, I don't think they can really do anything," Aaron said. "And neither can we."

"We can," Grandpa Sam said. "We have to." And already he was again knocking on the door. This time it was Scott, looking savagely pissed, who answered.

"We told you to get the fuck out of here," Scott said. "Now get the fuck out!"

"I would like my bag," Grandpa Sam said. His arms hung loosely at his sides; his voice was aged but firm: "We'll go when I have the bag in my hands."

"We don't have your fucking bag, you dumb asshole," Scott raged. "Get it through your fucking head."

"I know you have it. I'll leave when you give it back to me."

Scott seemed more puzzled than angered by Grandpa Sam's demands. His eyes bounced between Aaron and his grandpa as if trying to grasp some impossible fact. Aaron smiled stupidly, trying to communicate some unspoken sympathy with Scott, but quickly reined himself in, ashamed. Joel and Karl were both yelling in his ear in unison: Man up, dude! Get with it! This is your grandfather—you have to back him up! Aaron crossed his arms and glared at Scott, trying to exude testicular confidence, and for a microsecond he thought there might be a breakthrough in the offing. Scott's eyes were crinkling into some kind of pained wince. Maybe he was seeing the light at last, preparing to invite them inside.

But that wasn't the case. Scott had only been choosing which one of them to punch. By whatever terrible circuit of reasoning, he chose Grandpa Sam. It wasn't a strong punch—it was almost a push—but it was enough to knock Grandpa Sam off balance, and as he stumbled backward toward the steps, Aaron grabbed at his arm, turning his body a few degrees. He was latched on, but the weight was too much, flooding his arm and sending them both tumbling down the steps, onto the concrete walkway.

Aaron managed to slow their descent enough that the landing was not catastrophic. He hit the pavement first, and his arm cushioned his grandpa's impact, the dead weight smashing into the padding of his forearm, the caps of his knuckles. It had been a long time since he'd scabbed his elbow, but he could tell by the scraping pain that he was leaving skin on the cement.

"Grandpa! Are you okay?"

Grandpa Sam was lying on his back, staring into the sky. He looked almost relaxed, or at least resigned, and a single tear nested at the corner of his eye. Aaron wasn't sure if the tear came from pain or distress or some symptom of old age—his eyes were always watering to some degree—but inside Aaron, any ambivalence about their investigation was now gone. He still wasn't sure if Kari had stolen his grandpa's bag of gold, but he knew for a fact he wanted to kill Scott in the most painful way possible.

"Grandpa," he said again. "Are you okay?"

His grandfather grumbled. The same frustrated grumble that came out when he opened the refrigerator. He was all right.

Aaron prized his arm out from under his grandfather's body and stood up. He was helping his grandfather to his feet, assessing the damage, judging it minor, when suddenly a loud crash rang in his ear and a gust of pain blew through his head. The night jarred in his vision, and suddenly his face was in the scrubby grass.

It took him a second to realize that he'd been punched and another second to realize Scott was already on top of him, punching and slapping and calling him a stupid fucking faggot-face faggot bitch. Between punches, Aaron caught blurry glimpses of Scott's hateful face, all sweating brow and flashing eyes. He looked monstrous, demonic, his eyes slitted, his teeth clenched, his thin lips curled back. New nodes of pain sprang up on Aaron's face and shoulders, his ear, his neck. One of his arms was pinned, he realized, and that was not fair.

One hard pelvic thrust, and Scott was momentarily gone, and a surge of adrenaline poured through Aaron's system. He felt at once feather light and ironclad. His arms and legs were fiery machines. He grasped Scott's hair and threw him onto the ground and got down to the job of punching him repeatedly in the head. He relished the smashing of his knuckles on the bones of Scott's skull and face. Scott wasn't heavy, and he wasn't strong, and Aaron gloried in the attempt to rip out his limbs and squash his head like a grape.

Scott didn't give up easily, though, and all too quickly Aaron's superpowers seemed to fade. Scott rolled over, and the two of them landed side by side in the dirt. Scott scrambled on top again, and for a time his blows became indefensible, banging into Aaron's head and temples with impunity. Aaron grabbed him, trying to squeeze his life out like toothpaste, and somehow they rose to their feet again, using each other for leverage. Locked in a choking embrace—Scott's breath, his body smell, the detergent he used, his deodorant, invading Aaron's senses—the two staggered around the yard, whispering into each other's ears.

"Get . . . the . . . fuck . . . off . . . my property."

"Fuck you, man, fuck you."

"Gonna . . . kill you, bitch."

They were still clamped in their violent slow dance when the strobing red of police lights splashed the scene, and moments later an octopus of beefy hands dragged them apart.

Aaron and his grandfather sat in their car, waiting to give yet another statement to the police. The lights flashed on the surrounding walls and sidewalk, but calmly and silently now. Some kids had gathered to watch, and the police were talking to Kari and the bloody Scott. Occasionally their voices jumped, but they never carried far enough to reach Aaron, only spiraling out of reach into the night.

Aaron's face ached. He could feel his lips inflating. If he closed his left eye, he could practically see his upper lip down below his nose, the puffy skin hovering like a hot, red cloud. Or maybe he was just seeing the throbbing pain itself, a stinging aura around his mouth region. He touched his lip with his tongue, tasting the metallic blood, and winced, knowing it must be gnarly.

"How's my lip, grandpa?" His voice was thick and muddled, even to himself. He was glad he'd at least managed not to cry.

His grandpa looked over. "You got punched," he said.

"Yeah, I noticed that. But how does it look? Do I need some ice?"

"Wouldn't hurt."

Aaron tongued his lip some more. "It feels like a watermelon," he said, and flipped down the mirror for an inspection. "It's as big as a watermelon. Jesus."

But his grandpa wasn't listening anymore. He was busy watching the police officer walking ever so slowly in their direction, closing the distance at the glacial pace of authority. He was on his way, his gait said, but on his own terms. He would bend them to his will in every tiny way possible.

The officer leaned in the window, stern-faced, and Aaron's grandfather was talking before the first question was asked.

"These people have something of mine," he told the police officer. "A bag they took from me at the restaurant where the girl works. You can see what they did to my grandson. We came here to get the bag—"

"You two can't come around here anymore," the cop interrupted. "You come within five hundred feet, you're under arrest. You get me?"

Driving away, Aaron wanted a soundtrack that would somehow articulate the night's pain and humiliation. He wanted all the night's fear and stupidity bundled into a single, propulsive package, the overflowing rage brought into some pattern. He swished through the iPod, caressing its clitoral button until he came to his preferred setting: AC/DC. AC/DC was good for this kind of night. "Back in Black" especially. The raging, militant riffs were dependably transporting. The album made the aftermath of a pointless street fight seem not only normal but honorable.

The first blasting chords caused his grandpa to recoil, and he reached for the buttons to turn the volume down. But Aaron was already there, guarding the stereo's glowing face.

"Please turn it off," Grandpa Sam said. "Much too loud."

"I'm listening to this, Grandpa, all right?" Aaron said. "I like it."

"It's too late for that, sweetheart. It's time for bed."

"No," Aaron said. "I like this. We're listening to this. Just deal with it."

And so they drove to the La Quinta Hotel in Dublin, the speakers flaming with Angus Young's guitar, his grandpa hunched over, arms crossed, the tongues of the highway licking at the balls of their feet.

16

Terminal Island: the hardworking colon of Los Angeles. Terminal Island: the last stop on the long journey of western water from the inland mountains to the sea. Terminal Island: the final chamber before the city's workhorse life fluid was put down and jettisoned once and for all.

Terminal Island: maybe the doorway to rebirth.

Anne drove through the gate, properly in awe of the significance of the site. For years she'd wondered about the mysterious architecture behind these walls. Driving past, she'd caught glimpses of strange loading bays and placid containment pools, quiet smokestacks and busy catwalks, egg-shaped domes, blank aprons of concrete, pipes of all diameters, adding up into a bewildering engine of industrial power, all of it neatly and yet confusingly crammed into this 2,800-acre footprint in the middle of C.H.U.D. country, mere yards from Los Angeles Harbor. Even today, invited inside at last, she marveled at the size and complexity of Terminal Island, crowned by the low-flying planes coming down toward the runways of LAX.

The small parking area was mostly empty, and as she jockeyed into a place in the narrow band of shade, she felt her dread of the coming meeting spiking in her nerves. The anxiety wasn't necessarily an unwelcome feeling. She'd come to see it as a harbinger of a good performance on her part, the sign of high mental focus and clarity of thought, but in this case, she had to admit, the nerves were jangling a little more than she wanted, pushing her into the realm of nausea and mild discombobulation. Rifling through her papers, trying to organize her bag, she did her best to put the nerves out of her mind. If only she knew what Charlie Arnold was thinking about the Document, which she'd sent him three days ago, she would feel so much better.

The Document was something Mark had cooked up, a twenty-page booklet on the subject of something called a hydrodynamic cavitation reactor. It was an impressive graphical display, rife with diagrams, bullet points, and many inscrutable mathematical formulae, as far as she could understand it describing a technological leap in the realm of carbonated water. The science was far beyond her, just a bunch of squiggles on top of unlabeled grids, but she understood the general gist: the hydrodynamic cavitation reactor was a technological breakthrough of the highest order, with transformative potential in all categories related to wastewater management, and major disruptive ramifications for the future of water-delivery systems in general.

"What is cavitation, exactly?" she'd asked Mark upon first receiving the Document, her ten minutes of scrutiny not garnering much insight.

"Bubbles," Mark had explained over the phone. "Turns out a lot happens when a bubble pops. A lot of energy gets released. Cavitation is basically an attempt to harness the energy of tiny bubbles while they're imploding. People have been thinking about it as a possible alternative energy source for a long time. But it turns out there are applications for clean water, too."

"What are the applications?"

"Well . . . ," There was a long silence. "That I can't exactly explain."

The beauty of the Document was exactly this coy refusal to disclose its own object. There were blueprints of newly patented water-jet pumps, plunger pumps, and bypass throttle valves, but because the central technology was still technically in development and specific information remained proprietary, the ultimate black box in the middle was not viewable. In place of hard evidence, the Document made promises. It promised, for instance, a machine capable of destroying all waterborne organic contaminants and organic microorganisms without any residual chlorine or carcinogens in the by-product. It promised a cost-neutral pilot project with no risk whatsoever to Los Angeles's budget, funded and administered by BHC Industries. In convincingly flat, bureaucratic sentence fragments, it promised a future in which low-cost drinking water was not only cheap and available to all but forever replenishable.

In essence, the Document was a tantalizing mirage, a Trojan horse built of vague, hopeful assertions. The estimated budget was a fiction. The underperforming German pilot project of two years previous was not mentioned. The precise details of the private funding consortium, BHC Industries in partnership with German research conglomerate EMU Unterwasserpumpen, were left unstated. But the mirage didn't have to be deep, Mark reasoned. It had only to last long enough to beguile Charlie and the other relevant city officials into handing over the permit. After that, the mirage could plausibly disappear in any number of ways—scientific, seismic, financial—without raising suspicion. So long as the permit existed, legally establishing BHC as the gatekeeper to whatever technology eventually won the day, it didn't matter—the monetizing of the permit could begin in earnest. They could start selling their futures, bundling their options, whatever it took to awaken the animal spirits of the marketplace and bring the mirage to reality.

A mirage. A Trojan horse. But was the Document a lie? Anne asked herself as she gathered her papers. Locking the door, her copy of the Document tucked in her canvas bag, she had to admit, yes, it probably was. But it was a lie of a certain softness and edgelessness. It was a lie without any clear victims. And, assuming the world was in fact moving in the direction of the lie, that really made it less a lie than a prophecy of sorts, didn't it? A smart bet. In any case, she was merely the emissary of the lie, the ignorant mule go-between, able to plead innocence at any step along the way. Her reputation might end up tarnished a bit, she might look a little dumb, her ramrod brother would be appalled, but her actions would never be construed as outright criminal by a jury of her peers. Entering the building, she was doing a pretty good job of stilling the slosh of bile in her gut. She had to start thinking like Mark now, thinking like the devil. She had to go sell it.

The man at the desk who took her name and buzzed Charlie was slow in the way of an aging surfer, his face a blistered and pocked wreck of precancerous flesh. Once, long ago, he'd probably been an Adonis among men, but the pleasures of youth had taken their toll. He spoke her name into a phone with a gravelly, twangy monotone and told her to sit, then sank into a near coma. Thankfully, Charlie was soon down, pleased to welcome her to his kingdom of shit.

"Welcome to the machine," he said, holding the door and directing her deeper inside. "You want the grand tour?"

"Actually, yeah," she said. "I've always kind of wondered about this place."

"Well. Allow me to fulfill your lifelong dreams . . ."

He took her up a flight of echoing stairs, through a metal door, onto a landing, through another metal door, and out onto a mesh walkway skirting the main building, all the while talking over his shoulder about the various attributes of the facility:

"So, Terminal Island is one of the four major treatment plants in the city," he said. "We get about sixteen million gallons of wastewater through here on a daily basis. Sixty percent of which comes from industry, the rest from private residences. We can go as high as forty-two million gallons in a major storm if we have to."

"Has that ever happened?"

"Not even close."

They continued along a catwalk and arrived at a platform overlooking the entire compound. In the distance the harbor shone in the sun, and up in the sky the smug face of the Alaska Airlines logo passed by on a descending plane. Shouting over the engine's roar, Charlie pointed out the Terminal Island headworks, where the wastewater entered the system and where the largest incoming solids—from branches, plastics, rags, down to sand and other gritty materials—were removed by a series of bars and screens. From there, he gestured, the fluid flowed on to primary treatment—covered, underground, oxygen-rich aeration tanks in which most of the solids sank to the bottom and bacteria consumed most of the rest. The bacteria and the finest solids were then separated from the wastewater in clarifiers, and some of the biomass was sent back to the aeration tanks for additional treatment. Secondary effluent was treated to remove the very smallest solid particles. Coagulant was added. Then the fluid was pumped through microfiltration membranes, then through reverse osmosis membranes. Then it was chlorinated, then dechlorinated, all preliminary to disposal in Los Angeles Harbor and injection in the Dominguez Gap. Anne wasn't exactly sure what she was meant to glean from all this information. Was he giving her some kind of test? Or did he think he was taking a test? She wasn't sure who was supposed to be testing whom.

"The water comes out of here cleaner than the water you drink," Charlie finished as another plane descended overhead, half drowning him out.

"So why don't we drink it?" she wondered loudly.

"Well, it's pretty stepped on by the time we're done," he said. "It smells weird. Technically, it's very clean, but we only use it for industrial purposes anyway."

"What did the city do before all this?" she asked.

"We used to just dump the raw sewage out there." He pointed at the horizon. "Hard to believe, but the world is actually getting cleaner around here. You remember what the air and water used to be like in this city."

"I remember," she said. And she did. She remembered the smog alerts, the oily runoff in the gutters, the incredible quilt of litter on the roadsides and in the arroyos. The city was cleaner in some ways. No point in mentioning all the ways it wasn't, though, too, such as the pharmaceuticals in the reservoirs, the carbon emissions, the leveled foothills, the faraway, eradicated forests. If the world was getting less polluted, it was only because there was less of it to pollute. The world was practically used up.

"So I looked at the stuff you sent," he said. "Pretty interesting."

"Isn't it?" she said, gulping the warm air from the ocean breeze. On the way over, she'd decided that understatement was going to be her tactic today. All opinions would derive from Charlie, and she would only respond positively or negatively. He'd be the one to explain the plan as he saw it; she would concur; and in this way she would lead him onward to whatever conclusions were already forming in his head, never indicting herself.

"I hadn't heard about this patent pending," he said. "I knew people had been working on cavitation for a while. But this is a big step."

"So they tell me."

"No chlorine. No nothing."

"Yep."

"The effluent will be better than the water out of a tap."

"Yeah."

"And your guys really think people are going to pay for water that's already been used?"

"So they say."

"They're crazy."

The sun blasted a patch of water far out in the harbor, a sheet of pure white radiance, and seagulls drifted on the torrents of air. Charlie didn't seem to notice any of the scenery, however. He was too busy wrestling with his own knotted, inner objections to care.

"I think they're banking on a catastrophic shortage," she said. "They're pretty positive that someday people will pay for used water. They have the resources to lose a little until then."

"Not a bad bet. It's going to cost some dollars, though."

"True," she said.

"And the city should really be the one building this reactor," he said. "The city should be keeping its own water in the public domain."

"But the city won't," Anne pointed out. "It can't."

"The city won't, it's true," he agreed. "The people won't pay for it. So we'll all end up paying for the water later. We won't plan ahead and keep it ourselves, but we'll pay for it later. God, it's pathetic. It looks like a very elegant idea, I'll hand it to your guys."

Anne's heart hurt, watching her old friend bend over for this reaming. Charlie's long life of shouting in the streets, carrying placards, bawling out real estate developers in the name of the people, flashed before her eyes. He'd spent his entire adult career stewarding the public interest with almost nothing in the way of gratitude or material reward. And now he was girding himself to hand over the people's most precious possession, its water, to the agents of speculative capital. It was a reaming she hadn't really appreciated until this moment. But she quickly put the sadness out of her mind. The market was going to make it all better in the end. The market would solve the problems with its money magic.

"Why a thousand years on the permit?" he asked, zeroing in on the very kernel of the Document's true purpose.

Because asking for a million years sounded preposterous, she didn't say. Because everyone dreams of a thousand-year *Reich*.

Instead she said: "The investors need some security. They're ready to move on the construction as soon as possible, but they need a guarantee of access to the resource. A thousand years establishes the point. They lose it if they don't use it. But they want a commitment from the city. That part's not negotiable."

He stared at the harbor, unseeing.

"Yeah. Makes sense."

He had a few more pro forma questions, and when they were answered to his satisfaction, he walked her back to her car, telling her all about the egg-shaped digesters and the fertilizer that squirted out of them into the hauling trucks. But during the whole walk she knew the real meat of the conversation had not yet even been touched. She could tell by Charlie's rapid acceptance of the Document, and by the airy tone of his tour, that a turn was still somewhere in the offing. The topics thus far didn't merit a face-to-face meeting, and Charlie might have been deeply into waste, but he was not one to waste anyone's time.

"If this pans out," he said, "we're talking about a game changer."

"That's what I'm starting to see," she said. "I didn't understand the science at first—I still don't—but I'm starting to see the significance."

"It'll be big, believe me."

"Oh, I do."

They reached the parking lot, and she started digging around for her keys, but sure enough Charlie seemed unprepared to let her go. He leaned on the car, hands in pockets, mulling something over until she finally asked him what he was thinking.

"Your friends are probably going to lose a lot of money on this," he said. "They definitely won't see any dividends for a very long time."

"They're into risk," she said. "They see a lot of money in the long haul. And, like I said, they can afford to wait."

"You're going to have to talk to Randy Lowell. Or maybe you already have."

"You're the first one they wanted to reach out to. They're still waiting to bring this to Randy. If you have any ideas about how to frame this for him, I'd love to hear them."

"No idea what that redneck will say."

They stood silently at the car as men in jumpsuits affixed a nozzle to a truck and filled it with bioslurry, and as the slurping, sucking, chugging sounds grumbled away, as if as an afterthought, with great effort to sound super casual, Charlie got around to what he really wanted to say all along.

"So. I wanted to tell you about something I've been thinking about. I mean, if you still have a second, that is."

Here it came. "Of course," she said. "That's why I'm here, right?"

"You guys are doing some great work, obviously," he said, warming up. "This project is very exciting. And you and me—we've been doing some great work, too."

She nodded attentively, and Charlie leaned forward, his eagerness rising. He wasn't the sort for seduction. Now that the ice was broken, he just blundered on through.

"What I've been thinking," he said, "and I've been talking about this for a while with my staff, and with the mayor's office, too, is a new regional department for environmental communications. Some kind of sustainability czar for the whole region. We all know the city is one part of a much bigger regional sustainability problem. And we know there's a lot of information falling through the cracks. We've got programs happening all over the West right now. This one here." He tapped the Document, peeking from Anne's bag. "This is important. What we need is someone who can coordinate everyone's message. Someone working between your office, my office, all the other bureaus in the state, other states, too, and getting the word out. We did a survey last summer and found out almost no one outside Sanitation knows what we're doing. There's so much innovation, so much good information being generated, we need someone to organize it and get it out there . . ."

He went on, comparing the new position with other positions of a similar cast. It could be comparable to a drug czar or the head of the National Security Agency. A coordinating agent. Through the whole of his presentation, Anne bobbed her head in constant, unquestioning agreement. She'd heard him talk about this idea before. It seemed as if he'd been talking about it for years. What he wanted was a Goebbels of sustainability. A propaganda minister to broadcast the news of his injection process and whatever his next unprecedented achievements might be. But she made every effort to pretend to hear it as if for the first time.

"Yeah. Absolutely. Makes sense," she said.

And when he eventually came to a natural pause, she asked straight out, "So what do you need from me, exactly, Charlie? How can I help?"

Charlie, too enthused by his own pitch to detect any reluctance or skepticism in Anne's voice, barreled onward:

"I want to get this position funded. And at the right level. I want this to be a real position. I don't just want to fold it into someone else's job description. I'm willing to throw down for the office space and fund most of the operating expenses, all out of my budget. But I need a contribution from Susan's budget to pay the salary."

The screw had turned. The sharp tip had twisted and circled back in the mealy wood, digging deeper. The lie was asking for another lie. How many turns would it take before the thing was done?

"How much are you talking about?"

"If we want to attract someone with skills, we need to lay out at least a hundred fifty grand," he said. "That's still going to be a major haircut, compared with whatever someone's making in Palo Alto."

"You have someone in mind?" She allowed a tinge of distaste into her voice. The only question was which of Charlie's lieutenants would take the post.

"No, no," he demurred, obviously lying. "This is all just thinking out loud right now. This is the first I'm talking about it . . ."

"Let me see what I can do."

Two minutes later Anne was driving away. Not a single diagram or pie chart had been brandished, nor a single catchphrase deployed. Her guns had remained holstered. Either she had just massacred her enemy without a single shot, or she had been massacred—she wasn't sure which.

But, settling back into her sun-hot car, she felt light and free. Massacrer or massacree, she was pleased with the meeting.

The cards had been dealt, and now all the players wanted their piece of the action. It was in all the jostling and deal making that the ultimate compromise of reality came into being, that the future got made. The lying she'd done today was all part of the grand, wonderful game of reality.

Pulling out of Terminal Island's lot, she could see the palm trees of Venice shining like Roman candles, the sun bouncing off more cars than she could count, a million spiking stars in every direction.

She drove with the windows down, warm wind blowing in her hair. If anything, she felt the opposite of remorse. As it turned out, after all these years, she'd been waiting to get her fingerprints on the future and haul in the bucketloads of cash. Who didn't want that? Make me an offer, she thought. Lay me out on the stone altar and draw your pentagram of blood on my breasts. Plunge in the obsidian dagger. I'm ready to sell this soul, and cheap. Here she was, on the verge of perpetrating a gigantic, elaborate grift on her community, on the city for which she had fought so hard, so long, and all she could feel was fantastic. Driving down the river of cars, colors streaming on either side, she wondered: How many lies before nothing is the same? Before the whole world is made new? If Mark were there, she might have kissed him.

17

A blue Jeep was parked near his RV.

What the fuck was that about? He sure as hell wasn't expecting any visitors today. That was the whole point of this place. The location had been selected expressly for its inviolable privacy, four hundred yards from a road, backed against a desert wilderness of soul-testing dimensions. There was almost no way a Jeep could end up at his doorstep by accident. So what the fuck?

The Jeep looked like a rental, even doused in dust. The windshield was all beige, barring the double swipe of the wipers. The plates were California. He didn't see a driver anywhere, and for a moment he wondered if someone already had a high-power scope on him. Were the crosshairs on his forehead, probing for entry points? But no, he thought. What self-respecting shooter would park his Jeep right out in the open like that?

Creeping ahead, eyes on the vehicle, Ben was bothered even by the angle of its placement. It was parked so arrogantly at his front steps, as though someone had just cruised in and carelessly jammed on the brakes. The front tires were torqued, and he could see the smeary skid marks behind the rear tires where the vehicle had slid into place on the dust pack. Quietly, he unholstered the Beretta M9 he'd taken with him on the morning's hike to Comprehensible Bowl and gently laid his backpack on the ground, freeing his shoulder. Stepping lightly the last few yards into his base camp, he made for the cliff wall and hugged the rock as soon as he was within touch. His main arsenal was in the RV, but his M9 was sufficient for his current purposes.

It took only a few seconds to spot the intruders. They were over on the far edge of his yard, near the cliff, tucked into the coolest midday shadow, sleeping. Two men, arms flung over their faces. Both powerfully built. One white, one black. The white guy's arms had some shitty, amateur tattoos, possibly resembling a dragon or an eagle. The black guy's arms were unmarked. But already Ben didn't need any more clues. He knew exactly who these guys were. Those arms belonged to Doobie and Slick, his brothers from SEAL Team 7.

He holstered his gun, his cells still tingling with concern. What the fuck were Doobie and Slick doing out here? They'd never come uninvited, although maybe they would; it was hard to say. But most likely they wouldn't, and that meant there had to be some official reason for this invasion, some ulterior, bureaucratic motive. A dark thought blew into his mind: What if Command knew what he'd been doing the past few weeks? What if Doobie and Slick were here to arrest him? It made him sick to contemplate. Or was it possible they had some other terrible news to deliver? The only thing to do was stomp over to their shadow and find out.

"Trespassers," Ben grumbled, approaching the supine bodies. "Just my goddamn luck."

"The hermit returns," said Slick, opening one eye. "About fucking time, dude."

"Moses down from the mountain," said Doobie, not bothering to remove his burly arm from his face. "Where's your tablets, dickweed? You lost your fucking tablets already? God's gonna be real pissed if you lost his tablets."

"No stone tablets anymore," said Slick. "Tablets are old-school, man. God just beams all his shit into your brain these days. Isn't that right, Mac?" Mac was short for Maccabee, or the Last Maccabee, the most enduring of his team nicknames, slapped on him almost two decades ago. Among all his nicknames, he disliked it the least.

"Wireless communication," Slick went on. "God don't use no tablets anymore. God upgraded."

"We don't get signals out here, anyway," Ben said, joining the banter. He was still concerned about their motives and watched them closely for any sudden movements, but if they'd come to ambush him, they were following a strange protocol. He didn't sense any imminent threat to his person. "This air is too clean for signals."

"No fucking shit, the air is clean," Doobie said, finally sitting up and planting his feet on the ground. He pulled his phone from his pocket and tapped the glass. "Dead air, more like it. I can't get shit out here. Can't get my scores. No idea if my boys are up or what."

"Braves today?" Slick said.

"Braves by three. You know it."

"Ha! Good luck, son. You never learn."

And with that, Doobie and Slick wandered off into baseball esoterica, leaving Ben on the sidelines, as usual. He followed the jock talk more than he normally would, seeking subtexts in the names and numbers, but he couldn't find any.

And what about the Moses stuff? Was there some under-current to that he didn't understand? He didn't think so, not from these guys. Doobie was always talking Old Testament in Ben's presence. He was a giant, ginger-skinned guy from Geor-gia, raised by Evangelicals, and he'd never met a Jew until his first day in BUD/S with Ben. To this day, Jews remained a great novelty in his life, objects of major historical significance. He enjoyed nothing more than reminding Ben of his Chosen status.

"God must've told you to get your boys a beer by now, " said Doobie, interrupting his own rant about the Braves' batting or-der. "What kind of God you got out here, anyway? I heard your desert God is a jealous God, but this is just inhospitable."

"So I guess you guys are staying awhile," Ben said. "That's cool. Make yourselves at home. Bathroom's over there." He pointed at a rock. "I'll see what I got in the fridge."

"Don't knock yourself out, bro."

Ben left his old friends talking in the shade, knowing they would reveal their purpose only when they were good and ready. These guys had driven for hours, they hadn't seen him for months, they wanted to bust his balls for a while before they got down to business. They wanted to feel him first.

Walking to the RV, he reassured himself that the signals were normal, as far as he could tell. On the other hand, though, the guys knew that normal was exactly how they'd normally be expected to act. So it was possible the very normality of their behavior was just a disguise for their true, abnormal agenda, which was what? The thought chilled him. Were Slick and Doobie here to bring him in? Was it possible they were perpetrating an elaborate trick of normality, acting exactly as they would have acted if they had no suspicion at all? His paranoia jumped, hit a wall, and jumped again. There was no way to know and no way not to wonder.

Inside his RV, the questions continued to attack his mind: What did Slick and Doobie know? What were they hiding? What were they unable to hide? He cracked the mini-fridge and pulled out three Hamm's, wondering, wondering. As much as people had ridiculed Rumsfeld and his gnomic formulation about known unknowns and unknown unknowns, the sentiment made perfect sense to him. Some things you knew you didn't know, and some things you didn't even know you didn't know. Both had the power to kill you.

He set the three beers down and took his LR-308 from the closet in the bedroom. The nerves in his body were mildly spazzing. All the doubts and worries and speculation he'd been keeping under control in the desert were now flowing back through the gates. His silent peace was once again disturbed.

In the two weeks since completing the Mission, he'd been doing pretty well, all told, although much had transpired. The event had gone off more or less as planned, but the aftermath had been harder to predict. If the goal had been something surgical and discreet, he hadn't succeeded. The news of Michael Holmes's death had gotten out quickly and been judged significant, and had become widely commented upon.

The story had achieved a low to medium level of infamy. It wasn't a huge story. It didn't open a hole in the very fabric of the mass media, as Ben had momentarily feared it might. It was no O.J. trial, no 2000 recount, no octuplets. It wasn't one of those black holes sucking the nation's head into its own asshole. And because it was not all-engulfing, Ben found it was hard to gauge its size at all. To him, a person with a vested interest, the story obviously seemed pretty big. He spotted it on TV in the bar, on magazines at the grocery store. But to most people, the event probably registered as a mere curiosity, a minor tag among the thousands of tags that flowed over their screens and crawled out of their phones. Michael Holmes, a powerful corporate leader, had been shot. So what? Among the elite who were the event's true audience, he had no way to gauge the reception at all. His one conduit to that world was gone.

A few days into the story, he'd posted a brief, anonymous message to the *New Orleans Times-Picayune* (Why not let a little guy break the story? was his thinking). The message was succinct, including certain salient details verifying his author-ity, and linked Michael Holmes to the metastasizing cancer of American imperialism and American digital totalitarianism. It ended with a threat: Let Holmes and his fellow fascist oligarchs beware. We will hunt you down if provoked.

His note had stoked another round of media hypervent-ilation, and the black hole had momentarily dilated but never achieved terminal suck. The note had been read and discussed, but never on the merits of its arguments, only as the ramblings of a madman. Even the people who might have secretly agreed with him were appalled by his tactics. The note mainly became an object of ridicule. Most everyone agreed, Holmes was a good guy, a consistent supporter of the arts, a great dad.

Ben had been taking daily refuge at Comprehensible Bowl, awaiting the final death rattles of the news cycle and thinking about next moves. And now these guys were sitting outside in the shade of the bluff. He had to wonder what wheels had been turning outside his view. What unknown unknowns were already on his trail?

He pulled back the curtain and watched them. No guns were visible. No gestures or eye movements to make him suspect hidden schemes. He'd known these guys a long time; he could read them. He and Doobie had parachuted into Costa Rica back in BUD/S together. They'd fought off a whole bar full of frat guys over a ping-pong game the first day they met. He knew Doobie's wife, Tiffany, and the whole insanity with her breast cancer when she was pregnant. He'd known Slick almost as long. He'd once stitched a gash along Slick's inner thigh that led practically to his ball sack. He might have saved Slick's balls that day. That was a bond you couldn't easily break.

And yet, what did the past mean at this moment? What did any of the time he'd spent with these guys tell him about why they were here right now? He might well walk out the door and find them standing there with their .45s drawn, yelling him down, pushing his face into the dirt, all the cute little banter nothing more than a ruse. The smell of his RV was musty and hot. The window needed fixing. Maybe the best move he could make would be to walk out the door with his own Beretta in hand, hog-tying them and getting the hell out of town. If it came to it, he could probably smoke both of them before they made it to the car.

The sudden inside-out world he'd dropped into was dizzying and terrifying. To kill his brothers? To think that might possibly become the only course? No, no. He wasn't going there, not yet.

He pulled three beers from his mini-fridge and realized he already had three beers on the counter and put the first beers away. One thing he knew—he wasn't climbing into any cars with them, no matter what.

He plucked his LR-308 off the counter and placed it just behind the front door on his way out, and left the door ajar for easy access. His Beretta was still in the back of his waistband. If the guys pulled anything on him, he might be able to roll inside and get hold of the major firepower.

Their guns weren't out when he got back into their shadow. Doobie and Slick were still lying on their rocks. He set their beers near their heads and took a place in the sun, near his tools.

"Thanks, Moses," Doobie said, draining half his beer in one draw. "This beer is nice and cold. That's the sign I've been waiting for."

"We owe you one, God," Slick said, toasting the sky. "You did us a solid this time."

"Make 'em last," Ben said. "These are about the only beers for fifty miles in any direction."

"Oh, we brought some," Slick said. "We just wanted one of yours."

"Glad you still remember your old friend, beer," Doobie said. "Thought you were just eating dirt out here."

"Yeah, how come you hate the city so much, man?" said Slick. "How far out you need to get, bro?" Slick was from New Jersey, a true loudmouth son of Bayonne. He couldn't believe that Ben was a Jew at all. Ben resembled none of the Jews of his childhood, with their forelocks and coats, bawling out some contractor on their cell phones at the edge of a construction site.

"I love the city," Ben said. "I love all you city people, eating and shitting on top of each other. Sitting in your cars all day. Turns out I just love all of you a lot more when you aren't around."

"Moses is a sensitive dude," said Doobie.

"He's not gonna like what we have to tell him," said Slick.

Ben's nervous system flashed with fireworks, but he kept himself still.

"We hate to interrupt your precious alone time and all," Doobie said, "but it couldn't be helped. There are some powerful men who want to talk to you, dig? Even more powerful than God."

Ben's inner fireworks exploded. His blood shivered with adrenaline. Still, though, he played it calm. A minefield was opening in front of him, and he had yet to understand its geography, let alone map a way through. He needed to stay put, that was all.

"So this isn't just a social visit?" he said, and pulled on his beer to cover up his gulping throat.

"Oh, it's social," Doobie said, laughing. "We miss you and everything, if that's what you're worried about. We still cry every night since you left, if that's what you need to hear. That's the main reason we're here."

"That's right, queer," added Slick.

"But as long as we were driving all the way out here to lay sweet eyes on you, Command wanted us to deliver you a little message, too. They've got a little freelance job, if you're interested."

"They couldn't just call?"

"Would've just called, but you don't make it real easy, Mac. And then there's that beautiful face of yours. I need to refresh my memory for, you know, my nightly scrolling." He mimed a few slow, loving strokes of an invisible, giant, curvaceous dick, adding some ball play at the end for extra comedy. "Had to deliver the message in person."

"I didn't know I was up for any jobs," Ben said.

"And yet you filled out the application by being alive. So that's the first question. Are you open to a job? There's only one answer."

"Just tell me the fucking job." Ben said. He hoped he was hitting the right tone between nonchalance and prickly amusement so as to maintain the illusion that all was normal on his end, too. Doobie's next words rattled him even further, though.

"You watching this whole Michael Holmes thing?" Doobie said.

Ben gagged and tried to contain the look of shock and dismay on his face. The shrieking insect sound of fear was rising in his ears, and the fight-or-flight fork in the road was fast approaching. The only thought that kept his gun in his pants was one that said: If these guys are trying to take me in, they are coming at it all wrong. Why would they bring up Holmes unless they had absolutely no idea what was really going on?

"The world is fascinated," Ben said. "Big news story."

"World's fascinated 'cause it's fascinating," Doobie said.

"I'm fascinated," Slick agreed. "Celebrity death is fascinating by its nature."

"Weird, isn't it," Doobie said, "how famous death means more than normal death. I still remember the day the *Challenger* blew up. Everyone was so fucked up about it. Boo-hoo. These famous people are dead. My uncle died that week, too. No headlines about him."

"Dude, you're fucked," said Slick. "Those people were heroes. You can't compare your uncle to them. They were American astronauts."

"I'm just saying, death is death. Everyone is special."

"Takes a special dude to say that."

"Okay, okay," Ben cut in before the conversation could go too pear shaped. "What's the job? Jesus Christ."

"We just got briefed," Doobie said. "Here's the deal. Whoever it was that smoked Holmes was a pro gunslinger. Very efficient, very knowledgeable. The FBI went over all the forensics with us. This wasn't some amateur job. Dude had training."

"And? So?"

"And so, it changes who they're looking for, bro. And it changes how they want to go about the looking. This isn't just a search for some fuck-up psycho out there anymore. They figure they're looking for a real soldier. Someone with medals. That's how good the kill was. And for once, they seem like they're thinking, because they think it might take a soldier to find a soldier. That's why we're here. You knew him."

Ben's skin jangled, and he felt sweat streaming on his back. It was incredible that they'd gotten this deep into the conversation and he still wasn't sure where it was going. Were Doobie and Slick the hunters here, and was he the prey? Or was he the hunter, about to be hired to hunt himself? The conversation could still break in multiple directions. He hoped to God this whole stupid back-and-forth wasn't just a prelude to the guns coming out. But a SEAL knew when to creep quietly and when to sprint, guns blazing. He was still in the creeping-quietly phase of the operation, if barely.

"They want your help," Doobie said. "You're an intellectual. You might be able to see something we're missing here."

"'A sniper with brains.' That's what they want. For some reason, Stack said you fit the description."

"Maybe he felt Mac's brains with his dick when Mac was deep-throating him that time," Slick said to Doobie.

"Nice, hot, wet brains," Doobie riffed. "Oh yeah. Feel those brains with my big head-shed dick."

This went on for a while, a long digression on the mechanics of mind fucking, Ben's pussy brain, the proper use of contraception while brain fucking, brain dental dams, all of which allowed Ben to squint patiently into the sun, hiding his explosive sense of relief. This was simply too absurd. They would never present such a ludicrously, aggressively coincidental cover story just to bring him in quietly. Of course, there was still the slightest chance they were triple-fucking with him, but he didn't rate their skills that high. There were just SEALs, after all, not spies, not actors. They weren't capable of thinking that many steps ahead. The SEALs and Rangers, they were generally pretty stupid guys with extremely high pain thresholds and usually some kind of brutalizing childhood experience goading them to action. They were physical specimens, killing machines. They weren't spooks.

"They've got some leads?" he said when the subject of his labial brains was done.

"They've got some information."

"So you want me to help you find the guy who offed Holmes," Ben said, and couldn't help but laugh out loud.

"He thinks it's funny," Doobie said.

"Moses wants us to ask him why it's so funny," Slick said. "Fuck him. I'm not asking."

"I'd like to give the guy a medal," Ben said, rubbing his eyes. "I hated that motherfucker, Holmes. The world's better off without him."

"Thought you dug Holmes," Slick said. "You kept his ass alive a year, right?"

"I never liked him."

"Well, maybe they'll let you pin a medal on the dude before you shoot him in the head," said Slick. "Doesn't really matter to us. Point is, you've got four hours to get your ass to Twentynine Palms. They've got a command room in DC. Plane's waiting. They're going to be ready for you in the morning. You in or what?"

Still, he didn't get into their car. He didn't trust them that far just yet. Better to stay paranoid as long as possible. But he agreed to meet them at the airport at 2100 for a red-eye to Dulles. They would fly all night and head straight to the comm room for a complete debriefing, and from there he would throw down whatever speculations he might have to add. The other attending parties, he learned, would be Colonel Taymor, plus a few HUMINT and SIGINT guys, desk jockeys from the academy, most likely. The report they produced would go straight up the line to the Joint Chiefs, depending on what course of action they suggested. He predicted the whole process would take a week. He would pick up a day rate of three grand plus per diem.

Hilarious.

18

Aaron's grandfather was born in 1922 in Kraków, Poland. He had four brothers and three sisters. His father was a tinker studying to become a schoolteacher. His mother often cooked beets. The neighborhood where his family lived was called Kazimierz, a warren of cobbled alleyways and pocket squares peopled by tradesmen, cabinetmakers, grocers, and horses, centered on the comings and goings at the communal well.

That made Grandpa Sam seventeen years old when the Nazis invaded Poland. Of course, Aaron already knew that. But did he, really?

The storytelling had begun suddenly. Returning home to the hotel, late, hungry, they'd shuffled into the room. After food had been ordered, before cable, the words had begun to flow. Aaron wasn't sure what to do at first. His video camera was not far away, but he didn't want to scare his grandpa back into silence, so he sat on the edge of his queen bed, the sheets crisp with bleach, and listened.

His grandfather's memory of the invasion was vivid and sparse. He presented his images like small, precious heirlooms. Sitting in La Quinta, the air conditioner wheezing and burbling, he told Aaron about his mother tying the white armband with the blue Star of David onto his coat sleeve, the breadline queuing up at four in the morning, often dispersed by German dogs and soldiers with wooden truncheons, the rabbi paraded in the street and shorn of his beard, then forced to urinate on the Torah. He remembered the rabbi's shriveled, weeping, unbearded face in the fresh spring light, he said. He remembered the rumors of Jewish gravestones being used to repave the street.

In 1941 the Jews were consolidated into the ghetto of Podgórze, and Grandpa Sam's family abandoned their house for the town of Dabrowa, where a cousin of his mother lived. They walked the dirt road hauling the few bags they'd been allowed to take from their home, and as soon as they arrived, the Nazis took all the men of the village away and shot them. It happened in a field on the edge of town after they'd dug their own graves, they were told, and from that day onward Grandpa Sam never saw his father again.

His mother took the children back to Kraków and they found lodging in a pigeon coop on the roof of a building in Kazimierz. In 1942, the deportations began, and one by one his family members were lost. His mother was shot in the street. One of his brothers went to the camp Plaszow, another brother to Belzec. His sisters went to an orphanage, en route to Birkenau, or so he thought. Much was left out in the telling, and the daily life of the occupation was barely mentioned. It seemed he'd winnowed his memory down to a simple, streamlined tale, though the main events were unmistakable: one by one, everyone was swallowed by the earth.

In 1943, Grandpa Sam was taken from the street and loaded on a train without windows or water. He could still hear the sound of a woman crying nearby, unable to stop. Through the slats of the wall, he could catch glimpses of frozen fields rushing by, stone walls, distant chimneys smoking. When he deboarded, weak and afraid, he was at Plaszow, where he worked in the clothing factory, producing uniforms for the German army. He didn't give many details of his time at Plaszow, only that women were beaten and lorries were loaded with the sick and infirm, who were shot. Soon Grandpa Sam was being loaded into another train, enduring another terrible passage, and then he was entering the walls of Auschwitz.

His first image of arrival was of naked old men. The new prisoners were put into rows of five, two yards apart, and commanded to strip off their clothes. He remembered the sagging, wrinkled chicken skin of the old men's bellies, their yellow, clawed toenails. The guards shaved all the prisoners' heads, though to say "shaved" was too kind. They were not shaven; they were shorn like animals, and hosed down, and taken to the Lager.

In his description of the Lager, he became much more precise, as if he'd committed the dimensions of this hell to memory or done research after the fact. The Lager was a square about six hundred yards in length and width, he said, surrounded by two barbed wire fences, the inner fence electrified. In the Lager were sixty wooden huts, called blocks. There was a brick kitchen, an experimental farm, various huts with showers and latrines, one latrine for each six or eight blocks. Eight blocks at the end of camp comprised the infirmary. Block 24 was for skin diseases; block 7 was never entered; block 47 was for the political criminals; block 49 was for the *kapos;* block 37 was the quartermaster's office and the Office for Work; block 29 was the brothel, served by Polish *Häftling* girls.

He recalled ghoulish encounters with the German guards—
shouted, half-understood orders he still heard in his dreams.
He described unpredictable beatings that still ached in his
bones and told about terrible scenes of murder and fratricide.
He talked about his work in a sand mine, hauling dead weight
for no other purpose than the expansion of his very death factory. He talked about his diet of rotten potatoes, thin soup, and
occasional stale bread. The bread always defied Aaron's imagination in these stories. What was this bread, exactly? He could
never quite imagine it. Was it heavy bread, hard bread, brown
bread? Did it come in loaves, slices, buns? How much life could
a person squeeze out of this simple bread?

Some of Grandpa Sam's stories seemed a little misremem-
bered or vague or even shaped by some other source material.
Some of the details frankly seemed like they came from movies,
like the shining leather coats of the SS or the flashing monocle of
Dr. Mengele. Even the people digging their own graves bordered
on cliché. Genocide cliché, Aaron thought. What a heinous notion. But the world had made it so.

But then there were some details that rang very true.

The day, for instance, his grandfather was called with the
rest of the prisoners and lined up in the vacant lot in the Lager
yard. The men were all commanded to step forward, but for
some reason Grandpa Sam understood that stepping forward
was a death sentence. He pretended to drop something from
his pocket, a little scrap of paper, and bent over and held back
a few steps, letting the other men go forward, and all the other
men had been killed.

Aaron hadn't heard about the gay *kapo* in the camp, either.
This *kapo* was a cruel overseer who took sadistic advantage

of the prisoners, his grandpa said. At some point the men conspired to kill him in the showers. One man on each arm, one on each leg, and together they smashed him to death on the concrete floor. They lifted and smashed, lifted and smashed. It was hard to say whether his grandfather had held an arm or a leg that day or if he'd merely watched. How did one ask such a question?

Grandpa Sam was not a great storyteller. His mind was by no means a steel trap. He made his report in a flat voice, and he didn't look at Aaron during the telling. But it was clear that some of the things he'd witnessed in those days would not be unremembered.

Soon, after pizza was delivered, they were into the days following the liberation of the camp, and Aaron heard about his grandfather and another prisoner carrying a legless survivor through the woods of Poland to the German border. They traveled for days, if not weeks, with the man on their backs, crossing streams and ravaged meadows, trading him back and forth, hoping to find their way to the rumored DP camps. They'd schlepped his weight all the way to the gates of Berlin, from which point the legless man had survived and gone on to a distinguished career in life insurance in the Canadian province of Ontario.

When they came to Grandpa Sam's train voyages after the war, his fruitless search for his family, his tattoo as his train ticket, Aaron knew they'd reached the end of the tale for now. They'd skipped over many parts, and the phrasing hadn't been elegant, but they'd gone all the way, just as he'd hoped, from the innocence of the shtetl to the darkness of the war to the bright American life ever after. And Aaron, for his part, hadn't recorded a single word of it. His video camera was somewhere deep in his backpack, charged and sleeping. The words had been spoken in the hotel room and left there to memory.

When the talking was over, Grandpa Sam remained on the edge of the bed, breathing heavily, as if he'd been hauling stones, and then, predictably, turned on the TV, fumbling with the unfamiliar remote.

"It's amazing what you forget," he said, scrolling the menu.

Aaron helped him find a station with Sam Waterston solving crimes and sat beside him and watched the show for a while. When the commercial came on, he rubbed his grandfather's round, cement-hard shoulder, listening to the TV instruct them to buy pharmaceuticals and luxury cars, and when the show came back on, he murmured to his grandpa that he might take a walk. He wanted to think his own thoughts for a while.

"You're sure?" his grandpa said. "It's so late."

"I just want some air, I think," Aaron said.

"Well, be careful out there."

"Of course," Aaron said. "You want anything?"

Grandpa Sam thought about it, or possibly just stared at the TV, happy for the intrusion. "No."

The streets of Dublin were empty, only a few scuttling figures moving among the neighborhoods of corporate office parks. Aaron wandered aimlessly, passing streetlights and bark-dust beds, spotting security cameras tucked everywhere. The eyes of surveillance seemed to find the dull, eventless streets of Dublin fascinating.

He passed a few people waiting for the bus, talking about manicures and cheap restaurants, and thought about his grandfather and his mom. He had the facts now, but, in a way, the facts didn't change very much. In the end, whose family tree didn't hold mass murder somewhere in the branches? Everyone at the bus stop—Chinese, Japanese, Salvadoran, Indian—they'd all been on both sides of the gun at some point in history. Some became dentists, some became soldiers, like his uncle, but they all got the same lesson. He'd read there were more slaves in the world now than when Lincoln signed the Emancipation Proclamation.

He skirted a mall and wound up in front of the cinema multiplex, smelling the fake popcorn butter and bathing in the flashing lights. The lobby was nearly deserted, with only a teenage boy in a garnet uniform with a vacuum cleaner and a cardboard cutout of Hugh Jackman. A depressed-looking woman sat encased in the ticket booth, awaiting her last customers of the night.

He bought a ticket for *X-Men,* the story of a hunted genetic minority involving diabolical medical experiments, and trudged into the theater. Somehow, he thought, he was going to find a way to tell his family's history someday. Somehow, he would find a way to pull back the skin of the world and point at the dripping teeth and acid underneath. Look, he'd say, this is what we do. This is who we are. He would nurse the plan in darkness until the proper time came, telling no one, just in case he failed, but he didn't want to fail. He wanted to tell the world. He had no idea how.

19

Every once in a while Anne realized just how little Susan thought of her. Not that Susan thought little of her in the sense of undervaluing her as a person, just that she literally never thought of her, period. Anne was quite sure, for instance, that Susan didn't know where she lived. Why would she? She didn't know what was going on with her dad, and she probably wouldn't even recognize Aaron if she saw him, even though she'd met him at least fifteen times over the years. To Susan, Anne's life outside the Bureau of Sustainability was a complete blank, a flicker of shadow behind a thick veil of professionalism that was really, in the end, more like rank disinterest on her part.

On the other hand, Anne knew everything about Susan's life. She knew about Susan's husband, a doctor of obstetrics, and the infidelity of 1998; she knew about the family vacations to Madrid and Vieques; she knew about the travails of Susan's kids at Occidental and Evergreen, respectively.

It occurred to Anne that this must be the very definition of power, this blatant differential in consciousness. If ever there was a question of who wielded the power between two people, just look at who did all the thinking about the other one: that was the subordinate. Look at the one plagued by worries about the other's dietary needs, the other's social commitments, the other's domestic schedule: that was the subordinate. The thoughtless, memoryless one: that was the superior. In every relationship, there was a king and a serf; it had always been so.

Anne wondered if, taken to its extreme, this principle proved that God never thought about His creation. His complete ignorance was the ultimate measure of His power. Maybe so.

In any case, with Susan being nine time zones away, in Zurich, Anne realized she had no choice but to schedule their Skype meeting at two in the morning, Los Angeles time. Susan surely had no idea exactly what the time difference meant, and it would never occur to her to worry about any inconvenience on Anne's end. Anne, on her side, didn't want Susan alerted to any of her ulterior motives going into the conversation, and that meant she didn't want to create the slightest bit of turbulence in Susan's pretty little executive head. Thus, she resigned herself to the 2:00 AM call.

Staying awake was not easy. She downloaded a memory-improvement app and played some brainteasers as the clock edged past midnight, and around one o'clock she art-directed her computer's frame—pointing her camera at a chair in the corner of her living room, adding a happy-looking bouquet of pink roses, a pile of books, turning on all the lights, making sure no black windows were visible. It was too late to call Aaron, though she was sorely tempted. The radio silence on his end was becoming so obnoxious, just a few unforthcoming texts dribbling in a day, telling her nothing. It was like a stiff, invisible arm keeping her at bay. He knew exactly how little to give.

Of course Susan wasn't there on the first call. Nor the second, nor the third. But forty-five minutes later, on attempt four, Susan picked up, full of zesty apologies. "Sorry, sorry," she said. "The traffic is so fucking bad here!" Her pixelated face was rupturing and remaking itself on the screen, a scramble of data, and her voice, only vaguely synced to the picture, paused for large gaps of silence. The bad connection was aggravating, but not fatally so. How many satellites and way stations had these pulsations of energy traveled through before illuminating her box? That was another God question to ponder.

"I thought this town was supposed to run like a machine, but no," Susan said, unfreezing again. "Nobody knows what's going on here. I thought I'd be back at the hotel half an hour ago. Really sorry, really sorry."

Anne reassured her that everything was fine and dutifully asked how the trip was going. It was nearly three in the morning now, and she couldn't have cared less, but she asked out of reflex. Their conversations always began with this stream of one-way disclosure. Whatever Susan's day held, it became Anne's burden, too.

"Zurich is really fucking annoying," Susan said. "They keep giving me little tiny potatoes and cheese, like that's a real meal or something. These little, round, boiled potatoes and a few hunks of cheese on a huge, white plate. That's it. I mean, one time, that'd be fine—maybe it's traditional or something—but, like, eight times? Come on. How about a vegetable here? And then these Belgians I'm stuck with. Jesus. All they do is bitch about America, like I'm the fucking president or something. 'What about your blacks?' 'What about your Indians?' 'The poverty on the reservations is truly a shameful secret.' Like I don't know this. I'm, like, first of all, they're not 'my' blacks or 'my' Indians. You got that? Second of all, how about you go get some of your own blacks and Indians in your country, and then we'll talk, all right? I don't remember King Leopold was that cool to the fucking Congolese."

Anne was accustomed to Susan's charismatic complaining. Her negativity was a form of bonding, and for years at a time, it could be charming and inclusive in its scope. Look at these troubles we are enduring together! Look at these struggles we are overcoming! Look how little I'm enjoying my self-evident power and glory! Only occasionally, when Anne fell out of sync with her boss's agenda, did the routine become alienating, like now.

"The Belgians are really serious people, though," Susan went on. "God, they have such tiny, little technical questions about everything. I don't know what the hell I'm supposed to tell them half the time. I'm just like, 'I wish Anne was here! She'd know.' They all think you're a figment of my imagination."

"Ha."

"But seriously, they want to know the exact budget of the Richmond solarization program, down to the individual cells, the ad budget, everything. Can you get that to me? In some kind of organized file?"

"I'm not at the office right now, but when I go in, yeah, no problem . . ."

"Oh, no hurry. Anytime in the next day or two is great. Hey, are you at home right now? What time is it in L.A., anyway? Shit, it must be so late."

"It's kind of late," Anne allowed.

"We don't have to do this now."

"No, no. Now is good." Anne said, wishing she were able to help herself from letting Susan know what kind of suffering she was enduring, but she wasn't that strong.

"Okay, well, let's not keep you up too much longer. So, what did you need? I've got another panel in an hour. I should think about what I'm saying."

Already, Anne could see Susan's attention subdividing. She'd begun reading her email scroll alongside Anne's face on the screen; the telltale darting of her eyes gave her away. And the brief tapping of her fingers on the keys came next, the trickle of sound floating into the microphone and across the globe.

Maybe this wasn't the best time to make a pitch. Certainly, there was nothing Anne would have loved more than to say good night and climb into bed. But Anne knew that the success of her plan depended on a gradual, sidelong approach. And so, even though it was three in the morning and the only sound outside was an almost impossibly distant ambulance siren and her bed was only twenty feet away, she forced herself to slow down and claim all of Susan's attention.

She began with a summary of the past few days at the office, giving Susan a microscopic account of the many meetings and phone calls and little administrative chores she'd been handling alone, all the unseen fires she'd been putting out. She plumped each episode into a catastrophe narrowly averted, and she was rewarded with a string of small gasps and murmurs of great appreciation and concern. Anne rarely made this kind of bid for sympathy, and she was glad to find Susan was taken in by it. But of course she was taken in. Susan was not crazy, after all. She was wholly loyal and compassionate as long as you dragged it out of her.

Gradually, in among the litany of labors and small-bore gossip, Anne slivered in news of her meetings with Charlie Arnold, so that by the end of the conversation, among the final summary bullet points, she was able to return to the subject of Charlie and casually mention the request that had motivated the whole performance in the first place: can we free up a hundred fifty grand for Charlie's regional sustainability czar?

"Is he still on that trip?" Susan asked, perplexed. Her relationship with Charlie was a complicated blend of ideological affinity, personal competition, and mutual hunger for scarce civic resources. The idea of making a donation to Charlie's pet project was not immediately enticing.

"We would share access to everything the new department generates. Charlie sees the position as like a lobbyist, PR agent, and pollster all in one. We'd all get the reports, and we'd all use the agency as a kind of in-house consultant. The point would be to create . . ." Not synergies—that sounded too canned, too stupid—but what, then? "Collaboration opportunities."

Susan was barely listening anymore, shifting her attention back to the other windows of her screen. For all Anne's gradual approach, Susan easily grasped the nature of the power grab before her. She was a professional politician, after all. She could see a quid pro quo sneaking from behind.

"Tell him we already have a communications director, thank you," she said, tapping away. "I don't really see the value add on our side. I assume this new guy lives in Charlie's building, too, right? Sounds like we'd be paying for a new staff position in his world. Tell him thanks, but no thanks."

"He did a survey last summer. Ninety-five percent of the public has never even heard of our bureau. Eighty percent of public *employees* have never heard of our bureau."

"I don't care about Charlie's survey. As long as the mayor and the city council know about us, who cares? They're the ones who approve our budget. We don't need PR the way Charlie seems to think he does. Tell him to find another sugar mama. Honestly, he thinks we've got so much fat? It's offensive."

"I'm totally with you," Anne said. "I agree, it's all kind of ridiculous. But here's another thing to think about, too, all right? Just as a thought."

"What?"

Susan was on the verge of complete disengagement. The curtain of distraction was already lowering onto the stage, the pulleys squeaking, the heavy velveteen drapes sliding their cuffs across the boards. Anne took a deep breath, mentally donning her brightest tap-dancing shoes for one last shuffle before the crowd. If this last encore didn't do the trick, her cause was lost.

"We still have that budget line for Vicki's job," she said, "We need to use it, or we won't have it next budgeting cycle. One thought is, we could shift it over to Charlie's position and then reevaluate the allocations next year."

"We can't keep Vicki's salary in our budget otherwise? Seriously?"

"Use it or lose it, that's the law," Anne said, with much more confidence than her knowledge necessarily merited.

"There must be other ways to keep it."

"Maybe. But I don't know what they are. And this is right here."

"Vicki's salary is how much?"

"Almost eighty."

"So we're really talking about kicking in seventy above and beyond."

Susan paused in her texting to stare into Anne's aperture once again. She tightened her lips, manipulating the abacus in her mind.

"Okay," she said. "Agreed. What else you got? We've got to get you into bed."

Anne couldn't sleep until five o'clock in the morning, her gut was churning so much over all the lies and half lies she'd been telling. She tried viewing them from every possible angle, seeking vulnerabilities, gaps, rationalizations, until finally the lies were like a barrel rolling in the water, not a single thought sticking anywhere. At some point she finally drifted off for two hours and dreamed feverishly about job interviews.

When she stepped out of the shower, there were two calls waiting. One was from Aaron, informing her that he and his grandpa were staying an extra night in Oakland. They'd run into some car trouble and were waiting for a piston to be replaced. Nothing to worry about; they were having a fine time, bonding in an intergenerational way.

The other call was from Temo, the Fijian caregiver with the illustrious résumé, and, seeing his name in her palm, her heart leapt. The message was short and mildly garbled, but the mere fact of its existence implied good news: surely his last client was either dead or almost dead and he would soon be available for a new detail. She didn't even get dressed before she called him back and asked if he would meet her for coffee ASAP.

"Of course," he said. His voice was calm and cheerful, lit with a lovely, sun-kissed accent, the voice of a mature, grounded human being. "Next week is quite open for me. And the week after that—"

"No, no, how about now?"

"You mean, this very moment? Today?"

"If possible. Yes."

He chuckled and agreed. He had to be flattered that she was so eager to see him. Two hours later she was sitting at Urth, in Santa Monica, eating a granola parfait with a man from Fiji who might well become her new family.

Fijians, it turned out, were a dark-skinned, sturdy-looking people. At least this one was. She guessed Temo was about fifty-two years old. He had a wide, mature, sad face the color of maple syrup, and his body was thick and strapping but gently curvaceous, his wide chest framed by soft, sloping shoulders. His hands were large and soft and clean. Physically, he was exactly the handler an old, infirm person might need. Powerful yet gentle. Strong yet sensitive. Competent but not cynical. She'd been through a thousand racial-equity seminars and gave annually to the L.A. Anti-racist Alliance, but she was doing her best not to imagine him in a grass skirt.

Personality-wise, Temo seemed right, too. He was straightforward, simple, perhaps unimaginative, but definitely alert. He was not an intellectual, not a wit, but possibly a deep, insightful thinker. Maybe the slightest hint of superiority was in there, too. Maybe a slight hint of theater to his sad eyes as he half smiled, almost pityingly, and refused her offer of coffee. He seemed precise, self-effacing, mildly superior, obviously a good person. Nothing about him caused her any doubt.

They talked about Fiji to start. He still had a wife there, he said, and he had a daughter in Germany, recently married to a private in the U.S. Army. His village was outside Sigatoka, on the southern coast. He loved Fiji very much, and he went back every year, bearing gifts for his relatives and their growing families. He'd built his mother and aunt homes in their village, good homes, strong enough to weather a tsunami. He had a home there himself, and someday he would go back to retire, but not anytime soon.

He'd been in the United States for ten years, he said, and about the question of his citizenship, he was slightly cagey. She did not push the issue. If Deep Throat didn't care about Temo's legal status, she didn't care, either, and it wasn't as if she were running for office or anything. They were all just people here, weren't they? Ben was the only one who might have a problem, and he wasn't around.

"It is a blessing. I am the luckiest man in the world, getting to share this time with my clients and their families."

"That's a wise way of seeing," she said.

"It is how it is."

It was the crucifix that sold her. Normally, she hated seeing crucifixes around people's necks, these stupid, sanctimonious ornaments of someone's private belief. What did God care if you advertised your creed? But on this day, sitting in this fragrant restaurant, surrounded by bearded men peering at laptops, pedicured mom triathletes with their pink smartphones and canvas totes, she was glad for the unfashionable statement of old-time belief. Maybe Temo was one of the good Christians. Maybe he took the Christian service ethos to heart. Maybe he was an honest-to-God lover of his fellow man. For some reason, against all evidence in the history of the world, she found the crucifix to be not a reminder of the Inquisition, as usual, but a signal this man wasn't going to fuck her over.

They parted ways, promising to talk again in the coming few days. They hadn't talked about money yet. The cost of his heart and hands was not going to be cheap. He was contracted on a monthly basis, and he lived in Encino, and his car needed repair. Sundays off for church. She wasn't sure if his fee was negotiable, but she decided not to try talking him down at this moment. They had time for that.

Alone, she finished her parfait, an excellent confection of nutty, house-made granola and creamy, Greek-style yogurt. She refilled her coffee and scrolled through the messages of the past hour, enjoying a rare moment of calm.

With Temo at her dad's side, helping him eat, helping him bathe, making his bed, driving him to the store, she would finally be free to relax and concentrate on all the other chores of life. With Temo in the house, she could get a decent night's sleep. Maybe she could see a movie some night. Maybe she could even go on a date someday. Unthinkable.

She scanned the room, gauging the men as possible paramours. There were at least three that she would entertain. At least three she would allow to ravage her as long as they evaporated into smoke immediately thereafter. If, perchance, something was brewing with Mark, she should get in a few shags before the final threshold was crossed. For practice, if nothing else.

The feeling of great tranquillity and peace lasted approximately ten minutes. She was sliding her phone into her purse, wondering if the rumpled receipts had aged sufficiently to be discarded without a look, when a sudden, curdling intuition of wrongness entered into her heart region, clutching at her innards. The coffee in her mouth suddenly became bitter and strange. The corners of the table sharpened into deadly points. What had she done?

Here's what: She'd just met a man named Temo from Fiji, and, after talking to him for all of about forty minutes, she'd hired him to tend her own father in the final, dying days of his life. She'd subcontracted her most sacred duty in life, barring the raising of her own son, to this . . . this . . . what? Who was this man, Temo? She had no idea. She'd barely understood numerous of his anecdotes, let alone checked out if anything he said was true. Meanwhile, her father, the flesh that had formed her, the fire that had sparked her, was counting his hours left on this earth. She'd decided, almost without deciding, that she would skip out on nursing his body from the world. She'd decided, without truly understanding the consequences, that the man who'd raised her, who'd endured the worst that humanity had ever devised, who deserved a king's death, would die with a stranger.

She couldn't breathe. What kind of person outsourced her own father's death? She stumbled out of the café and down the stairs, holding on tightly to the handrail. The sun hit bleakly on the sidewalk, revealing every spot of oil and gum, every broken straw and bent bottle cap. In a flash, forty-five years of her father's love—precious hours of him swaddling her as a baby, feeding her as a toddler, reading to her in bed, driving her, holding her, sending her to the best schools, not communicating much but never giving any inkling of doubt as to his devotion, his utter, unconditional love—filled her body. He'd given her everything he had, and she'd turned around and hired a ringer. All her father's love burned in her throat, down to her intestines. The great test had come, and she was failing.

She walked past the car, not ready to seal herself into its shell, trying to calm down. Blurry figures passed by. Cars roared. She had arguments. No one would judge her for this. This was simply how society was organized now. The division of labor demanded this kind of transaction.

But since when was society the arbiter of the good? Had we developed so much freedom that we'd become free from responsibility itself? What was this life for, if not this? Who took care of Temo's family?

She kept walking down the boardwalk, the long cement ribbon limning the edge of the continent. The sand was stomped with footprints, and the eye of God was on her. The heat of the sky was burning on her back, a hot hand on the nape of her neck. People traveled past her, forward and back, mumbling private incantations. She felt stuck in the old dreams of early motherhood. All those terrible dreams of misplacing Aaron in a store, losing him in a crowd. The horrible dream logic of looking and looking and never finding. Now the dream feeling had entered the waking life.

She passed the spot where the opening credits of *Three's Company* had been filmed and descended into the dregs of Venice. The path became clogged with mangy hippies selling their pipes and papers, sweat-shellacked roller skaters, homeless children begging for drug money, each person more fried than the last. She walked farther, passing the aerosol paintings of Jim Morrison and Jimi Hendrix, the saints of American hedonism; the T-shirt emporiums, these swamps of bad taste. "The eight stages of tequila . . ." "Where's my bong?" She entered a cloud of patchouli that seemed to cling to the air like tendrils of ivy.

She walked for fully half an hour without spotting a single person she could honestly talk to. The people were all so warped by their failed fantasies. They were future lizard kings, future shamans of rock and roll, nihilist punks, black hustlers, archetypal bums, all of humanity, none as terrible and selfish as she.

At a fish-and-chips shack, she turned and shuffled in the direction of the water, cresting a dune not far from the pier. The swell of sand was like the body of a giant, sleeping pig, she thought, and on the other side gray palms stood like sentinels guarding the tide. Beyond the trees was a gate to the endless expanse of salt water. She walked the plank of the pier toward the severe truth of the horizon.

She stared at the Pacific. Out there, she knew, under the water, the shit of a whole society once flowed. Torrents of warm piss, geysers of cornwater, chugging from some giant pipe into the briny depths. Through the clouds of waste swam sharks, octopi, jellyfish, lampreys, blind skates, bottom feeders of unimaginable shape and girth. Out there, under the thin glaze of silver light, everything she could see, an ocean of shit.

20

Colonel Owen was not a war fighter. He may have been many other things—a creature of great beauty and dignity, the maintainer of closely cropped, ghost-gray hair, the owner of an astonishing, angular jaw and a fatless waist, the wearer of a pressed, fitted uniform—but he was not a war fighter.

He was a paper pusher, and in that, in a sense, he was a fighter. He was a fighter of the one, true, never-ending war within the armed forces—namely, the war for bureaucratic supremacy amid the executive class. Like many of the executive soldiers of his ilk, he'd pitched in during a few battles in Grenada or something, maybe sprayed a wall with bullets in Somalia, tagged along on a patrol or two in Sarejevo, and had then proceeded to spend the remainder of his career ensconced in the head shed, outflanking commission reports, strafing his competitors for promotions, capturing the affections of generals' wives. The mission before him this morning was exactly within his skill set: the writing of an eloquent and ambiguously incendiary memo.

The forensic report presented to Colonel Owen in the presence of Ben was a tantalizing document, surely a puzzle worthy of many meetings and memoranda, maybe even the raw material for a whole suite of memos. Colonel Owen seemed to have a nearly sexual attraction to the report. And Ben had to admit, he was impressed by some of the deductions the report writers had made, though mostly just relieved that certain crucial elements of his activities had been plainly misunderstood. The investigators had discovered his shooting perch, of course—that was a simple line to draw—and they'd figured out his opossum trick, too. The pit had been uncovered merely hours after he'd fled, purged of forensic evidence, just as he'd intended. They'd also found his boat, which they understood to be a ruse.

But they'd also gotten some things wrong. They'd assumed the shooter was assisted by a getaway driver, for instance, unable to believe he could have crept out of their cordon on foot. They speculated he'd had a spotter, too, which made the search potentially for three people, a conspiracy. He was also pleased to learn that his shot had been as clean as he'd suspected. The news reports had been vague on that matter. But sure enough, the bullet had entered Holmes's temple and deposited his brain on the geraniums as gently as a teacup onto a china saucer.

The meeting in Colonel Owen's office, a plain corner room overlooking the Potomac, went on for two hours, with many interesting twists and turns. The initial presentation of the forensic information went quickly, after which much of the time was spent developing a psychological profile of the possible perpetrator or perpetrators in question, which was fun. It was almost like being a guest at your own funeral, your own autopsy, exactly the kind of conversation a person was never privy to in waking life. Ben listened with fascination, too pleased to appear deferential among the brass.

"The perp is obviously frustrated," said Colonel Owen, showing his leather soles on his desktop, "angry with his own lack of recognition in the larger world. Old story: He comes out of the services, and he can't integrate back into daily life, can't get those warm fuzzies he's used to. No one knows what he did over there. No one knows what he's capable of. His self-perception and his recognition in the world are not syncing up anymore." The colonel's tapered fingers clasped one another in an elegant braid and, as elegantly, unbraided. "He doesn't think the world is listening to him. He cracks. It's classic PTSD. A bid for attention, even the bad kind."

"He's not stupid," said the HUMINT guy, Jerry. He was a pumpkin-headed Indian data whiz, unimpressed by the guess-work thus far. "Fairly literate. The letter was coherent, grammatical."

"Assuming he wrote it."

"You think he didn't write it?" Ben said. "Who else would?"

"A friend. Or maybe it's plagiarized."

This suggestion offended Ben—how could the perpetrator, i.e., he, have plagiarized something so obviously tailored to the mission at hand? Not to mention the self-evident originality of the letter's whole slant. But he didn't have time to make his case. The next suggestion offended him even more:

"It's not plagiarized," said the SIGINT guy, a featureless twenty-something with wire-rim glasses, too young even to have built a face. "If it was plagiarized, it'd be a lot better written."

"What do you mean, 'better written'?" Ben said. "The letter is good. It gets right to the point. The argument is clearly stated. The demands are plain. It's written for a general audience. What else would you want in that kind of letter?"

"It's functional, sure," said the SIGINT guy. "But it's also demented and illogical. That's a big handicap."

"Illogical?" Ben said. Now he was getting pissed. "How is it illogical? Seems pretty straightforward to me."

"The guy is obviously totally warped by his raging martyr complex. He blames the world for his own pathetic delusions of persecution."

"Blames the world for his own pin dick," chimed in the HUMINT guy.

"Let's just say he's no scholar—put it that way," Colonel Owen said, trying to rechannel the conversation back into more productive directions. "But he is a thorough, detail-oriented, foresightful risk taker. We can agree on that."

"He knows how to shoot a guy in the dark," agreed HUMINT.

"I found the letter provocative," Ben said. "I can't say I've ever seen that exact argument made in the public sphere before. It took synthesis. That's critical thought." Ben could see he wasn't going to win anyone over with his literary criticism. But if nothing else, his opinions further muddied the waters as to the perp's identity, so he could rationalize sharing them.

"A SEAL, possibly," said Colonel Owen, moving on.

"Maybe a Ranger," said SIGINT.

"A Green Beret," Ben added, expanding the pool. "The skill set this guy shows is not unique to the SEALs or the Rangers. Assuming it was one guy. I'm still interested in the idea of a trio."

"I think the letter says SEAL all over it," said HUMINT. "The whole operation says SEAL to me."

"Why's that?" Ben asked, offended anew. The motivation for this mission had nothing to do with his SEAL training. If anything, it cut directly against the SEAL mentality. He hadn't learned how to think for himself in the goddamn SEALs. He'd learned how to jump out of an airplane and how to slit a man's throat, but he hadn't learned to think. He'd learned all his thinking on his own.

HUMINT had a point, however: "Only a SEAL would be this full of himself."

Ben exited the debriefing room in a state of smoldering pique, but also exhilaration, and in possession of a hard file of classified data, his homework for the week. At the next meeting, everyone would come bearing plausible theories based on closer scrutiny of the forensic information, ready to formulate the best, most penetrating, most richly imagined memo the Joint Chiefs had ever seen.

There were still hours left in the day, so Ben took a jog along the mall, trotting past the brooding Lincoln Monument, the occult Vietnam Memorial, and toward the penile Washington Monument. He circled the base twice and headed west, until his run ended at a statue of Albert Einstein a few blocks down the mall. Now here was a true hero, he thought. A scientist and a humanist, a man of genius and tolerance. Perhaps the most beloved Jew of the last century, barring Bob Dylan.

It was standing there with Albert Einstein that Ben conceived his second mission. The meeting with Colonel Owen had been undeniably thought provoking, and he'd come away happily undiscovered as the perp in question, but the conversation had also confirmed his suspicions about the first mission's ultimate failure. It was now painfully obvious that his message had been misunderstood. It had been too subtle, he saw, too tightly focused. He'd overestimated the power of a singular statement to impress meaning on the oligarchy's consciousness, let alone the citizenry's. The news cycle had shredded the statement's significance almost before it had emerged, and the whole event had been treated as an isolated crime as opposed to an indictment of society—not that it mattered, anyway, because it had been lost so quickly in the morass of competing information, buried in all the subsequent mudslides of data. How had he ever thought that a single mission would alter the nation's destiny?

Leaning on Einstein's knee, he could see it was going to be necessary to establish a larger pattern if he wanted to convey his whole meaning. A compelling story demanded multiple plot points, a gripping motion of action and suspense. This was just remedial rhetoric. He was going to have to carry the lesson through a series of examples. Only then would he seize the zeitgeist in the way he desired and inspire his fellow patriots to rise up.

Back at his hotel he logged on to the Web, and within five clicks he had the next mission in hand. The target this time would be none other than Shane Larson himself, reviled host of *The Shane Larson Show,* whose daily remarks reached some 3.4 million citizens of the United States. Among all the celebrated politicians and culture heroes of the world, Ben thought, Larson would serve as a true wake-up call to the sleeping potato people of the nation. His death would shock them and jump-start the corroded critical faculties of his once-determined people. Shane Larson, grandson of Goebbels, the voice of the very industrial communication technology that had created fascism itself.

Another two clicks, and Ben knew how the Mission would go down. Two weeks hence, Larson would be making his annual pilgrimage to the Bob Hope Invitational, a golf tournament in Palm Springs and a veritable magnet for bloated media icons of all color and stripe. The tournament would occur on the Indian Canyons Golf Resort, a renowned course at the base of the San Jacinto Mountains. The weekend's schedule was posted on the invitational's site, with the entire celebrity guest list emblazoned in a banner at the top, and a convenient map of the links and their relation to Palm Springs' downtown core.

Toggling through the site, Ben felt as if the world was speaking to him, sending him clear signals. He was touching the deep energies of the universe, whispering directly to the dark matter itself. The idea of terminating Shane Larson on a golf course was obscurely thrilling. The long sight lines of the fairways would prove excellent for shooting, and the crowds could well work in his favor. He wouldn't hide in a hole this time. Instead, he'd hide in the jungle of humanity, blending into the docile herd itself. And then there was the symbolic register. A golf course named Indian Canyons. That said it all, didn't it? In this, he was taking a lesson from bin Laden himself, the great genius of modern mass communication. Say what you would about his craven attack on the World Trade Center; the event stood as one of the most effective spectacles of the young century. Against the society of spectacle, he had cast a flaming spectacle. Against the Great Satan of images, he had flung an indelible image. In turning the Twin Towers into pillars of flame, bin Laden had waged his ancient Muslim iconoclasm using the very tools of the modern Occidental icon. His fundamentalist mind had conceived and directed the ultimate episode of *Jackass*.

Drinking beer in the hotel bar, Ben contemplated his new mission until it became a certainty. The first mission had laid the groundwork. The second would deliver the true apostate message. Let the world contemplate the violence upholding the golf course. Let the world contemplate these green oil slicks expanding over the West. Let the world contemplate the true meaning of this leisure as Larson bled out in the rough.

He flew back to California and drove directly to Palm Springs, arriving in the punishing heat of midafternoon. The week of meetings with Colonel Owen had gone much as expected, generating almost nothing in the way of usable information but much in the way of "areas for further discussion," many of which were currently heading up the line of Command for review. It was obvious nothing was going to happen on that front for months, and, as none of the current arrows of suspicion pointed remotely in the direction of Ben, the time seemed ripe for his next action.

Just west of town, at the base of the San Jacinto Mountains, he located the entrance of the Indian Canyons golf course and took the measure of the fence line in the hard desert light. He stared at the shadowless grass and the receding fan palms and the low, modern clubhouse shimmering like a mirage in the distance. He kept on moving and parked at the end of a cul-de-sac near the eighth hole, where trailheads led into the nude, brown mountains overlooking the course. Hiking the blazing earth, taking the heat like a shower, he thought about the hallowed golfers of yesteryear. Bob Hope, Dwight Eisenhower, and Jack Benny had golfed here. Walt Disney was an Indian Canyons golfer, too. He'd owned an estate along the second hole, and the grotesque fountain on the eighteenth hole, a blue lotus flower, had been his gift. And from these thoughts Ben moved on to thoughts about the Cahuilla Indians, the original denizens and namesake of these canyons. They'd grown melons, squash, beans, and corn in this earth. They'd walked this land, breathing this clean air, before the putter and the iron had ever been imagined by man.

Walking on the dry earth, he could feel the spirit of the Indians inside him.

The day was still too bright for trespassing, so Ben hiked deeper into the desert instead. He climbed the canyon walls and crossed into God's country, the stark rock-and-sand wilderness stretching to Utah. As usual, he didn't see God, but he might have felt His hand on the back of his head, keeping his eyes off His face. Yes, Ben could feel the hand of God on his skull even now. He could feel God, as always, behind him, out of sight.

He mounted a ridge and arrived at a perch overlooking an arid playa. Cloud shadows glided below, glowing gray on the white earth. Sunlight speckled his arms and neck. The clouds changed and then changed again, casting new shapes on the white bed. He breathed the desert air deeply into his lungs, taking in the smell of nothingness itself—nothingness tinted with fine sand, baked rock, and sage. He breathed again, drawing particles of desert-clean oxygen into the tiniest branches of his capillaries. The scent of Afghanistan, Iraq, Kuwait, every God-blighted desert on every continent of the world. It was the smell of a perfumed abyss.

He remembered Kuwait. He'd seen his first desert sandstorm in Kuwait—this vast, orange-brown cloud approaching over the emptiness. He'd watched it billow and grow, getting wider and darker, until finally it had engulfed him, sending him into a torrential blackness like he'd never known. It was like a mine shaft collapsing over and over again, a furious vortex of sand and blackness. Fine grit swarming into his hair and his ears, scraping on the panes of his goggles. The memory of the sandstorm blurred into other desert memories. His asbestos gloves on the hot barrel of his M60, the Pig. The donkey-dick radio antennae on the desert patrol vehicle. The woman with the yellow Chinese grenade on the street of Nasiriyah, destroyed by his .300 Win Mag.

The desert before him was like a movie screen, bouncing his own thoughts back at him. He watched two shit-head civilians driving their car into the middle of the firefight in Ramadi, those stupid, stupid fucks, ignoring his flash grenades, not even noticing the mangled bodies on the ground, until finally one of them took a bullet in the knee, and they'd managed to limp away, bleeding but alive, into the alley. How lucky could two assholes get? Much as he tried to slow his thoughts by watching the clouds on the desert floor, their pulsing, shifting grace, he couldn't get there. That was the speed at which his mind should go, he thought, the speed of a cloud. The speed of God's breath over the land. If only he could get his mind to slow down, he thought, he might still be all right.

Night came, and he returned to the golf course. He parked a mile away and walked through the cold desert air under the moonless sky.

He climbed the low fence and stalked the fairways with the infrared goggles he'd bought that afternoon at the army surplus store. The goggles attached to a helmet and allowed him to walk with his hands free, casting a beam of visibility into the darkness from his face. The greens were moist and springy from their twilight watering, and the smell of cool, mineral earth mixed with the smell of desert rock. The green luminosity of the goggles made the manicured landscape look like a fairy playland—the glowing green palm trees, glowing green grass, glowing green golf carts parked in sleeping rows. The whole world overflowed with a fuzzy life force, green energy bursting from its starlit skin.

The moon was on the horizon. A tiny sliver. He goggled the moon, and the moon turned green in his lenses. Was there life and heat out there in the cosmos? He believed so, yes.

He prowled to the fourteenth hole, the fifteenth, scanning the landscape for clean shooting lanes, catching sight of the giant white whale of the hospitality tent already erected near the clubhouse patio. In that giant tent Shane Larson would soon be mingling with his fellow plutocrats. They'd all crowd inside and eat their seared tuna and drink their pinot gris and smoke their cigars as the descending pyramid of adjuncts and toadies thumbed their phones on the sidelines. From thousands of miles away, shrimp and avocado would be delivered in refrigerated trucks. From every corner of the world, useless women would be assembled to talk about their children's yoga practice. And when the party was over, the tent would be rolled up and shipped to the next celebration of nothing.

Ben stared at the tent, sick to death of his argument with America. His mind was like a broken record on the subject, the needle turning in the rutted grooves, causing him physical pain. It was like a tattoo in his brain. Over and over, the same lines. This land had been a land of bison and beaver, and now it was a land of *Angry Birds* and vape shops. This land had been a land of Crazy Horse and Mark Twain. Now who? He'd thought these thoughts so many times over the years, releasing the same toxin of hatred into his blood, that the thoughts almost seemed to think themselves. Once again, he realized he was composing his open letter to America, laying out his branches of logic, polishing his dagger clauses. To know that his repeating thoughts had some eventual outlet and would someday find shape and audience gave some solace. The killing of Shane Larson was only a crucial means to his artistic ends.

He was taking a piss in the rough near the seventeenth hole when he spotted five teenage boys scuttling over the fairway. They moved in a hunched lope, trying and failing to cross the golf course without being seen. He watched them going from cover to cover, sometimes rolling into positions as if they were on some covert op. He stood against the tree trunk and observed them with his blazing night ray. They were terrible creepers, to a man, too drunk and stoned to walk straight, let alone execute a mission, not to mention they were pushing a wheelbarrow with a scronking, rusty wheel.

He watched the boys stumble up the slope of the eighteenth hole and skirt the weedy pond, making their way toward the billowing, white hospitality tent. He'd avoided the tent, not wanting to get too close, but listened as the boys clanked around inside the fabric walls. When the boys emerged he understood what all the grunting and clanking had been about: in their wheelbarrow they now carted a gleaming, silver keg.

He watched the boys come and go from the tent two more times, aglow in the infrared lenses, spilling their life energy onto the grass. They looted the tent of two kegs, ten cases of imported beer, numerous bottles of gin and vodka, some mixers, some snacks, and many promotional golf balls. Throughout the robbery, they could barely stop laughing, they were so shit-faced. And Ben had to laugh along with them from his hideout near the rushes. What buffoons. What funny, devious boys. What good, solid, all-American kids.

21

They arrived in L.A. by dusk, under a melting sherbet sky, and Aaron helped his grandfather into his house and turned on the heat. He cooked the chicken breasts they'd bought at the store, plated them with unsalted green beans. He ate with him and waited while he changed into clean sweatpants and took his place in the leather recliner.

The silence of his grandfather's house was usually very simple in its tedium. Aaron was well accustomed to the long minutes of no talking, the hours of dull nothingness. But on this day, after driving home on I-5 empty-handed and humiliated, crushed on either side by the expanses of the central Valley, the silence seemed somehow shameful, an unbroken note of remorse and self-reproach.

"Should I turn off the heat?" Aaron asked.

"Whatever you want."

"Still hungry?"

"I'm fine, sweetheart. Don't worry."

In the last days of their Oakland trip, exactly nothing worthwhile had happened. The police hadn't returned their calls, and the newspaper had carried a single item, a novelty paragraph in the crime pages, not as though anyone read the newspaper, anyway. As the hours in the hotel had crawled along, they'd almost been able to feel the gold dispersing out into the world, getting pawned for video-game consoles or zirconium necklaces, exchanged for stereos and guitar amps, transformed into meth and Molly, never to return.

Aaron had made one more trip to the Bagel Café, hoping to trade a few words with the employees in private. He'd cornered one of the Mexican dishwashers, a hulking man with a hair net over his face like a funeral veil, but the language barrier had been too steep. The guy had no idea what Aaron wanted, and, sadly, neither exactly did Aaron. He'd talked to the other waitresses, but they were generally cold, protecting their friend. If they knew anything, they'd pledged to keep quiet about it. He'd even talked to Kari herself, the culprit, invading her space as long as he could bear and trying to wheedle any kind of information out of her, whether indicting or exonerating, he didn't care.

"Look, someone stole his gold," he said. "I'm not saying it was you. But if you have any ideas, I just want to know what they might be . . ."

Kari walked the tables before opening, collecting half-empty ketchup bottles and carrying them to the counter for refilling. "Get out of here," she said. "If I knew anything, I would've told the cops, all right?"

"Maybe there's something you're forgetting," Aaron said. He watched her closely for any signs of deceit, not that he was sure what those signs would be. Shifty eyes? Nervous tics? The sudden dampening of her armpits? "If you could just talk it through with me, maybe you'd remember. Where were you when it happened? What did you see?"

"I didn't see shit."

He left in disgust. If she was too ignorant, or uncaring, or worse, to comprehend his family's tragic story, he couldn't get through to her. He and his grandpa had spent another day watching TV, fielding worried calls and texts from his mom, before giving up and driving home. And now here they were, puttering in the same, silent, miserable, defeated house. He'd never thought he'd miss the old, merely uncomfortable silence, but he'd trade it for this grievous silence, swimming with anger and regrets, any day.

"I just can't fucking believe it, you know?" Aaron said without any prompting, while his grandpa went through the junk mail. "What the fuck is wrong with people, Grandpa? Shit."

"It doesn't matter," his grandpa said. "Truly, it doesn't."

"It does matter, though," Aaron said. "It matters. A lot."

"It's only money, sweetheart. Once it's gone, it's gone."

"It's a lot more than that."

His grandfather didn't reply. He was beyond caring, as he had been almost from the start. After the first night he'd given up and stayed in Dublin only because of Aaron's wishful thinking. He just sat in his chair and looked through the envelopes, settling back into his familiar home life. But Aaron didn't want to leave the subject of their trip undiscussed. He wanted his grandfather to know how deeply he was in this with him. He wanted him to understand that all the shame and disappointment he might be feeling was also Aaron's shame and disappointment. But it wasn't easy to express anything like that in words.

"I know it's only money," Aaron said. "But that's really fucked, too, don't you think? Why do people need the money that badly? Why is that how everything is organized? Money.

And some people don't have it. I don't even blame the people who took it, exactly. Whoever took it, I don't know, maybe they needed it. I blame everything. Life is just fucked."

His grandfather continued looking through the envelopes that had stacked up in his absence. There were coupons, fundraising pleas from Greenpeace and B'nai B'rith, and mostly yellow and green and white envelopes from credit card companies and insurance conglomerates, fishing for the octogenarian suckers of the world. Grandpa Sam piled his envelopes into a neat stack on the end table, refusing to throw them in the garbage, where they belonged, and as he shuffled for the bathroom, he mumbled something in Aaron's general direction. Aaron asked him to say it again, and he spoke up a little louder.

"Life is good," he said. "That's all I know, honey. Life is good. It's good to remember."

For once, Aaron was the one who said nothing. How did one respond to a platitude like that? The words just hung there, inert. "Life is good." He'd seen the movie with that Italian actor, Benigni. Or "Life is sweet"? "Beautiful"? Whatever.

He watched his grandpa hobble unsteadily to the bathroom, carefully setting his envelopes on his bureau for later review. Grandpa Sam didn't know much, Aaron thought. He was pretty ignorant of the whole modern society that surrounded him, technologically illiterate. He told terrible jokes to waitresses in diners, and he was politically out of whack, a one-issue Zionist. But on this topic, maybe he possessed an unassailable authority. On this one, gigantic, all-encompassing topic, he might be irrefutably wise. If he said life was good, then it was true, life was good. Aaron was willing to

take it as the only undeniably true thing his grandfather had
ever told him.

He drove home and found his mom sitting in the living room,
staring at her computer screen. She closed the shell as he
stepped inside and got up to hug him, smothering him with
her smiling, grateful, unconditional attention.

"You're home!" she said. "How was it? Tell me everything! I
want to hear all about the trip."

"It was okay," Aaron said, enduring her hug with his
backpack still strapped to his shoulder. He'd been hoping to
avoid a lengthy debriefing. The familiar smell and temperature
of his house was already causing him itchiness to leave.

"What happened?" she asked, sitting on the couch with an
expectant look in her eyes. "You guys have been gone for days.
I'm so curious."

"Oh, I don't know," Aaron said. "We just, like, you know,
drove up there and came back." He didn't even know where to
start.

"Did you get a flat tire or something? Is that what you said?
Something must've happened."

"Yeah, I guess. I mean, not really."

"Did you see his old house?"

"No. We mostly just sat in the hotel. Watched TV."

"Did you . . . talk?"

"A little."

"Well, that's good, I guess. Hey, what happened to your lips?"

"Nothing!"

She looked hurt by his anger, but he didn't know what to do
about that. It wasn't his job to satisfy her every emotional need.

He stalked to the kitchen and made himself a peanut-butter-and-honey sandwich that he carried directly to his room, and he shut the door.

Lying on his bed, he wondered why the mere idea of sharing his thoughts with his mother seemed so repellent to him. He wasn't afraid of her judgment. He didn't think that she'd punish him or think less of him for anything he might say. If anything, it was exactly the opposite of that. He was afraid she'd love everything he told her so much, she'd never let him stop. She would drink it up so thirstily, he'd be stuck feeding her the rest of his life.

So instead of saying anything, he listened to the Velvet Underground, cranking his speakers so that the room filled with the throbbing drone. He lay there on the bed, communing with the guitars, the arrogant, incantatory vocals, and lost himself in the glittering dust motes near his head.

He stayed home only a few hours before going out again, this time to meet Joel at a diner in Chinatown. At last, given the chance to recount the whole adventure to an interested third party, he blossomed into a storyteller, and he was pleased by the loyal amazement his friend displayed in return. Joel seemed intuitively to understand all the sickening ironies of the Oakland experience, all the depths of evidence about how fucked up the world truly was. He was an expert in the nuances of the absurd.

"It is unreal, dude," Joel said, grinning. "Out of control! Gold."

"No shit, right?" Aaron said. His Budweiser was almost gone, and he wasn't sure whether to try his luck ordering another. He didn't want to push it with his flimsy fake ID. He'd already told Joel everything, from the factory farm to the fight in Kari's front yard, leaving out no detail except for the part about jacking off in the bathroom at that crucial moment. That passage had been revised into a very long shit on his part.

"I can't believe it," Joel said. "The widow . . ."

"I know."

"And, most of all, I can't believe your grandpa wanted to listen to Steppenwolf."

"That was very possibly the most terrifying part."

They talked it all through again, the fight with Scott, the red wave of rage that had crashed over him. And, as usual with Joel, the talk eventually turned to Mexico and their coming trip. How incredibly pathetic was it, he wanted to know, that no one besides them seemed to have even the slightest desire to go down there and see the true country for themselves? He wasn't talking about Cancún or TJ, but the real pueblos of the nation's heartland. Considering how utterly dependent Americans were on the people and culture of Mexico—not just on the guys who came up looking for jobs, but on the whole families and extended families and communities they left behind—everyone in America should be mandated to drive around down there and pay homage. Joel topped off his revolution talk by revealing he'd found another van for sale. They should go look at it soon, before someone else beat them to the punch.

Aaron said okay in his usual tone of near commitment, still unsure what he wanted to do. He definitely didn't want to mention that he had a plan with Karl in a few weeks to see a sun dance on a mesa in Indio. It was going to be a very special performance, Karl claimed, a true urban tribal sun dance ritual, complete with a guy impaling his nipples with hooks and attaching himself to a tree and dancing his way outward until the rings broke through his flesh. The invitation had arrived through Karl's friend Monica, and the gathered crowd would be among the royalty of L.A.'s underground, the very community of fascinating personages that would swirl around the sunporch on a nightly basis. Karl was working on scoring them peyote for the soiree.

Aaron parted with Joel and drove back home, still not ready to go inside the house. Instead, he walked around the neighborhood, peering in windows, thinking. Nothing about the future had gotten any clearer since Oakland. He was still the same mealy, indecisive, superficial person he'd been a week ago.

A part of him wished his dad were still at home. He wished he could walk into the living room and find Barry lying there on the couch with his rum and Coke on his stomach, ready to lay down his abstract wisdom. Not that he couldn't predict what Barry would say in this particular situation—i.e., nothing helpful whatsoever. "This is the kind of decision a guy has to figure out for himself, right? You don't really want anyone else making your big decisions for you, do you?" Then he'd flip sides on his Captain Beefheart record and pour himself another drink. But still, it would have been nice to hear it from his dad in person.

When he reached the 7-Eleven, he figured he'd turn around and start back to his darkened house. He wandered past the empty park again, the sleeping fire station, these streets he'd walked almost every day of his life, and wondered if they all led to the same place in the end. To a land of enchantment or a land of righteousness, or some incredible combination thereof.

To a land of bitterness and desperation. They might lead to some country he'd never heard of before, some island he could never chart. They all led toward something called manhood, whatever that meant. He could feel it out there, just around the bend, and fuck if he knew what kind of man he wanted to be.

22

Mark gave great PowerPoint. He was a master of the technology, in complete command of the moving boxes, darting arrows, cascading bullet points, and subdividing frames within frames, at all times ready with a steady patter of anecdotes and jokes sprung from the graphical interface. He delivered his rap on the glories of cavitation with great ease and transparent organization. But at the same time, he was not too slick or too practiced in his talking, not full of obvious bullshit. He didn't use the empty jargon of the faker.

His audience, admiring his skill, rewarded him with its rapt attention. They laughed at all the appropriate moments, scribbled notes during the information-rich passages. It wasn't an easy crowd, either. Seated around the conference table in this plush, flickering cave in the upper aeries of city hall were Charlie Arnold, commissioner of Sanitation, Randy Lowell, senior city councilman, and the mayor's chief of staff, Bill Bailey, whose authority in the mayor's office was unquestioned. Each was a king of his own fiefdom, and each was ensconced in his own executive throne, equipped with a perfect-bound book filled with four-color infographics as a take-away prize— the Document. Simply getting these men in the same room at the same time had been a superhuman feat of scheduling, and the idea of pleasing them all en masse was a feat of nearly impossible charisma. A labor for a modern-day Hercules. But here was Mark, modern Hercules, pleasing them all.

"The water wars are not a question of if, but when," he said, images of postapocalyptic armies limping through desert landscapes flashing behind him. *Road Warrior,* with Mel Gibson wreathed in smoke from oil fires on the horizon; *Waterworld,* with Kevin Costner drinking his own urine on his catamaran; *Dune,* with Kyle MacLachlan riding the sandworm.

"I like that guy," Mark said, and paused to point out a screaming, flailing figure deep in the background of a *Soylent Green* still. He seemed to be doing the splits. "James Brown, seventies apocalypse version."

He paused for an appreciative burble of laughter from the paladins and continued, asserting that humanity was on the cusp of a global war over the one truly precious substance on earth, the substance of life itself, and that it was a war that would make the wars over the other stuff—gold, land, and oil— look quaint in comparison. He alluded to a few of the crazy water-hoarding schemes of the past, like shipping blocks of ice from the Arctic to the Arabian Peninsula, or damming giant rivers until their flows were reversed, to illustrate the postulate that the winners of the water wars would be those states and municipalities that had started planning for the crisis thirty years ago, while those communities that were just figuring out the stakes were basically already fucked.

The homework had been well done, if Anne did say so herself. The audience didn't seem to notice the scarf work, the sleight of hand. They had no idea the boxes flashing on the screen were in fact empty boxes, the diagrams mere fiction.

Around the conference table they stared at Mark and his screen, grinning like idiots.

"Hydrodynamic cavitation probably sounds like another crazy scheme, I'm sure. What is cavitation? Cavitation refers to the formation and immediate implosion of small cavities in a liquid. These liquid-free pockets are also known, more commonly, as bubbles. So cavitation refers to the making and collapsing of bubbles to create shock waves of energy that can be harnessed in any number of ways. There are applications for wastewater purification and also for alternative energy production. We've been making some enormous leaps lately. Quantum leaps."

Now Mark was entering the most treacherous passage, exiting the soft, irrefutable social-theorizing section and traveling into the unforgiving plains of hard science. He moved lightly through the minefield, talking briefly about orifices and venturi, inertial and noninertial reference frames, and disambiguation, delivering pithy, impressionistic explanations of the tangled equations that materialized and disintegrated on the screen. And then, soon enough, he was out of the desert and back onto gentler terrain, talking abstractly again, if not poetically, about the promise of the future, the challenge of sloughing off humankind's historical aversion to reused water, the imperative of evolving into the next golden chapter of civilization.

The pale light of the screen shifted on the dark walls. The men's faces were unreadable. Anne's skin prickled with heat. The lie was fully in blossom now, unfurling its dark petals. And Mark muscled through toward the end, subliminally pitching his talk in the direction of the city councilman, Randy. He knew Charlie had already been bought. He was getting his sustainability czar. He knew the mayor would accept his subordinate's judgment. He loved the secrecy as much as the promise. The one who needed convincing was the bulldog, Randy Lowell.

"This is next-level technology," Mark said. "Not only will the hydrodynamic cavitation reactor create an incredible new surplus of usable water for the city; it will also create hundreds, if not thousands, of family-wage jobs. The implementation of BHC's project, when it comes—and it will come soon; it's only a matter of some final confirming experiments—will place the City of Los Angeles at the forefront of a new wave of green technology."

His next bullet point materialized on screen, a dollar sign.

"The revenue we predict the program will generate is somewhere in the region of five hundred million dollars a year. The city shares in that revenue at a level commensurate with its investment. This amounts to a lot of discretionary funding for schools, roads, whatever the city leadership chooses.

"And this is the killer thing," he said, summoning his final bullet point and staring directly at Randy Lowell's shadowy chair. "This city won't ever need to worry about federal clean-water standards again."

He paused to let this magical nugget of information dapple in the light.

"Think about that," he went on. "Los Angeles will step off of the regulatory grid. BHC Industries will become the sole customer for the city's wastewater, and that means the city's wastewater will no longer be flowing into the public ecosystem. It will be delivered into the possession of a third party, and that third party will have the pleasure of interfacing with the EPA, the Fish and Wildlife Service, the IRS, all of it. We'll be responsible for diverting the water, cleaning the water, sending the water back through the system, and we will be responsible for making sure the water conforms to federal standards. The dirtier the water we get from the city, the better—we don't care. We can handle it. Los Angeles gets to walk away from the Washington table. Say bye-bye to the feds. Bye-bye, regulators. Bye-bye, lawyers. Bye-bye, everyone."

This bullet point entered the brain of Randy Lowell and exploded its magical contents. He became a little kitten in the hands of Mark Harris.

The questions following the presentation gave the impression of some toughness but were in fact anything but tough. "How soon will the reactor be ready to go online?" "What kind of tax incentives would BHC Industries need to commence building its facilities?" "What are the chances of a Nobel Prize?" The barb was plunged deep in their cheeks. It was so easy, especially with his beautiful assistant standing there with him the whole time, a lovely, sequined distraction. Anne might as well be doing a pole dance for these fuckers. Every ounce of trust she had ever built in her career was tossed on the floor. Here she was, pasties shining, spinning her tassels.

"Amazing stuff, Mark," said Charlie. "We'll start circulating the paperwork ASAP."

"Mind-blowing," said the mayor's man. "A real honor. Thank you for bringing this to us."

"You hit it out of the ballpark," Randy said. "We'll talk and get back to you very soon."

Anne saw no way of avoiding the grotesquely expensive celebratory dinner with Mark afterward. They ate deviled quail eggs with smoked salmon, pan-roasted flatiron steaks with hazelnut *romanesco,* and sat under geometric paper-and-wire lampshades in view of a vertical garden of succulents. Anne tried her best to enjoy the incredible meal, but the food was like clay in her mouth. She had to fight the impulse to vomit, or bolt, or hurl insults at Mark. But she forced the glorious food and wine down. She'd done all the sinning. There was no point in forgoing the reward.

Mark was seemingly not tormented by the day's charade at all. He'd come around to her devilish plans and saw no reason to look back now. If anything, he seemed to relish his meal with extra gusto, scarfing it down like a teenager. Afterward he ordered a ludicrously expensive shot of scotch, like a simmering fire of peat and honey captured in thick cut glass, which he sat caressing, marveling at the day's success.

"I don't want to be counting any chickens or anything," he said, sated, "but, fucking A, Anne, that was good today. Those guys are fucking pysched. Am I right?"

"Everything can still fall apart, believe me."

"Ha. I like your attitude. Negative, all the way down the line. Life is full of pleasant surprises that way, isn't it? Stay negative, and the worst almost never comes."

"Or at least you get a lot of confirmation."

Mark rolled his scotch in his palms, chuckling in the back of his throat. "But just for the hell of it," he said, "let's pretend for a second that the best happens. Pretend all the paperwork goes through. Pretend we just slayed the dragon. What do you think happens next? What's the encore?"

"You tell me."

He sipped his amber fire, letting the heat infuse his skin. "I'm thinking we have a window open here," he mused. "There are literally hundreds of other wastewater properties out there that we could probably acquire if we moved fast enough. This is the time. We've got this gap between signing the contract with the city and"—he searched for the proper euphemism here—"shedding the obligations of the contract. In this little window we have a magic amulet in our hands. We've set a precedent. If we move fast enough, we could potentially consolidate a much bigger pool of rights than just L.A."

"It would cost you a lot."

"More money to make in the long run. I consider it an investment in the future. If the pool gets big enough, the returns could jump in scale. Think about it. If we had Phoenix, San Antonio, Houston. Think about the Ogallala Aquifer. That's the water supply for the whole breadbasket of America, and it's about to bottom out. The middle of the country is a hollow shell. They need to start reusing. If we can consolidate all the rights west of the Mississippi, we have something. We can start on statewide acquisitions. Deal with governors' offices. It would mean scaling up and moving fast, though."

"Lords of the American Shit Water."

"We'd be sitting on the biggest wastewater reserves in the world. Think about it, Anne Singer."

"Maybe you just need a trip to Vegas. Get this out of your system."

"Anyone can spin a roulette wheel. That's for chumps. This is the real shit here, Anne. We're making a bet on reality itself. I feel this one down in my balls."

"That's how you read the future? With your genitals?"

"I like the future in my hands, baby, that's right." He mimed cupping a giant pair of nuts, rubbing them in his face. "Hell yeah, that feels good. Oh yeah. The future. Right here. Time is my bitch."

At other moments, Anne would have laughed, but in this case she only rolled her eyes. "God."

"All I'm saying," he said, cutting the theatrics, "is this might be the moment for you to consider joining the private sector, Anne. I like how we're working together. This all wouldn't be happening if it weren't for you. I can see it'd be a little awkward, I guess; you'd have to answer some questions from Susan. But who cares, right? What's she going to do? I think you need to quit this city gig and push on BHC full-time. This is happening."

"I don't have any connections outside Los Angeles," Anne said. "You've pretty much tapped me for what I'm worth."

"Don't sell yourself short, Anne." Mark was refulgent with his scotch in hand, ready to bequeath pardons and favors. Or was this his form of a proposition? "It's not just what you bring to the deal; it's what you make of it. I've seen how you operate. You set up all these introductions, but you also helped create the presentation. You already did the work. You deserve it. It's your due. Think about it. But think fast."

Anne stared at the remains of the steak on her plate, the smears of grease and fat among the demolished leeks. She told Mark she would think about it, not even knowing what the "it" really was.

Driving home, she felt queasy. It wasn't the food, though the dessert of elderflower crème brûlée didn't help matters. Rather, it was the feeling of some terrible judgment coming due, of storm clouds gathering on the horizon, pregnant with lightning. She wasn't sure exactly how her fate was darkening, but she could sense the violent weather ahead.

She got home, and Aaron was out, per usual. The next afternoon, he appeared for a span of hours, finally. He still wouldn't say anything about his trip to Oakland, or about anything else, for that matter. He was so evasive and lethargic, she had to wonder sometimes if he was on heroin. Was he that dumb? She still wasn't even sure if he was planning to go to college or not. Every query about applications was met with the same quick exit. If only he could understand that she didn't give a shit about the degree. She only wanted him to go so that he wouldn't regret it later on. Don't let yourself get bullied by those college boys out in the world, she wanted to tell him. You can waste your life with that chip on your shoulder. But he wouldn't listen. He might be on heroin. Wouldn't it just be too perfect if the terrible news she was anticipating turned out to be her son's addiction to hard street drugs?

She set up a meeting with Temo, this time with her dad in tow. Temo always answered her texts within seconds, and that was something positive, anyway. She arranged a lunch date between the two men with herself as chaperone.

At some point, the initial storm of guilt over hiring Temo had faded away and settled into a small knot in her chest, tightening and loosening, depending. She'd talked to three friends about the dilemma, and all of them had reassured her that her decision was fine and natural. Of course, they all had parents in convalescent homes or on their way to homes, and they needed to rationalize their own life choices, but they were people she generally respected and whose moral fiber was regarded as stronger than most. If only she had someone else on her team, she thought, someone with whom to share the burden, it would be such a help. But the fact was, she was the only one.

What would Ben say? she had to wonder. Now, that was a laugh. For all her brother's big talk of duty and valor and patriotism, his sense of obligation always seemed to lead him in some far-distant direction. She'd left him five messages, and he hadn't called a single time since their dinner, and she knew for a fact that he hadn't called their dad, either. Her dad always called the second he heard from Ben. Ben is in Africa! Ben is off protecting Israel! Ben had a lot on his plate, Anne was sure, but when it came down to his own family, he'd just never really been there at all. It was a shame. Her brother was a man of such passionate convictions, and they only ever seemed to demand more blood.

She and her dad met Temo in a park. The meeting was inconclusive. Her dad was not exactly happy to greet his new babysitter. He found the whole arrangement degrading. But Temo revealed himself to be adept at negotiating her dad's brand of geriatric petulance. He was a smooth, patient, unhurried man, and Anne could see in his small gestures, the way he hovered near her dad's elbow without touching him, ready to catch him if necessary, the way he never rose to the bait of her dad's griping, that he understood the proper boundaries. He was on hand to protect her dad from physical harm, nothing more. She felt lucky, and for a moment the branches of dry lightning that had been flashing in her nervous system dimmed and receded.

Storm clouds didn't appear at work, either. Susan got home from Norway and seemed extra-happy and optimistic about the future of the bureau. She'd already apparently forgotten the deal she'd approved with Charlie and had moved on to new visions, new goals. She called Anne into her office to discuss the bureau's five- and ten-year plans, which seemed absurdly grandiose but which also went a long way to reassuring Anne about her own future. It meant Susan valued her and she hadn't been exposed as the terrible, conniving person she was, at least not yet.

Sitting at home, watching the snakes of light bouncing off the birdbath's water, onto the stucco wall, she wondered if maybe everything was going to be fine. Aaron was a good kid with good prospects, most likely not on heroin. Her brother was doing his best. Maybe Temo had been sent by a higher power. Maybe the BHC project was only a tiny blip on her time line, a deviation in an otherwise upstanding life. As of yet, no real transgression had even occurred. A few papers were circulating and accruing signatures. Some lawyers were feeding on the chum of their hourly negotiations. In the everyday fluxation of life, the moment-by-moment experience of reality as she most commonly understood it, nothing had really happened at all. So she'd hired a helper for her dad. So she'd given away the city's wastewater. All of it was so incredibly abstract next to the delicate lavender of the flowering honeysuckle growing against the back fence, it barely seemed to exist.

23

You could always get unmarried in life. You could switch jobs. You could get fat and turn around and get thin again. You could change your haircut a thousand times. But there was one thing you couldn't ever change, and that was being dead.

No, you couldn't ever stop being dead once you started. Death was the great and ultimate threshold of human experience, the one-way door through which no one ever returned. You could swap houses, you could make water into ice and back into water again, but being dead, that was the one irrevocable, unchangeable state.

Curtains for you, Shane Larson, Ben thought. In ten minutes, the curtains would be drawn once and for all on Shane Larson's life, and there would be no putting Humpty Dumpty back together again. Perched on the roof of Palm Canyon Resort, his rifle cradled against his chest, breathing slowly and methodically, Ben waited patiently for the next pivot point of his own vengeful life to arrive. You could never stop being dead; nor could you ever bring someone back to life once you'd greased them.

His eyes remained fixed on the third hole of the Indian Canyons golf course, framed over the white lip of the resort roof. He'd chosen the Palm Canyon for its slight elevation; it was the only three-story building near the perimeter of the links. The third hole was not his favorite choice—he might have preferred a higher number, if only for the drama of letting the tournament play out—but overall the third hole was acceptable. There were at least three exit routes nearby, paths going north and south along South Palm Canyon Drive, and a vast, empty scrubland stretching west into the mountains. Plan A was to evacuate on the street using the pickup truck he'd stolen the night before, joining the flow of traffic, finding his car downtown, making the trade and drifting quietly away. Plan B was to evacuate on the street by foot, melding with the street traffic and reconnecting with his car and continuing on as per Plan A. And Plan C, should he need it, was to flee into the mountains. The nest itself was very solid. He could see the lima-bean green abutting a glittering pond at the end of an alley of palm trees. He could see a swath of the mountains sheltering the valley from the wind. He could see an immensity of cornflower-blue sky extending into infinity.

This was a beautiful place to exit the world, Ben thought. Shane Larson was a lucky man in that regard. He would exit the planet in sunlight and fragrant desert air, surrounded by adoring fans, or at least admiring fans, or at the very least people who recognized him. He would avoid all the suffering of the elder years, the decrepitude and disease. He would not slowly wither until his mind was soft cheese and his family didn't know what to do with him. He would go out in the greenery of the Indian Canyons golf course without a moment of pain. Or maybe just one very brief moment of pain. Depended on how well the shooting went today.

Ben had arrived at the Palm Canyon at three in the morning, wanting privacy for the scaling of the wall and the choosing of precisely the right spot. The resort-goers had been sleeping, and he'd nestled in under the star-throbbing sky. He'd seen the sun rise over the San Jacinto Mountains, the wind-planed clouds turning pink and orange and the dome of existence gradually filling with color. He'd heard the desert birds awaken, including one strange type that made noises like R2-D2, greeting the day with a funny, computerized bleep-bleep-bloop song.

Over the hours, the human world had come to life. The golf course had picked up employees. The tournament spectators had trickled through the front gate in their BMWs and Lexuses and hybrids, claiming parking spots with smooth self-confidence. From the sidewalk, the voices of the men floated in the air, talking about all the petty garbage of their privileged lives. From the pool area, the squeals of the children had begun. Ben had overheard numerous complaints about wives, lawyers, neighbors, contractors and subcontractors, many grousing complaints relating to people's own revolting wealth. He'd overheard at least a dozen men he would have gladly killed if only their deaths would have meant anything to people. But he'd waited stoically for the one man he'd come to make an example of, Shane Larson.

Doom on you, Shane Larson. Doom on you for all your lies.

The third fairway was a lush, green carpet leading to the spotlight of the putting green. The tournament had begun midmorning, and the players had been wending through in clusters. The gallery had been shrinking and growing but generally sticking to about fifty or seventy-five bodies. Ben had been monitoring the progress of the overall competition on his phone, reading the ticker tape of the incoming Twitter feed, and he knew Larson had begun playing and was already four over par after only two holes.

He was not in the running for golf victory today. The third fairway was waiting, only an occasional bird breaking the airspace. It was almost noon when Larson's group ambled into view, with its attendant caddies and spectators in tow. At last, two hundred yards away on the fairway, the target had presented himself.

Ben watched as the golfers selected their locations and stabbed their tees into the ground. He watched as they made their final calculations for windage, slope, and distance and straddled their balls, squaring their shoulders. He could see the naked napes of their necks as some turned and spoke to their caddies, the vulnerable spots of their temples, their ribs. And then one by one they teed off, swinging their silver clubs like scythes. He lost sight of the balls as they sailed in the sun, carving mountainous arcs, and caught sight of them again as they made their landings with delicate plops near the green. The balls rolled the final distance to their resting places and shone whitely on the turf, waiting, only seventy yards away. The gallery clapped. He could hear one meaty set of palms in particular amid the soft clatter.

The golfers were coming in his direction, and one by one they approached the green, crouching and scoping their lines of attack. They weighed their options, balanced their minuscule judgments, and all the while Ben watched and measured as well. It was all a form of golfing in the end.

Shane Larson putted second. His lime-green shirt and giant black watch shone brightly in the sun, as did his white arms, the consistency of uncooked dough. He waddled over the nubby grass with the overfed confidence of the truly rich, his backside a foreign country. He dug his thumb in his nose, not caring who saw, he was that rich. He approached his dimpled ball, separating himself from the bystanders, and took sole possession of the green apron. He crouched to his knee, angled his head. He stood and shook his leg.

Ben watched him in the crosshairs of the scope on his Ruger Varminter, the fat body flattened on the lens. The gun had come from a dealer he'd found on Craigslist, located in Barstow, and it was not yet familiar in Ben's hands. The stainless-steel stock was heavier than he would have liked, and he'd never used the .204 Ruger ammo before, but it had been priced to sell, and there'd been no questions asked. He'd gone to the man's shack with no ID, only his SEAL insignia, and had blustered his way through the deal with anecdotes of killing in foreign lands, and that had been enough. The guy had treated him like royalty, never even asking about the driver's license or full name.

The temperature was moderate, with no humidity. The wind was nil. The distance was approximately seventy meters. The target was large and ready.

Shane Larson stood still, preparing for his putt, but just before the final pendulum swing, Ben made his move. The trigger pull was three pounds. The barrel was twenty-six inches of alloy steel. He sent the bullet streaking. There was no arc to the bullet's flight. The bullet entered Shane Larson's chest on the right side, somewhere near the logo for the global communications conglomerate that transponded his radio signal, and seemed to bounce around in his rib cage, shredding his organs. Mid-putt, Larson's face blanched with puzzlement as he stared at the wound that had suddenly opened in his chest cavity.

Hole in one.

The crowd didn't understand what had happened. For three long seconds, no one realized anything was amiss. Shane stumbled back two steps and turned a woozy half circle, his putter extended from his waist like a dousing rod. Then the putter dipped, and he pitched forward, getting hung up on the shaft and dangling there, three-legged, as a bloody bubble grew in his mouth. The bubble was thick and viscous, and popped, splashing blood on his chin and lips. Finally his weight shifted, and he tumbled onto the ground, a sack of potatoes.

Even then, the crowd only dimly comprehended what they were seeing. Death was so incongruous here, in this oasis of leisure. Maybe Shane Larson was just joking around. He had a reputation as a kidder, after all, and he was an entertainer by trade. But as he lay there, unmoving, blood coughing from his mouth, the crowd gradually became more alarmed. Murmurs of concern began circulating as the group mind apprehended that something had definitely occurred, something was crazy. A few fellow golfers hurried over and knelt down and waved for their caddies. One hand rose in the air, covered in blood, and fear traveled through the herd like an electric shock.

Screams commenced, which Ben took as his cue to wipe down the rifle, stow it in a corner for eventual discovery, and crawl on his elbows to the far side of the rooftop to begin his retreat. The access stairway led down to the third-floor hallway. From there he would walk quickly to the emergency stairwell leading to the lobby, and from there onto the courtyard patio–pool area of Palm Canyon. He doubted the docile herd of suburban families and hipster weekenders would even notice him in his cargo shorts and Crocs, and he would walk through them quickly and quietly, heading out the front door to the nondescript truck he'd stolen. In two hours, he would be sitting where everyone already assumed he was, in his desert quarry, next to his RV, drinking a cold, watery domestic beer.

As he crept to the rooftop stairs, however, there near the door, gaping at the scene of mayhem on the golf course, was a janitor holding a bag of Taco Bell and a smoldering one-hitter. The janitor was probably twenty-five years old, just a kid, with coffeecolored skin and facial hair groomed into a razor-thin wedge along his jawline. He was standing directly between Ben and the stairs, eyes agog, processing all the unbelievable information streaming into his brain.

There was no question he understood what he was seeing. He'd been on the roof in Ben's blind spot the whole time, Ben realized. He'd probably heard the whisper of the suppressor, smelled the gunpowder in the air. Even now he was memorizing Ben's features, burning his eyes and nose and mouth into the hard drive of his mind.

Ben's first thought, the thought he was trained to have, was to kill him. One quick twist of his neck, and it would all be over. No one was watching; all attention was fixed on the green. He could just rise up and snap the guy's neck and end this problem right away. But Ben couldn't seem to make the decision and engage his hands quickly enough. He just lay there on his elbows as the kid scooted away to the far side of the roof, and Ben let him go, knowing he had just made everything much, much more difficult for himself.

◎

The plan had to go on, however. He leapt up and pushed his way through the roof door and hurried down the stairs as anticipated, walked breezily through the carpeted lobby, wended his way through the ludicrous pool area. He made it out the front door to the sidewalk and all the way to the truck without incident. He got as far as the driver's seat, reaching down to hot-wire the engine, before he realized plan A was not going to work. The janitor was surely watching him from the rooftop, reporting his every movement to the 911 dispatcher. And even if the janitor hadn't called the police, the roads were too congested to drive on. The tournament traffic was clogging all the arteries, assassination notwithstanding. The truck was a no-go. He would have better luck escaping on foot.

So Ben climbed out of the truck and started hoofing his way down the sidewalk, going north. He walked briskly, scanning the passing pedestrians for any suspicious looks or gestures, but he didn't see anything suspicious. He walked, hands in his pockets, ass tight as a screw, aiming for La Verne Way, where maybe he could join with the crowd at the Smoke Tree Village Shopping Center. He had a change of clothes in his backpack, and the janitor had possibly been too stoned to memorize his features all that well. It would be the word of a white guy against that of a Latino guy. In that, he had the advantage. Ben also had a fake driver's license to show if need be. He picked up his pace, noticing that the car traffic wasn't as bad as he'd thought, and, passing a burly, garnet Cadillac at a stoplight, he contemplated a carjacking but decided against it.

He passed Granada and Warnock Fine Arts, and he was just starting to feel the claws of the crime scene slackening on the muscles of his back, the poison talons withdrawing, when he heard calls from behind, telling him to stop.

"Halt!" "Stop!" the voices said. He ignored them at first, praying they were aimed somewhere else, but a quick glance over his shoulder told him he was fucked. A trio of policemen was sure enough charging in his direction, jostling their guns out of their holsters as they shambled in pursuit.

Thank God they'd been stupid enough to give him warning. He bolted, charging ahead, and then immediately zagged hard to the left, jumping a low wall into the yard of an elegant, mid-century mini-estate. He sped through the lush, fragrant desert garden, a gallery of succulents and palms, until reaching the rear wall, and blew out of the backyard into a landscape of Paleolithic nothingness. He sprinted full tilt for the beige mountains of the San Jacintos, weaving in and out of giant tufts of sage. If he could just make it across the half mile of scrub brush, the land would lift him up and away, and he would enter a world of stony seams and caverns with all their innumerable trajectories of escape.

Thank God, again, the cops were so pathetically slow. By the time they finally emerged from the palm trees and bougain-villea, Ben was already halfway to the foothills, and by the time he began scaling the lowest layer of rock, they were already slowing down, their legs shot. They weren't firing at him yet, thankfully, not even symbolically; they didn't seem to have the nerve or the authority for that, and he was most of the way up the first pile of sediment, a tumble of hamburger-sized nuggets deposited a century or two or three ago when some ledge finally gave up and yielded to gravity.

He arrived at a band of powdered dust and set to the next wall of rock, attacking the splintered boulders that seemed to grow from the dirt. The cops were no longer in sight, blocked by the slope of rubble, but Ben could see the golf course over his shoulder, the palms and the boxes of the surrounding homes.

His breath filled his ears as he climbed, and a glaze of sweat covered his skin. He felt strong, grasping the stones, pulling himself upward toward the beige ridge. From a distance, the mountains had been a study in brown, but up close there was coral, green, yellow, and every shade of taupe. He climbed past beautiful succulents, cacti, yucca. He achieved another level, and the whole of the Indian Canyons golf course spread into view. He could see that the gallery was still gathered at the third hole, surrounding Shane Larson's bleeding body, and an ambulance was nudging its way through the parking lot, siren flaring. A few stick figures were prowling the rooftop of the Palm Canyon Resort, likely investigating his nest, but they weren't looking toward the mountain. The cops down below were invisible, probably still struggling to make the first plateau.

He wondered if Shane Larson was dead. He wasn't confident that the shot had finished him. He wasn't sure if he'd ever know.

He climbed over a bed of shale, feeling the old war feeling spiking in his blood. His vision was so clear, it looked as if everything had been cut out and put back in place, outlined vividly for his personal apprehension. If he could get to the top of the ridge before they sent helicopters, he could make it. He could survive out in the desert as long as need be. Mother Ocean is your home and solace. This used to be ocean. This whole basin, all the way to Washington State, had once been plunged under prehistoric water, home to dinosauric whales and octopuses. Thus, this was his element. He was a SEAL. Those pathetic motherfuckers following him could never keep pace.

As he jogged a narrow trail, winding higher and higher, the war feeling thrummed alongside an even older feeling, the feeling that had prepared him for the war feeling in the first place. This feeling, this energy, was from childhood. The feeling of hide-and-seek, fox and hounds. The game of chase. One kid searching, picking up allies, until only one kid remained. Ben had carried this deep, gold-hued feeling in his bones since the beginning of time. He knew in that gold haze his mother lived somewhere. Hers was the spirit infusing those days. The feeling went back all the way, so far, there was nothing before it. Alone, his mother alive. And even in that feeling, a yearning. His first feeling, already missing the past. The golden age was only the most potent moment of wishing to be elsewhere. The sense of wrongness was fundamental, original to life.

He climbed past an eagle's nest knitted into a skull-like cliff. He mounted a formation of sandstone. Already, he was within sight of the first ridge, putting him into the realm of the wilderness, many more ridges ahead. The grid of Palm Springs was below him, spreading over the desert's skin like a festering wound, and he kept climbing into the desert.

He humped west, toward the ocean, toward his sister and father and nephew, not knowing exactly if or when he would find them out there. He was more concerned with the people behind him than the people out ahead. The men with guns chasing him were his first priority. He didn't believe in death, but he believed in jail, and he didn't want to go to jail. He willed himself onward, knowing he had to keep up a decent clip. At some point he'd find a cave. He'd go mujahideen and take refuge in the brutal, cultic land of stones. But for the moment he needed to push. He had enough water for a day or two, and hopefully he'd find some spring or small stream along the way, even an ice pack on a plateau rim. His eyes lifted to the giant clouds trailing their vapor, these immense reserves of water floating overhead, and cursed them for keeping it all to themselves.

He jogged into a canyon, stepping lightly over rock and pebble, sand, gravel, passing terraces of slick, unbroken sandstone. From afar, the landscape looked bleak, but up close there were a million hiding places, a million rifts and wrinkles and seams. He went farther, and the walls rose on either side, becoming parallel faces thirty or forty feet tall. A half mile in, he wasn't sure he'd made a good decision, but he still wasn't sure it was bad, either.

He arrived at the end of the canyon, where the walls tapered to a single corner, and he had no choice but to climb or turn back. He wasn't going back, he knew that much, so he found a foothold and a handhold and began inching his way up. The going was slow, hand over hand, but soon he was midway to the open sky. He continued finding crevices and shelves until he reached a point where he couldn't find a decent handhold anymore. There were still fifteen feet to go. He managed to swing his backpack around to his front and flattened his spine against one wall and pushed against the other with the soles of his feet. He waited for a minute, his arms and legs trembling, and pushed upward.

It took twenty minutes, but at last he swung over the edge onto a new vista. The land descended in a gentle grade to an open playa, white salt rime and blanched dust. In the distance he could see a mound of reddish rock with sheltering coves punched in the side. To go there would mean being exposed for a few minutes on the plain, but he saw no choice. He'd be exposed in any direction. Gliding like a Paiute, he made his way toward the giant mound. He was already wishing the night would come, but he knew he still had hours of light to endure. He wanted to put in distance.

The mound turned out to be the size of a stadium, and Ben climbed the spill of porous rock leading to a ledge. He walked the ancient, natural trail and found a series of shallow caves lined up in a row. The birds seemed to like the caves. They were padded with straw and bird shit. They had probably hosted humans in the distant past, granting sweet southern exposure in the cold months, shelter in the hot months, a nice mix of sun and shade. It was a good place to huddle for a while, until night fell and he could move in the darkness.

He squatted and gazed at the playa and prayed to the God of America. The God of this land was not the God of the Israelites, that vaudeville thunder machine. The God of America could go for years without making an appearance, and then, with a ripple, transform the world. Here: an elk. Here: a serpent. Here: an army of conquistadors crossing the desert in their burnished armor. Someday the God of America would visit Palm Springs and smite those people in streams of lava. But in the meantime it would appear in the form of wind in the long grass, frost on the basalt peaks, geysers of dust on the playa. Ben sat in the cave's mouth like the long-ago humans, looking out the socket at the baking landscape, awaiting the spirit's magic. As they had tried to coax the spirit awake when they'd needed it, and had tried to coax it back asleep, so did he.

He took an inventory of his backpack, even though he knew exactly what was in there. His food amounted to five Clif bars, some cashews, and a destroyed banana. His clothes were a shirt, a pair of socks, and his Oakleys. He had a short length of rope, a Swiss Army knife, a gun, a first-aid kit—the basics.

Once in the late afternoon he heard a helicopter, the whup-whup-whup over the whining engine, but he never saw the source. The sunset was glorious, a torrid scene of magenta and purple, and he fell asleep midway through, waking up to find the moon in his eyes. It was a bright moon, almost full, blanking out the surrounding stars and casting a silver, enchanted light on the land. In the moments of waking, Ben thought he saw figures below, not police or the FBI, but bodies that were shimmery and vaporous. Desert fairies, jinn. They disappeared before he could pull focus.

He shook his head, clearing his senses, and set out walking under the star-killing moon. The moonlight lay all around him like hoarfrost. He descended and skirted the rock stadium, aiming toward the next barricade of ridges. The moon was so bright, he could make out a ridge five miles away and the faint outline of the succeeding ridge behind it. He had lots of land to cross, lots of time.

He came to a crevasse and jumped it. He mounted a gentle hill and walked alongside a meadow-type expanse. He was whistling to himself when the blast of white light ignited in his face. The light came as a brutal shock, a total violation of his senses, and it was accompanied by harsh yelling and the roar of engines. Who was this? But he really meant: How? How could this be? How had they found him? There'd been no helicopter sounds or even footsteps. Where did this disembodied light suddenly come from? How?

"Halt! Halt or we will shoot. We are not fucking around here."

He stumbled away, blinded, but the lance of light stayed on him. He could hear voices yelling, telling him to get down, lay flat, and feet scuffling and thwacking on the dry earth. He stumbled and ran, his shadow skitting and flashing on the ground ahead. He could find a gully or arroyo of some kind, erect some wall between him and the light. Ahead, he caught glimpses of rutted furrows, tire tread, and cursed himself for his stupidity. He'd been walking next to a dirt road all this time! He'd been walking on the shoulder of a road! For all his sneaking, all his climbing, all his praying, he'd ended up on a BLM service road, pinned in the iron arms of the grid.

He could hear underwater voices and feel heated air, bullets flying past his cheek. He dug for his Beretta and shot wildly at the lights behind him. In the corners of his vision, he could see the pale tulips of muzzle flashes. He kept telling his legs to run, but they were too heavy. He could imagine that he was shot, losing blood, but the pain had not reached his brain yet.

He fell to the ground, his face flat against a powdery swell. He rolled onto his back to see the stars pulsing above. Shafts of light fried out the blackness, but it didn't matter. The blackness was inside him now, spreading through his cells, seeping into his mind. No noise, no color, no heat was getting through, just blackness within blackness, a roiling withdrawal of his senses. Into this blackness he fled.

24

Was it terrible of him to want coffee first? It was terrible, he knew. It was a sign of pitiful weakness and massive, disgusting selfishness on his part, but on the other hand, in the long run, what difference did it really make, assuming all the bad news was true? If something genuinely horrific had happened to his uncle, as it supposedly had, the precise timing of his arrival at the Desert Regional Medical Center in Palm Springs, whether 12:17 PM or 12:32 PM, was of almost no consequence whatsoever. Aaron's uncle would be in the same boat no matter what, and once he arrived, there would be only unremitting awfulness to deal with, so the way he saw it, he might as well have a cup of decent coffee in his hand when he got there.

The coffee stop took longer than planned, the line being incredibly slow in the Starbucks drive-through, and by the time he pulled out of the parking lot en route to the Desert Regional Medical Center, it was actually 11:11 AM, slightly later than his worst-case scenario. More texts had been coming in from his mom during the drive, urging him onward at great haste. He now knew his uncle was in room 435, north wing. He knew the prognosis was still unknown.

"Unknown" was better than some options, he thought, watching the dot on the GPS inch along the screen. "Unknown" wasn't "dead" yet. "Unknown" might not even be that bad. He'd talked to his mom three times so far over the morning, and each report had been "holding steady." When the initial news had landed, around 8:00 AM, his mom had told him that his uncle had been involved in some kind of chase in the desert in Palm Springs. She'd been told by the police that he'd been injured, but no one would confirm how. The details were hazy, if not contradictory, but the death of Shane Larson, the radio guy, was also part of the story. They claimed that his uncle was in critical condition and that the Life Flight helicopter had been delayed or possibly not called until too late. But also that the Life Flight had never arrived.

So even the information they had was unreliable. There was so much bad information out there, he'd reassured her, so many false memes. Fake articles passing for real news; opinions masquerading as facts; sheer idiocy becoming sanctified as significant and never going back. Aaron had learned long ago to distrust all data until confirming it with his own eyes, or at least a couple of reputable news sources, and this case seemed especially true in that regard. He would wait and see what the day presented, and until then he would refuse to get too worked up. Hopefully it would all get resolved before his grandpa ever had to know.

He'd borrowed Joel's car to go meet his mom, and the drive to Palm Springs had further worn away his concerns. The desert was such a beautiful, boring landscape, it repelled the very idea that life-changing events were possible. How could a sudden, terrible event be possible in this geologic nullity? How could a man who'd made it through firefights in Afghanistan and Somalia possibly meet his demise in Palm Springs? It made no sense.

During the drive he'd been in contact with Karl and Joel, both of whom were monitoring the day's events on the Internet. It was from them he'd learned some other disconcerting tidbits, namely, that his uncle was being called a terrorist and a serial killer. But again he put the rumors out of his mind. The Internet was so demonstrably untrustworthy, one had to dismiss most of what it said as a matter of course.

He drove on, letting his mind wander to images of sex and gold, both things he'd like a lot more of in his life, almost enjoying the spell of air-conditioned suspense. His mom was such a drama queen, he thought, always ready to declare an apocalypse. Take off your shoes or you'll track radioactive dust in the house. The earthquake that destroys Los Angeles is already three hundred years overdue. Soon enough all would be divulged. Until then, he'd take an hour or so to think about Dana Star in that green halter top she liked, drink his coffee, and drive incredibly fast through one of the most gorgeous landscapes on earth.

The Desert Regional Medical Center was a strange complex, half Mission church, half science-fiction colony on the moon. Under the desert sky, with the bell tower butting up against the glass skyways and the beige brickwork, Aaron could almost convince himself he was stepping not into a medical facility but into a humongous bank branch from the not-so-far future. He hurried through the front doors with his strong, lukewarm coffee in hand, unable to enjoy it for the small pangs of guilt the delay had cost him, for he was in full seeking mode now, searching for his uncle's room, speed walking and even trotting for stretches down the hall.

The nurse at the desk was sharp and no-nonsense. Aaron uttered Uncle Ben's name, and after a brief glance at her screen, the nurse pointed him to the third floor, intensive care. Entering the elevator, pushing the button, he was almost surprised by the ease of the transaction. He hadn't had to provide ID or anything. He could be anyone. Although he guessed not many people were actively trying to sneak into this building.

Rising, he wondered again what was in store. Most likely, he was on the verge of a great deflation. Life so rarely made good on its patches of suspense, offering at least a thousand near misses for every promise of dramatic sparks. If his own healthy body was any indication, nothing painful was going on in this hospital at all, and momentarily he'd only have to turn around and drive home.

The extreme realness of the situation hit him only when the elevator door parted and he caught sight of his mother, wailing. She was crumpled in the waiting room, clutching the arm of the chair, the only person in a long, empty row. Her face was contorted, and her shoulders were convulsing. She pulled her hair and wrung her hands. He'd never seen her like this, not even close, and at once all the petty meanness he'd been harboring toward her lately vanished from his system. All the shame he felt in her presence disappeared, to be replaced by a powerful drive to protect her and return her life to some normalcy. He knew without a doubt his own arrival would help, and he hurried directly to her side, feeling the blood in him freezing over, conducting every tiny tremor of perception. Why in God's name had he stopped for that coffee? That was something he'd never forgive himself for, not in his whole life.

"Mom," he said.

His mother reached out and felt for him, gripping his arm. "My brother, my brother," she said. "He's bleeding."

For a moment her face emerged from her mask of hair, another mask of mucus and tears. He held her by the quaking shoulders, and her body felt incredibly tiny and fragile. She buried her face on his chest, and the full, true weight of what was happening entered him, sinking into his stomach and guts, turning him into lead. Uncle Ben was his mother's brother. They'd grown up in the same rooms, spent their mornings fighting over the same bathroom sink. They'd endured the death of their mother together. They'd watched their father grow old. Ben might not appear to his mom in the flesh very often anymore, but that didn't mean he wasn't in her thoughts at all times, or that he wasn't in the fiber of her very nervous system. Down in the depths of her memory, in the honeycombed chambers even Aaron himself didn't know, he was in there, and he always would be.

The sobbing kept rising and falling, the keening of a broken animal, and eventually Aaron glanced around the room, realizing that he and his mother were not alone. The waiting area was populated by other people, some of whom looked like patients or relatives of patients, but some of whom were dour-looking men in uniforms. There must have been at least a dozen cops or other agents of government authority in the small space, politely pretending Aaron's mom was not racked with pain. They were careful to keep their eyes on their magazines and phones, but they were definitely watching her, scrutinizing her grief. They remained in their posts as she gathered herself together and took some deep breaths and closed her eyes. They all waited while she wiped her face and wiped her nose. Either she didn't notice that the room was full of watchers, or—more likely—she didn't care.

"It isn't looking so good," she said in a low voice, with hard-won composure. "I talked to the doctor, and he told me some things I haven't told you yet. I don't want to tell you. But I'm going to have to tell you some things because I need to talk this through."

"Tell me," he said. He beamed his full attention on her face, wanting only to help his mom through this tribulation. The cops and other patients evaporated from his mind, as did the voices of Karl, Joel, and everybody else that usually chimed in to guide his actions, or keep him from acting, as the case might be.

She told him her brother had been shot in the head. The doctors called it a transtentorial gunshot wound. She hadn't understood what they meant at first, but it meant the bullet had gone in one side and out the other, which was not a good situation. He'd also been shot in the leg and the butt, but those wounds weren't so concerning. It was his brain that was the problem. His vital signs were all okay, his heartbeat was steady, his lungs were inflating, but everything above the brain stem was in major trouble. They'd done a CT scan and found evidence of intercranial hemorrhage. "Destruction of brain architecture," the neurosurgeon had said. He'd also talked about bony fragments and bilateral skull fracture, all of which sounded very grim.

"So where is he now?" Aaron said.

"He's on a ventilator in the ICU."

"Have you seen him?"

"They won't let me in. But soon."

"And so . . . ?"

His mom shook her head with stunned slowness. "I don't know," she said.

"So what do we need to do?"

She breathed deeply and girded herself.

"Ben doesn't have a spouse," she breathed, "and he doesn't have a living will that anyone knows of, so the medical-decision power goes to the next of kin. That means Grandpa. I know you just drove all the way out here. I should have been thinking more clearly when I first called, but I wasn't. I think the first thing you have to do is drive back and get him."

Grandpa Sam was waiting when Aaron arrived at his mailbox. For the first time in recorded memory, he was ready and waiting. He had a fanny pack belted around his waist, a thermos of water in his hand. He was sitting on the curb, the house locked behind him. He was climbing into the car before Aaron had even stopped.

"You were at the hospital?" Grandpa Sam said, arranging his provisions on his lap. "All the way in Palm Springs?"

"I was."

"And you saw Benny?" He sounded at once vacant and disturbed. Aaron had rarely heard his grandpa talk about his son, and when he had, it had always been Ben, not Benny. But today was different from other days. Uncle Ben was with them again, and time was getting all mixed up.

"No. Not yet."

"Is he okay?"

Aaron paused before saying anything. He'd assumed his mom had been telling his grandpa everything she'd been telling him, but maybe that wasn't the case. Maybe she was keeping the worst news from him until the last possible moment. If that was the strategy, Aaron didn't want to be the one to spring anything unexpected. If today's events were coming as a shock to his mom, what they meant to his grandpa, he could barely imagine. Your son is a killer. Your son has been shot. An army of pundits and citizen-bloggers is dissecting the significance of his actions and ideology, invading every corner of his public record, casting judgments on his very life. Aaron didn't know if Ben was okay. No one knew. That was part of the whole ordeal.

"I don't know," Aaron said. "We really don't know that much yet."

Grandpa Sam received the news with a truncated grunt, followed by another question: "Does he have a good room?"

To that question Aaron didn't know how to respond. Good room, bad room, what difference did it make? If Grandpa Sam was asking if his son had a nice view or a loud roommate, he was out of his mind. And maybe he was. His son, the soldier, was out in the desert, comatose, accused of great crimes. It was enough to crush anyone's spirit. Aaron watched uncomfortably as his grandfather tried to twist off the lid of the thermos, holding his water between his knees, and finally tucked the thermos between his thighs, giving up. His hands continued trembling, and he put them on his knees.

"A good room, yeah," Aaron said, recognizing that the right answer had nothing to do with the truth right now. "I'm pretty sure it's good." And with that they headed back into traffic, plagued by yet a new kind of silence—anguished, curdled, borderline nauseous. After all they'd been through, all the miles they'd put in, Aaron could only guess as to the deep, inaccessible feelings roiling in his grandpa's body. The feelings were in there, he knew. They might be far away, and cloaked in thick fog, but they were definitely in there. And whatever they were, whatever one called them, they had to be utterly hellacious.

They entered the waiting room to another burst of tears from his mother. The sight of her father seemed to knock her back like a fist. She recovered quickly, though, and gave them the most recent report. Uncle Ben was attached to life support. He also had a bolt attached to his skull, a monitor for the intercranial pressure, or brain swelling. His liver and his lungs were fine. They would hear more about his brainwaves, or lack thereof, soon. None of the information seemed to be getting through to Grandpa Sam, however. He listened with his head bowed, and when the report was over he had only one question: when could they see Ben?

"I don't know that yet," Aaron's mom said. "They haven't said anything about that. He's still in critical condition, Dad. No one is saying anything about visitors."

"Who do we talk to about seeing him?" Grandpa Sam said. He only wanted to see his son, nothing else. He could make the diagnosis himself if they'd just let him through. His voice didn't sound very urgent on the surface, but Aaron knew by now just how resilient his grandfather could be. Woe to the cop or G-man who would stand in his way.

"There are a lot of reasons why we can't see him," his mom tried to explain. "He's still in really delicate condition. And there are legal factors."

"We should be able to see our relative," Grandpa Sam stated.

Aaron wasn't sure whose side to take, or if there even were sides, but in the end he didn't have to decide. One of the men pretending not to listen stepped forward and flashed an FBI badge

and asked Grandpa Sam to please come with him and answer
some questions. For whatever reason, Grandpa Sam complied,
possibly thinking the man would lead him to Ben, and Aaron and
his mom were left to themselves. The only thing to do, it seemed,
was to find seats in the waiting room and settle into the life of the
hospital, possibly the life they would live until the end of time.

Aaron killed a few minutes firing off texts to Joel and Karl,
hoping they knew enough to avoid sharing anything with the
public at large, and glanced up to find nothing had changed.
He took the dimensions of the room and noticed the hospital
was in fact a lot grosser than he'd first realized. The floorboards
were speckled with grime. The lights were at once harsh and
dim, with numerous missing tubes among the overhead fluo-
rescents. The air was too cool, the smell too sharply antiseptic.
The TV was much, much too loud. His mom, who was also
staring ahead, and also seemed to be sensing the general shitti-
ness of the institution, shared with him a look of rue.

"I hear Eisenhower is even worse," she said.

"So we're lucky, I guess."

She shrugged. "You know, if you're hungry, you can go find
something. There are places not too far away."

"Why?" he said. "Do you want anything?"

"No. I'm fine."

"Then I'm fine, too."

He wasn't going anywhere. He was planning to stay at his
mom's side as long as this took, he'd already decided. When she
pulled her phone from her purse, he allowed himself to pull
his iPod from his bag, but he didn't turn it on yet. He held it
loosely in his hands, staring at a nurse, then a man cleaning his
fingernails, waiting for the right moment to ask the question

that had been nagging him for hours and that he had to think
was nagging everyone else, too.

"So," he said eventually, "what do you think is, like, going
to happen?"

"I have no idea," she said. Her attention had become absorbed in a medical website featuring a reasonably professional-
looking logo. Her scrolling was by turns quick and measured.

"Is he going to"—he debated how to phrase this—"make it
through all right?"

"I really don't know," she said.

"They haven't said anything?"

"It sounds like there are cases where people come through.
A few, anyway. That's all I know."

His mom continued scouring the website, then another,
and Aaron went ahead and inserted his earbuds, spinning the
wheel until he came to *Zuma*, by Neil Young. As the consoling
chords of "Barstool Blues" flowed into him and the world knit
into its spell, the room filled with a wistful, piercing light. The
people seemed to slow down, and the ugly corners turned
more inviting. His mom, hunched over her phone, continued
her tapping, unaware of any changes. Aaron wished she could
relax, but he knew there was no point in saying anything.
Throughout all the campaigns, all the coalitions, he'd never
once seen her pause to rest. Even now, with so little hope, she
kept on fighting, learning the names of every nurse and doctor
in the hospital, figuring out the definitions of every Greek and
Latinate medical term they used. Her focus amazed him.

The song was still playing when his grandfather returned,
already seemingly exhausted, and took a seat near the fish tank.
He looked over at Aaron and allowed a deep communication of

submission to pass between them. Aaron was almost relieved when the wordless look finally ended. How could it be possible, he wondered, that his grandfather's fate, already so harrowing and immense, was still not yet done?

He looked out the window as a cluster of birds lifted together from a concrete bench, swatting light from the air. The song ended, and he skipped ahead to "Cortez the Killer." Neil's sound was that of the trees, the earth, and the clouds themselves. He'd come to California and found songs seeping from the ground, cracked rocks and found songs inside. People should build totem poles out of boom boxes and stick them on every corner of every street in America and play Neil Young songs twenty-four hours a day, Aaron thought. He wanted to live inside Neil's music for the rest of his life.

Late in the afternoon a doctor came and delivered the latest prognosis, much like the ones before. Uncle Ben had suffered a serious head wound, he said. The bullet had gone through the skull above the temples, and the brain was extremely damaged. As with every report, new bits of information came out, unseen facets emerged to light. This time, they learned more than they ever wanted to know about the danger of brain herniation, or the possibility of brain matter squeezing outside the structures of the skull, through the nose. Thankfully, the doctor said, brain herniation didn't seem to be a danger for Ben, but forever onward it was a horrific image that would never leave their minds.

"So, is there anyone who specializes in this kind of thing?" Aaron's mom asked pleadingly. "Are there programs? Or treatments?"

"None that I'm aware of."

"Is there some time frame we're looking at here?"

"That's impossible to say."

Almost as an aside, she asked if they could see her brother, and to their surprise this doctor said yes, of course. He was a new doctor, and Aaron and his mom were careful not to betray any doubt by looking at each other. Either the regulations had suddenly changed, or else no one had told this doctor they existed in the first place. They knew better than to seem alarmed.

The doctor turned and led the three of them into the ICU, taking them through the electronic door controlled by the inside nurse. They glided past shrouded rooms holding other mangled patients, catching glimpses of legs in traction, purplish toes, green monitors broadcasting inscrutable, large-font numerals. Aaron followed his mother and grandfather into the main control room, peopled by nurses in scrubs, and then into the room where his uncle was being kept, and suddenly there he was, sleeping. He lay in bed surrounded by big, metal boxes, gridded screens, and the Darth Vader rasp of the ventilator. His face was bruised and scratched, his mouth distended by the plastic breathing tubes. In his nose was another tube. His head was bandaged in thick, white gauze, with two wires extending from the top. His arms looked limp, held in place by the spiderweb of IVs. His legs were only half-covered by sheets and showed nasty cuts and abrasions along the hairy thighs.

As a final insult, there were handcuffs on his right wrist, attaching him to the metal railing of the hospital bed. And sitting beside him was a military cop, keeping watch. Aaron's mom gasped at the sight of the handcuffs, but the cop was not ashamed. He had his orders. He sat like a statue, doing his duty, feeling for no one. The fucking prick.

The doctor nodded the guard off, and he stood and
stationed himself in the far corner of the room, making way for
the family to approach. Any feelings of hope were blasted by
the scene. They shuffled closer, Aaron staying with his grandpa
and going to the right of the bed, his mom going left. His
uncle's gown was disarrayed, and along his shoulder the edge
of a tattoo was visible. It seemed to be a sentence, but Aaron
could make out only the first words. "We sleep . . ." We sleep?
Tattoos weren't allowed among his people, were they?

No one else seemed to notice or care, however. Aaron's
mom choked and sat on the bed's edge, clasping her brother's
hand while his grandfather knelt, head bowed. Thin, watery
tears spread over his cheeks and the barrel of his body shook
and he pulled a hand towel out of his pocket and swabbed his
whole face. He'd come prepared.

Aaron watched his grandfather weeping over his uncle's
body. He didn't know what to think. His mom rarely talked
about her brother, but they were a part of each other, he could
see. Her entire body was suffering with him. To see her in
such a tortured state was almost frightening. The depths of her
animal feeling were darker than he could have known.

The ventilator continued its gasping intake and output.
The doctor hovered in the doorway, and the guard stood with
his hands clasped. Aaron could feel his phone vibrating in his
pocket, filling with messages from his friends, but right now
they would have to wait. Standing with his grandpa, a single,
terrible question tolled over and over in his head: How good
is life now, Grandpa? he thought. Your family got murdered.
Your gold is gone. Your son is a killer and now he's broken and
bleeding in the desert. Tell me, how good is life now?

25

The organ harvester had amazing timing, Anne thought. Either that or the medical establishment had some kind of PR company on retainer, some data-crunching consulting operation sending out secret announcements to the relevant bureaucrats, because the minute her brother's official brain-dead status came back positive, the call came in. Anne had put the guy off at first, but he'd been persistent, and at last she'd relented. So for more than half an hour that morning, she'd talked to him—an utterly normal dude who probably coached his daughter's volleyball team and bought his hardware at Home Depot—about the future of her brother's innards.

The man had given her the hard sell. Her brother was young and healthy, he said. He hadn't done any drugs or even drunk in excess. His blood type was common. Thus, he was an excellent candidate for donating his kidneys, heart, lungs, liver, all of it, for the benefit of humankind. Talking to the organ harvester, Anne had felt as if she were trapped in some Ancient Egyptian myth. Ben wasn't even dead! He was still breathing, and they were already talking about spreading his organs over the land as if an army might grow from his dismembered pieces. It seemed insane. She'd been preparing for her dad's disintegration, not her brother's. She never could have imagined a punishment this grotesque for her actions. It was just like God, though, wasn't it?

Though by another light, she could see, the organ harvester was utterly reasonable, too. Of course the organs should go to the needy. Of course children and mothers should live on with her brother's recycled tissue. And yet she couldn't even begin to get herself to entertain the deal. Some primal part of her couldn't let go of the superstitious feeling that it was simply macabre.

The waiting room was more crowded today, she noted, nibbling her dried fruit and nuts. After four days, it was becoming almost like a refugee camp. Two more families had entered in the night and staked out their own pitiful sections, and from overheard snippets of conversation, she gathered they were there with car-crash victims. They were waiting for news of full-body CT scans, blood tests, blood marrow transplants, she wasn't sure exactly what. She didn't have the strength to question the grief-stunned fathers and brothers or make small talk with the terrified women staring at the posters of pastel mountains and forests throughout the room. All she could do was watch the children playing with their blocks, blissfully ignorant of everything, not knowing that behind every wall people were dying in slow agony.

Anne's own shanty was neat and well ordered. She had her dried fruit and a bag of trail mix from Whole Foods, some rice cakes, and a water thermos. That was it. Her main goal at this juncture was just to stay hydrated. And, lo and behold, her thermos was empty. Once again, it was time to make the voyage for a refill. Something to do.

She'd come to prefer the drinking fountain near the elevators, where the stream was stronger and she didn't have to touch the mouth of her thermos to the spigot. She'd even come to consider the walk a form of exercise. She got up and took the long way around to stretch her legs and catch a view of the mountains outside the eastern windows, ghosted by her reflection in the panes of glass. After days of sleeping in chairs and brushing her teeth in public sinks, she took her pleasures where she could.

Afterward, she went to the room and visited Ben. She'd become an expert in the procedure for entering the ICU, picking up the phone and saying her name and waiting for the double doors to swing open, all controlled by an invisible nurse at the deep inner desk. The military cop was still sitting there, still rigid and blank. She hated him so much. How many hours had he watched her sitting next to her brother, watching the machines blow air into his lungs and suck air out? In that time she'd memorized the tubing running from his body to the machine, the nasogastric tube sucking his stomach clean through his nose, the TPN feeding him through the IV. What had this guy learned?

She'd done her share of talking to Ben while she sat there, even though Ben didn't respond to anything she said. Mostly she'd been recounting stories from their youth. She'd talked about the little creek down the road with the big, white rock they'd dubbed Alcatraz, and the rafts they'd built every summer, all of which had inevitably capsized. She'd talked about the days of sliding down the golden hill across Alpine Drive on the flattened cardboard boxes and picking the foxtails from their tube socks. She'd talked about the night at Bruce Misner's house in high school when everyone was doing nitrous hits and she'd passed out and Ben had sat there with her until the world had come back to her eyes. She'd entered many forgotten rooms of memory, whole wings of the mansion unvisited for years. None of the stories made it through his sleep.

This time she just sat, watching him breathe, or, rather, watching the machines breathe. His mouth was warped from the plastic tubing, and the pores on his nose were oily and black. For some reason his hair needed brushing, though she had no idea why. He didn't look evil, even though that was what the people on the news said. He wasn't evil. No more than anyone. He was just a product of the system that created him, that was all. He was a soldier doing his job, which was killing. He'd just killed the wrong people this time. No one on the news wanted to say that. If anyone was evil, it was her, the one who'd betrayed all.

And in the end, it was much bigger than that. It was all just God's killing, wasn't it? God murdering God. God in one form rising against God in another. All God's hilarious rising and smiting of Himself. God must love it on some level, she thought. God, the Grand Inquisitor. From the very beginning, He'd been at his little game. On the first day, He'd laid out the railroad tracks, constructed the huts and the bunkers of the Lager; on the second day, He'd rolled out the concertina wire, erected the electrified fence; on the third day, He'd built the gas chambers and the ovens; on the fourth day, He'd penned in humankind. The rest of the week, He'd tortured them, starved them, pitted them against one another, dangled hope, only to yank it away, given them dreams, dashed them, made them hurt. And on Saturday, He'd herded them into the showers and burned their gray corpses back into the sky. God, the great SS man in the clouds.

She held her brother's limp hand, hating him for all the moronic, God-like killing he'd done. Why hadn't he ever listened? She'd been on him his entire life about the killing of brown people in distant lands. What was the point? Why the bizarre faith in the men who sent him to war? She'd even yelled at him about it again in his coma. She'd worked herself up and found herself yelling at his unconscious face. You really think there are good guys and bad guys in the world? You stupid fucking idiot? Good guys and bad guys. What fucking idiot believes that? That was what you took from Dad's life? More killing? Fuck you, Ben. Grow the fuck up.

But, holding her brother's hand, staring at his bruised eyelids, his loose lips, she didn't yell anymore. He looked so helpless in the bed, so heavy and thick and disheveled. She didn't say anything. Their argument was over. There was nothing to say. He was basically dead.

She returned to the waiting room and called Mark Harris, who'd become her lifeline to the outside world. She still wasn't sure if she wanted to join his team, or become his lover, or report him to the SEC, but she liked the sound of his scheming voice right now. He didn't bother asking about her brother, either, and that was nice—his intuition was correct in this regard yet again. Of course he wanted to know the details—everyone did—but he respected that she didn't want to talk to him about any of that. All she wanted was to be a part of the living world.

"Any word from the city yet?" she asked.

"Still waiting on the contracts to come back. No word."

"Seems like they're taking their time."

"Always takes a long time with this kind of stuff. This is still the fast track. We're still at the beginning. Don't worry. You doing all right?"

She hung up before things could get personal and texted Susan but could barely force herself to tap out a whole message.

She preferred watching Aaron napping on the middle row of chairs, a bunched jacket as his pillow. He'd been in the waiting room most of the time, too, and whiskers were sprouting from his delicate teenage chin. Soft, patchy whiskers, the shock troops of more whiskers. So the long march was already that far along, she thought. God was herding her son into the mountains, preparing to plunge in the bayonet the moment he stumbled in the snow. What would happen up there in his mountains, she wondered? Would he starve? Would he lose his limbs? She watched him sleep as time flowed over him like clear water over stones. Already, God was taking him away from her. The sadist. In a matter of months, he'd be gone.

The time had passed so quickly the past seventeen years. He'd only just arrived. For a fleeting second he'd been a baby, and she'd held him to her chest, feeling his weight, and then the next second he was a man, walking into the woods.

Her father was in the corner, staring in the general direction of the goldfish tank. Flashes of gold and black and red squiggled in the cube of water. His eyes were bleary and pink. His sweatshirt was splashed with yogurt from lunch the day before. He'd aged ten years in the past twenty-four hours. His hands hung empty between his knees.

Maybe it was all her fault, she allowed. The thought kept occurring to her throughout the days. She picked up an old copy of Sunset magazine and wondered yet again if maybe she'd brought this plague of bad luck on the family with her less-than-perfect behavior. But she refused to believe it. Look at all the sick, immoral fuckers out there who got through without a scratch, she thought. If this was her punishment, it surely went far, far beyond the crime.

She watched her son and her father, wondering what the hell God was trying to do. It would be so easy to believe there was no God at all. It would be so simple just to think that human fate was meted out purely at random, the function of some insane, broken machine. Some people got rich, some people found love, some people were crushed by boulders—you never knew. And yet, back of the days, there always seemed to be some infernal design, didn't there? Some kind of intelligence exploiting our invisible weaknesses, some consciousness relishing the ironic twists of fate. For every man and woman and animal and plant, a customized suffering, an elaborate machinery of personal, indescribable pain. This was probably the reason she'd made herself hard inside, she thought. She'd never wanted her goodness to invite death and disease into her body.

She got up to stretch her legs and sat down again. The air-conditioning was too cold, and the guy in the corner was showing much more ass crack than any person should.

Yes, there was a God, Anne thought, watching the Mexican nurse walk in one door and out the other. There was a God, all right, and God, She was such a fucking bitch.

She went back to her brother's room. The white nurse came in, and Anne watched her go about her chores, checking charts, emptying the bag of urine. Her hair was long and smooth and red, held in place with a leather barrette. Anne imagined a country life with a woodstove and pickle jars, a single cow to milk in the morning.

"The doctor will be here in about an hour," the nurse said.

"Great," Anne said. "Thank you."

"You're doing okay?"

Anne just laughed, and the nurse left, unperturbed. She was a saint, that nurse, walking into this inferno every day to tend to the dying, pulling God's victims from the pyre. Doctors were one thing. They lived in the glory, hauling in their shitloads of money, driving their SUVs to the country club. But nurses, they were the true saviors.

The neurosurgeon arrived three hours later, his tardiness no longer surprising. Anne had fought for this man because he was reportedly the best, and she almost took his tardiness as a good sign. Want the job done right? Ask a busy person. She knew that old saw was true; she'd lived it.

Dr. Salt was always late, but at least he didn't hurry once he arrived. He sat with Anne and her dad and explained the diagnosis again in great detail, showing all the appropriate consideration and compassion that the circumstances required. He was a bit remote, but he was thorough. He had a shiny bald pate and homely features; his knuckles were tufted with hair. Throughout the talk, her dad was silent. The information was no different this time around. Ben's brain was still wrecked. The electroencephalogram still showed nothing happening, brain wave–wise. The real discussion today was not so much about Ben's condition but rather about what happened next, because very soon they would have a decision to make.

"So there's no chance for a change in condition?" Anne said, voicing what she assumed was her dad's main, ongoing question. "None at all?"

"No," the doctor said, not harshly, but with no trace of ambiguity in his voice whatsoever.

"There's no operation to do? No intervention? Or therapy?"

"No."

"Would it make sense to get a second opinion?" Anne said. "I think we want to do that. Don't we, Dad?"

Her dad nodded thickly, too sunk in his despair to muster anything more.

"I can set you up with some other doctors," Dr. Salt said. "But I can tell you they're all going to say the same thing. Ben can't live any longer on his own. Without the ventilator he will naturally die. I think it's time to start thinking about Ben's quality of life now. I'd urge you both to think about what he'd want in this situation."

"He'd want to live," her dad muttered, and Anne and Dr. Salt avoided looking at each other out of deference to his pain.

"Of course he would," Dr. Salt said. "But the question is, would he want to live in this circumstance? That's the question you need to ask yourselves now. You need to put yourselves in Ben's shoes and think about what's best for him in this moment. And going forward."

"What about the police?" Anne said.

"What about them?" the doctor said, not understanding.

"They probably want to kill him themselves, don't they?" she said. "Don't we have to keep him alive for that?"

The doctor made a show of seriously pondering the question. It seemed not impossible that the state would want to exact its punishment in some capacity. Of course, it would be utterly absurd to kill a dead man, but the world had seen much stranger things. Was Dr. Salt almost smiling behind those glasses? This kind of lunacy was the spice of life, after all, just so long as the lunacy wasn't your own. He would go home tonight and talk about this conversation with his wife or mistress. But if the idea amused him, he kept it well hidden.

He touched her hand lightly and spoke in a soft, serious voice, only for her ears.

"I'm not thinking about the police right now," he said. "The police are not my concern. Or yours. Your concern is only your brother and what's best for him and your family. Okay? So put the police out of your mind. Don't think about that here. That's for another day."

Anne loved this doctor.

Anne sat with her father and her son in a corner of the waiting room, pondering what to do. For many minutes they sat there silently, staring at the floor. Anne's dad was ultimately the one who had to make the call, and Anne had no idea what he was thinking. She didn't know what she wanted to do, either. Among her tests, this was a new one, utterly unpredicted. All her worries about her dad had obscured her own clarity of judgment. Was she ready to do this already? After only four days, was she prepared to say good-bye? The hours had been going so slowly, but there hadn't been that many of them yet. She sensed Aaron was ready. He understood the gravity of the situation, but he was also the most objective, having logged so little time with Ben. He was able to see Ben as a mere patient.

"It isn't looking so good, is it?" she said to no one in particular.

"Nope," Aaron said, in a way that let her understand he wasn't being flip.

"I think Dr. Salt is right," she said. "We have to think about Ben's comfort here. I know he isn't feeling anything right now, but the way he is, it just isn't right. It isn't how he'd . . . Oh God . . ." Her chin and mouth crumpled, and she couldn't go on.

"This isn't how he'd want to be," Aaron said, gently continuing her thought.

"And even if something happened, and he somehow comes through," she said, "then what . . . a life in bed? No brain activity? Eating through a tube? He's never going to think and feel again. And even if a miracle happened, what after that? The death penalty? My God. I mean . . . What do you do with that?"

"That's not what we're thinking about now," Aaron said.

Still her dad wasn't talking. He was rocking in his seat, massaging his thighs. He'd conferred with a rabbi earlier in the day, but it hadn't seemed to change anything for him. Anne still wasn't even sure how fully he comprehended the situation.

"What do you think, Daddy?" she managed to ask him.

Her dad's eyes remained on the floor. The footsteps of a faraway nurse made a screech on the linoleum. The wheel of the food cart clicked on its axle. Aaron sighed, tracking on some sad tangent of thought.

"Daddy?"

Still he didn't move, but eventually his rusty voice emerged from his mouth: "There is always hope," he said.

Anne looked over at Aaron, who raised his eyebrows a degree to confirm he'd heard the communication. The words had registered. There's always hope. That's what her dad, the legal custodian, had said. But what did this mean, practically speaking? Aaron didn't offer any response, because what did a person say? There's always hope. They weren't crazy words, not uncomprehending of the circumstances, but they weren't helpful, either. There would have to be some interpretation ahead.

And so they waited.

The morning was unendurably long, a slow trickle of seconds, a hot, gritty ooze of minutes, and at last the afternoon came on. Anne killed fifteen minutes staring at some kid playing a video game on his stupid plastic console. Over his shoulder she could see the screen, where hunchback orcs were losing limbs to the slashing blade of a ranger's scimitar. It was another cruel joke, obviously, but eventually it went beyond a joke. She stared openly as the slack-jawed kid wallowed in that awful, ugly, pastiched world, bathed in that awful, gray, computerized light, giving himself over to the stiff-moving avatar. He poured himself into this crude, digital puppet, unaware of anything in his physical vicinity, lost in the meaningless but obligatory killing of subhumans.

What does Ben want? She asked herself Dr. Salt's question. He wants to go, she thought. He wants to be released from his cage. He wants to release us, too, and send us back to our productive lives. That was her best guess, anyway. That was what she'd want in his situation. Or so she thought. There was always what people said they wanted, and then what they really wanted, confronted by the pyre of death.

In Ben's healthy life, what would he have imagined for himself? He'd have wanted to die in battle, she thought. And in that, he'd gotten his wish. He'd made the whole world his battlefield, and he'd taken many of his foes with him. And how did she herself want to go? Fast. Hit by a bus. An anvil on her head. A piano falling out a fifth-story window. She vowed to start walking in more construction zones as she got older and more brittle. Postmenopause, she'd start living very much more dangerously. She'd never sin again.

Do you believe in anything after? Dr. Salt never asked this question, but it was where the other questions led. On this question, she hated to hazard a guess. Her deepest intuitions went something in the vein of mulch—the beatific dissolve of carbon-based life into organic dirt. Maybe, possibly, it felt good. The dissolve was maybe even a form of ecstasy. Maybe even sexually pleasurable, in a way. Slowly, slowly, the flesh melted into rich earth, gradually growing back into the forms of life, as flowers, spreading as pollen in the wind, carried away by honeybees. A tree is water becoming light. The prospect made her want to choose her burial ground very carefully.

In the evening, the nurse came again. Anne still loved her, but she'd come to dread the sight of her. This angel of mercy and death. So wonderful and so unwanted. She told Anne that Dr. Salt had arranged a meeting with some other intensivists and specialists in the hospital for a second opinion. Ten o'clock was the agreed-upon time. They would meet in the conference room, if that sounded all right.

"That soon?" Anne said.

"He thought you wanted more feedback. Isn't that right?"

"Okay."

The nurse went away, and Anne told her dad and Aaron about the coming meeting. They didn't question the need. They remained in their seats, killing their time however they could.

At the appointed hour they proceeded to the conference room and waited as the doctors trickled in one by one. There were five of them in all, one young, one gray haired, three with glasses—what were the chances? Dr. Salt presided over the meeting, explaining some of the more recent charts and the vital statistics, and afterward Anne and her dad went down the line, receiving all the experts' ultimate opinions. Is there any chance of a change? Is there any reason to prolong this process? No, no, no, no, no. They were all in complete agreement, straight down the line.

The doctors filed out, returning to their rounds. Dr. Salt stayed. The family sat around the conference table, basting in the windowless room, testing the new ground they'd come to.

"Grandpa?" Aaron said. The silence of the room was thick enough, it almost swallowed his voice. Anne was mildly astonished that he was the one taking the lead in the conversation, but it made a certain sense, too. He and her dad had come to some new understanding. He was the one who should preside over this monumental family conversation. He was old enough. "What do you think?" he said.

Grandpa Sam sat at the end of the table, the weight of the universe pressing on his back. He understood what all the doctors had said and what their group diagnosis meant. He hadn't missed a trick. He hadn't been prepared to make the decision previous to this meeting, but now, at last, there was truly no hope at all. Over four days, the hope had never truly existed, but only now was the final, fading echo of hope gone, too. Faced with the row of doctors, he bowed to their collective authority. Here was the threshold he'd been waiting to cross. The days of agony had gone on long enough.

He looked at Aaron with resignation.

Aaron waited an appropriately long time to answer the gaze, allowing the weights to settle on the scales.

"I think we need to let him go."

Grandpa Sam looked at Anne. She nodded her assent.

He stared at the wall, weighing the scales one last time in his own mind, and he nodded. "Okay."

So the words had been spoken. The judgment had been handed down. Anne's mouth was suddenly dry. Her fingers and toes were numb. She stared at the poster about sanitary hand washing, trying and failing to understand the graphic. Had they really just made the decision? This was the very hour? This was what she was looking at when she pulled the plug on her brother? It seemed so. This was the chair she would be sitting in. This was the clock. This was the chair and this was the clock that had been waiting for her since the beginning of time. This was the room that God had created long ago and dressed for her. This was the sound of an air-conditioning vent He'd decided on to accompany this act. These were the clothes and this was the taste in her mouth. All the details seemed wrong. They were so random, so absurd. She was so unprepared.

"Now?" she said, almost choking, as Dr. Salt stood. He nodded once and exited the room and waited in the hallway for the family to follow.

Here I am walking down the corridor to kill my brother, she thought, passing the doors of the offices and restrooms. And here are the faces of the nurses who see us walking. She followed Dr. Salt's footsteps through the ICU doors and down the inner hallway, past the other cells holding their broken bodies. They entered Ben's room, Dr. Salt first, then Anne, then her dad, then Aaron, and, last, the white nurse. The military cop stood to the side, trained at last.

"Take those off," the nurse said with gratifying disgust, pointing to the handcuffs. Anne could tell their vigil had worked some power on the nurse, bringing her over to the terms of their struggle, and that was something. The cop unlocked the handcuffs and placed them in his belt.

"What do we do?" Anne said.

"You just wait," said the nurse.

The nurse started by removing the endotracheal tube. When the tube was withdrawn, she shut down the ventilator, and the rasping sound ended with a chuckling rattle. Next the nurse removed the brain-monitoring wires. She took out the nasogastric tube and the two IVs, gradually returning Ben to his natural self. He lay there in the bed like a rude piece of clay. He already appeared to be losing his shape. His skin was softening, waxy, with red bumps and welts on his forearms. His breathing was getting slower and more shallow, but it didn't stop. They all watched him, his chest still rising and falling, waiting.

"How long will it take now?" Anne whispered.

"It might be an hour," Dr. Salt said. She could smell the Tic Tac in his mouth, an almost overpowering fume of artificial mint. This is the smell, she thought. "It could be six hours," he said. "We can't say exactly. His body is healthy. We'll see."

Anne looked at the nurse, not even knowing what to ask.

"What do we do?" she said again.

"You can say good-bye," the nurse said.

Anne tightened her jaw. She stepped forward and sat down in the seat at the side of the bed. She laid her hand on top of Ben's hand. His hand was warm, positively clammy, and his knuckles were thick and strong. The life in the body was almost vigorous. She kept her hand on his warrior's hand, utterly unsure they were doing the right thing.

"We're with you right now," she said quietly. "We are always with you, Benny. We're right here. Dad?"

"B— B—" Trying to utter his son's name, her dad broke, sobbing. For a second Anne worried that he'd gone insane, that the sobbing might never end. He crouched over and shook his head, as if he'd ruptured from reality, and she could feel panic gathering in the base of her mind, but thankfully the feeling didn't go any farther. She could see her dad hadn't dropped over the edge after all. He knew what was happening and how to behave. His tears were exactly appropriate to the situation. Soon he'd recovered himself and taken a place beside the bed. He held his son's hand as the muted thrum of the hospital surrounded them, and Aaron, her son, took a place at the foot of the bed.

Together, they watched, focusing all their attention on this still-living being before them. Anne was very grateful her son and father were there, adding their thoughts to the pool of concentration. She was focused so hard, she could almost feel the life force receding. And as her awareness of his receding life grew, she began to feel the life in herself as well. There was a living energy that bound them, a single, living energy of which they both, they all, partook. The life of her brother was the life of everyone, and as his life energy ebbed, it ebbed back into the life energy of everything. Her own life energy was part of it, as was the life energy of those pitiful schmucks in the waiting room, trapped in their shapes, with their weird faces, all of them, one. In the presence of her brother's dying form, she felt every human hierarchy dissolve. The fact of this existence, its myriad eyes and minds, dwarfed every human ambition and pretense. Names, money, status, all of it was nothing. There was no fucking way she was giving the people's water to Mark Harris.

She kept watching, examining her brother's every pore and stray hair for a final time. Ben's chest rose and fell, each breath a struggle. To live without him sounded so miserable and wrong. She couldn't imagine being in that world. She sobbed suddenly, comprehending the finality of the experience. They were standing at the door to the center of creation here, and it was a one-way door. Ben's voice would never speak to her again. She would never feel the burl of muscles in his back, the brawny hardness of his elbows. She would never feel his gaze on the side of her face. She saw the coming absence with such clarity, in the way she should have seen it all the time, the fog of distraction peeled away. God, she hoped Ben knew how much she loved him. He knew, didn't he?

She stared at the metal bar of the bed, too blighted to think or feel. It was two more hours before Ben's breathing finally ended. The doctor drifted in and out, checking, but when the last moment came, he wasn't there. Anne had heard a body lost 0.02 ounces at the moment of death, the weight of the soul, but she didn't know if that was truly the case. She felt the moment of passing, though, the final shudder and giving up, as if some immense chasm had been crossed. The cup poured back into the ocean. She and her father and son sat there with the body, in a state of shared bewilderment, not talking, not understanding a thing, not even trying.

At some point the nurse came into the room and asked them something, but Anne didn't hear exactly what she'd said. "What?" she said. To turn around was beyond her strength.

"Would you like to shave him?" the nurse said.

Still Anne didn't understand what she was proposing. "Now?" she said.

"Now is a good time," the nurse said. "Some people do. Some people don't. It's up to you."

Anne was quiet. No one had told her anything about shaving her brother's corpse. No one had prepared her for that intimacy. She wasn't sure what the proper response should be. It occurred to her that she could plausibly say no, beg off, and no one would think any less of her. But truly, she had no choice, did she?

She looked down at Ben, at his empty, lifeless face. It was the face she'd known from the beginning of time. It was the face that had greeted her every morning of her youth. It was the face she'd summoned in her mind every time she read the newspaper. She looked at her son, tears streaming over his cheeks. She looked at her dad, head bowed. Fuck you, God, she thought. Of course I'll shave him.

26

In Ben's dream, he was in heaven. He assumed it was heaven, anyway. No one had told him as much, but the world resembled the pictures of heaven that everyone knew as heaven. Stretching below him was a landscape of pink cumulus clouds, big, round bulbs coursing slowly with the atmospheric wind. Above him arched a deep, blue-black sky marbled with stars, and in its highest zone flocks of shimmering beings flew across the dome, leaving multicolored contrails in their wakes. He knew without being told that they were higher forms of some kind, probably angels. And he knew they were the source of the booming, glorious music that filled the air and filled his body to the core. The music was a chant coming down from above, raining through him, a profound, enveloping bombardment of harmony.

He knew it was a dream, and yet, on some level, he knew it wasn't that, too. It was a dream and not a dream, not that it mattered either way. For even if it was a pure dream, even if this was a vision manufactured entirely in the chemical factory of his own mind, it was still a clear testament to the miraculous foundations of reality itself and didn't diminish one bit the glory of the experience of God.

A brilliant rainbow flared across the curve of space, the sheer cliché of which convinced him it had to be a dream. He was still experiencing the activity of his mind, and that meant he was still alive. But what a mind he'd been given to imagine this!

His body, such as it was, floated over the cloudscape. He wasn't going very fast, just cruising at a gentle clip, and he enjoyed the soft air, the sweet scent, the overwhelming sense of oneness and connection to everything that existed. Sometimes voices came to him as if seeping into his dream from behind many walls. He caught the sounds of his sister, his nephew, and possibly his dad, murmuring to each other very far away. He wanted to say something to Anne, to reassure her that everything was all right, even better than all right, glorious, but the desire to speak didn't connect to any bodily machinery. The synapses didn't extend into any hands or tongue. The electrical charge fizzled somewhere and stopped before making the connection. He couldn't find any arms to move, or a mouth to open. He couldn't find the breath to push out of his throat over his nonexistent lips.

The voices faded, and he continued flying. The stars and moons and gleaming asteroids of the universe drifted above. He could see the churning of a thick nebula, the speckled rings of a jeweled planet. He laughed at the cosmic splendor of it all, and the laughter seemed to vibrate through him, breaking him into happy shards, shaking him into happy pieces. The laughter carried him into a whole different realm of being. His laughter was like a disintegration into God Himself.

He opened his eyes, and he was whole again, relatively speaking. He could see the stars and the planets above, and he could also tell that a presence had joined him. Did he believe in angels? Well, he did now, in this moment, anyway. He turned to the angel and discovered she was a young woman with a pleasant face, high cheekbones, and pale-blue eyes. She had golden-brown tresses, and her eyes were familiar and full of a welcoming joy.

I know you, the angel's eyes said. And Ben smiled into her eyes, knowing her as well.

They both laughed—an angel!—and again he shook to tiny pieces. When he opened his eyes again, the angel was still there with him, and he was incredibly glad. They were beaming at each other, so pleased they had finally found each other. Had she been with him all this time, he wondered? Had she been watching over him in Kuwait and Afghanistan? Had she watched him in youth karate class in Sun Valley? If so, she'd never allowed the slightest clue to drop. But it didn't matter now, because she was fully with him, and he assumed they would be together on some level for eternity. He would most definitely never forget her, even if this ended. This moment would never leave his mind.

He realized he and the angel were on the move. Together, they were bobbing through the celestial wind, surrounded by many flashes of bright, vivid color. Tangerine, cadmium, canary, and iridium, all vibrated in his vision, and he realized, much to his amazement, that they were riding on the majestic wing of a butterfly. Absolutely insane! There were millions of butterflies streaming all around them, an ocean of butterflies! Carried along by butterflies, Ben and his angel, his being-partner, glided over a landscape of verdant earth, wild meadows, dappled woods, laughing and disintegrating into each other as they flew. To ride a butterfly seemed to be thrilling even for an angel.

He'd never felt a feeling with someone that was so perfectly clear, so perfectly open. Without words, they understood each other. We will show you things, she told him. You will know everything very soon. I trust you, he said. I'm ready. And all around them the butterflies shivered and shimmered in the light, flashing powder blue, indigo, pastel orange, and peach. All the while, the wind on their faces remained steady, fragrant, and warm.

They exited the forest, and the butterflies spun upward into the sky. They became like a cyclone of color, rising higher, and Ben and his angel rode along in their funneling motion. It was a wild ride, better than any roller coaster, and as they reached the upper levels of the atmosphere, he could see the black pane of outer space approaching ahead. The blackness was not exactly space, though, he could see. There were no stars or planets in the blackness. It was more like a pool of oil, perfectly black, and before he could ask the angel what they were zooming toward, they passed through into the blackness, and the butterflies began bursting out of existence all around them. Pop, pop, they sizzled into smoke. Ben found himself suddenly floating in absolute blackness, not sure whether the angel was at his side or not. There was no light to see her by, no light by which to see his own limbs. The clouds and trees and sky were all gone from view, and only blackness existed. It engulfed him like a substance, soft, granular, warm, and absolute.

That level of darkness didn't last long, though, because almost immediately a spot of light appeared, flickering and growing into a compact, silver orb. It was an interpreter orb. Ben knew this somehow without being told.

The blackness—illuminated softly by the orb—took on shape and texture. Ben found himself in a cavernous stone hallway lit with flaming candelabras and heavy, candle-studded fixtures on the ceiling. The shining orb was floating up ahead, beckoning him onward, and he walked deeper into the hallway, over massive paving stones. He heard the sounds of laughter and talking somewhere, many voices echoing on stone walls. He followed the sound, hoping his being-partner was somewhere nearby.

The interpreter orb led him under a Moorish archway into a large banquet room where two long, oaken tables were set. At the tables sat all the men and women he had ever killed.

Ben stood in the doorway, feeling great dread run through him. Fearful, awful intuitions spilled through his chest and into his arms and legs, numbing him. He recognized many of the dead. He knew them by sight, from the glass of his scope or the images of his dossiers. He'd killed these people in every corner of the world, and now, for some reason, they'd been assembled in this dank Valhalla of his mind. This was still his mind, wasn't it? He had to think he was getting to the limits of his imagination here. But he felt resigned to whatever his mind was giving him. This was how it should be. The truth of his life was on the verge of being disclosed, the final, ultimate shape was taking form, and he had no choice but to submit to its totality. It was only right that the answer to the question of his life would go through these men and women. They were his riddle. It was his duty to receive the answer humbly.

The dead didn't seem to notice him at first. They were all too involved in their own boisterous talk and what seemed to be an endless series of toasts, accompanied by the clanking of huge bottles and steins. Many of them were still mangled, still bleeding, even. A man with half a head, a boy holding his dismembered arm. From Kabul? That kid? There was Jorge Martinez, the Hyena. And Milan Maric. And there was Larson.

So the shot was good after all. This suggested something, but he didn't know what.

Where am I? he asked, for his angel had appeared at his shoulder again.

Where do you think? she said, without any judgment or even any real inflection.

Am I in hell? he said. If this was his judgment, he wanted to rise to the occasion.

She shook her head. No, this place doesn't have a name.

He had other questions for her, but he didn't have time to ask because his dead had spotted him at last. They'd begun rising from their seats and stumbling closer, almost like shambling zombies. They didn't seem vengeful or violent, exactly. They just had their own questions, their own truths to understand. As they drew closer many of them began talking at once. The book of dead faces opened, page after page. Ben looked deeply into each victim's face and understood each of their lives in full. He saw all the dead's experiences as husbands, mothers, brothers, fathers, sons. He saw their families, he understood their ideologies. Holmes appeared, expressing discontent that he'd missed the chance to tell his son an important fact. There were certain things I wanted him to read, he expressed. There were things he needed to read. I could have saved him so much useless pain and suffering. All of it is right there, and he doesn't know.

Ben knew everything his dead had ever known, which meant, he realized, he was knowing things he couldn't possibly truly know, which meant he was moving beyond the limits of his own finite mind. Was this still his mind's activity? Or was he in the throes of something else, something divine? Was he creating this information to shock himself in some way?

Or was this information flowing into him from another consciousness, another source? The reality was literally beyond his comprehension.

The dead continued to gather, crowding around him, and fed him with their information. This dead boy had lost his elder sister to pneumonia. This dead woman had loved her neighbor's husband. The pain from the bullet that had severed Maric's spine flared strangely in his chest. And as his victims divulged their secrets, they seemed to comprehend Ben's own secrets as well. They saw the shape of his life, and they understood his unique destiny. Their natural anger and recrimination gave way to a more tragic acceptance of his ignorance. They didn't forgive him, they communicated. But they didn't doubt he was real.

He felt the need to tell them something. He didn't want to apologize, exactly, because he knew it was too late for that, and what choice had he had in the creation of his fate? But he felt the need to utter some words to commemorate this ultimate congregation of enemies. Probably there was a prayer for this moment, a kaddish for himself and his collective victims. A blessing for the greatness of their shared creator. But if there was, he didn't know the words, and he couldn't make any sounds, anyway. He still had no throat.

He turned to his angel in wonder and shame.

What can I do? he said.

There's nothing to do, she said. You're doing it.

I want these people to hear me, he said.

They hear you, she said. They know what they have to say.

I want them to know I saved people, too.

No, she said. You actually didn't save any.

But—how can that be?

Killing isn't saving. Killing can't give life.

But more people would have died. Many more.

How could you ever know that? There is what is. That's all.

She didn't say any more. She just turned and left the room. The dead were turning away, too, returning to their tables, and Ben understood it was time for him to leave. He followed his angel into the darkness, and soon the sounds of the dead were fading away, replaced by his own footsteps on the slick, damp stones. The orb returned, floating at his shoulder, shedding light on the steps, and Ben hurried to keep pace with the angel as she slid through the stone maze. She was going quickly, losing herself in the shadows and reappearing just as she slipped around corners. The sound of voices whispered through the cracks in the walls, the muffled voices of Doobie, Slick, his nephew, Aaron. It seemed he was being haunted by the living now.

At last she stopped, and he managed to catch up. They'd arrived at a new room, much smaller than the other, with walls of similar stone. It was dank, like all the other rooms, and had wet straw on the floor, and a vibration of terrible doom.

Where are we now? Ben said. He was breathing hard, and he didn't like this room. He couldn't see into the corners, it was so dark, and the walls seemed incredibly thick. They might be a mile underground, for all he knew. This was not anyplace he wanted to be.

This is your room, she said.

But I don't like this room, he said.

You don't have a choice, she said.

I can't have a different room?

No.

He peered into the shadows, trying to gauge the room's dimensions, but the darkness was too immense. Could he get used to this room? He couldn't say. He couldn't even get a fix on the edges in any direction.

How long do I have to be here? he said.

That depends, she said.

Does everyone have a room like this?

No.

Ben peered again into the shadows, finding nothing, and when he turned back he found that his angel had changed. He wasn't sure when it had happened, but she was no longer a simple peasant girl anymore. She was at least twelve feet tall, and she was emitting an intense white light. He could barely look at her without blinding himself in the whiteness. He raised his hand, squinting into her light, trying to find her, but she was no longer there. Inside the light, her features were shifting. For a moment he glimpsed rainbowed ram's horns, fish eyes, rotten teeth. There were goat features and snake scales. The fire coming from her was not only bright but hot, and he had to draw away. But still the room was impenetrably dark.

Now is the time, the angel said through her shining flames. I hope you're ready.

The time for what? he called. The fire was so powerful, he could barely hear.

I think you know.

Are you taking me somewhere else?

No. It all happens here now.

Am I going home?

No. You're never going home.

I'd like to go home, please. One more time.

She smiled sadly and expanded toward him, aflame. He tried crawling backward, but there didn't seem to be a floor anymore. The room had become all empty black space.

Is this going to hurt? he cried.

I'm afraid it is. Very much.

And again the face of the angel turned inside out, mashing inward, and coiled with many colors. Turquoise and magenta and ebony and violet, the colors of a mandrill, the colors of a rare, poisonous fish. Flames shot from her shoulders and off her head, and she grew even larger, in explosive blasts, tearing out of herself, until she shone like a white-hot star.

Ben, crouching in the void, could hear the roar of flames all around him. And as the flame grew hotter, devouring all, the angel touched him, and the physical pain was beyond all comprehension. It was everywhere, like a knife scraping the inside of his veins. He'd never felt the underside of his skin, but he did now. Layer after layer peeled away, more layers than he could imagine having. The pain poured through his body, concentrating in different centers, his thigh, his stomach, his back, a roving tornado of pain. He felt his bones being pulled out of his body with pincers, the ganglia of his veins dragged out of his muscles. The nets of his fat were ripped from his meat. And somehow when his body was gone the pain remained.

Still his mind and his vision were there. He could see light. People talked about seeing a light in death, but this wasn't the light they described. It wasn't some aqueous pool of light overhead, some gentle light at the end of the tunnel. This wasn't the cool, white light surrounding laughing loved ones as they welcomed the departed into the pearly gates. This light was like fireworks. The most incredible, gorgeous display he'd ever seen. He could see many-colored explosions in his vision, streamers, bursting geysers, blossoming flowers, pinwheels, and jellyfish. He saw slow trails of pink and yellow and gold smearing against the warm blackness. It was the Fourth of July times ten thousand. Soundless, shimmering, beautiful light. It was the light of his own life pouring through his body's many branches and roots.

All the while, the waves of pain came and went, a crashing ocean of pain, for hundreds of years. The fireworks burst and sizzled behind his eyes. And between the rushes of pain, through the pyrotechnics, a final taste filled his mouth, a sweet taste, a taste he knew. But what? And a thousand years later the answer finally came. The taste of clean, sweet honey on his tongue.

27

Sometimes Aaron wondered how this city once must have smelled. Back before internal combustion, before asphalt roads, before the oil derricks, back when the orange blossoms and bougainvillea were in bloom, the lavender and eucalyptus, and nothing had trampled it all down and beaten it all to shit and fucked it over until there was almost nothing left. It must have been like heaven on earth in Los Angeles until the people came and paved it all over. If it was this heavenly now, imagine what it must have been before.

Aaron was sitting in his backyard, soaking in the sun through the lemon tree. On the end table were his cup of black coffee and his juice and his everything bagel with chive cream cheese. The newspaper was within arm's reach, but he hadn't touched it yet; he was too satisfied simply to sit.

He wasn't even supposed to be in L.A. this afternoon. The plan had been to vacate the city two days earlier and cross the border into Nogales yesterday. After Nogales he and Joel were planning to cruise down the middle of Sonora before bending over to the west coast, ending up in a town called San Blas, beloved by the more robust hippies on the gringo trail. From there they would putter over to Guadalajara and Mexico City and end up in the Yucatán, visiting pyramids.

All was in readiness. The van he and Joel had bought was ready to go, all packed, freshly tuned, sitting in Joel's driveway. But the very day before their departure date, everything had come to a sudden, grinding halt when Aaron had received the call about his grandfather.

Grandpa Sam was dead. After eighty-seven years, he'd died as he'd lived his American life, in his recliner, watching *CSI: Miami*. According to Temo it was a peaceful passing, but of course he would say that.

Aaron was saddened by the news, of course. He loved his grandpa deeply. But his death had not been unexpected, and in a way it was surely for the best. For the past three months, Grandpa Sam had been struggling, and he'd taken a few perilous falls. The hospice nurses had been coming around, helping with the cleaning, leaving trays of green beans and meat loaf, reporting to his mother that the time was most definitely coming close. The Chabad people had been sniffing around, too, talking about G-d and the new temple they were building, trying to coax Grandpa Sam into donating his house to their organization, which had pissed him off greatly. He might have been old, but he was not confused: My house goes to my daughter. Never talk about my house again.

He'd always been such an indestructible barrel of a man, and in the past three months, he'd become frail, unable even to walk around the park one time. "What happened to Samuel?" he'd said. "What happened to Samuel?" The answer was, he got old.

In the Jewish faith, Aaron had learned from his uncle's passing, a funeral occurs as quickly as possible after death. Grandpa Sam had died on Wednesday; thus, the funeral was scheduled for this very Friday afternoon. His departure for Mexico with Joel would still be able to happen by the end of the week, only a few days later than expected.

Sitting under the lemon tree, he tried to feel the proper reverence and nostalgia his grandpa's death deserved, but mostly he ended up thinking about his backyard. He'd spent many mornings in this spot, pondering his life. He wasn't sorry to be leaving, though, even if this spot knew him so well. Had he made the right decision? That was another question.

The decision to go to Mexico had come in a kind of flash. It had happened back in July at the sun dance, a very interesting ritual. The day had been everything he and Karl had been led to expect. Late in the morning, out in the desert, a paunchy, heavily modified dude had hooked himself to a juniper tree and proceeded to shuffle in ever wider circles under the thrumming sun, over the hours entering a trance of endorphins. The dance had gone all day, the man's nipples distending and bleeding, his voice moaning and chanting, and the crowd had been rapt, amazed.

But somehow Aaron hadn't been that moved. He'd stood there with everyone, watching the bloody scene in the dust, interested, curious, extremely baked (no peyote that day; the deal had fallen through), but never truly, wholly engaged. He hadn't ever been able to shake the sense of the rite as a mere fiction, a wishful, ersatz version of a tradition that had lost meaning at least a hundred years before. Other people had claimed the sun dance was a revelation to them, but he'd realized, driving home, that Mexico was his way. He liked these people, but he needed to cover more ground before he committed.

His mother wasn't happy and harangued him into promising that he'd reapply to colleges within a couple of years, but at least Karl had been understanding about his decision, and they'd promised each other to keep in close touch, notifying each other as to all the amazing and not-so-amazing experiences they were having. The sunporch would still be there when Aaron got back, and, assuming Karl was still ensconced there and didn't have a roommate, he was welcome to move in whenever. Or go to college. Or do something else. Whatever. No one could really say what would be happening in six months. The whole world would have been rearranged five times by then.

His mom came out to the yard, already wearing her funeral clothes, a dark woolen skirt and dark blouse. She looked nice, but mostly just exhausted and fretful. The past two days had been crazy for her, what with dealing with Chabad about finding the *shomer* to sit with the body, cleansing it and saying the proper psalms. She'd also made all the arrangements with the funeral director, with whom she had a budding friendship now, what with her brother's death so recent in memory, and dealt with the man at the florist and the guy making the headstone, and gotten a start on all the banking headaches. She'd ended up breaking into her dad's bank account only after the prompt "Left arm" had flashed on the screen. His bank account password was his concentration camp number! How could it ever have been otherwise? She'd had to consult a photo of Grandpa Sam holding a cat to get the digits right, reading the numbers off his forearm with a magnifying glass. She'd also sent out all the funeral invitations to all the relevant people, fielded everyone's condolences, and had his house cleaned. She looked as if she'd lost five pounds since last weekend.

"You should really eat something," Aaron said, and pushed his bagel in her direction.

"I can't," she said, staring at the lemon tree. "Too much to think about." She rubbed her palms on her skirt, erasing the creases, already looking damp with sweat. "God, God, God . . . ," she muttered without even hearing herself.

"Juice at least?" he offered. He held his juice out, and she took a sip but didn't seem to notice what she was doing. She might not even have known she was standing outside in the morning sun.

She took a deep breath and rubbed her hands on her creases. And then she walked back into the house, still muttering to God.

On the way to the cemetery, they had to stop to pick up Aaron's dad. Barry was running late, of course, and when he finally came ambling out of his apartment complex, he was wearing an idiotic T-shirt with Spuds MacKenzie, the party-animal dog, emblazoned on the chest. What was he thinking? Otherwise, he was decently attired, for him, at least. He had on clean chinos, shoes with closed toes. His long, blond hair was pulled back in a neat ponytail. But the T-shirt was a truly bizarre choice. "Unbelievable," his mom whispered as he approached the car. Aaron just lightly sighed.

"So that's what you're wearing?" Anne said as her ex-husband crawled into the backseat.

"I figure I'm going to have to rend it," he explained, "so I didn't want to wear one of my good shirts, you know?"

"You don't have to rend it," Anne said. She was beyond arguing with Aaron's dad, but merely making a point. "You're not actually related."

"I was, though," Barry said. "For an important period of my life. I think it's a good time to honor that relationship with your dad. Anyway, I'm okay to rend this shirt. I don't even hardly wear it."

"Haven't been going to too many funerals lately, I guess?" Aaron said, smirking.

"If you don't want to rend it, don't rend it," his mom said. "He wouldn't care."

"You don't think he'd care? I think he'd like someone rending their shirt. Wouldn't you?"

"I know for a fact he wouldn't care."

That eventually settled the question. Grandpa Sam didn't care, and Aaron's dad had another shirt in his knapsack for the post-rending get-together, and he changed as they drove. No one really minded either way. He could have worn the Spuds MacKenzie T-shirt, for all they cared. They were not religious people, after all. They were Californians above all else.

The grave site was at the end of a cul-de-sac at the edge of a neat suburban neighborhood. The site was becoming a familiar stomping ground for the family of late. Aaron's grandmother was buried there, his uncle, now Grandpa Sam. Over the years, they'd deposited their share of bodies. His uncle's grave was still lacking a headstone, as he'd been in the ground for only a season. When it arrived it would bear the word "Peace." But they placed rocks on all the graves and contemplated their dead.

"That headstone guy better get it right this time," Anne said. Years ago, they'd had to swap out Aaron's grandma's headstone when they realized the name had been misspelled. Aaron had heard his mom on the phone going over the Hebrew spelling letter by letter this time.

"Go minimal," Aaron said. "Just get a blank one. Or do one of those laser portraits, like the Russians do."

"I just want mine to have a question mark, that's all," she said, staring at her mother's grave.

"Sounds good to me."

"Maybe the words 'She Never Knew.' But that's it."

"You got it, Mom. I'll remember."

"God, I can't believe we're even talking about this," she said. "It's so morbid. Let's stop."

There was a tent and some chairs set up. The turnout was a little better than expected. Aaron didn't know why he should be surprised by that fact. His grandfather had lived in Sun Valley for upward of forty years. He'd belonged to many groups. He'd even been a Mason for a spell. He'd always enjoyed the company of other people. He'd always wanted to belong. Maybe he'd thought an official group would hide him if the bad days ever returned. But no, Aaron thought, he'd just genuinely liked people; it was nothing more complicated than that.

There were guys from the gym, dating back to the bodybuilding days. People from the office. People from the bagel shop he frequented. Bizarrely, there was even Jackie from the bank in Oakland. She told Aaron that she and his grandpa had exchanged some endearing emails during the last months of his life, and, as she happened to be in town anyway, she'd wanted to pay her respects. The lost gold had never been found, not even close, but Grandpa Sam had managed to wring one last friend from the world before kicking off.

They all shook Aaron's hand with screwed-up eyes and frozen smiles. He didn't enjoy talking to them, but he appreciated their presence nonetheless. He knew these people had been taking care of his mom the past few days, and they'd continue to take care of her over the next few months, when he was gone. They were bringing her lasagna and enchiladas, weeding the yard, checking in around bedtime. They were all good, decent, middle-class people who understood the value of human life and their place in the community.

There were a few ringers in the group, too. The Chabad rabbi had brought out some young Hasidim for the event. The funeral of a Holocaust survivor was after all a rare and significant event. These were young men who would never otherwise partake in such a sacred day. His grandfather's passing was a trophy death to be shared with the community at large. Aaron didn't resent them being there. His grandfather was his own portal into history. Why should he not guide others into history as well?

The rabbi was much younger than Aaron had expected, not remotely the bearded patriarch of the imagination. His beard was a scrabbly, reddish thing, the kind one saw in a rock club or at the gourmet coffee shop. He was thin and with it. He handed Aaron a chic business card, half the size of a normal card. He was a graphic designer on the side? What a drag, Aaron thought. This was not the place for coolness of any kind.

But once he began the ceremony, he channeled a deep, hallowed force. He began by reciting the blessing of the Lord God, King of the Universe, and at once became the voice of ancient power. The ancient ways were truly reassuring in the face of this loss, Aaron thought. Someone, please tell us what to do. It doesn't matter what. Whether you believed in the words or not, it didn't matter. The point was only that the same words had been uttered since the beginning of man's consciousness, and the tone was authoritative yet gentle. Whereas the gringo sun dance had seemed wishful and contrived, this ritual seemed dignified and mildly frightening. The window of human history opened, and one could see backward into the eons, if darkly.

According to the rabbi there were four signal animals to emulate in Jewish tradition: the leopard, the eagle, the deer, and the lion. Be bold as a leopard, light as an eagle, fast as a deer, and strong as a lion, and you will do the will of your Father in Heaven. He turned to Psalm 23, and Aaron couldn't help but cry. "'Though I walk through the valley of the shadow of death, I fear no harm, for you are with me.'" Who had walked deeper into that valley than Grandpa Sam? No one.

The words took their inexorable course, and soon Aaron was being instructed to help bear the coffin to the grave. He rose and took a corner, feeling the weight of the plain, pine coffin with his grandfather's body inside. He shoveled dirt onto the wood, splashing the Star of David.

After the service, Aaron's mom thanked the rabbi for his hard work. She reached out and touched his shoulder, immediately withdrawing her hand as if she'd touched a hot burner.

"Oh, sorry," she said.

The rabbi shrugged. "I didn't see anything," he said.

Aaron liked this rabbi.

They held a reception at his grandfather's house, but not many people came to that. Just Aaron, his mother, his father, Temo, the caregiver, and his grandfather's old friend Joe, a fellow survivor from the oldest days in the Bay Area. Joe told them stories of Oakland, of the jobs in the beginning, the dances, and his memory was a little better than Grandpa Sam's. If only they'd had this gathering when Grandpa Sam was alive, Aaron thought, they might have captured another image or two.

Aaron wandered the rooms, eyeing the debris of his grandfather's life. The final cleaning was going to be a motherfucker. He sat in the recliner in which his grandfather had died, listening to wind chimes gong and gong.

The night before he left for Mexico, he got incredibly high and took a last walkabout through the neighborhood that had reared him and oppressed him for so many years. He walked through the lamplit streets, one empty spotlight to the next, and up the hill, past the high school, down into the arroyo.

It was a hot night, and down in the arroyo the crickets were thunderous, louder than he'd ever heard them before. He walked through the narrow valley of oak trees, under a tunnel of overhanging boughs, with crickets ringing in his head. He passed from one cluster to another, through a long channel of changing tones. Chirrup, chirrup, chirrrrup. There were areas of long, low notes, areas of high, shrieking notes. The crickets' voices gathered and faded, replaced by new voices, new patterns. He walked for ten full minutes through the tube of singing crickets. The whole black corridor was vibrating.

He woke up to sun on his bed, his last morning at home.

So this is the day I leave home, he thought. He stared at the ceiling, counting the divots. Here is the light on the day I leave home. This is the temperature on the day I leave home. Here is the shirt I'm wearing on the day I leave home. What a fantastic day it is for leaving home.

He got up and showered in his mother's shower. He loved this shower, with its darting needles of hot water, the smooth, burgundy-colored tiles on the floor. He loved his mom's towels, the smell of detergent in the plush fabric. He would miss them. He would never forget them, he was sure.

He ate breakfast in the kitchen with his mom. She was still drained from the funeral, but she was already moving on to the next obligations. She had a big meeting later in the day with her old boss, Susan, that was causing her much stress. She'd just recently gotten a big promotion to become something called a sustainability czar, and now she didn't report to anyone except the photographers for the newspaper and the city magazine, which seemed to love running interviews. Then, tomorrow, she was taking yet another trip up to Portland to visit the guy she told him was most definitely, in no way, shape, or form, her boyfriend, but whose very existence had to be kept shrouded in secrecy lest the powers that be smite them all down. She claimed she'd never done it with him, that the very thought repulsed her, and yet she also said she was breaking things off with him, professionally speaking, but somehow never did. Somehow the calls and texts kept coming, week after week. She liked him.

She acted blasé about the significance of their final meal, pretending it was just another day, like any other. She wasn't one for ceremony if it could ever be avoided.

"You packed some aspirin?" she said.

"Yeah."

"Band-Aids? A whole first-aid kit? You might need that."

"In the glove box. No worries."

But when the tinny honk of the van sounded out front, she had to steady herself on the sink to keep from falling down. She crouched there at the counter until the spasm of tears passed, her head hanging, her breathing ragged and harsh.

"I'll be back, you know," Aaron said. He was still at the table, holding his spoon. "We're just driving around for a while, that's all."

"I know, I know," she said. She sniffed and forced a tight smile in his direction. The light from the window made her hair glow but cast a shadow onto her face.

"I might even be back soon," he said. "Who knows? We might hate it down there."

She smiled again, this time with a wise, knowing demeanor. Her gaze was focused on someplace far outside the room.

"No," she said, dabbing her eyes. "You won't. That's not going to happen. You're going to like it out there. I know."

"How do you know?"

She wiped her eyes. The sound of the van's rolling door drifted in through the window. "Some things, baby, I just know."

In the driveway, Joel was rearranging the bedding in the back of the van, making room for Aaron's last bags of clothes. Already, the camping gear and books and various mechanical and travel manuals were packed into the makeshift drawers they'd constructed in back, under the thin mattress. The tools were stashed; the rope was coiled and tucked near the wheel well. The only thing left, really, was to climb in and go.

"Hey, Ms. Singer," Joel said, slamming the back flip-up door. "Nice day, right?"

"Nice day for driving safely, Joel," she said.

"We would never speed, Ms. Singer, if that's what you mean," he said, mock aghast. "Your son is the biggest pussy driver in town, in case you didn't know."

"I'm glad to hear it."

Now there was truly nothing left to do. The van was fully loaded. The gas tank was brimming. His money was stowed in his secret compartment. His mother stood waiting for a final hug, and dutifully he hugged her for the last time before leaving. She held him for a long time, feeling the skin of his neck, the muscle of his shoulders. He submitted to the final frisking and held back the surge of heat shooting into his own nose and eyes, turning away to keep the flush of tears from coming. Then he climbed into the van, and they were gone.

They were only around the corner when the first joint came out, a big fat one rolled especially for this auspicious occasion, filled with the purple-haired bud scored from the dispensary on Fairfax. Joel lit the tapered end and took a long, savoring hit and passed it to Aaron. The sweet, skunky smell fogged the van.

"So, what do you want to hear?" Aaron said, getting down to the important business at hand. As passenger, Aaron's job was navigation and music selection, most importantly the latter. The past few weeks had entailed major downloading of new material for the long plains of highway ahead.

"Something good," Joel said.

Aaron scrolled through the options, taking a few more small hits off the joint. It was a difficult choice. The music of this moment should be just right. Nothing too mellow. Nothing too harsh. Nothing overproduced. Nothing too raw. Nothing he'd heard ten thousand times before. Nothing untested, either.

He settled finally on Lynyrd Skynyrd. He'd downloaded a few of their albums the year before, and he'd listened to them

a few times, but not overmuch. He'd half listened to the song
"Freebird," the hoary arena anthem, and it seemed like a funny
time to boot it up. The joke of the song was so old, so hide-
bound, he'd never felt the need to investigate. "Freebird!" they
yelled at the shows. He'd been yelling "Freebird!" since before
he ever knew what the hell "Freebird!" meant.

Open with the punch line, he thought. Why not?

He depressed the button, and the information siphoned
into the wires to the speakers.

It took only a few seconds to see why this song was so
beloved. Why? Because it fucking ruled! Immediately, he was
in thrall to the slow, surging bass line, the smoky, inevitable,
not-even-thatembarrassing lyrics. Already, he could feel the
throb of the song aiming him toward the flaming, cokey guitar
solo burning up ahead.

> But if I stayed here with you, girl
> Things just couldn't be the same.
> 'Cause I'm as free as a bird now
> And this bird you cannot change.

Okay, the lyrics actually were kind of embarrassing, but
they bore such a direct relationship to Aaron and Joel's current situation that they almost became something else entirely,
a kind of prophecy. Methodically, the guitars built until they
peeled away from the song itself, becoming a whole new thing,
a sprawling labyrinth of sound celebrating everything that existed in their range of audibility. Outside, the palm trees shimmered against the blue sky, etched with hazy cirrus, rocking
to "Freebird." The cars zoomed by to "Freebird." The song rose

higher and higher, mounting plateau after plateau, becoming more and more desperate, almost unhinged, but never once losing control, not even close.

The climax seemed to go on for an hour, and Aaron sucked in every note, followed every coiling, cornering trail as it lasered through his mind. He loved this stupid fucking song. He loved the racist assholes who wrote it. He planned to listen to it again as soon as it ended. And he could tell Joel was loving it, too, the way he was grinning like a sated cat, eyes half-closed, hand draped on the wheel. I-5 stretched ahead of them, a great, gray strip into the southern unknown, and all around them the world was ablaze with music. Aaron raced straight into it, right into the heart, as if he were hearing its song for the very first time in his life.

ALSO BY JON RAYMOND

*The Community: Writings about Art in
and around Portland, 1997–2016*

Rain Dragon

Livability

The Half-Life

ACKNOWLEDGMENTS

Many people contributed invaluably to the writing of this book.

First and foremost: Fiona McCrae, whose faith is a gift, and whose almost supernatural editorial instincts made the book a thousand times better; and Bill Clegg, brilliant writer, reader, agent, and friend.

In the realm of research: Jason Bell provided much-needed medical information; Megan Ponder and Michael Rosen shared crucial insights regarding municipal governance; Ronin Colman helped with guns; and Tom Cody supplied not only a big idea, but a splash of personal charisma as well.

Great thanks to everyone at Graywolf, especially Steve Woodward, who discovered the title. And to everyone at Tin House, a family to which I feel beyond honored to belong—with extra arrows of gratitude shooting to Tony Perez, editor, writer, and mensch extraordinaire.

And for all these readers I am tremendously grateful: Heather Abel, Domenick Ammirati, Julia Bryan-Wilson, Sean Byrne, Emily Chenoweth, Steve Doughton, Todd Haynes, Cheston Knapp, Camela Raymond, Carole Raymond, Richard Raymond, Kelly Reichardt, Michael Shamberg, Mattathias Schwartz, Rob Spillman, Pauls Toutonghi, Storm Tharp, James Yu, and Tony Zito. And most of all, my grandfather's old friend, Bill Kaye.

JON RAYMOND is the author of the novels *Rain Dragon* and *The Half-Life*, a *Publishers Weekly* Best Book of 2004, and the short-story collection *Livability*, a Barnes and Noble Discover Great New Writers selection and winner of the Oregon Book Award. He is also the screenwriter of the film *Meek's Cutoff* and cowriter of the films *Old Joy* and *Wendy and Lucy*, both based on his short fiction, and the film *Night Moves*. He also cowrote the HBO miniseries *Mildred Pierce*, winner of five Emmy Awards. Raymond's writing has appeared in *Tin House*, the *Village Voice*, *Bookforum*, *Artforum*, *Playboy*, *Zoetrope*, and other publications. He lives in Portland, Oregon.